Ringfence

Samke S. Mhlongo

DISCLAIMER

This book is inspired by a number of stories and experiences shared across the African continent, which are weaved into the author's figment of imagination. The book does not represent and is not intended to portray any person's real life. Accordingly, no one character is to be construed as being representative of any one person. The author has used and created names, occupations, locations, dates and fictitious scenes to highlight certain social, financial and legal messages. Any similarity or resemblance to actual persons, occupations, events and locations is purely coincidental. The legal and financial information contained in this book is for informational purposes only and is not intended to be advice. Should you wish to embark on any legal or financial journey based on what is contained in this book, the author strongly recommends that you obtain professional advice before doing so.

Text © Samke S. Mhlongo, 2020
Published edition © Lötz Publishing, 2020
Author photograph © Gilly Gilmohr, 2020
Cover, design and typesetting by Gregg Davies Media

Originally published in South Africa in 2020
by Lötz Publishing
Johannesburg, South Africa

Lötz Publishing
WE BELIEVE IN THE MAGIC OF BOOKS

ISBN 978 0 620 88094 7

Printed and bound by XMD Books, Cape Town

CONTENTS

DEDICATION

For every woman
that is done being strong

FOREWORD

On Friday, 11 August 2017, a group of six women huddled together in a small hotel room at The Hyatt Kilimanjaro in Dar-Es-Salaam, for what I thought would be a light-hearted afternoon of networking and making merry. Earlier that day, I had addressed over 200 women from across the continent that were gathered for the inaugural Graça Machel Trust Women Advancing Africa Forum. Immediately after my talk, my good friend and fellow activist, Renée Ngamau, pulled me aside and told me there was a dynamic young lady from South Africa that I absolutely had to meet, who also had an inspirational story of trial and triumph.

Little did I know that by sunset, there would not be a dry eye in the room. Not only had Samke, the bright-eyed and wide-smiled "Babygirl" (as I call her), shared a journey so unbelievable for her tender thirty-two-years of life, but, one by one, the rest of the women in the room had also revealed their tales of oppression and abuse at the hands of the men, society and judicial system that is meant to protect them.

From South Africa to Mozambique, Tanzania and Kenya, the theme in that hotel room was the same – these women were silently suffering.

Three years before I was born, whilst delivering the Opening Speech at the First Conference of the FRELIMO women's league, the late Samora Machel stated:

"The Emancipation of women is not an act of charity, the result of a humanitarian or compassionate attitude. The liberation of women is a fundamental necessity for the revolution, a guarantee of its continuity and a precondition for its victory."

More than four decades since my father uttered these words, it is clear that the revolution is not complete. Africa has attained political and economic emancipation, yet the emancipation of women remains elusive.

It's a sunny afternoon here in Maputo as I pen this foreword, on the eve of the fifth anniversary that saw me brutally attacked by the man that had claimed to love me. An attack that left me permanently blind in my right eye and yet ironically, left me seeing clearer than ever before, just how far we still have to go on the journey of justice for women. It is on this journey that *Ringfence* proves a crucial roadmap for all who read it.

Ringfence depicts the intimate, private and public dilemmas faced by four African women whose upbringing had positioned them for comfort and success. We follow them as they navigate womanhood as global citizens, living in a society steeped in traditional African culture and customs. Their stories gently highlight the intricacies and complexities of the different types of gender-based violence against women, the connections between toxic masculinities and the ever simple-yet-sophisticated ways in which women ignore oppression, manipulate their existences to ensure survival, or ultimately embark on the courageous quest to break away from it. From Cape Town to Nairobi, Rome to Lagos, and Harare to Singapore, their stories span across geographies and yet confront the dark spheres of the same, seemingly desirable world. *Ringfence* is not only effortlessly witty, humorous and captivating, but Samke also manages to provide financial and legal insights crucial for a woman at every life stage.

I could not put this book down as I was invaded by laughter at sharp-tongued Lolo's antics, shock at naïve Qhayiya's rude awakening, tears at Nala's continued betrayal by those she trusts, and surprise at Runako's compromise. This compromise may be far more common than we imagine. But most of all, I was imbued with a sense of great pride at every turn of the page. Pride that our Babygirl had kept the promise she made on that teary afternoon in Dar-Es-Salaam, of turning her personal pain into purpose.

Ringfence could not be a greater gift for women living during a time such as this. A time where women's financial circumstances force them to remain in abusive relationships, making them susceptible to gender-based violence. A time where a woman is murdered every three hours in South Africa! A time where the South African conviction rate for GBV-related crimes is only 3% of reported cases. A time where only 22 of 56 African countries have adopted laws that criminalise GBV. A time where nearly one billion women worldwide are affected by GBV, with less than 10% of their perpetrators being convicted. A time where women face secondary victimisation from the very healthcare organisations, police bodies, judicial systems, friends, family and society meant to protect them. It is for a time such as this that *Ringfence* proves an invaluable asset to help women identify and potentially avoid instances of abuse. Where this abuse is currently occurring, *Ringfence* empowers victims to more successfully leave such relationships and shines a light on some of the pitfalls that line the long walk to freedom.

Acclaimed poet and civil rights activist Maya Angelou said:

"Each time a woman stands up for herself, without knowing it possibly, without claiming it, she stands up for all women."

Babygirl is standing up for herself with this brave and daring book. Without knowing it, her bravery has strengthened me on my pursuit to continue standing up for myself, standing up to the judicial system that in 2020 overturned the guilty verdict previously passed against my attacker, and in standing up, I stand for those who continue to suffer in silence. I press on in my journey because I know that a state of injustice will never prevail. And on the road to justice and emancipation, *Ringfence* is an invaluable companion.

Aluta Continua!

Josina Z. Machel

Maputo, October 2020

www.justice4allwomxn.org

PROLOGUE

THE MISSION

"A speaker of truth has no friends"

— AFRICAN PROVERB

Eko Convention Centre, Lagos
November 2019

Qhayiya Dana sat nervously in the front row of the Eko Convention Centre in Lagos, her face fixed firmly on the stage for fear of seeing the over 2 500 women behind her.

Considered Africa's largest gathering of women in business and leadership, WIMBIZ had always drawn large crowds at its annual conference. Qhayiya doubted it would be different this time.

She could feel her heart pounding at the thought of getting on stage in the next fifteen minutes. Especially since, she was likely the only South African in the room, not because South African women did not attend the conference, but because tensions between the two countries were high. Violent outbursts between South Africans and Nigerian nationals living in the country had become a frequent occurrence over the past two months.

Qhayiya shifted in her seat to pull her dress down discreetly. Adrenalin coursed through her body. She'd even forgotten that she hadn't eaten in nearly two days. Food was the least of her concerns at the moment. The reaction to her opening address, from thousands of the continent's most powerful women, was.

The crowd clapped politely as she made her way onto the stage. She took her seat at the far end of the panel.

One by one, the rest of the panellists made their way up. A few minutes later, the Programme Director said the words Qhayiya had dreaded, "I now hand you over to our Panel Moderator."

Qhayiya's tummy rumbled as she walked across the stage to the podium. The crowd murmured in confusion. *What was she doing?* Moderators spoke from their seats and not the podium. THAT was reserved for the Programme Director and keynote speakers. She put one foot in front of the other, praying to God that she would not trip and fall. She hated the shoes she was wearing and had packed them 'just in case'. Over time, the suede had softened, and the back of her heels kept popping out with each step she took.

This is why I needed the Valentinos, God, Qhayiya thought reproachfully.

The glass podium was now in front of her, the conference spotlight firmly fixed on her.

Qhayiya had traversed over 42 563 nautical miles, made 726 diary entries and cried 147 tissue boxes worth of tears to stand at this podium.

She was crystal clear on the gamble she had to take at that podium. Crystal clear on the culture she had to shift on her friend Nala's behalf. Crystal clear on the laws that denied her friend Lolo justice. Crystal clear on the stigma that was holding her friend Runako hostage in a lifelong sentence. And Qhayiya was crystal clear on the debt she had to settle, once and for all.

She no longer worried about the reaction of the audience. She was here to speak her truth. She was here to speak her friends' truth. She was here to speak women's often unspoken truth.

ONCE UPON A TIME

"If you don't know where you're going, any road will take you there"

— GEORGE HARRISON

Food Court, University of Cape Town
June 2006

*T*he winter holidays that usually flew by had dragged for Nala Kalenga, the self-appointed queen of Umhlanga Rocks' social scene. It had been less than a year since her father's passing, and as tradition would have it, she was not allowed to be out of the house after sunset.

This practice had killed her social life and made her miss hubbly smoking sessions at her cousin Liyana's house, Thursday drinks specials at the yacht club, and the highlight of every Umhlanga Rocks teenager's social calendar that year – Tyson Cooper's farewell party. He was the hot American boy, returning home after spending two years in the country.

Nala had always treasured visits to her dad's house. Umhlanga Rocks was a far cry from the sleepy village of Shongweni, where she had been raised by her maternal grandmother, Blossom.

Granny Blossom was kind but very strict and had kept her granddaughter under lock and key. The matriarch's two daughters had both fallen pregnant during university. Perhaps keeping a close watch on her eldest granddaughter's activities was Granny Blossom's way of ending this cycle.

It was the first week of July, and the three-week holiday Nala had spent indoors with her siblings and stepmother Audrey had finally come to an end. Nala couldn't remember ever being this excited to be back on campus, perhaps not since January that year, when she had received the first tranche of her inheritance. She had gone on a three-day shopping spree that made her the envy of UCT's fashion elite, especially her best friend – the de facto leader of their girl squad – Tshenolo 'Lolo' Motsepe.

Lolo was outspoken, bordering on brash, and Nala doubted they would have been friends had they not met in boarding school as socially awkward, brace-faced tweens.

Throughout her teenage years, Lolo's rebellious nature had been dismissed as a way of coping with her parents' acrimonious divorce. The divorce had ripped her from the lap of luxury in the leafy suburb of Houghton in Johannesburg. It left her mother, Aunty Nandi, scrambling to pay rent on a two-bedroom flat in the less-affluent neighbourhood of Killarney and provide daily upkeep for Lolo and her younger sister, Koketso. Meanwhile, their father, Uncle Harvey, had continued to live large with his mistress-turned-housewife in their family home.

From the tender age of thirteen, Lolo had vowed never to be subjected to the same treatment her mother had faced. This birthed her dysfunctional relationship with men and money.

At twenty-one years of age, the Motswana beauty was a year older than the rest of the students in her stream, a consequence of having taken a gap year after Grade 12 to au pair in France. The official PR story Lolo sold was that she had decided to travel through Europe before embarking on her university studies.

In reality, she had forfeited her bursary with a leading audit firm by deciding to pursue a marketing degree instead of one in Accounting Science.

The trouble was, without the bursary, Lolo's mother had no way of putting her through university. After her ex-husband's fortunes turned, she had cashed out all her investments and maxed out all her credit lines keeping her daughters in private school.

Poor Uncle Harvey hadn't bargained on his second marriage falling apart after he lost his three largest construction clients to his competitors. Not being one to sacrifice Harvey Nichols for Harvey Motsepe, the ousted businessman's mistress-turned-housewife-turned-ex-wife soon found herself in the arms of the newest king of low-cost-housing development, but not before taking her ex-husband for a hefty settlement and a tear-inducing alimony. After all, Mrs Motsepe II did not have a tertiary education and had been 100% dependent on her husband as a stay-at-home wife. What court would deny her the right to maintain the lavish lifestyle she had become accustomed to?

Lolo's dad was a financial delinquent, and working part-time was out of the question for the girl schooled in the Natal Midlands. Lolo's gap year bought her mother time to approach her employers for a loan.

Instead of using this opportunity to save for her subsequent years of university, Lolo took her mom's gesture as permission to live large on the money she was making in France. It was during this time that her taste for designer items intensified.

While a Guess handbag was considered the ultimate status symbol by the fashion-forward girl on campus, Lolo casually carried a Takashi Murakami multicoloured Louis Vuitton pochette. A holiday fling she'd met while touring Toulouse had bought it for her.

To remind naysayers that hers was authentic, and not the 'inspired' version, Lolo would periodically bring the Louis Vuitton carrier bag to campus too. Not only had she lugged it all the way from Rue Croix Baragnon to Johannesburg, AND onward to Cape Town; she also carried it around as she went about her school day, as she was doing now.

"Nala!" Lolo shouted with glee in her hoarse, slightly baritone voice. "How are you, babe?" She nearly toppled Nala with an overenthusiastic hug.

"I'm good, my Lols, how are you?" Nala replied. "Aren't you cold?"

Cape Town winters were cold and wet, and Lolo's outfit of a denim mini skirt, Puma boxing boots, white vest and calf-length puffer jacket did very little to protect her exposed thighs from the elements.

"Cold? Where? It's so warm. African winters are not really winter, hey! When I lived in Saint-Nizier…"

"Au paired!" Runako interjected as she took her seat at the food court table. "You didn't LIVE there, you AU PAIRED there. Big difference! And it was for only nine months!"

"Well, welcome back to you too, biatch!" Lolo said, unperturbed by her ex-campus roommate's jab, as she fixed herself two rice cakes topped with hummus and cucumber slices.

Runako 'Ru' Madzonge was from one of the wealthiest families in Zimbabwe. Although she wasn't arrogant, she certainly wasn't shy of flaunting the family fortune. The youngest of three children, and the only girl, the second-year law student had no competition as the apple of her father's eye, who also happened to be governor of one of Zimbabwe's largest provinces. Runako's political lineage had likely secured her the appointment as President of the Diaspora Students' Society (DIASOC) for the 2006 academic year. It certainly wasn't her grades or her pursuits in student activism, as the former were mediocre, and the latter non-existent.

But DIASOC members knew that one phone call from darling Ruru to her father Governor George Madzonge, about a student permit issue here or urgent travel assistance there, meant the issue would be resolved in a matter of hours. This alone was enough to earn her enough votes to become head of the 500-member student organisation.

"How was home, Ru?" Nala smiled.

"It was so-so. Actually, how do you like my new gift from Mama and Papa?" Runako beamed, pulling out a brand new MacBook Pro from her laptop sleeve.

"And what did you do to deserve such a lavish gift from the *rents*[1]? I know it wasn't your semester marks!" Lolo scoffed; her tone laced with a touch of jealousy.

"As if yours were any better!" Nala exclaimed, trying to quell an impending flare-up of Lolo and Runako's sometimes bitter rivalry.

"You know my father. He said he feels uncomfortable with me working late in the computer labs, so he decided to get me my own laptop!" Runako giggled.

"You! COMPUTER LABS!" Lolo and Nala exclaimed simultaneously before bursting into laughter. They knew full well that Runako did not go anywhere near the computer labs. It was probably just another story she sold her father when she missed one of his daily 8 pm calls to her waterfront apartment.

Runako's suggestion was ludicrous for another reason. She and her friends regularly skipped lectures and seldom struggled through assignments by themselves. They preferred, instead, to purchase class notes and private tutoring lessons from the students they referred to as SRBs – students with a Strong Rural Background.

The derogatory term was used by many of the privileged students on campus to refer to those students from small or rural towns, whose studies were being funded by a bursary or scholarship. They were often mocked for their unpolished English accents, and repetitive wear of free faculty tee-shirts paired with blue, bootleg jeans faded from wear, not design.

The 'Sons of' and 'Daughters of' had fostered a mutually beneficial relationship with the SRBs: 'You attend lectures and help us with our assignments; we'll pay you handsomely and make your university stay more comfortable.' The campus elite knew just how little a scholarship or bursary stipend did to fund university life, especially in Cape Town!

"Hello, girls" came a familiar voice from behind Nala.

"Miss Q is in the house!" Lolo exclaimed, throwing her arms in the air for a hug.

"Miss Lolo's in the house!" Qhayiya exclaimed back, bending over to give Lolo a hug.

"Darling, have you lost weight?" Runako asked sincerely.

"Yeah, she definitely has. Are you on diet pills again?" Nala agreed, cocking her head to the side to get a better view of Qhayiya's shrunken behind.

"Not this time, babes. My mom's put me on this hectic eating plan and taken out a gym membership for me," Qhayiya replied, eyeing Nala's sweet and sour chicken noodles before pulling out a takeaway niçoise salad and a sachet of balsamic vinaigrette.

Qhayiya 'Q' Dana was obsessed with her weight. Having grown up chubby, she was teased for it all through high school. She had insecurities brought on not only by her physical appearance but also by her family's financial standing.

Unlike the rest of the group, the Xhosa teen didn't come from a wealthy family and had a modest upbringing. Born and raised in Port Elizabeth by a single mother, Qhayiya moved to Kwa-Zulu Natal at the beginning of Grade 8 to attend boarding school. Her mother, Aunty Pat, had moved to London, where healthcare professionals earned a much higher salary than in South Africa.

On her nurse's salary, Qhayiya's mother had made many sacrifices to send her daughter to the exclusive girls' only high school, where she, Nala and Lolo first met and became friends.

Aunty Pat made sure to remind her daughter that there was only enough funding for her high school career. She would need to earn high enough grades to secure herself a scholarship for her tertiary education. The hardworking finance and economics major had managed to do so, with seven distinctions to boot!

"What is that awful smell?" Runako exclaimed.

"Hey! It's rude to speak about someone's food like that," Qhayiya frowned.

"I'm sorry, but that tuna honks, babe," Runako insisted.

"Glad someone finally said it..." Nala concurred, casually paging through the latest edition of the ELLE magazine.

"Now, now, ladies," Lolo interrupted. "Let's not be mean to Miss Qhayiya over here, who is just trying to prevent a repeat of the first year spread. Instead, can we draw our attention to our outfits for Thursday night? I'm thinking we skip class tomorrow and head to Cavendish in the morning."

"Oooh! The R75 sale starts tomorrow, right, Lols?" Nala beamed.

"Yes, ma'am. And we'll be there to bail out all those poor clothes," Lolo smiled, slowly rubbing her hands together as though she were cooking up some evil masterplan.

"I hope you're not going to drop us again, Q..." Nala said reprovingly.

"I don't do it on purpose, Nala," Qhayiya said softly. "And to be honest, I'll have to miss even more shopping dates going forward. Not only did my mom put me on a strict diet over the holidays, but she's also put me on the 50/30/20 budget."

"Budget?" Runako choked.

"What on earth for?" Nala commiserated, looking at the rest of her friends in confusion.

"Well, as you guys know, my mom's not been feeling too well lately, and she can't take on as many shifts as she used to. She's basically cut my allowance in half, and given me a budget tool to help me make do with the little I'll have going forward."

"*Eish*[2]! That sucks..." Lolo agonised with her friend.

"Big time!" Runako concurred.

"So, explain this 30/40/20 thing you're on," Nala asked casually. "If it's half as good as your diet, then I'm in!"

"It's FIFTY. THIRTY. TWENTY," Qhayiya chuckled. "It's basically a budgeting hack she read about in some book where the author suggests you spend 50% of your money on your needs, 30% on your wants, and 20% on savings," she explained.

"Great! Clothing is a need, so we're on for tomorrow," Lolo argued.

"Nice try, Lols, but no. I have enough clothes for me to be decent on campus. Any more clothes I buy would be a want, not a need," Qhayiya countered. "And I'm already spending my weekly WANTS allowance on Thursday night, so I'll have to give tomorrow a miss."

"I'm impressed, Q," Runako said, contemplating. "Papa's always stressed the importance of living a frugal life."

"That's rich, coming from the man that bought his twenty-year-old daughter an Audi TT and a waterfront apartment," Lolo snickered, shaking her head and grabbing the magazine out of Nala's hands.

"Jealous!" Runako mouthed and rolled her eyes.

"Anyway…" Nala interjected, clearing her throat. "What's our colour scheme for Thursday night, Lols? Are we doing all white again?"

"I'm thinking all black," Lolo mused.

"Before you guys continue, please excuse me. I need to head to a meeting with my stats tutor. I'll see you at supper, *neh*[3]?" Qhayiya said, standing up and starting to pack her bags.

The Ivy Night Club, Camps Bay

The winter north-westerly was on full display in the Mother City that night. And yet, despite the strong winds and heavy rains, The Ivy was teeming with scantily clad babes in their late teens and early twenties, ready to usher in the second semester of the year.

The Ivy was not only Camps Bay's premier nightclub; it had also become the preferred *Phuza Thursday*[4] watering hole for the local student elite. With drinks priced at three times more than those at the more student-allowance-friendly establishments such as Obz Café and the Claremont Bowling Club, The Ivy was the place to see and be seen by, the 'Do you know who his/her dad is?' crowd of the city.

Nala's braids swayed at the small of her back as she snaked her way through the crowd to the beat of Nelly Furtado's *Maneater*. The psychology major with a heart-shaped face and flirty eyes created quite the stir as she sashayed past in black thigh-high boots and a matching off-shoulder mini-dress that barely covered her ample derrière. Nala was unmissable; her melodic laugh, exaggerated expressions and wide smile made her stand out in a crowd.

If you didn't see her, you heard her. And if you hadn't seen or heard her, someone would undoubtedly point her out to you by the end of the night.

Either way, she commanded attention whenever she was in the room, and she revelled in it.

Nala was making her way across the VIP dance floor, back to her seat, when a warm, honeyed voice came out of nowhere and offered her a drink.

The voice, with its slight French accent, belonged to none other than twenty-two-year-old Blaise Ilunga. Blaise wasn't usually described as the hottest guy in the room, but his cheeky grin, cocoa skin and chiselled features gave him an allure that raised many a girl's curiosity. At 1.9 metres, Blaise was taller than the average guy on campus. And his years of playing first-team basketball at one of the continent's most expensive boarding schools gave him the bearing of someone far more handsome than he was. Perhaps, it was this swagger that secured him a response from the braided maiden who was notorious for shutting down male advances.

"If you buy me a drink, you'll have to get one for all my friends, too," Nala shouted over the music. She pointed to a table of three similarly underdressed women, that were chatting and laughing with a group of young men gathered around them.

Blaise recognised them instantly as the Belters – a group of second-year students renowned for dating only the richest boys on campus. He and his friends had tried unsuccessfully to infiltrate the friendship made up of girls that were insanely beautiful, always impeccably dressed, and highly intelligent.

Making a quick mental calculation of the maximum damage the girls could do to his budget for the night, Blaise figured he was suitable for their best attempt and decided to indulge Nala in a bit of power play.

"Order what you want," he called back, giving her a cheeky wink.

"What I want?" Nala chuckled provocatively and leaned closer so that she wouldn't have to shout. "Are you sure?" she taunted, turning to him with an 'I dare you' look. She waited for him to back down at the potential dent her drinks order would make to what was undoubtedly Mommy or Daddy's black card.

Blaise, knowing full well what Nala was playing at, simply smiled and turned to summon a waiter.

"*Monsieur*[5]! Four bottles of your finest champagne please, to that table," Blaise said, pointing to Nala's friends. "And keep them coming."

He turned back to Nala and took a brief moment to enjoy the look of defeat written all over her face.

"Will that be all, *Madamoiselle*[6]?" he teased.

"Yes, that will be all," she smiled. She paused for a second before lifting her bangle-laden arm to offer him a handshake. "I'm Nala."

There was no way Blaise Ilunga was going to accept a handshake after winning so thoroughly. Nor would he pass up the opportunity of marking his territory for the night. Instead, he put his arm around Nala's waist and gently pulled her towards him. He whispered in her ear, "I know exactly who you are... Just like you know who I am, too."

Nala giggled, immediately annoyed with herself for giving up the game so soon. There was no use in pretending that Blaise didn't impress her. Or that she didn't know – as he rightfully pointed out – exactly who he was.

Even if she hadn't met him casually at a number of campus social events, she would have recognised him as a member of the Muzungus – a group of four wealthy guys in third year, famous for driving around campus in their mothers' hand-me-down SUVs and notorious for entertaining girls on their parents' tab.

The Muzungus were made up of the four high school friends from the Republic of Azalia, the island country off the coast of Pointe-Noire.

Established in 1904 after the discovery of oil and gold, Africa's 55th country was a melting pot of people from all over the continent. The former British colony had attracted the best talent on the continent and quickly grown to its current population of 18 million spanning nine states.

Making up the Muzungus was Blaise Ilunga, great-grandson of the pioneering Gabriel Ilunga, founder of the largest national bank in Azalia.

Blaise's parents ensured that their son remained in the top three Accounting students each year, through private tutoring and strict monitoring of his marks. As the son of the current Chief Executive of Azalian National Bank (AZB), Blaise was being groomed to one day step into his father's shoes and continue the great Ilunga banking legacy.

The next member of the Muzungus was Geoffrey "Junior" Okello II, son of Geoffrey Okello, Prime Minister of Azalia. Quarter-to-handsome with an athletic build, Junior's unkempt dreadlocks, tattooed arms and numerous piercings spoke of one trying to be everything BUT the model first son of Azalia.

Enrolled for a degree in politics, philosophy and economics at his father's behest, Junior spent his days on Hiddingh Campus researching his true passion instead – Fine Art. It was only then that the young man with a permanent 'can't be bothered' look on his face, truly came alive.

Then there was engineering student Kobe Mensah, who was the exact opposite. Firmly focused on pleasing his family, Kobe was plain arrogant and always pretended not to recognise the rest of the Belters, even though Runako had introduced them numerous times.

Many blamed his muscular body and soccer-player bow legs for his dismissive demeanour. The Belters knew better. Thanks to Runako's on-again-off-again *situationship*[7] with Kobe over the past six months, they had it on good authority that Kobe was from THE Mensahs. The oil-field-owning Mensahs of Azalia.

The Mensahs were also the reason none of the Muzungus had ever been spotted at Cape Town International Airport. They flew the boys to and from Azalia on the family private jet, of course!

Finally, there was João Morreira, the anchor of the group in the looks department. João was born and raised in Azalia, but his family had relocated to the US during his early teens. Thanks to his green eyes from his Portuguese-British mom, and square jawline from his Azalian dad, João was by far the most handsome student in the Law Faculty, and most unapproachable of the group.

João was known for spending excessive effort and money chasing down and entertaining a girl, that is until she started showing interest in him. At that point, he would dump her for the next conquest. João had a string of broken hearts to his name. One name, however, had managed to elude him successfully thus far. Lolo Motsepe.

Nala was still trying to figure out whether Blaise was the subject of the latest Muzungu rumour making the rounds on campus when he spun her around and started singing along to the Marvin Gaye and Tammi Terrell classic.

"Listen, baby!" he belted out, throwing his head back, and pleased with himself at his recent show of might.

Nala sang along, the attitude forgotten and the nostalgia transporting her back to her childhood days when she had danced to the very same song with her late father. He picked up where she had left off, making mountain shapes and flowing river motions with his arms as he sang. She giggled at the silliness of it all.

The Azalian charmer boy and sheltered daddy's girl danced cheek-to-cheek to the soul train classic, lost in the magic of the spark they had ignited. The fire of their love story had the power to bring warmth and light to those around it or to destroy everything in its path. Especially each other.

There, in the dark, on the packed dance floor, no one noticed the little girl begging for a father's love. She twirled with reckless abandon, safe in the arms of a little boy desperately seeking validation. She needed saving. And he, like the rest of his friends that were growing tired of living under the shadow of their fathers' wings, wanted to play the hero.

Canterbury Place, Newlands

The sun was already high in the clear blue sky by the time Lolo opened her eyes. The blurry surroundings slowly came into focus, and she didn't recognise where she was.

Her eyes moved from the white ceiling to the white fitted cupboards, over to the right where the wind had blown open the white French doors, and back to her left where she found... OH, CRAP!

"João, get up and take me home immediately!" she blurted, sitting up. She was mad at herself for breaking her vow never to fall victim to João Morreira's charm. She and the Belters had always pitied the poor campus girls that believed they could win the heart of the known playboy.

"Huh...?" João mumbled.

"I said, wake up and take me home right now!" she insisted. "I guess you finally did it – ticked the mighty Lolo Motsepe off your hit list. Congratulations!" she growled defensively.

"Dude! That's not what you were saying last night though," João grumbled. The slight American accent that was previously charming was now plain annoying.

"I can barely remember leaving the club, so how the hell do you expect me to remember what I said?" Lolo argued.

"Relax... It ain't that deep." João turned over and went back to sleep, leaving Lolo embarrassed at how blasé he was about their first sexual encounter.

Sure, Lolo was a known liberal when it comes to sex, openly sharing her belief that a woman has full rights over when and how she uses her body. But that didn't mean she doesn't revere sex or the bond that comes with being connected to another.

But clearly, sex meant much less to João than it did to her. The year-long cat-and-mouse game she and João had played was clearly just that to him – a game. What a disappointment!

The girls must be so worried, she realised and reached for her phone. She had nine missed calls and three unread text messages:

(08:01) Ru: Babe, are you okay? Been trying to call you

(08:50) Q: Are you ok, Lols? We missed you at breakfast this morning.

(09:17) Nala: João – 1, Lolo – 0

A response to any of their messages now would result in a thirty-minute phone call, with each of them, to explain in excruciating detail how she had landed in João's bed when just hours before, she was lamenting the foolishness of the girls giggling at his effortless charm.

Gingerly, she placed her phone on the bedside table, deciding she'd deal with the aftermath of last night's events when she met the girls at dinner.

It was hard to believe that João Morreira, dubbed one of the biggest players on campus, looked harmless and innocent, as he lay fast asleep next to her.

She slipped off the bed to use the loo and, on the way back, took the opportunity to look around the bedroom for clues as to whether or not there was currently a woman in João's life.

On João's dresser was a framed family picture of him with his parents and twin sisters, a collection of fragrances, a pair of hair clippers and a plastic container with US dollars and Azalian pound notes. On his nightstands sat a lampshade, with João's phone lying face-down on his side of the bed. Other than that, his bedroom was spotless.

There was not a stray strand of hair (natural or synthetic) on the floor, no mascara lying around, not even a lonely earring stopper under the bed. Nothing. Except for a blue, foil condom wrapper, presumably from the wee hours of that morning. *At least he used a condom*, Lolo thought to herself.

Perhaps the nightstand drawer held some clues and, after gently pulling it open, she uncovered some crime novels, a pack of headache tablets and three unopened boxes of condoms. *How much sex does this guy have?*

"Next time, come on a Wednesday," João suggested sarcastically, still lying with his back turned to her.

"Excuse me?" Lolo jumped, startled and embarrassed that João had caught her, red-handed, snooping through his belongings.

"Wednesday. The cleaning lady comes by on Thursday mornings so if you want to snoop, come through on a Wednesday," João explained drily.

"I wasn't snooping, João," Lolo bluffed cheekily, "I was looking for a charger. My phone is flat."

João turned to face Lolo with a naughty smile on his face.

"Dude, come on! You have a Sony Ericsson. NO ONE has the same charger as you."

"Urgh! Piss off, João," Lolo capitulated. "Anyway, since you're up, can you take me home now? I'm already late for class!"

João burst out laughing.

"It's cool, no need to pretend with me. Everyone knows the Belters hardly go to class!" João chuckled, sitting up and propping his pillows behind his back. "Check it out. The boys are coming over for breakfast later. Why don't you chill with us and I'll drop you back home after that."

Dining Hall, Tugwell Residence

It was just after 6 pm when Lolo did the Walk of Shame from her residence parking lot, dressed in João's size XXL Rocawear baseball jacket and size 13 flip-flops.

Her 'barely there' dress from the night before disappeared under the oversized jacket. Lolo felt the eyes of fellow Tugwellites, streaming in and out of the entrance hall, were staring disapprovingly at her for coming back from one of THOSE nights.

She SO wished they knew that the reason for her late arrival was innocent. She'd spent the day eating, laughing and watching sports with the Muzungus.

Lolo had sworn never to be caught dead hanging around the Muzungus and had repeatedly chastised Runako for letting Kobe waltz in and out of her life thanks to their ongoing situationship. However, João's latest conquest found her time with the Muzungus surprisingly enjoyable. They were charming, smart, and incredibly witty.

It had been a surprisingly fun day, but now, Lolo was grateful to be home at Tugwell Hall, which, according to its residents, was home to the most beautiful girls on campus.

A healthy rivalry existed between the residences on the main campus of UCT, with the Fullerites (residents of Fuller Hall) considering themselves the academic elite, while the Baxterites (residents of Baxter Hall) and Tugwellites chided them for being too stiff.

The Tugwellites, on the other hand, prided themselves on being well-rounded students that balanced their studies with a very healthy social life. Fullerites and Baxterites looked down on them as lacking in focus.

The Baxterites, well, they were caught in the middle, always trying to outdo the Fullerites in their academic marks. But, also not wanting to be left out of all the fun the Tugwellites seemed to be enjoying constantly.

Such was the hierarchy of UCT's campus residences. After a quick shower and change, Lolo walked into the dining hall where the latest fashion, hook-ups and breakups were the fodder of conversation, as opposed to, say, the possible religious meaning behind Van Gogh's *Café Terrace at Night*.

"Oh! She lives!" Nala exclaimed.

"Tshenolo Gloria Motsepe! Where have you been? We've been worried sick about you," Qhayiya agreed.

"Can you two grandmas calm yourselves down to a panic?" Lolo said cheekily. "I'm fine. I was with João."

"This whole time? I hope you didn't sleep with him," Runako opined as she played with the evening's meal of pizza and fries. "He SO won't respect you if all it takes to get into your pants is a bottle of champagne at the club!"

"Paid for by HIS FRIEND I might add," Nala said, referring to the bottles of champagne Blaise had sent to the girls' table.

"How the hell does this one still have access to the dining hall?" Lolo asked, pointing to Runako who had moved out of res at the end of the prior academic year.

"Don't change the subject," Qhayiya said disapprovingly.

"Which means they did it," Nala said, nodding her head before taking another sip of her pineapple juice.

"Fine! We did! So what?" Lolo snapped.

"And? Is it true what they say about Azalian men?" Nala asked excitedly. She raised both index fingers to indicate size.

"Dunno to be honest. I don't even remember getting to João's place," Lolo replied casually.

"Yeah, you were pretty drunk when you insisted on leaving with him last night," Runako nodded thoughtlessly.

"Just like YOU were when you left with Kobe!" Lolo deflected.

"Well, I hope you're going to report João, like you did Gitongo," Qhayiya said quietly.

She was referring to an incident the previous year when Lolo had reported a fellow student to campus security for attempted rape. This resulted in the termination of his scholarship with a leading investment bank, and him subsequently dropping out of university.

A dedicated student, exceptionally gifted at mathematics, Gitongo had tutored Lolo over several weeks to help her improve her subject marks ahead of the final examinations. Lolo's flirty and playful manner had unfortunately been grossly misinterpreted by the boy from a rural village in Azalia.

On the last of many late nights at the far end of the library, Gitongo made a sexual advance on the girl he thought had mutual feelings for him. He mistook her resistance for the coyness he had apparently been raised to expect from NICE girls. It was only when she kicked him in the groin, and then ran towards the library exit in tears, that it dawned on him that she had actually meant it when she said 'No'.

"Don't be silly, Q! I'm obviously not going to report João. This is different," Lolo replied offhandedly.

"How so?" Qhayiya persisted.

"Because… as much as I hate to admit it, I was bound to give it up to João at SOME stage!" Lolo replied, taken aback by Q's tenacity.

"And Gitongo?" Qhayiya pressed on.

"Gitongo! In what world would I be caught sleeping with an SRB?" Lolo grimaced, turning to Nala and Runako for support.

"Uhm… so Gitongo gets reported for something that ALMOST happened and loses his scholarship, but João, who is actually guilty of rape, gets away scot-free because he's what – from a rich family?" Qhayiya asked, incredulously.

"Awkward," Nala coughed.

"That's uncalled for, Q," Runako frowned.

"It's not uncalled for. I'm just wondering how safe I am with you guys if different rules apply depending on who you are," Qhayiya said archly. "For all I know, you guys consider me an SRB too, since I'm here on a scholarship and my family is not as rich as yours…"

"Dude! Seriously?" Lolo said dismissively. "We've been friends since we were in high school. You're one of us! I can't believe we're even having this discussion. I'm too hungover for this…"

"So…" Runako sighed loudly, "I can't deal with tonight's menu. Who's down for Nando's?"

"Ooh, sounds good – let's!" Nala squealed.

"I need to watch my diet, you girls go ahead," Qhayiya declined. After the startling disclosure about her budget the previous day, her friends knew to let the white lie slide without comment.

"Lols, please spot me R100," Nala asked sheepishly. "My mom's late with my allowance again."

"Sure, hun. But are you sure everything's okay? There's always an issue with your money now?" Lolo asked.

"Of course, it is," Nala replied airily. "The investment she put my inheritance in is very strict with how many withdrawals she can make. That's all."

2

ROW E, CLOUD 9

"Do not think there are no crocodiles just because the water is calm"

— MALAY PROVERB

Parsons Green Train Station, London
December 2007

*P*arsons Green looked more like the London Runako was expecting, in contrast to the unattractive, box-like designs of the houses in Bromley-by-Bow where she would be staying for the next six weeks.

It was sheer serendipity that Runako's visit with Qhayiya and her mom coincided with Kobe's annual Christmas trip to his family holiday home in Kent.

The original plan was for all four Belters to spend Christmas together in London, but Nala had pulled out suddenly when her mother advised they'd reached the investment withdrawal limit for the year, and João insisted Lolo spent New Year's Eve with him in the US.

It had been a blissful eighteen months since that fateful night at The Ivy when Blaise decided to make a move on Nala. Thanks to Blaise and Nala's blossoming romance, the Belters and Muzungus had started spending more time with each other, resulting in two additional relationships. Lolo and João had built on the bond they had formed after Lolo spent the night at João's place, and Kobe and Runako decided to formalise their situationship into an actual relationship.

Runako had found Kobe to be very different once he decided she was more than just a casual fling. Instead of the indifferent boy she'd spent many late nights with, he was a delicate soul that showered her with attention and gave in to her every whim. It was his elaborate gestures of affection that had won her over and made her hope that Kobe would be much more than just a university sweetheart.

But things weren't always rosy for UCT's new favourite couple. As with all public relationships, several girls started trying their luck with Kobe in the hope that they, too, could be on the receiving end of such royal treatment.

Determined not to lose her status as one half of the hottest couple of 2007, Runako guarded her relationship fiercely.

As the months went by, many wondered how the standoffish girl had managed to tie down the elusive hunk for so long. Cynics dismissed their romance as nothing more than the typical Muzungu courtship – spectacular to behold and fleeting in nature. They were wrong, because not only had Runako's relationship with Kobe lasted longer than any other girl had managed, she was about to be introduced to Kobe's family, starting with his sister, Kate.

Parsons Green Lane was buzzing with locals and tourists going about their Christmas holiday business, seemingly unperturbed by the harsh winter weather. Runako and Qhayiya, on the other hand, shivered uncontrollably through the cold as they walked from the tube station to their destination.

Luckily, it wasn't long before they came upon the iconic Victorian façade of one of London's most popular pubs – The White Horse. Set in classic pub style with a grand dark-wood bar, matching leather Chesterfield sofas, and open fires, the home of the largest beer selection in Parsons Green was also home to the Sloaneys – the millennial version of the Sloane Ranger.

First brought to prominence in 1982 with the release of The Official Sloane Ranger Handbook, the phrase was coined to describe London's conservative middle- to upper-class twenty-somethings. They came from wealthy families, had weekend homes in the countryside, and donned the unofficial 'uniform' of navy gilets and pearls, ala Princess Diana in the 1980s.

The two Belters, who were usually the envy of their peers for their flamboyant lifestyles, were about to walk into a sea of teens and twenty-somethings that would likely consider THEM as SRBs.

Hailing from the country's most expensive schools, the Sloaneys spent their days shopping on Chelsea's King's Road, before retreating to their family country estates in the shires for Christmas. They were from money; LOTS of money.

"They're all so chic!" Runako exclaimed as she walked through the doors of the popular bar.

"No, they're not! They look like freakin' farmers. What's up with the gumboots and life jackets?" Qhayiya asked, referring to the ubiquitous outfit combination of riding pants, wellington boots, and quilted gilets.

"Oh, sweet, sweet, Qhayiya!" Runako exclaimed, placing her arm condescendingly around her friend's shoulder. "Have we taught you nothing? What you see here is country chic. These people, my dear, are wealthy, not just rich. To your untrained eye, those are merely 'gumboots'. But those of us in the know understand the comfort and stylishness of Hunter wellingtons. And those 'life jackets' are actually gilets. Looking at the design, I'd bet they're probably Barbour. Darling, this fashion is for people that actually OWN horses, not just pose with them at the races. Know what I mean?"

"They still look like farmers to me, babe," Qhayiya sighed, rolling her eyes.

"Whatever, Q! I'm so getting myself a pair of Hunters before I go back home. Remind me to ask Lols and Nala if they'd like a pair too. Oh! And keep an eye out for Prince Harry, I heard he likes to hang around here," Runako whispered in her friend's ear, her eyes darting about excitedly.

"Please don't tell me you're also a 'Harry Hunter' now," scowled Qhayiya, obviously underwhelmed. "The only person you should be keeping an eye out for is your boyfriend, Prince Kobe of the House of Mensah. Remember him?"

"Urgh!" Runako grunted at her killjoy friend.

The conspicuous pair walked awkwardly through the bustling crowd to the upstairs dining section where Kobe had said they were to meet.

His two-week stubble gave him a rugged maturity, and Runako's stomach went into a tighter knot with each step she took towards the party of six. At the table, she recognised Kate. Kobe's older sister looked, even more, intimidating in real life than in Kobe's Facebook pictures. Her deep-set eyes, high-arched eyebrows and aristocratic nose confirmed her no-nonsense reputation.

"Hey, Baby Cakes!" Runako squealed as she gave a seated Kobe a big hug from behind.

"Baby Cakes! That's a first," Kate teased, running her hands through her jet black, straight-cut bob.

Not moved by his sister's teasing, Kobe rose to his feet and gave Runako a warm hug and kiss before turning around to introduce her to everyone.

"Guys! Please meet my 'Baby Cakes', Runako, and her best friend, well one of her best friends, Qhayiya. But you can call her Q. Ru arrived yesterday so please introduce yourselves, and let's show her a good time!"

Kobe took his seat as Runako and Qhayiya went around the table greeting everyone, starting with Kate, who was sitting on Kobe's left.

"Nice to finally meet you," Kate said, giving Runako a firm handshake and courteous smile. "This is my boyfriend, Oliver."

"You can call me Oli. A pleasure to meet you both," Oliver said with a cheeky grin that, at a quick glance, made him favour Robert Downey Jr.

Next to Oliver sat Kuukuwa and Afia, Kobe's cousins on his mom's side, who were both studying in London. The pair stood up excitedly and gave their cousin's new girlfriend and her bestie warm hugs.

"I'm Kuukuwa. Everyone calls me Kuku! And, oh my gosh, you guys are so fabulous. How did my cousin bag a girl like you, Ruru? You don't mind me calling you Ruru, right?" Kuku babbled excitedly, adjusting her jeans over her ample bottom.

"Uhm… no, of course not!" Runako replied, caving under duress.

"Move over, sis!" Afia said, pushing her sister out the way. "I'm Afia, known as Fifi. You guys should totally hang with us!"

"Totally!" Kuku agreed.

"And not our boring cousins over there," Kuku said, motioning to Kobe and Kate with her head.

"That's very kind of you. Thank you," Runako replied gratefully.

"Yeah, we will. You guys look like fun," Qhayiya concurred. Kuku and Fifi took their seats as Runako and Qhayiya continued with the introductions.

"I'm Chinara, but everyone calls me CJ!" the familiar-looking woman smiled, stretching out her hand for a handshake. "It's a pleasure to finally meet you. I've heard so much about you." CJ was annoyingly beautiful with almond-shaped eyes, deep dimples and long thin braids that disappeared behind her back.

"It's a pleasure to meet you too, CJ. You look so familiar…?" Runako fished.

"Really? I'm pretty sure we've never met before," CJ replied.

It dawned on Runako that CJ was the girl she'd seen in many of Kobe's Facebook photos from high school. "I'm sure I'll figure it out," she chuckled, uncomfortably.

"Who's CJ again?" Runako whispered to Kobe as she took her seat next to him and started paging through the menu.

"She's Kate's friend," Kobe said dismissively, taking another sip of his Pilsner Urquell draught.

"But she looks so familiar," Runako insisted, not quite sure how to broach the subject without letting Kobe know that she'd studied all of his Facebook posts.

"Don't know where you might know her from," Kobe shrugged and turned to Qhayiya to suggest she try the Scotch eggs as a starter.

Continuing the conversation would cause unnecessary tension, and unravel Runako's plan of presenting herself to Kobe's family and friends as the perfect girlfriend. Besides, she reckoned it would be better to broach this subject again in private.

Craft beers and Pimm's cocktails flowed as the group recounted stories from their childhood, tales of their travels, and their career aspirations.

"So, Runako, I hear London's your favourite city in the UK. Kobe prefers Essex," Kate said snidely.

"Why Essex?" Runako asked, naively.

"Not NECESSARY, Kate," Kobe said, shaking his head.

"Because that's where CJ's family lives, of course! Kobe had the hugest crush on CJ growing up, and Daddy even had to send the jet to fly her down to Azalia for Kobe's school leaver's dinner," Kate chuckled. "Kobe didn't care that she was, what, three years older than him."

"That's hilarious," Runako said disingenuously, wondering if Kobe's awkwardness was an indication that he still wasn't over his childhood sweetheart. "So, where are you based now, CJ?"

"I'm based in Durham. A small city not as vibrant as London," CJ smiled in reply.

"She's not just based there; she's doing her master's at the business school there. Don't be fooled by the pretty face, my friend's a very smart cookie..." Kate winked again.

"Kate, I know you're a cutthroat lawyer, but seriously, you don't have to defend me. Besides, tonight's about Runako, not me," CJ said graciously.

The tension between Kate and Runako was palpable, but the rest of the guests were oblivious to it. They were caught up in various conversations in their little corners of the table.

At 9 pm, it was time for everyone to head home, and Kate offered to get the bill.

The group said their goodbyes with promises that they would 'definitely do this again' before Runako, Qhayiya and Kobe left London.

"Spend Christmas with me," Kobe whispered as Runako slowly pulled away from their goodbye kiss.

"I can't, baby," she whispered back. "I came here to spend time with Q and Aunty Pat..."

"Okay," he shrugged. "New Year's Eve, then. I know she's one of your best friends, but you're my girl now, and she'll just have to understand."

"Baby, please don't make me choose..."

"Okay..." he exhaled slowly, "I'm not happy, but okay. At least come to Kent after Christmas, to meet my parents. It's only an hour away, and I'll pay for everything."

"You really want me to meet your parents?" Runako beamed.

"Of course! You can't leave without Kwame and Corah meeting their *bi harusi.*[1]"

"Okay," Runako giggled, "I'd love to!"

Air kisses and hugs were exchanged as the group said goodbye before Runako, Qhayiya, Fifi and Kuku went in one direction, and the rest in another.

"What are you girls doing for New Year's Eve?" Fifi asked as the quartet walked back to the tube station.

"We don't have any plans yet," Qhayiya replied.

"Well, then you should join us. We've been invited to a party at Two Degrees, one of the most exclusive members-only clubs in the world," Fifi bragged.

"Sounds lovely!" Runako smiled. "My father's a member of a members-only club with establishments in New York and Singapore. I've always been curious to see what goes on in there..."

"Really? You're in for a treat then!" Kuku nodded conspiratorially. "And do you know whose guest list we're on? Obinna Okonkwo"

"What's *Okonko Mikonko*?" Runako laughed.

"Okonkwo, not Okonko! Or maybe you know him as Obi Okonkwo?" replied Fifi. Then, astonished, "Have you guys never heard of Obi? Kuku, they don't know Obi..." Fifi's eyes were wide as she turned to her sister in shock.

"Who is this Obi you're on about, and why should WE know HIM?" Qhayiya shrugged.

"Because, he is only like the eldest son of Mr Felix Okonkwo, founder of one of the largest shipping companies in Nigeria...!" Fifi exclaimed. She threw her arms in the air in exasperation when Qhayiya and Runako's expressions remained nonplussed.

"Oh. He's Nigerian..." Runako said, doubtfully.

"And... what is that supposed to mean?" Fifi frowned.

"It's just that... Nigerians tend to be...you know..." Runako stuttered. She scrunched her face and shook her head disapprovingly.

"You need to change your attitude babe. I don't know what your experience is with people from Nigeria, but they're not all dodgy," Fifi assured her.

"Exactly!" Kuku jumped in. "And Obi is from a very good family. His father is a very well-respected businessman that has won numerous international business and philanthropy awards!"

"Well, if he's from THAT kind of family then I guess we could..." Runako said sheepishly.

"Do me a favour when you get home tonight, yeah? Just look up Obinna Okonkwo on Facebook. And in case you're confused as to which profile is his, he's the guy standing next to Diddy in his profile picture."

"He parties with Diddy?" Runako exclaimed, mouth agape.

"Fifi, what's your number?" Qhayiya said, her phone unlocked and opened to her dialling pad. "You had me at international business awards."

33

Aunty Pat's flat, Bromley

It was nearly 10:30 pm by the time the giggling duo arrived back at the council flats where Aunty Pat was renting a room. The building was a far cry from the sorbet-coloured, Georgian row houses she had imagined her London accommodation would be; a consequence of watching Notting Hill too many times.

Instead, the property was a modern structure with an unattractive, box-like design. It looked like a row of brown brick Monopoly houses with black-tiled roofs. Inside was a shared kitchen area, TV area, and bathroom. The four bedrooms each had a padlock.

Were it not for Aunty Pat being a night nurse, her double bed would have been too small for all three of them, and Runako would have had to arrange alternative accommodation.

The two friends changed into their fleece onesies, before heading into the kitchen to unpack the evening's events over a cup of PG Tips.

"She's so annoying!" Runako complained as she stirred another teaspoon of sugar into her tea.

"Junior did say Kate was difficult," Qhayiya replied. "I wouldn't take it personally if I were you."

"You and Junior have been talking quite a bit these days, hey…" Runako said, raising her eyebrows and smiling suspiciously.

"Yes… because that's what friends do," Qhayiya responded dismissively, mirroring Runako's expression.

"Anyway, what was up with Kate bringing Kobe's high school sweetheart to my introductory dinner? That was rather distasteful of her, I must say!"

"But they're friends, *kaloku*[2]! I didn't take you for the paranoid type, Ru."

"I guess you're right. I'm the one Kobe likes, and he wouldn't have invited me to spend Christmas with his parents if he wasn't serious about me, right?" Runako smiled mischievously, waiting for Qhayiya's reaction.

"You're spending Christmas with his parents?" Qhayiya asked, her expression annoyed.

"No, I'm spending Christmas with YOU and Aunty Pat, but on the 26th, I'm heading to Kent to meet my future in-laws. Let's just say, you guys can start referring to me as 'Mrs Runako Rose Mensah'. Better start practising!" Runako beamed as she blew on her tea before taking another sip.

Christmas Day had come and gone, and Runako lay in bed, thinking back on the day's events. Aunty Pat and her work friends had tried to put on as warm a Christmas celebration as they possibly could. However, there was still something rather sad, and even incomplete, about the day.

It was a women-only gathering at the home of one of Aunty Pat's friends. Each of the women, all of African descent, had brought with them a home-cooked dish from their country. Aunty Patience, the hostess, and a nurse from Zimbabwe, cooked *sadza*[3] and a pot of *amacimbi*[4] and Aunty Pat brought *samp*[5] and a traditional beef stew. Aunty Cynthia, from Kenya, brought a bucket of fluffy *mandazi*[6]. Both Aunty Esther from Ghana and Aunty Nneka from Nigeria brought a large pot of party *jollof*[7] rice, and spent the whole afternoon asking everyone to vote which was better.

The small party of seven had spent the afternoon eating, retelling stories from childhood, drinking Alizé and sparkling wine cocktails, and dancing to old-school classics such as Ashford and Simpson's *Solid As A Rock* and Womack and Womack's *Baby I'm Scared Of You*.

Before long, however, the cheerful house had turned into a group counselling session with the women recounting how much they missed their homes, some their children, and their families. They also lamented how difficult it was that family and friends thought life in a foreign land was tea and crumpets, when in fact it was long work hours, extremely expensive, and brutally lonely.

With its fast-paced lifestyle and unfriendly inhabitants, Runako understood why London could be lonely, and she was even more delighted to be seeing Kobe the following day.

Two Degrees, Knightsbridge, London

I'm glad I came, Runako thought to herself as she, Qhayiya, Fifi, and Kuku worked their way through the bustling crowd. She'd been in two minds about spending New Year's Eve with Kobe's cousins as he was uncomfortable that his girlfriend was being hosted by another guy. A *Nigerian* no less!

Fellow Africans had a poor perception of Nigerian nationals, based on the unfortunate few that gained worldwide notoriety for their "creative" economic activities. Many Africans used this sample to make an inference overall. An exercise that was hugely skewed and fundamentally flawed.

Now was not the time to be thinking about Kobe's misgivings. Runako was at THE hottest party on the London social calendar – New Year's Eve at Two Degrees. Established in 1974, the Grande Dame of Knightsbridge high society played trusted hostess to Hollywood and Windsor royals alike. Two Degrees was accustomed to putting on a spectacular show for her guests, and tonight was no different.

No expense had been spared to convert the high-rise banquet hall into a gilt and glitter Brazilian wonderland. It brimmed with svelte *passistas*[8] that looked like birds of paradise in their elaborate feather headdresses and ostentatiously bejewelled costumes.

Fire breathers stunned the crowd with their dangerous and enchanting routine. The live band performed an authentic rendition of Reinaldo's *Retrato Cantado de um amor*. In a flash, the girls had been transported from miserable Knightsbridge into the heart of Rio.

"There they are!" Kuku shouted over the music, pointing to a table of four men in their mid-twenties, just ahead.

"Wow! You didn't mention how HANDSOME your friends are," Runako squealed.

"Told ya' you could do better than my nerdy cousin," Fifi teased.

"Hey! Don't talk about my Baby Cakes that way," Runako mock-scolded in Kobe's defence. The young men had risen from their seats for Kuku to make the introductions.

"Ladies, meet our host, Obi, and his friends Uche, Ozee and Tobi," Kuku pointed to each of them in turn. "And gentlemen, you know my sister and me. These are our friends Runako and Q, they're at uni in South Africa."

"Q? What's that short for?" Obi asked genially as he invited everyone to take their seats.

"It's short for Qhayiya. I personally prefer to be called by my full name, but I know the click sound is difficult for some," Qhayiya replied coolly.

"Qha-yi-ya," Obi tried gamely. "Did I get it right?" He had a naughty smile and a friendly air about him. Runako was a little jealous that Qhayiya was getting all the attention, a departure from the norm.

"Yes, you did," Qhayiya giggled with surprise. "Very well done!"

"Obi, won't you please teach me how to pronounce your surname? I got it horribly wrong when the girls first told me about you," Runako interrupted coyly. She leaned forward in her seat and rested her cheek on her shoulder. "I wouldn't want to offend our gracious host by mispronouncing his surname."

"O-KON-kwo," Obi mouthed slowly. His lush beard gave way to a wide smile set in dark gums as he watched Runako make an attempt at pronouncing his surname.

"O-BEEN-uh, O-KON-kwo," Runako said in a sultry voice.

"Well done! I think that deserves a toast," Obi winked. He stopped a waiter that was passing by and whispered something to his ear.

In what felt like mere seconds, the waiter returned with two bottles of Ace of Spades and an ice bucket. A second waiter soon followed with platters of *pão de queijo*[9], salsa, and assorted grilled meats.

Once everyone had received a glass of champagne, Obi proposed a toast, looking squarely into Runako's eyes.

"Here's to the nights we won't remember, with the people, we will never forget!"

Maryland, USA

Five and a half thousand kilometres away, Lolo sat, mesmerised by the tiny snowflakes frosting up her aeroplane window. Minutes felt like hours as she counted down the ninety minutes her flight would take to get from New York City to Arlington County. João had already commandeered most of Lolo's time during the year and had insisted she spend New Year's Eve with him at his family home in Potomac.

The flight finally touched down at Reagan National Airport. After collecting her luggage, Lolo made her way to the Hudson News store where they'd agreed to meet. She spotted João, and ran into his arms for a long, passionate kiss that would definitely have elicited rude remarks from onlookers, had they been back in South Africa.

João helped Lolo with her luggage, and they made their way to the parking lot, where he snuck in another quick kiss before closing the car door after her. Mrs Morreira's seafrost green Jaguar S-type cruised down the George Washington Memorial Parkway as João navigated his way towards his family home.

Grit, grass and gravel crunched under the weight of the luxury sedan pulling up to the gates. Up ahead lay a brightly-lit, Georgian Colonial-style home with sprawling lawns. It was magical!

Snowflakes fell gently on the twinkling Morreira home, picturesque with its snow-capped roof and Christmas lights. "Damn..." Lolo sighed under her breath, careful not to be too obviously blown away by her boyfriend's home. The gates slowly swung open and João inched his way up the driveway, past a magnificent Cavalli Fountain and around to the front entrance of the house.

"Dude! You didn't tell me your dad has a Bentley!" Lolo exclaimed as João came to a standstill next to the luxury sedan parked in front of one of the four garage doors.

"Nah! That's my godfather Uncle Stanford's new car – latest model Bentley Arnage."

"Well, your godfather better not have a hot, young son otherwise you're in trouble mister!" Lolo teased, stepping out of the Jaguar and retrieving her jacket from the back seat.

"I'd like to see Charles try!" João winked as he lifted Lolo's bag and locked the car.

Lolo followed João's lead and took her Timberlands off at the entrance, placing them carefully behind the door. The entrance hall opened onto a two-storey foyer and dramatic split staircase. The foyer had a large dining room to the left, with the living room and kitchen to the right.

Upstairs were five large bedrooms, all en-suite. The master bedroom was located on the third floor with its own living area, walk-in closet and exquisite bathroom.

The smell of beef roasting in the oven greeted them, and Lolo's mouth salivated at the thought of having a traditional English meal for dinner.

"Do I look fine?" Lolo whispered, pointing to her outfit of skinny blue jeans, cream-coloured turtleneck, and a Burberry-print snood, which she hoped would give João's parents the message 'I'm classy but not a prude, presentable but not trying too hard'.

"Nah… you look smashing," he whispered back reassuringly, planting a quick kiss on her cheek and giving her backside a naughty squeeze.

"Okay, then, let's do this!" Lolo mouthed, before taking hold of João's hand, who led her into the living room where she would meet his dad.

Two gentlemen were in deep conversation when João walked in, and he had to address his father twice before catching his attention.

Mr Morreira was even more striking than in pictures. He was toned with broad shoulders, and even though he was seated, Lolo could tell that he was much taller than his son. Clean-shaven with short, greying coils for hair, he looked much younger than his fifty-five years. His universal features could have passed him off as coming from anywhere between Cape Agulhas and Ras ben Sakka.

"*Papai*[10], meet my girlfriend, Tshenolo," João introduced her.

"Good afternoon, Mr Morreira. It's a pleasure to meet you," Lolo said. She reached out to shake his hand and found herself in an involuntary demi-curtsey.

Raul grasped Lolo's hand and remained seated as he greeted her.

"Tshenolo, you are welcome. João told us it's your first time in America. How are you finding it?" he enquired, his voice deep and hoarse. His accent was far more Azalian than American, unlike that of his son.

"Oh, it's lovely sir, but freezing. I didn't know it would be this cold!"

"We are used to the cold, isn't it, Stanford?" Raul replied casually, letting go of his young visitor's hand.

"Certainly, my good man. Three and a half decades living in England and America will do that to you," concurred Stanford. His accent was

British and posh. His rich baritone suggested a man very familiar with the finer things in life.

Although born and raised in a mining town in Azalia, Stanford De Sousa left his city of birth at fifteen to complete his schooling at a prestigious boarding school in the UK.

He then read for a mining degree before landing a job at a global mining firm in London, thanks, no doubt, to his family's sizeable mining assets back in Azalia.

During the 80s, Stanford met Raul while shuttling between Azalia and the UK, and the two had been close friends ever since.

"Uncle Stanford, please meet my girlfriend, Tshenolo," João continued the introduction. "Lolo, this is my godfather, Uncle Stanford. He owns the beast we saw parked outside."

"Lovely to meet you, sir," Lolo said, automatically.

A consummate gentleman, the tall, bearded man rose to his feet, before offering the young newcomer a handshake.

"The pleasure is mine," he replied gently, flashing dark gums that contrasted the frost-white teeth set in them.

The mining tycoon was casual, yet debonair, in an outfit that was age-appropriate yet surprisingly fashionable. In theory, the combination of khaki chinos, a blush pink cotton shirt and a sangria-red jersey slung over his shoulders should seem odd. And yet, even eccentrically paired with burgundy leather tassel loafers and accessorised with a navy, pink and turquoise ascot, Stanford managed to translate the berry hues into Ivy League chic instead of an Eton mess.

"João – have you taken Lolo to meet *Mamãe*[11]?" Raul asked his son.

"Not yet, Papai, I wanted her to greet you, first."

"Aah, all right. You are welcome, Lolo," Raul assured her. "You said your surname is…?"

"Motsepe – my surname is Motsepe, sir."

"Motsepe? Okay, then Miss Motsepe – you are welcome."

Isabel Morreira was leaning over the open oven door, mumbling softly to herself, when Lolo and João walked in.

Short and plump, she looked like Grammi Gummi as she wiggled about in her marigold fleece tracksuit, periwinkle-coloured apron and brown sheep wool slippers. It was only when she straightened up to put the tray of herb-roasted heirloom carrots on the kitchen counter that she noticed the two intruders giggling silently at her mannerisms.

"What have I told you about scaring me like that, João!" Isabel scolded, before composing herself for her guest. "Apologies, my dear, for raising my voice in your presence."

"It's cool, Mrs Morreira. He kinda deserves it!" Lolo giggled nervously, using the opportunity to, hopefully, break the ice between herself and her potential mother-in-law.

"I didn't mean to scare you, Mamãe," João smiled naughtily. "Anyway, this is Lolo. My girlfriend."

"Lolo. You have such a lovely name," Isabel said, placing her oven gloves beside the tray and giving her guest a warm hug. Isabel was soft and cuddly, and smelled like fabric softener and melted butter.

"Thank you, Mrs Morreira, it's wonderful to meet you. And thanks for inviting me to your home," Lolo replied.

"Oh, it's a pleasure, dear. João wouldn't stop bothering us about his new girlfriend from South Africa," she chuckled.

Although Lolo and João had started spending more time together since their meeting at The Ivy, it was only in the past six months that they'd started seeing each other exclusively. Their love-hate relationship had grown into a deep friendship that culminated in a thrilling yet authentic romantic relationship.

What had also won Lolo's affection was that contrary to her

conclusions, João hadn't actually touched her the night she went home with him from The Ivy. He had instead put his pecker back in his pants when it became clear that Lolo was too drunk to consent to having sex with him.

Over the past eighteen months, Lolo had opened up about the pain her estranged relationship with her father caused her. And João had shared the resentment he felt towards his own father for the *small house*[12] he was secretly running back in Azalia. The young couple had agreed that marriage was an outdated institution that only served to ruin perfectly good relationships, and vowed never to subject each other to same.

"João, why don't you go catch up with your father while Lolo and I take care of supper?" Isabel said.

"Mamãe, I'm sure Lolo's tired after her long-" João started to advocate for her.

"No, dude, I'm good!" interrupted Lolo. "Later!" she winked at him.

"So, Lolo, João tells me your father is a successful accountant with his own property development company?" Isabel began, as she carefully poured the Yorkshire pudding batter into baking tray cups.

"Yes, he is!" Lolo lied. Although her father had qualified as a chartered accountant before venturing into construction, he was far from successful. Not now, anyway. "My dad wanted me to be an accountant too, but I told him numbers are not for me."

"I see... Was he not disappointed that you decided against a career in one of the more formal disciplines?" Isabel continued. "João mentioned that you're studying marketing."

"Uhm...not really. My dad considers marketing to be a formal discipline..." Lolo smiled awkwardly. She was slightly annoyed with Mrs Morreira's snide remark. She needed to find a way to change the subject, before saying something she might later regret. "Mrs Morreira, I believe you're a psychologist?"

"Psychiatrist, dear," Isabel corrected. "I'm a qualified medical doctor. I run my practice from an upmarket wellness centre down the road. You wouldn't believe how many problems the rich have!"

"Well, I'm surprised you still work at all, given that you and Mr Morreira are already so accomplished," Lolo inquired, pulling dirty utensils in the sink as she tried to make herself useful.

"I guess we are quite privileged," Isabel mused, "but that doesn't mean we can stop working."

"But Mrs Morreira –"

"Aunty Isabel will do," Isabel interrupted, placing her hand gently on Lolo's arm.

"Sorry, Aunty Isabel," Lolo blushed before continuing. "As I was saying, I believe running a home as lovely as this, AND supervising children at school on two different continents, AND managing fifteen investment properties, IS work." Lolo smiled coyly, embarrassed at having revealed her knowledge of the family's financial affairs.

"You know about our properties?" Isabel asked surprisingly, placing her hands on her hips.

"Yes. João told me," Lolo blushed. "He was encouraging me to take more interest in my dad's business and told me that *you* are actually the one that manages the family property portfolio."

"He did, did he?" Isabel said casually, adding more water to the boiling pot of peas on the stove. "I'd take his advice if I were you, especially since your father develops properties in low-income areas."

"I'd much rather invest in an apartment in Manhattan or Mayfair," Lolo said with dreamy eyes. She took the kettle from Isabel and placed it back on its stand.

"You mean you'd rather *live* there," Isabel winked. "But for investment purposes, you want to put your money in those residential nodes where people don't generally qualify for mortgages, as there'll always be demand."

"Sounds like you should have gone into investments instead of medicine, Aunty Isabel!" Lolo chuckled.

"Oh, I just love numbers! Won't you pass me the oven gloves, dear?" Isabel interrupted herself. "Raul thinks I'm mad for always watching CNBC and tracking the currencies. I'm always looking for the best time to fund our rand account for João's tuition, and our Euro account for Eva and Sofia's boarding school fees."

Isabel put her oven gloves on the stovetop and folded her arms in front of her chest, nodding to herself with pride. "In fact, do you know that it was my smart timing of the markets that funded the very ski trip that Eva and Sophia are on right now?" Isabel said smugly, pointing her index finger in the air.

"You're making my head spin with all the CNBC and currencies talk, Aunty Isabel. I don't think I'll be the kind of wife that bothers with all that stuff," Lolo joked.

Apparently, Isabel didn't find anything amusing about Lolo's statement. Her face suddenly turned cold, and her eyes steely.

"All that 'stuff'?" Isabel chuckled incredulously, before placing her hands on her hips. "Listen, my dear, I was just like you when I married Raul – young, naïve, and from an unknown family. I thought marrying up meant I would spend the rest of my life being wined, dined, and taken on trips around the world. Much like you find yourself doing now." Isabel took a step closer to Lolo and leaned one hand on the kitchen sink.

"But, my husband made sure I knew very early on that I would have to contribute to the wealth of this family, and not just take from it."

Isabel brusquely wiped her hands on a dishcloth, looking Lolo straight in the eye. "I hope you will adopt this philosophy, as well. It will help you make a fine wife to whoever you end up marrying one day!"

Secret Location, Cape Town - January 2008

It was the day of João's graduation and by now all of UCT knew the Belters and the Muzungus as the most enviable couples on campus. Although Junior and Qhayiya were still nothing more than just friends, onlookers assumed the octet was a union of four couples. News of Lolo and Runako's lavish Christmas holidays at their boyfriends' family homes had made headlines throughout January. It was assumed that Nala had spent December in South Africa by choice.

Many campus females' hearts were crushed when João changed his Facebook relationship status from 'Single' to 'In a relationship with Lolo Motsepe', a feat no previous girl had managed to achieve. João had then flooded his timeline with images of Lolo with his friends and family in Maryland.

To add insult to injury, João had chronicled what seemed to be every detail of their ultra-luxurious three-day tour of New York City, courtesy of his father's Centurion Card. His timeline was littered with images of the couple on a helicopter tour of Manhattan, ice skating at Rockefeller Center, having breakfast at The Four Seasons Hotel, getting cosy at Bemelmans Bar, and chasing down famous artworks across various galleries.

The lovebirds had posed in front of the *Portrait of a Young Swiss Woman*, the famous work dubbed 'the black Girl with a Pearl Earring'. And next to Annibale Carracci's *Portrait of an African Woman Holding a Clock,* one of the most famous portraits of a black subject from the Baroque era.

Their romance hadn't slowed down when they returned to South Africa, and daily public displays of affection had become the norm. Lolo had further cemented her place as first in line to marry João after she sacrificed spending time with her family, to return to Cape Town early for João's graduation.

The Morreiras had announced that they wouldn't be able to travel to South Africa. João's father was being bestowed with national honours for his contribution to trade relations between Azalia and the USA, on the very same day.

The Morreiras offered to throw their son a graduation party, for him and twenty of his closest friends, to make up for their absence. Knowing how extravagant Raul and Isabel could be, what was meant to be an intimate dinner among friends would surely be one of the highlights of the Cape Town social calendar.

"Dude! Are you sure you have no idea where we're going?" Lolo beamed from the back of the BMW X5, as the six-car motorcade sped down Nelson Mandela Boulevard.

"Negative!" João replied, shaking his head. "Only my parents, Junior and his dad know the venue."

"Junior really outdid himself today, hey! Asking a whole Prime Minister to arrange a government motorcade to escort us to your party. I'm glad your country recognises the VIP I am!" Lolo chuckled, adjusting her posture to match her new status.

"What I recognise is how FINE you're looking in this outfit!" João smiled, placing his hand on the section of thigh peeping through the slit of the black, floor length, sequined halter-neck gown.

"I know!" Lolo grinned, pretending to adjust João's bowtie.

"Seriously though, why did those two insist on my graduation dinner being a black-tie event?" commented João, lifting his chin while she fiddled with the garment in question. "Knowing my parents, we're still going to feel underdressed when we finally arrive at this 'secret location' of theirs."

"What? Speak for yourself!" Lolo teased as she looked out the window and tried to figure out where the vehicle was headed.

The motorcade skilfully sped through the winding roads up Lion's Head, sirens blaring and blue lights flashing. They turned into Nettleton Road, one of the most sought-after residential addresses on the African continent. A few minutes later, the car stopped in front of a cliffside property that looked like nothing more than a high wall shooting straight into the sky.

A white-gloved butler reached for the door as soon as the car stopped, and an usher escorted them into the elevator.

The doors of the elevator pinged open when they reached the fifth floor. The elevator had reached the top floor of the six-storey home suspended over the highest point in Clifton. Lolo and João found themselves stepping out into the sky!

The entertainment area led onto the bar, where the glass floor swept to surround the infinity pool that merged with the Atlantic Ocean. Leading South African soprano, Pretty Yende, sang Puccini's *O Mio Babbino Caro* to an enthralled crowd. Throngs of white-gloved stewards moved about gracefully serving champagne and canapés to João's guests.

Lolo marvelled at the panoramic views. "I think I've died and gone to heaven!" she sighed.

"Actually, not quite. But I'll be sure to let my father know you were impressed by his home," said an unexpected voice.

"Charles!" João exclaimed, his jaw clenching at the sight of the speaker.

"Always a pleasure to see you, my good man!" Charles responded, tilting his champagne glass towards João, who held his own firmly to his chest. Lolo remembered that João had mentioned his bitter rivalry with Stanford De Sousa's son, even though their families had been friends, their whole lives.

"And you must be the beautiful Lolo," Charles continued, proffering his hand. "My father didn't do you much justice, I'm afraid." He bowed slightly and gently kissed the back of her hand. As he did, a flood of dopamine coursed through her veins, thanks to a whiff of bergamot and black pepper that caressed her olfactory senses before fading.

The thirty-one-year-old heir to one of Azalia's largest mining companies smelled absolutely devourable and was also devilishly good-looking. Frequently mistaken for Ghanaian-British fashion designer Ozwald Boateng, Charles De Sousa's two-metre frame, hawk-like eyes and Cupid's bow lips made him as alluring as he was intimidating.

"It's a pleasure to meet you too, Charles," Lolo blushed.

"What brings you to town?" João asked coldly, wrapping his arm around his girlfriend's waist, and pulling Lolo closer to his side.

"I'm on a stopover on my way to Mozambique, actually. I've got a meeting with our Foundation's project co-ordinator." Charles' expression became sombre. "We're building emergency housing for the people displaced by the floods. The havoc caused by the cyclones is terrible!" he finished, his face and tone sincere.

"Wow, that was quick. The flooding happened what, only a few days ago?" João queried.

"Well... my mom's relatives were among those that lost their property in the flood. Even though they've been divorced for some years now, my father still makes sure Mom and her family are taken care of. He likes to keep an eye on matters that are close to his heart. Nearly as much as you do," Charles teased, his gaze going to João's hand on Lolo's hip, then travelling down the curve of her body, lingering on her exposed thigh.

Sensing the tension between the two men, Lolo moved to diffuse the potential flare-up.

"This really is an incredible place your father has here!"

"You've seen nothing yet! Let me show you around, and I'm not taking no for an answer. João, excuse us, please," Charles said, taking Lolo by the hand and escorting her towards the elevator.

The elevator opened onto the basement floor, and Charles led Lolo down a dark, narrow passage to a windowless space filled with the smell of rubber and fuel. With the flip of a switch, Lolo found herself standing in the entrance to the garage. It looked more like a dealership showroom, complete with a bar and seating area. Inside were six cars, all covered, except for one.

"Welcome to the petrol station!" Charles said, spreading his arms wide to include all the cars in front of him.

"Why is this poor guy not under a cover?" Lolo asked, pausing next to the Mini Cooper with a Union Jack on its roof.

"Oh! You mean Jackson? He's still too young. Once he's a bit older, maybe he'll get a jacket," quipped Charles.

"You do realise these are just cars we're talking about, right?" Lolo chuckled.

"No, my dear. These are classics! And you are staring at about fifty million rands worth!"

"Bullshit! Why would your father spend so much money on things that lose value? I'm sorry, but I don't find that very impressive," Lolo replied, sceptically.

Charles paused and gave Lolo a cheeky grin before grabbing her glass for a refill at the bar.

"Ordinarily, your misgivings would be valid," Charles began, popping open a bottle of Nicolas Feuillatte Brut from the bar fridge. "However, the cars in here – well, except for Jackson – actually appreciate in value. And technically, my father didn't buy these cars with his own money."

"What do you mean?" Lolo asked, accepting her glass of champagne from Charles.

"Let me show you what I mean. Pick a car!"

"Okay… let's go for this one," answered Lolo, pointing to the mound right in front of her.

Charles handed his glass to Lolo and lifted the cover of the car she'd chosen.

"A woman with taste! 1955 Mercedes Benz 300 SL Gullwing. I'd say this bad boy is easily worth a million US dollars; paid for by Azalian Mining International in 1977. New York Stock Exchange," Charles rattled off smugly.

"What do you mean, paid for by Azalian Mining International?" Lolo asked, peeking through the windows of the shiny car.

"Pick another one. You'll soon get the picture."

"Alright, then. This one," Lolo said, turning around to point at the unusual shape behind her.

"Ah! Our gift from the Chinese!" Charles heaved the cover off the next car. "1965 Shelby 427 Cobra. Paid for by Hong Se Properties in 1998. Hong Kong Stock Exchange. My father believes this baby is worth about half a million US."

"Okay, now I'm really confused," grumbled Lolo, fingertips to her temples. "And I think you're doing it on purpose!" She frowned at him with dramatic disapproval.

Charles laughed heartily before retrieving his glass of champagne from Lolo and taking a long, slow sip.

"Look, these cars are bought with the money my family made from various stocks over many years. Look at the number plates carefully. The Merc is 77 AMI – AZ that shows the year it was bought, and the share code of the company whose shares were sold to fund it. Now, look at the Cobra: 98 HSP – AZ. The car was bought in 1998 using proceeds from selling stock in Hong Se Properties. All legit!"

"Wow! Is that why you said your dad didn't use his own money to buy these cars?" Lolo asked, tilting her head questioningly.

"Exactly!" Charles beamed as he ushered Lolo back to the elevator to show her around the rest of the property.

"Basically, we have my grandfather to thank for three of the classics you saw in there. Every twenty or so years, he used to review his portfolio and take his profits from stocks that have super-performed. My father adopted that same habit, and that's the money he used to fund his luxuries, which in themselves are usually investments."

"But how did your grandfather get those stocks to begin with? No one just wakes up with a huge portfolio!" Lolo said irritably. She was growing tired of Charles' never-ending explanation.

"You're right! It started with my great-grandfather. He believed that any money earned must be put to work a few more times before it is spent," Charles said seriously, as the elevator doors closed. "He used to plough his wages into various small businesses, which my grandfather inherited and grew into big businesses. My grandfather then used the profits from *those* businesses, to invest in property and in the stock market."

The lift stopped, and the doors opened on the third floor of the house, which contained five sea-facing bedrooms, all en-suite. Charles gestured for her to step out first.

"My father continued this tradition when he took over the reins of the family business and investments, and also added to the classic car collection when the time was right." Charles grinned, waiting for her reaction.

"So basically your family will never run out of money as you're never spending your capital!" Lolo said. "Spot on!" Charles winked, as he placed his hand on Lolo's upper arm to lead her down the passage.

"Watch your step," he warned, as the tiles gave way to a carpet so deep-piled it threatened to entrap her pencil heels. "Would you believe that this house pays for itself? My father rents it out for R50,000 per night, thanks to a view I like to call God's window. Come see this!"

Lolo looked around the opulent suite, trying not to gape, as she walked towards the balcony.

"Wow!" she exclaimed, looking out at the spectacular sunset over the Atlantic Ocean. "I can see why someone would pay a pretty penny to wake up to this every morning!"

"Indeed! The Cape Town summer season covers the mortgage for the whole year, and we have the house for the rest of the time, to use as we please! Like hosting a graduation party for your little boyfriend..." Charles teased.

"João! Shit! I need to head back..." Lolo panicked as she turned to hurry back to the elevator. João would be upset that she'd been gone for so long, with Charles De Sousa, no less!

"Hey!" Charles protested, grabbing Lolo's hand and pulling her towards him. "I was thinking...would you like to spend the night? I'm all alone here, and there are plenty of rooms for you to choose from. In the morning, we can hike up Lion's Head, and later go for lunch at our family friend's wine farm in Franschhoek."

"Uhm... That's sweet Charles, but I'm sure João would rather be in his own bed, thanks," Lolo deflected sheepishly.

"As he should be," Charles whispered. "The invite wasn't open to him; it was for you."

"Charles!" Lolo snapped, yanking her arm back. "What the hell do you take me for?" She retreated from him, flustered. "João's my boyfriend, and your fathers are friends, for goodness sake!" She marched towards the elevator, her heels clicking a quick staccato on the marble floor.

"You're not seriously in love with him, are you?" Charles asked derisively as he easily caught up with long strides.

"And what the hell is that supposed to mean?" Lolo asked, perplexed, her finger frantically pushing the elevator button.

"Don't you know this is all just a game to him? Taking you home to meet his parents doesn't make you special!" Charles planted his hand on the button, his arm barring her way.

"Now I see why João cannot stand you! You're nothing but a little boy who uses his daddy's toys to try and win girls over." She put both hands on his forearm and pushed hard. "Now if you'll excuse me. I've got my MAN to get back to!"

The elevator doors pinged open, and Lolo marched in. She turned around and gave Charles a look that let him know he was not welcome to accompany her. Charles stood in place, regarding her with pity.

Lolo hurried back onto the fifth floor as Kobe, flanked by the Muzungus, called for everyone's attention. Lolo spotted Q, Nala and Runako standing up front, and squeezed through the crowd to join them. As soon as the hubbub had died down, Kobe placed his arm around João and proposed a toast.

"To my mate, João Morreira, I can't believe you made it! From writing off your mom's car during our first year and walking away from the scene without a scratch..." he began, before handing the microphone over to Junior who was standing to his left.

"To getting us backstage passes at the Mandela concert because the organisers thought you're Drake," Junior continued. The crowd roared in laughter as he handed the microphone to Blaise.

"To partying with you all night and then watching you ace your exams the following day. You still need to tell us how you did that!"

"It's that Morreira winning gene, man!" João shouted into the microphone. The guests cheered and broke into loud applause.

"João, buddy," Kobe continued, "I, together with the rest of the Muzungus, are proud of you and the man you've become, and we're honoured to be celebrating this special day with you." Kobe paused and looked up to the sky as if holding back tears. After a few moments, he looked back at the Muzungus before continuing with his address.

"Gents, we'll soon be going our separate ways. João is heading to Azalia to start with his law articles, and Junior is moving to Joburg to intern at the Azalian Embassy. Luckily, I'll still have Blaise around who's staying in Cape Town to start his audit articles, while I play around with some oil as a junior engineer."

Kobe shook his head mockingly as the guests laughed politely at his joke. The Muzungus wrapped their arms around each other and huddled together.

"Promise me, gents, that we will not lose the friendship we have here. As much as this celebration is for you João, I'd like to propose we toast to friendship."

"To friendship!" the party cheered as bottles of G.H. Mumm flowed, and Pretty Yende serenaded the guests with the Cape Town Philharmonic Orchestra accompanying her.

"So, you're leaving me then, João?" Natasha smiled when Lolo managed to re-join him after fighting through the throng. Natasha was one of João's closest female friends, and Lolo despised the cosy body language she always adopted when around him. Although João vowed that they'd never shared anything more than a platonic friendship, Lolo wasn't so sure Natasha was satisfied with the status quo.

"Afraid so! My parents will kill me if I don't get admitted to the Azalian bar. They're scared I've lost focus because my grades slipped last year. They blame HER for the distraction," João smiled at Lolo, who had possessively slipped her arm under his tuxedo jacket and wrapped it around his waist.

"Good thing you're moving away from the distraction then," Natasha winked.

"There are telephones. Emails. Jets." João smiled. Natasha frowned for a moment, trying to figure out what João meant.

"Oh! You guys will continue seeing each other then?"

"Yes, ma'am! I'm not done with this one yet..." João gave Lolo a naughty wink before giving her a peck on the cheek.

Lolo blushed and rested her head on his shoulder, giving Natasha a loaded look to remind her who the main girl in João's life was. Then she lifted her head to whisper in João's ear.

"I have a very special surprise for you when we get home..."

Franklin Securities, Sandton, Johannesburg
February 2008

Qhayiya's heart beat painfully in her chest as she walked into the high-rise building situated at 54 Gwen Lane. It suddenly hit her that she hadn't been alone in a new environment since her first day of boarding school in Grade 8. Throughout high school, she'd had Nala and Lolo by her side, with Runako joining the friendship in the first year of university.

Now she was alone – starting a new job, in a new building, in a new city, by herself. Qhayiya so wished she could be back on campus with her friends, who were still together to complete their honours year. Having to complete her honours degree while working, was just another reminder that although Qhayiya had spent years with the Belters, she still didn't feel that she truly belonged.

It seemed that she was always the outsider – too rich to be accepted by her cousins in the Eastern Cape, and too poor to have the same options as Lolo, Nala and Runako. Qhayiya was always *too something*. Hopefully, this day would mark her entrance into a world where she was the perfect fit.

The lift doors closed as quickly as they had opened, but not before fifteen eager professionals of all ages, shapes and sizes squeezed their way into the metal cubicle. Two stops later, the doors finally opened onto the fifth floor, where Qhayiya would be embarking on the very first day of her investment banking internship.

Qhayiya sat, patiently waiting to be collected from the reception area of Franklin Securities. The space was ultra-modern and highly intimidating. The grey wall-to-wall carpeting and glass interior gave one a sense of a cutthroat environment, while the friendly trio of receptionists in matching navy-blue suit jackets and crisp, white shirts with floral scarves added warmth and personality to the otherwise cold aesthetic.

A few minutes later, a nervous-looking young woman named Chloe sat down next to Qhayiya. After striking up a conversation, the two interns recognised each other from UCT and established they had some mutual acquaintances. However, they had never been introduced to each other.

An HR co-ordinator escorted Qhayiya and Chloe to the 27th floor where the auditorium was situated. The foyer was abuzz with the chatter of excited interns, milling around as they waited for the day's proceedings to begin. Among them were Brooke and Caitlyn, who Chloe had befriended on the day of their psychometric tests.

After cautious introductions centred on which university each had graduated from, and which other firms they'd been accepted to, the four friends took their seats at one of the round tables and quietened down as the facilitator called for everyone's attention. Miss Justine Stevens, the HR business partner, introduced herself and took the group through the two-day induction programme. Justine's green eyes twinkled against her pale face as she ran through Franklin Securities' company policies.

Speeches from various members of management and the executive blurred into one another as Qhayiya, and her new workmates passed around Post-It notes. These lamented the tediousness of the agenda; described how they could not wait for the cocktail session with the rest of the firm that evening; and wished that the three interns on the Banker Development Programme (BDP) would stop asking so many damn questions!

After tea, Justine took to the stage again to facilitate the Financial Fitness session, which would focus on helping them understand their payslips.

"Okay, guys, for this section of the employment contract I'd like you to pull out your dummy payslips. The reason we use dummy payslips is that not everyone is starting on the same salary. Also, I must reiterate that it is a dismissible offence to discuss your earnings with your colleagues. I hope we're all clear on that?" Justine said firmly and turned to face the payslip example projected onto the big screen behind her.

The leader of the talkative group of graduates on the BDP raised her hand yet again, as she had done all morning, and Qhayiya and her table all grimaced their irritation at the same time.

"Yes, Pamela?" Justine acknowledged the young woman.

"Ma'am, why are we are not being paid the same when we are doing the same work?" Pamela asked. Her two friends nodded their agreement, whispering, "Ya," behind her.

"That's a very good question, Pamela, but your qualifications are not the same, so the expertise you bring to the organisation will not be the same," Justine defended. "May I remind you that your group is entering the workplace with only a matric certificate, while your colleagues have undergraduate and even honours degrees."

"She's so annoying," Qhayiya mouthed silently to her newfound friends as she rolled her eyes in Pamela's direction.

"But it's still the same work, ma'am! Are you punishing us because we can't afford to go to university?" Funeka added.

"Of course not!" Justine giggled nervously. "May I suggest we continue this conversation in private as we have a lot to get through?"

"Yes, please!" Chloe chirped.

Justine seemed highly embarrassed by Pamela and Funeka's questions. She struggled to hide it, but she proceeded to explain the concepts of cost of employment, gross earnings and net earnings.

"Yes, AGAIN, Pamela?" Justine sighed heavily.

"Ma'am, what if I don't want medical aid? My mom has a hospital plan that covers us, and I hardly get sick."

"And, ma'am," Funeka weighed in. "I can't afford to have medical aid for myself when my brother is staying at home without school fees. Can I please cancel mine, and take the money instead?"

Thami, another intern on the BDP chimed in. "Me too, please! My sister works at a call centre for a medical aid scheme, and during training; their supervisor told them it's not the law for people to belong to medical aid. So we should have the right to not join if we don't want to."

Brooke threw her head on the table in exasperation, while Caitlyn shook her head in disbelief. Justine took a deep breath and composed herself. "Colleagues, you raise very valid points. And you are correct. It is not a legal requirement that employees join a medical aid. However, because Franklin Securities operates on a cost to company basis, makes a medical contribution on your behalf, and has included medical aid as one of the conditions of service in your employment contracts, you are obliged to make a contribution towards medical aid.

Put differently, we have BUMPED UP your package, to cater for non-cash benefits such as the medical aid contributions. This means that even if we gave you the option of not belonging to medical aid, we still wouldn't give you that benefit as cash."

Justine paused to make sure the three interns were satisfied with her answer before continuing with her presentation. At 1 pm, half an hour behind schedule, Justine finally announced the group would be breaking for a one-hour lunch break.

Qhayiya and her new friends made a quick bathroom stop before tucking into the elaborate buffet spread laid out in the dining room.

"I can't believe those BDP interns. They were so rude to poor Justine!" Chloe said as she washed her hands in the basin.

"I know! Like, if you don't agree with the rules of the job, then why did you take it?" Caitlyn concurred, airing her hands under the dryer.

"I kinda feel sorry for them though," Qhayiya argued, "they raised some valid points!"

"Fine, maybe they did," Brooke conceded, touching up her lipstick in the mirror. "It's just not a great way to start your career by challenging EVERYTHING, especially since the firm is already doing so much for them."

"Right?" Caitlyn chimed in. "I'd give anything to be given a job straight from matric *and* have my tertiary studies paid for!"

"Agreed! Some people walk around with such an attitude of entitlement. Then they wonder why they aren't promoted into senior positions at work. Like, how do you expect to grow in an organisation when all you do is go around, causing trouble with everyone?" Chloe exclaimed while drying her hands.

The closed-door to a toilet stall opened and Funeka exited. "Would you like to repeat that to my face, Chloe?" Funeka asked archly, walking threateningly towards her colleague.

"Please don't hit me," Chloe whispered. She jumped behind Qhayiya, using her as a human shield. Brooke and Caitlyn darted for the door.

"Funeka," Pamela said, bursting forth from the stall next to Funeka's, "is this the girl that was talking about us?" Pamela winked at Funeka who folded her arms and nodded.

"Q! Say something!" Chloe begged, clutching on to Qhayiya's top.

"You guys..." Qhayiya smiled awkwardly. "I don't think Chloe meant any harm –"

"And you Qhayiya," Funeka interrupted, "don't think we didn't see you rolling your eyes when we were speaking. I guess you don't know what if feels like to be black and poor in this country!"

"Excuse me! I'll have you know that I didn't grow up rich!" Qhayiya replied defensively, her hands fixed firmly on her hips.

"Aah! So then you've just CHOSEN to forget what it feels like!" Funeka retaliated.

"What!" Qhayiya barked back. "Forgive me for not using my background as an excuse to be angry at everyone and everything around me!"

"You want to see angry?" Funeka yelled, shoving Qhayiya backwards who nearly tripped over Chloe who was still hiding behind her.

"I'm calling security!" Brooke shouted as she bolted out the door. Caitlyn followed behind her.

"YEYI, WENA[13]! I'll fuck you up!" Qhayiya yelled, shoving Funeka back with even more force than she had received.

"Leave her, Funeka!" Pamela shouted, jumping between the two girls. "She's clearly forgotten who she is." Pamela stared at Qhayiya for an angry moment. "Let me give you a friendly warning, sisi[14]. It's clear you won't stand with us in changing unfair company policies, that's your choice. But don't you DARE stand in our fucking way! Mas'hambe[15], Funeka."

The smooth lacquer-finish table suddenly felt cold and rough against Qhayiya's forearm as she made doodles all over her note pad. It had been two hours since her altercation with Pamela and Funeka, and she felt terrible for the way she'd handled their encounter.

It was true that she'd had a relatively comfortable upbringing and couldn't relate to the struggles they were going through. But why did they pick on HER when it was the rest of her friends that had said terrible things about them? Why was she the only one taken to task for not supporting their effort to change company policies?

Why did the colour of her skin bind her to a cause she knew nothing about and didn't sign up for, while her white friends got off without being held to account?

Qhayiya arrived home from the cocktail evening to a dark and empty apartment. She turned on the light and placed her bag on the kitchen counter. The feeling of loneliness overcame her once again as she collapsed on the couch and took off her shoes.

The sound of her phone vibrating in her bag jolted Qhayiya from her one-man pity party. The tiles were cold under her feet as she walked back into the kitchen. She reached for her phone and smiled when she realised who the message was from.

Of course, she wasn't alone in Johannesburg. She had Junior.

Junior's Place, Waterkloof

The imposing black metal gate rolled open as soon as the car lights approached. Three weeks of back and forth phone calls had finally culminated in an evening where both Qhayiya and Junior were free to see each other. A scrawny-looking guard in an ill-fitting Azalian uniform offered a salute as the black BMW 7-series went through the gate. The friendly chauffeur whose name Qhayiya had forgotten made a sharp left turn and came to a stop alongside two of the four garage doors.

The modest entrance to Junior's home stood in stark contrast to the impossibly high walls and security guard post it hid behind. Instead of a stately home, Qhayiya was greeted by a symmetrical bunker-style structure with two garage doors on either side of two large, low-lying windows, with a narrow walkway down the centre.

The chauffeur held the car door open with one hand, and with the other, offered to help his prized passenger out the car. Qhayiya carefully navigated her heels across the steppingstone walkway towards the large swivel glass door, where a petite woman in a three-piece housekeeper uniform was waiting. Qhayiya stepped through the door and found herself in a space that seemed to go on forever!

The open-plan house was as long as it was wide, with living spaces demarcated using cleverly placed furniture and pop false ceiling designs. Truffle grey and macaron cream decor complemented the warm maple flooring to create a cool yet intimate feel in the home.

Miriam, the housekeeper, escorted her guest to the TV area where she offered her a seat and something to drink. She returned with a glass of orange juice and a bowl of fresh fruit and advised Qhayiya that "Master Junior" would be with her shortly.

Qhayiya remembered that Junior had a weekly catch-up call with his father on Friday evenings, a routine he claimed to dread, but followed with military precision. Her heart began to race at the realisation that she had actually never been alone with Junior before. Although their friendship had developed over the years, they'd always seen each other with the rest of the Belters and Muzungus around.

With each passing minute, she wondered if she'd be able to sustain hours of conversation alone with Junior, without Lolo butting in with another crass statement. Or Blaise cutting everyone off to share one of his silly jokes. "Just be yourself," she thought to herself, as she paged aimlessly through the large book that she picked up off the coffee table.

"You also like Basquiat?" Junior called out from across the room, startling Qhayiya.

"Who?" Qhayiya asked. She turned around and watched Junior walk towards her. He was barefoot in a pair of stone-coloured drawstring linen pants and a form-fitting white tee.

"Jean-Michel Basquiat, the artist whose work you're looking at," Junior explained, pointing to the book in Qhayiya's hands.

"Oh! Never heard of him!" Qhayiya placed the book back on the coffee table and rose to her feet. "His work is quite dark if you ask me…"

"It's dark because he brings out the demons we keep so well hidden…" Junior smiled. He gave Qhayiya a lingering look before taking her in his arms for a hug.

"It's good to see you," he whispered in her ear. He gave her a peck on the cheek before releasing her from his embrace.

"It's good to see you too," Qhayiya blushed, "and this is quite the place you have here!"

"Place MY PARENTS have here," Junior corrected, reaching for the TV remote before navigating to the music channel. "I hope you're hungry," he said, smiling down at Qhayiya who had returned to her seat. "I told the chef to make your favourite!"

"Your chef made scallops and risotto?" Qhayiya beamed. She'd often told Junior of the heavenly delight that was the highlight of her trips to London.

"Don't be silly, Q!" he frowned, as he held out his hand and helped Qhayiya off the couch. "Please don't tell me you've changed now that you're a Joburg girl…"

"What do you mean?" Qhayiya chuckled as she followed Junior towards the 8-seater table in the dining area. Miriam appeared as if out of thin air, and hurriedly removed the silver food domes lining the table.

Qhayiya burst out in laughter when she realised what was on the menu that evening: baguettes, green salad, potato chips, masala steak, fried eggs and sliced cheese.

"We're having a *Gatsby*[16]? Seriously!" Qhayiya stuttered in between loud bouts of laughter.

"Yes, ma'am!" Junior winked, pulling out a chair for Qhayiya. "Your favourite meal after a big night out on Long Street!"

"You're so silly…" she smiled, shaking her head.

Junior and Qhayiya reminisced over their university antics as they indulged in the Cape Town culinary classic, washed down with vodka and lemonade. They also shared how different work-life was to what they had expected. Junior bemoaned his long days at the Azalian Embassy as a political analyst. Qhayiya shared her bathroom incident with Pamela and Funeka.

Hours went by effortlessly, and Qhayiya remembered why she considered Junior to be one of her best friends. Before long, Junior had opened up about the resentment he felt towards his parents for not allowing him to follow his passion in art. Qhayiya revealed her pain at losing contact with her father as a young girl, and that the only memory she had of him was that he used to call her *"MaMtolo[17]"*.

"I wanna show you something," Junior said as Miriam appeared to clear up the table. He walked around the table and pulled out Qhayiya's chair. She held his hand as he led her carefully down the stairs. He flicked on the lights and revealed a large, messy space with tables and chairs and paintbrushes and paint and paintings everywhere.

There were paintings lined up on the floor against the wall. Paintings hanging off the wall. Paintings on easels scattered around the room. It seemed the only surface without a painting on it was the futon placed in the centre of the room.

"Is this all you?" Qhayiya asked in amazement. She caught herself walking towards a painting of yellow rectangles against a black background.

"Some me…" Junior shrugged. "Some are pieces I've collected over the years."

"Which ones are yours?" Qhayiya asked genuinely. She'd always been curious to see Junior's work. Although his friends knew that he painted, no one had actually seen any of Junior's pieces. He had always been obsessively secretive about his work.

"They're all over!" he deflected while clearing up one of his desks. Qhayiya wasn't going to let him get away with hiding his talent when she was practically staring at it.

"Alright, then show me your favourite." She walked towards him and scanned the sketches lying on his workstation.

"Hmmm… that could take a while," Junior smirked.

"I've got time!" she said cheekily. She walked to the futon and sat down to take off her heels. Junior looked on with mild disbelief as Qhayiya continued to make herself comfortable. She lay on her stomach and held her head up in her hands.

"Told you I've got time!" she winked.

Junior chuckled softly as he plugged his iPhone into the speaker and scrolled to his playlist. He took off his shirt before walking over to another one of his worktables. Qhayiya willed herself to think only pure thoughts as she watched a bare-chested Junior lift a large canvas and place it on an easel. And as he squeezed different coloured paint onto his palette, while holding a paintbrush between his teeth.

Qhayiya's eyes tracked Junior's every move when she realised what was happening. She didn't want to miss a single moment of watching Junior in his element. Doing what he loved above all else. Tonight, she was going to see him paint. Junior placed his palette on the floor and reached for his pants pocket.

"May I?" he asked, holding up a joint. "It helps me work better."

"Sure… as long as you share."

"Q, since when do you smoke?" Junior frowned, shaking his head in disbelief.

"Since we're both opening up and trying new things," she shrugged, "like this dodgy music you're playing…"

"Hey! Leave my playlist alone," Junior snickered, as he lit up. "The Goo Goo Dolls are iconic, okay!"

"Yeah… whatever!"

The world turned hazy as Qhayiya watched Junior in action. She didn't understand why he kept turning back to look at her as he worked the canvas. She bit her bottom lip to stop herself from saying anything inappropriate as she watched his bare, sculpted back twist and turn and bend and straighten up with long brush strokes.

"There!" he said, moving aside to reveal what he had been working on for the past hour.

"That's just squiggles," Qhayiya giggled. She'd giggled at everything and nothing for the past thirty minutes. She was clearly high.

"Look closely," Junior said, as he walked towards Qhayiya. He sat down beside her on the futon and rested his arms on his knees. "It's you…."

"Really…Yeah…If I squint my eyes… and turn my head upside down… I can see me," Qhayiya mumbled slowly.

Qhayiya fell on her back and held her tummy as she continued giggling. She turned toward Junior and saw him smiling over her. She held his gaze and smiled back. Slowly, he lowered his face to hers. Time stood still as she shared the same breath as him.

Soft. His lips were so soft. The rough palm of his hand brushed against her cheek as he pulled back and kissed her again. Tenderly. Lightly. Gently, he climbed onto the futon and placed the full weight of his body on top of hers.

A wave of emotions came rushing in as the gravity of the moment became apparent to Qhayiya. Here she was, in the innermost sanctuary of a man that had kept himself hidden from her, and the world, for so long. In one night, Junior had opened up more to Qhayiya than he had done in the three years she'd known him. He'd given himself to her, and she was ready to give herself in return. She took a deep breath and allowed herself to surrender.

"It's my first time," she confessed.

"It is?" Junior confirmed gently. Qhayiya nodded silently in response.

"Then maybe we should wait…"

"No. I don't want to wait," Qhayiya whispered, "I want my first time to be with you."

"Are you sure?" Junior whispered, in between kisses to her neck.

"Yes… as long as you promise this won't change things between us. I don't want to lose you, Junior."

"I'm not going anywhere, MaMtolo…"

The Goo Goo Dolls' *Iris* played softly in the background, as Qhayiya and Junior's souls danced in and out of each other's bodies.

3

THE MOTHER WOUND

"The axe forgets but the tree remembers"

— AFRICAN PROVERB

Blaise's Place, Camps Bay Villas, Cape Town
March 2008

*T*hings are so different now, Nala thought to herself, shaving some parmesan into the prawn linguine she had prepared for dinner. Two months had passed since the Belters, and Muzungus were all together at João's graduation. Although Nala still had Lolo and Runako with her on campus, the honours year workload prevented the friends from seeing much of each other.

Runako spent all her days and nights in the law library. Lolo was constantly tied up in market research, and Nala found herself spending more and more time with Blaise, that was when she wasn't knee-deep in psychology essays.

Nala was spending so much time at Blaise's apartment, that Lolo often teased her for paying such a large rental amount for storage space for her clothing and furniture. Supper was ready, but Nala wouldn't be able to enjoy her meal before making a quick bathroom stop.

"AAAAAAAAAAAH!!!" Nala screamed, perched on the toilet seat.

"What? Is it negative?" Blaise asked as he barged through the bathroom door, eyes filled with equal parts of hope and anticipation.

"No, hun! It's positive. We're having a baby!" Nala squealed.

"AAAAAAAAAAAH!!!" Blaise immediately screamed in response.

"*Hawu* Blaise, why are you screaming like that? Don't you want us to have a baby?"

"Nala, *cherie*. It's not that I don't WANT to have a baby with you, it's just that we're not ready for a baby!" Blaise said as he crouched beside his pregnant girlfriend. "Nala, baby, you know I'm being groomed to take over from my father at the bank. I can't have a baby now. I can't risk not qualifying as a chartered accountant. And think about it. How will we afford a baby on my articled clerk salary of eight grand a month? I still get money from my parents!"

Blaise's reaction took Nala by surprise, and she couldn't believe that he was serious. Although they hadn't planned to have a baby quite so soon, settling down together and one day starting a family was something they had already discussed.

Blaise had given Nala a promise ring for their first anniversary back in September, to symbolise his commitment to their engagement when she completed her honours year. They'd also agreed to move in officially together at the end of the year since Nala was already spending most nights at Blaise's apartment anyway. Furthermore, they'd decided never to spend another Christmas away from each other!

Blaise's argument that they were financially unprepared for a baby was ridiculous. Together, they had R20 000 per month; way more than the average graduate couple! Nala figured that Blaise was in a state of shock and decided to reason with him instead of taking offence at his reaction.

"So? We can ask them for a little more, and I can ask my mom for more money from my inheritance –"

"Nala! You don't understand. My parents won't be happy about this," Blaise's cheek bulged as he clenched his jaw.

"Why not? Aunty Brigitte and Uncle Jean-Pierre love me! And your mom always calls me her bride."

"Nala, just because my parents jokingly refer to you as their bride over the phone, doesn't mean they ACTUALLY wanted us to get married."

"What do you mean, Blaise?" Nala demanded, stunned. "Why WOULDN'T they want us ending up together?" she asked in a small voice, and then burst into tears. "Am I not good enough, Blaise? Is my family not important or wealthy enough for me to marry into the great banking Ilungas?" she sobbed, accusingly.

"Don't be silly, Nala," soothed Blaise, holding Nala in his arms. "Of course, you are good enough. MORE than good enough! It's just that, my parents are VERY traditional, and have always thought it best that I marry a fellow Azalian woman who practices our culture and traditions."

Blaise rose to his feet and paced around the small bathroom with his hands on his head before stopping at the door and sighing heavily. As he turned back to face Nala, she noticed that the look on his face wasn't fear, but pity. For her! She didn't understand.

"Are you sure you want to keep this baby?"

"Yes," Nala whispered. "I want to keep the baby. But I don't want to do this alone. If I'm keeping the baby, then I want us to do this right…"

Blaise looked at her expressionlessly. "You want us to get married?"

"Yes..." Nala squeaked, tears still streaming down her face. "I vowed never to put my children through what I went through when I was growing up. So, if we're going to keep this baby, you need to promise me that we are going to raise it together. Me and you. Mommy and Daddy. In one house."

"Okay," he said, his expression uneasy, nodding his head slightly. "Okay..."

The young couple mulled over their decision for another two days before finally braving the phone call to the Ilungas.

Blaise had been particularly uptight, and Nala couldn't understand why. She and Brigitte were now practically besties, even sharing phone calls and texts between them without Blaise's knowledge.

In fact, Nala was more concerned with the phone call to her own mother Bayanda than she was with the phone call to Blaise's parents. He was likely just overreacting, and she offered to break the news to Brigitte first. Blaise's mother could then provide guidance on how to break the news to his father, Jean-Pierre.

"Was this your plan?" Brigitte asked, in a steely voice.

"Uhm... sorry, Ma?" Nala asked, confused by Brigitte's question. It was not the response she was hoping for.

"I asked if this was your plan." Brigitte's voice was threatening and the bond they'd fostered over the past year seemed all but forgotten.

"Uhm. I'm not sure what you mean by that question, Ma," Nala said hesitantly and chuckled nervously.

"Not sure what I mean?" screeched Brigitte. "Was it your plan to lock down my son with a baby after you realised he's from a wealthy family? I know how you South African girls love securing your meal ticket by trapping men with a baby…" Brigitte's voice rose louder and louder until she had to stop for a breath. A short one, before she continued her tirade. "So, I ask you again: WAS THIS YOUR PLAN?!"

Blaise, overhearing his mother's now screaming voice and harsh words, grabbed the phone from a visibly shaken Nala and left his bedroom.

You South African girls… Mrs Ilunga's words stung.

Nala's self-confidence collapsed as she processed the implications, horrified.

Is that all she thinks of me? A gold digger that wants to trap her son? So the endless hours spent on the phone meant nothing. My surprise Mother's Day INTERNATIONAL flower delivery – all because I was planning on trapping her son?

Nala was sobbing with disbelief and betrayal by the time Blaise walked back into his bedroom. Her crying came to an abrupt halt when she saw the look on his face.

Blaise's expression held more questions than it did answers. He was grey with shock. He collapsed onto the bed and told Nala that his parents were cutting off his allowance. They felt that he should face the consequences of his decision to have a baby with no financial help from them.

Nala had never seen him look this helpless before, and a flush of fear ran through her body. *What was he thinking? Did he regret their decision to keep the baby?*

She didn't understand why his parents would react so harshly when he had already completed his degree. Or… were they afraid that his new family responsibilities would stand in the way of his obtaining his CA (SA) qualification?

The Ilungas were a proud family that placed a high value on education. Jean-Pierre Ilunga held two master's degrees – one in Advanced Mathematics and another in Quantum Physics from the

University of Berkshire. Brigitte had an MSc in Economics from the London School of Economics, and Blaise's younger brother Olivier was the top student in his grade. Blaise had always been teased by his family for choosing to remain in Africa to complete his tertiary studies since they believed an international qualification held more weight. And now, there was another threat standing in the way of his professional success.

The thought that Blaise might be reconsidering his decision worried Nala, and she acted immediately to take charge of the fast-deteriorating situation. She leaned against his back and wrapped her arms around his waist.

"We'll be fine, right?" she whispered.

Her question was met with silence.

———

The conversation with the Ilungas had been a disaster. Luckily, things had been less bumpy with Bayanda, who promised to give her daughter all the support she needed – physical, emotional, financial or otherwise. Bayanda had also offered to break the news to Nala's grandmother Blossom and uncle Maanda, Nala's uncle on her late father's side.

With the comfort of knowing that Nala's family supported the decision, coupled with a newfound resolve to prove to his parents that he was now a grown man, Blaise gave Nala the go ahead to tell ONLY the Belters about her pregnancy.

———

Nala: Girls, Limnos date. 2nyt. 7pm sharp (16:00)

(16:48) Lols: Limnos? Y? Who's preggers? LOL!

Nala: LOL! Y wud u say that? (16:48)

(16:49) Ru: Limnos is 4 big news only bebz

(16:50) Lols: Babe! Spill.com. We're dying here.

Nala: I'm not sharing anything. C u @ 7 (16:51)

(17:35) Q: Hey! U guys better fill me in!

Limnos Bakers, Greenpoint

Limnos Bakers was one of Cape Town's premier patisseries and the girls' favourite meeting place for all life-changing news. That evening, the usually quiet patisserie was bustling with activity, thanks to a party of ten that was celebrating a hen night, and a couple that was clearly in the early stages of courting was sitting in the girls' usual corner spot.

The girls decided to accept the manager's offer of the secluded booth that was usually reserved for private bookings. Knowing that her order of a non-alcoholic drink would be a dead giveaway, Nala asked the waitress to give them ten minutes before coming back to take their orders.

"So you're keeping the baby then?" Runako asked, concern and worry written all over her face.

"Of COURSE! What sort of insensitive question is that, Ru?" Nala retorted.

"I didn't mean to offend you, babe," Runako said earnestly. "It's just that, you're still getting to know Blaise, and I wonder if you're ready to commit the rest of your life to sharing a child with him."

"Well, we'll just have to figure it out, won't we?" Nala spat. "Cause there's no ways I'm having an abortion – I was not raised that way!"

"You weren't raised to be having babies before marriage either, yet here we are," Lolo chimed in.

Nala rolled her eyes and faked a loud, sarcastic, yawn.

"Have you told Blaise's parents?" Runako asked gently.

"Yeah, we have. They were obviously happy for us," Nala lied. She didn't want to ruin the evening with the truth of what had actually happened. She gave Runako an eye that she hoped would make her back off.

"Well, that's good then," Runako placated, "I just know how wealthy Azalian families can be, especially because you're a South African girl."

"South African girl? What's wrong with South African girls?" Nala demanded.

"Well… let's just say my parents and some of their Azalian friends feel South African girls are not as conservative as say, girls from the rest of the continent," Runako explained.

"Your dad would know!" Lolo mumbled under her breath.

"Lolo, you will NOT speak about my father that way!" Runako screeched.

"Can you guys just stop it!" Nala growled, glaring at both of them. "I'm supposed to be happy and excited, and you're all just ruining it! First, it's Blaise's parents cutting him off, then he seems to be in two minds about the baby, and now you guys are here fighting and spoiling my whole celebration! This is so UNFAIR!"

"Cutting him off? You never said they're cutting him off!" Runako interrupted Nala's frustrated bleating.

Nala looked up, tears still running down her cheeks. "Yes," she sniffed. "They're cutting off his allowance, and he won't be allowed to access his trust fund until he joins the family bank. We're basically ON OUR OWN…!" She broke into another round of hiccups and tears.

"Nala, babe, calm down," Runako urged, taking Nala's hands into her own. "You've still got your mom and your inheritance to support you, right?"

"Uhm… yeah, I guess…" Nala answered, wiping her nose delicately.

"Good. And you'll start working next year and earn your own salary. All you need to ensure now is that Blaise finishes his articles and qualifies as a chartered accountant," Runako continued, emphasising her words with a pointed finger. "Because if he doesn't, they will blame YOU and he will forever be the black sheep in the family."

"Really?" Nala asked, drying her tears with another pink Limnos serviette.

"Ohhh, yeah," Runako confirmed, fatalistically. She stared at Nala, deadly serious until Nala nodded uncertainly, the clammy serviette still in her hand.

"Right. As long as you understand that, you guys will be fine. Besides, Kobe and I will be available to babysit anytime you need help," said Runako. "Now, where is that damn waitress so we can order a bottle of the finest, vintage OJ? No godchild of mine will be exposed to alcohol before their 18th birthday," Runako declared imperiously, placing her hand on Nala's tummy.

"You? Godmother?" Lolo disputed. "You've known Nala for two New York minutes. Nala, I'm the godmother, right? And Blaise will NO DOUBT make João the godfather. A perfect arrangement since we're not planning on ever getting married or having kids of our own. Your wittle bean will get a big inheritance from his rich Aunty Lolo and Uncle João."

The girls chuckled. Runako, the surprise diplomat, had managed to subdue the ladies' heightened emotions and lift the mood. The waitress appeared with a spread of salambos, marzipan sticks and Fabiola slices, and the girls laughed, drank and made merry for the rest of the evening.

"How did the girls take it?" Blaise asked from the couch when Nala arrived back at his place. She had been staying here for the past week.

"They're really excited, baby. They think we can make this work..." Nala bent over to give Blaise a kiss before taking a seat on the couch next to him.

"Really?", he asked optimistically as he sat up and lowered the volume on the TV.

"Yeah! In fact, I was thinking we should probably move into my place when the baby comes," Nala replied, smiling timidly, eyes shining.

"Mm... No offence cherie, but your place isn't big enough for the three of us," Blaise smiled ruefully.

"But your rental is like five times mine! And I don't think your landlord will be impressed with the damage a baby will do to her fancy furniture," Nala pointed out. "Just move to mine. I'm nearly finished furnishing it, and we won't need to buy much to make it baby-friendly."

"That's sweet, baby, but cheaper rental or not, the reality is that I will need to quit my articles and look for a job, and an affordable, family home," Blaise shrugged despondently. He held the remote control to his lips, something he did when he was deep in thought.

"Quit your articles! Baby, you can't!" Nala urged emphatically.

"Your allowance and my stipend are just not enough for us to run a household," Blaise replied vehemently. "I've been doing some research online on the cost of having a baby, and we're in for much more than just a fancy pram and loads of nappies."

He stared at Nala, her hopefulness and excitement obvious despite her worry. Blaise pulled Nala onto his lap and enfolded her in his arms before gently kissing her on the forehead and whispering, "I love you." Then he lowered his head to kiss her belly and whispered, "I love you, too."

Nala smiled and gently brushed Blaise's cheek. "I just wish you didn't have to choose between us and your family."

"You and this baby are my family now, cherie," he said softly, "and we're going to make this work."

Granny Blossom's house, Shongweni
July 2008

The buttery smell of Blossom Hlatshwayo's velvety maize meal porridge gently awoke Nala from her slumber. It transported her back to her childhood years where the familiar aroma would signal it was time to get ready for school. The same aroma woke her on the day of her lobola ceremony.

In just a few hours, the Ilunga uncles would be arriving at Nala's childhood home, to conduct the lobola negotiations.

It had been a whirlwind journey getting to this point. Firstly, Nala had to overcome the ridicule that came with being 'the pregnant girl' on campus. Then she'd faced constant criticism from Brigitte for being a "loose" girl with no morals.

Jean-Pierre had been much kinder to the young couple, being the first to give his blessing for Blaise and Nala to get married. Brigitte too had come around but insisted she would not recognise Nala, or her child, as members of the Ilunga family, unless and until the marriage had been concluded according to Azalian custom.

Nala and Blaise agreed to comply with Brigitte's request, and decided to proceed with the South African customs in the meantime. Blaise also wanted to conclude the payment of 'damages', the fine for impregnating a woman before marriage, before the baby was born.

Nala found herself asking her mom to make more and more withdrawals from her inheritance to fund an ever-growing list of needs. From day-to-day medical bills for her gynae visits to those bills that were supposed to be small, but seemed to grow by the minute. One of them being the cost of today's function.

Her inheritance had paid for the event's catering, decor, and entertainment. There were also the traditional outfits and accommodation for what felt like hundreds of aunts, uncles and cousins that suddenly took a keen interest in her life. She was grateful for the genuine ones, like her favourite aunt, Zizi.

"*Nana… usalele*[1]?" Zizi whispered. Only ten years older than Nala, Zizipho felt more like a sibling than an aunt.

"No… I'm up. What's up?" Nala answered.

"*Ngisacela uk'khuluma nawe*[2]. It's urgent," Zizi replied quietly.

"Okay. Let me quickly put on a gown and meet you *ekhishini*[3]."

Zizi had sounded worried and Nala, already six months pregnant, wobbled as fast as she could to the kitchen.

Granny Blossom's usually quiet home was already a hive of activity, even though it was only six in the morning. On a normal day, the modest three-bedroom house, with large front and back yards, was tranquil, occupied solely by the family matriarch, her last-born child Zizi, and Zizi's two children.

Thirteen family members and friends had slept over in every available nook and cranny of the warm home. In the passage, aunts and cousins were walking around aimlessly with towels over their shoulders and toothbrushes in their hands.

The team from the events company was already draping the framed marquee on the expansive front lawn, while the crew from the catering company was unpacking food and equipment on the back lawn.

Nala walked into the kitchen where Zizi was standing with a visibly furious Sis' Ntombi – the owner of the catering company commissioned for the day.

"Nana… Ntombi says she still hasn't been paid her deposit and she won't start cooking until that's been sorted."

"*Hayi bo*[4]! *Kanjani*[5]? I asked uMa to pay you when I first spoke to you in May, and she said she had!" Nala defended, her stomach feeling hollow.

"Sisi," hissed Ntombi, "I don't care who said what to whom. *Mina*[6], all I'm saying is that I've given you the benefit of the doubt as a fellow black person and you do this to me. I've been patient with your promises for payment, but my team and I won't start cooking until I receive the full payment. CLEARED, *kwi account yami*[7]."

"Okay, okay, okay! I'm sorry about that," Nala apologised. "Let me speak to my mom quickly. Give me five minutes."

Before Nala could storm off, Zizi called her aside so that they could talk in private.

"Nana…" she started, eyes downcast as she searched for words. Finally, she took a deep breath and looked Nala straight in the eye. "I didn't want to tell you this because I thought maybe I'd heard wrong. But I overheard uBayanda last night fighting with uNgozi on the phone about your money."

"Why would my mom be fighting with her boyfriend about MY money? It's got nothing to do with him!" Nala said, bemused.

"Well, apparently she only invested half of your money. The other half she loaned to him for a business idea he wanted to invest in. She just kept saying 'I trusted you. When will you repay the money? Nala will start asking questions when I can't pay her school fees next year.' That's what I heard her say on the phone *izolo*[8]."

"No… Zizi…" Nala moaned softly. "Please say you're joking."

"I'm sorry, my nana. I didn't want to tell you this now, but I don't think uBayanda forgot to pay uNtombi. I think she simply doesn't have the money to." Zizi rubbed Nala's upper arms sympathetically until Nala sagged into her embrace to sob on her shoulder.

She doesn't have the money. How could this be? Nala's entire livelihood depended on this money. How was she going to settle the balance of her school fees? How was she going to pay for the baby's upkeep? Or contribute towards household expenses? How could her mother have been so cruel? Especially since their relationship was finally starting to resemble that of a normal mother and daughter.

Historically, Bayanda had not been the epitome of a caring mother, something about her and Nala's dad parting acrimoniously after she fell pregnant.

Nala still carried the pain of having been neglected by her mother, the same pain that made her insist on raising her baby at her side. Bayanda and her daughter had grown closer since the passing of Nala's dad three years before, given the constant communication about Nala's funds and general wellbeing.

The two hard-headed women had, as a result, communicated more often than they previously did, creating the illusion their rocky relationship was on the mend.

This revelation, however, was sure to break it. Nala knew she had to play her cards carefully to salvage the situation, given Bayanda's history of causing scenes at the most crucial times. Nala stood at her mother's bedroom door and took a deep breath before knocking.

"Ma," Nala said in a low voice.

"*Yini*[9], Nala?"

Nala entered the room and stood by the bedside.

"uSis' Ntombi is saying she hasn't been paid yet. Have you paid her, or maybe you forgot?" Nala asked, diplomatically.

"*Hawu*[10]! Why is she being funny?" shrieked Bayanda, sitting upright. "Tell her I'll pay her on Monday! I'm just waiting for the money from the investment to clear."

"But she says she won't start cooking without her payment, Ma," Nala persisted. "She says she didn't even get her deposit?"

"*Pho uthi senzeni*[11]? What must we do right now?" Bayanda said evasively. "She's being unreasonable, man! I'll pay her on Monday. If she doesn't want our business, we'll find someone who does!"

"Ma, I'm not sure how to ask this..." Nala sighed heavily before continuing, "...but I really need to know exactly what is going on with my money."

"What do you mean what's going on with your money? I told you it's in a safe investment, and I didn't know there would be such a strict lock-in period," Bayanda said for the hundredth time.

"But why haven't I seen any statement, Ma? I've asked you for statements, and there's always a story!" Nala's voice rose as she forced out the disrespectful accusation.

"Yeyi wena Inala Hlatshwayo Kalenga! *Gada ukuthi ukhuluma nami kanjani*[12]! Who the hell do you think you are, speaking to me like that?" Bayanda hyperventilated with indignation.

"I'm sorry for speaking like that, Ma, but it's my money, and I deserve to see the statements for my money." Nala managed to keep her voice down, but distress made her speak quickly.

"I told you I'll send the statements! Are you saying I'm lying? Are you accusing me of lying? How dare you!" Bayanda screamed.

"You are, Ma! Yes, you are! You're lying!" Nala screamed back, voicing the unthinkable. "I know you gave half of my money to uNgozi for some business idea he had, and Zizi told me he lost it all! She heard you on the phone with him, and she told me!"

"Don't you dare forget who you're speaking to!" Bayanda tried to threaten, only to be cut off by Nala's furious anguish.

"And now you don't have money for my fees. I can't believe you lied to me and wasted my money on your boyfriend!"

"Yes! So what? I loaned my partner some of your money because he promised a better return than your investment. Sue me for trying to do what's best for you!"

Nala gasped for air at the admission. It took a few long moments to find her voice again.

"BEST for ME? You've never done what's best for me! You've always done what's best for YOU!" Nala's condemnation became an unstoppable juggernaut.

"That's why you've been lying for the past two years and why money is always short or always late. That's why you dumped me with your mother after I was born. That's why you never came to fetch me even after you finished uni, got married and had another child. That's why you never raised me or provided for me." The betrayal Nala had denied for so long was now naked and bitter in the back of her throat. "You've never loved me, Bayanda," she said tonelessly, "and now you've ruined my future."

Nala fell silent, weeping softly, her heart broken. *It's always been broken,* she reminded herself savagely. *You just wouldn't admit it.*

"YOU ruined MY future!" Bayanda accused shrilly. "I would have been rich like your father too, had I not fallen pregnant with you in university! Yes. I used your money," she said, in a low, taunting voice, before returning to a scream, "and I don't feel sorry about it! Your father owed me. He owed me for ruining my future. Owed me for going on to be a success when I didn't!"

Bayanda snatched a breath and bulldozed on. "And YOU! You owe me for sacrificing my future to keep you when he wanted me to abort you! So yes, I took your money and guess what, I deserve it and I'm not sorry. You want a statement. I'll tell you how much you have left in your investment – five thousand rand. I don't know how you'll settle your school fees at the end of the year. It's not my fault you decided to get pregnant before finishing school like you were supposed to. The money is finished – make a plan. I made a plan when I fell pregnant with you – you do the same. Now get out of here before I call off *umsebenzi wakho*[13]!"

Nala knew better than to call her mother's bluff as Blaise's family would be arriving in a few hours, and Bayanda was perfectly likely to carry out her threat.

Nala collapsed on the bed in the next bedroom, silent, and staring unseeingly at the ceiling. Tears rolled involuntarily down her cheeks.

She was too hurt to sob, too shocked to cry. So she just leaked, silently.

Numb, everything around her had gone silent. No thought trailed through her mind.

It was as if she had stepped outside of herself and was watching herself lying there, motionless, silent. Leaking.

Finally, her spirit reunited with her body, and her mind started racing. What was she going to do? How was she going to tell Blaise the money on which they had based their decision to keep the baby was no more?

How was she going to pay for her school fees? How did she end up in a position where someone who was a stranger to her, only two years before, now held her destiny in his hands?

How she wished her father was still around to make all of this right. How she wished he had left a will and placed her monies in a trust to be administered by people that actually knew how to handle money, and actually gave a damn about her wellbeing, instead of the courts casually handing it over to her mother. A woman who, apart from birthing Nala, had never really shown much interest in her.

How she wished…

Nala walked back into the living room, her eyes bloodshot and swollen from crying. Zizi and Granny Blossom had heard the shouting and commotion in the bedroom but seemed surprised that it had been this bad.

"What's wrong, nana?" Zizi asked, with palpable concern.

"It's gone... the money is gone... You were right, Zizi," Nala sobbed, collapsing into her aunt's arms.

"What does she mean, it's gone?" Granny Blossom asked Zizi.

"I mean it's gone, Granny. Everything. Bayanda only invested half of my money and gave the other half to that stupid boyfriend of hers." Reduced to sobs again, Nala took a while to pull herself together.

"Even the money she invested is down to five thousand rand. She put it in an investment scheme that has collapsed. How could she have been so stupid with my inheritance? Money that was supposed to look after me? How does the law just pay out so much money to people that don't even know how to handle the money?" Nala's voice trembled with confused disbelief.

"*Thula, s'thandwa sami*[14]. Don't cry, you'll upset the baby," Granny Blossom reminded her gently. "I'll pay uNtombi, and no one will cancel anything. After *umsebenzi*[15], please speak to your uncle about this. Maanda will know what to do."

They had arrived! Blaise's uncles had finally arrived, and as was the custom, they stood at the gate shouting the family's clan names and singing its praises. The negotiations were set to begin at 9 am, but the wise uncles knew to arrive at 8 am. They had left enough time for a little game of *imvula mlomo*[16], an attempt by the groom's family, to coax the bride's family, to commence with the negotiations.

Nala peeked through the bedroom window and saw four men, dressed in suits, standing at the gate. Blaise had also come with them, but was waiting in a car parked two houses down. He was not allowed onto the bride's family property until the two families had reached an agreement.

The uncles, known under the circumstances as *abakhongi*[17], continued singing praises until the Hlatshwayos and Kalengas were satisfied that their guests had paid them adequate respect.

Nala saw her Uncle Bongani make his way to the gate, to let *abakhongi* in, about fifteen minutes after their arrival.

Joining him was the chief negotiator, Maanda Kalenga, Nala's paternal uncle who had flown in from Cape Town that morning. And completing the negotiation panel from the bride's side was none other than the matriarch, Granny Blossom herself. She was an unusual choice given her gender, but an acceptable one since she was the head of her family.

Nala wished she could be a fly on the wall as the two families decided on the bride price. But she was strictly prohibited from emerging unless, and until, she was called. An hour later, Zizi informed Nala that she had been summoned to the living room.

Nala appeared, dressed in a floor length dress and *doek*[18], and knelt on the floor beside her gran. Her head remained bowed as was the custom.

"Inala," Maanda began. "*Uyabazi la'bantu*[19]?"

"*Yebo, Malume*[20]," Nala responded softly, not once lifting her bowed head.

"And you know what they have come here for?" he continued.

"Yebo, Malume."

"*Kulungile*[21]. *Usungahamba*[22]. *Sizok'biza futhi uma sikudinga*[23]."

Another torturous hour passed before Zizi returned, summoning Nala to the elders once more. Nala walked into the living room and saw Blaise seated next to one of his uncles, his head bowed in respect. She smiled, her heart full at seeing a whole Blaise Ilunga, of the great banking dynasty, seated on her grandmother's worn couch in her childhood home.

"Inala," Maanda began again. "Is it true that the man you want to marry is in our presence?"

"Yebo, Malume."

"I am told it is this one." Maanda shifted in his chair and pointed to one of Blaise's uncles.

"No, Malume, that's not him," Nala replied softly.

"Oh! Then I must have made a mistake. Could it be this one?" Maanda shifted in the opposite direction and pointed to another Ilunga uncle.

"No, Malume, that's still not him," Nala replied softly, grateful that her bowed head helped to hide her smile at her uncle's traditional antics.

"Hawu! I must be getting old. Could it be this one?" Maanda turned back and pointed at Blaise.

"Yebo, Malume. It is him I want to marry," Nala confirmed solemnly, and quickly placed her hand over her mouth to muffle an excited giggle.

"I see," Maanda said with equal solemnity. He then turned to Blaise and asked him if Nala was the woman he was here to marry, which Blaise confirmed with a simple nod of the head. "Alright, then. Let us continue, and we will call you when we are ready."

Nala returned to Zizi's bedroom.

She speculated how much longer it would take. At the same time, she was glad to see Maanda so invested in the process, since he had expressed his reservations about Nala taking this step so soon.

She'd made it clear, in the most respectful way possible, that she didn't want to wait any longer to marry Blaise. She didn't see the point. She was having a baby with the man and was practically living with him. So why wait? Reluctantly, Maanda had agreed and given his blessing for the lobola negotiations and traditional wedding ceremony to go ahead.

"Nana! Nana! They're calling you again," Zizi said excitedly, gesturing around the door for Nala to come, come now.

Nala jumped up, grateful to leave the bedroom and hoping she wouldn't return. It was nearly midday, and she was hungry and tired, having barely slept in all the excitement.

The negotiators were all in high spirits when Nala walked in, a sign that things had gone well. She sat down at her grandmother's feet and waited for the good news.

"Inala, we have concluded our business of the day and have agreed to a lobola amount with the Ilunga family," Maanda confirmed formally.

Zizi burst into ululation and Nala nodded emphatically at the news.

"However," Maanda continued, "both families agree that there is no use in rushing for payment, as we don't want to put the young Mr Ilunga under financial pressure. We have agreed the lobola will be settled in the week before the white wedding. I believe you have set a date for next year December. Is that right?"

"Yebo, Malume," Nala responded, her voice more confident with the happy knowledge that she was finally marrying the love of her life.

"Very well, then. I guess it's official. Congratulations to you both – Mr and Mrs Ilunga."

Granny Blossom broke out into ululation and was soon joined by the rest of the Hlatshwayo and Kalenga women who had been listening intently from the kitchen, for the signal that the nuptials were now official.

Malum' Maanda's house, Upper Newlands, Cape Town
December 2008

Saturday afternoons at Maanda Kalenga's household involved long debates about global politics and why younger generations should better appreciate bands such as Snarky Puppy.

This was complemented with wine-cellar-denting amounts of La Motte Sauvignon Blanc paired with Aunt Nakedi's signature cheese and fish board. Pan-toasted steamed bread, scallop and prawn ceviche, an assortment of soft cheeses such as Camembert and Cabécou, thinly sliced kiwi, roasted cashews and fresh roasted figs were accompanied by a jar of farm-fresh gooseberry jam.

Yes, visits to Maanda's were always pleasant, except for that one time when Nala was summoned to explain her teenage pregnancy, by a foreign boy, no less. There was no pregnancy announcement this time, but she felt the visit would be just as tense since she planned to tell Maanda about the state of her inheritance.

She would ask to see the statements of account and confirm if there were any remaining funds. As the executor of his late brother's estate, Maanda was best positioned to take her through the ins and outs of her inheritance pay out.

She also hoped for advice regarding her intention to take legal action against her mother.

Nala walked into Maanda's man cave, pushing Solal in his stroller, and found him sitting in his favourite position: TV on full blast, feet up on his leather pin-button ottoman, right arm on the couch's armrest with remote in hand, and the left hand balancing his crystal whisky glass on his ample abdomen. At a quick glance, he resembled Uncle Phil from *The Fresh Prince of Bel-Air*. In fact, his nieces and nephews called him Uncle Phil behind his back.

"Solal! How's my favourite grandson doing?" Maanda said, jumping to his feet and peeping at the sleeping baby. Baby Solal was snoring peacefully, an enchanting high-pitched rumble that sounded like a hundred teeny ants playing a hundred teeny talking drums.

At just two months, the little boy had already developed a cheeky personality – shunning his nanny whenever his parents were home from uni and work, and smiling at Nala whenever she called his name.

Solal was a cute little thing – a spitting image of his mother with a sharp chin, and big round eyes. Watching him sleep so peacefully always made up for the inconvenience Nala was facing as a result of having a baby while in university.

The greatest of these was having to spend an extra year on campus, as she hadn't attended the second semester of school. But it was a small sacrifice considering the prize – a bouncing baby boy and a loving fiancé.

"Oh, so now Solal gets greeted first?" Nala said, pouting and giving her uncle the puppy eyes she knew melted his heart every time.

"Never! Come here, my favourite niece," Maanda guffawed, taking Nala into his arms. Maanda insisted on cuddling with the baby boy and proceeded to take Solal out his stroller, careful not to wake him.

"Where's Blaise?" he enquired, lowering the volume on the TV as he nestled back into his signature position, with Solal now wedged between his arm and cushy belly.

"He's working late, Malume. Blaise started a new job as a Junior Financial Analyst last month. That is one of the reasons I'm here to see you," Nala replied.

"New job? Blaise quit his articles?"

"Yes, Malume," Nala said, the croak in her voice a dead giveaway.

"Hey! What's going on? Has Blaise done something to upset you? Because you KNOW, I'll be very upset if he breaks my favourite niece's heart." Maanda raised his eyebrows and lowered his chin, wordlessly insisting on an honest answer, as he waited for her to respond.

"No, it's not Blaise," Nala chuckled bleakly. "In fact, Blaise has been great. It's my mom, Malume. She and her boyfriend spent my inheritance, and now it's all gone. All of it. That's the real reason Blaise had to quit his articles. He did so because there wasn't enough money to give me an allowance over the past three months."

"What? When did this happen?" Maanda barked. "And why didn't you tell me earlier?"

"I… I also only found out in July, Malume, when we were going through the lobola negotiations. I didn't want to ruin the ceremony because you know how Mam'Bayanda can be when she's upset. I need your help to find out if there are any other monies due to me, and to sue her for the money she stole from me."

"Calm down, Nala, I don't think there's any need for that," he reassured her. "You still have money in your fund, all we must do is apply for a withdrawal. If you had told me, we would have applied for a withdrawal sooner."

"Really? So, there's like a lot left?" Nala squealed, hope resurfacing.

"Not a lot, but enough."

Nala deflated again. "How much is enough, Malum Maanda? Why does everyone keep hiding my money from me?"

"Hey! Watch your tone," he warned. "No one is hiding your money. Have you ever asked me about your inheritance?"

"Sorry, Malume, you're right. I've never asked you. Do you mind taking me through it now? I just want to know where I stand so I can plan my life better."

"Okay," he nodded. "I suppose you're an adult now and there's no need to shield you from adult conversations. Go fetch my laptop from the study and leave Solal with Nakedi," Maanda said, sitting up and handing the baby to Nala. "Oh – and ask your aunt to give us about an hour of privacy, this will take a while."

Nala returned a few minutes later with her uncle's laptop and settled in on the couch next to him.

Maanda explained that he gauged she was now old enough, not only to discuss the details of her inheritance but also to learn some facts surrounding her father's death. Facts that, for her own protection, he had kept from her in the past.

Maanda stood up and fixed himself another whisky before settling back into his seat. He stared into the distance, something he did whenever he was deeply conflicted.

"It was around 10:15 pm, on that fateful Friday night when I got a call from your stepmom to say my brother was in hospital. As you know, he had been involved in a car accident on his way back from a meeting in La Lucia."

"I took the first flight to Durban the next morning and found my brother unconscious. He had all these machines connected to him. The doctors explained that he had suffered severe brain and spinal damage, and was paralysed from the waist down. They also said he wouldn't be able to talk again once he recovered."

Maanda paused briefly, reaching out his hand to comfort his niece, who had not let out a sound, but had tears streaming down her face.

"The doctors asked us to give them forty-eight hours to monitor his situation, after which they would have a clearer picture of his prospects for recovery."

"Is that when he complicated?" Nala whispered.

"No, he didn't complicate. He remained the same. His condition did not improve."

"If his condition didn't change, how did he suddenly die?"

Maanda paused for a moment, took a deep breath, and then responded.

"I instructed the doctors to switch off his life support," he said gravely.

"What?! Malume... You killed Papa?" Nala gasped.

"I didn't kill your father, Nala, I was simply complying with his wishes," Maanda replied gently.

"HIS wishes?"

"Yes. I was your father's nominated Healthcare Power of Attorney, and he asked me to end his life if he ever became mentally and/or physically incapacitated. He was a very proud man, you know that?"

Nala nodded, no less horrified.

"The thought of not being able to feed himself, clothe himself, let alone speak, terrified him greatly. He always said he would rather be dead than to live that kind of life. That's why I decided as I did, my dear. I was simply obeying the request your father had made known to me long before the accident."

"I see... But since Papa was married, why didn't Mam' Audrey make that decision?"

Maanda let out a soft chuckle, the first time his face had shown a semblance of a smile since greeting his niece earlier.

"The Power of Attorney supersedes spousal rights, my dear. Meaning that, although your father subsequently got married, I still held the healthcare decision-making powers over his life."

Just then, Nakedi popped her head through the door. "I know you asked not to be disturbed, but I thought you may be hungry."

"Ooh, that smells nice," Maanda said, sitting up and clearing the TV remote and Financial Mail off the ottoman for Aunty Nakedi to place the tray of food.

"Made your favourite – blackberry, brie and rocket focaccia," Aunty Nakedi smiled, planting a kiss on her husband's cheek.

Nala scooped up a portion. "Oh, my gosh," she mumbled around the mouthful of food, her palm cupped under her chin to catch crumbs. "What's this black sauce? It's divine!"

"Balsamic glaze. I get it from an olive farm in the Karoo. They also have excellent olive oil."

"An olive farm? In South Africa?" Nala gawked.

"Yup. We grow olives too, darling!" Aunty Nakedi chuckled.

"Thanks for this, honey," Maanda smiled up at his wife. "Could you please give Nala and I another thirty minutes? We're almost done."

Nakedi, ever the gracious hostess, politely obliged her husband and left the duo to continue their discussion. She tactfully took her two lion-cut Löwchens, and the baby, to Kirstenbosch Gardens for a walk.

"Right! Back to the point – your inheritance. As you know, your father had done well for himself in business. However, your father died intestate, meaning without a will. "

"That's weird! Papa was such a smart and successful businessman. Why wouldn't he have drafted a will?" Nala listened with growing dismay as her uncle explained.

Litha had, in fact, drafted a will, but it had been deemed invalid since it was witnessed by only one person instead of two.

"Your aunt is very grateful that all the pain I went through to wind up your father's estate jolted me to create a Life File. It's a folder where I put all the documents I know will be needed when I die, including a valid will."

"That's smart, Malume. Do you keep it in the house?"

"No, my Life File is with my attorney. I don't want my wife to see my will before I die!"

"Why not?"

"*Hayi*[24] man, Nala, it's an African thing. Anyway, when your father died, the monies due to you and your siblings were paid into the Guardian's Fund because you were all minors. When you turned twenty-one, we transferred your portion into an investment for you."

"I see. But what about the monies paid to Bayanda?" Nala asked curiously.

"Oh, yes!" Maanda exclaimed as if he'd suddenly remembered what the point of the conversation was. He closed his laptop and placed it on the ottoman before continuing. "The monies paid out to Bayanda were proceeds from a life policy your dad took out when he started working. At the time of taking it out, he nominated you as one of the beneficiaries. He opted to have the funds paid to your legal guardian if he were to pass before you reached the age of majority."

"Was there another option, then?" Nala asked. She leaned forward to snag another slice of the focaccia, which was now cold.

"Yes… the other option was to have the funds paid out to a beneficiaries trust managed by the life insurer."

Nala chuckled as Maanda sneakily took the last remaining piece of focaccia out her hand.

"I wish Papa had chosen to put my money in the trust," Nala frowned.

"We can't wish away the past, Nala, only look to doing better going forward," Maanda smiled, wrapping his left arm around Nala's shoulders and pulling her to his chest. "Besides, you still have a reasonable amount left in your investment – enough to settle your fees next year. Pass me my laptop, and I'll give you the exact figure."

"You can mail that to me later, Malume. I'd rather focus on my mom. How do I handle this situation?"

"Well, the choice is yours. You can take legal action against her, but you'll need to provide documentation proving the misuse, like bank statements, investment statements, etcetera. And before you go ahead, I want you to consider the likelihood of recovering the monies and how much you estimate you'll recover. Don't forget to include the amount of legal fees you'll have to settle. And the further damage this would cause to your already fragile relationship with your mother."

"So, you're saying I should let it go?"

"No, I'm not saying what you should or shouldn't do. I'm just asking that, before you make your decision, you consider the merits of each option, and do what's best for you, in BOTH the short-term AND the long-term. Sometimes what's just is not always best. Sometimes we must give up the battle so we can win the war." He sighed, and looked at her fondly, his chin almost on his chest as he smiled tightly. "Welcome to adulthood, Nala... Welcome to adulthood."

Nala smiled back as ruefully, unaware that this was the first of many trade-offs she'd have to consider in the series of negotiations called life.

4

AZALIAN HOSPITALITY

"Only a fool tests the depth of a river with both feet!"

— AFRICAN PROVERB

Domestic Terminal, Cape Town International Airport
March 2009

*R*unako, Lolo and Nala laughed animatedly as they made their way through the boarding gates of Cape Town International Airport, ready to depart for Johannesburg. Despite still being based in Cape Town, time for social engagements had grown increasingly scarce, the trip out of town for Runako's bridal fitting provided the perfect opportunity to spend some time together.

Runako's mom, Maita, had been referred to a talented designer in Johannesburg and was flying in from Harare to ensure every cut was along the grain and every zipper had an eye and hook.

The two-hour flight to OR Tambo International Airport was filled with peals of Nala's loud laughter, Lolo's staccato profanity, and Runako's know-it-all superiority as the girls caught each other up on the happenings in their lives.

By the time the trio disembarked, rows 14 to 19 had intimate details of all the colleagues Lolo despised in her new role as Junior Digital Marketing Assistant for a leading fashion publication; Runako's impossible schedule trying to balance the workload of a master's in International Trade Law and the planning of a wedding in Rome, and Nala's frustration at being the oldest student in her honours class.

A choir of girly shrieks filled the arrivals terminal of OR Tambo International Airport as the girls spotted their friend waiting to collect them.

"Miss Q is in the house!" they screamed in unison, marvelling at the suited, corporate professional waiting for them on the other side of the glass sliding doors.

"Geez. I think I burst my eardrum," Qhayiya remarked drily, grinning from ear to ear.

"Oh, really? You think you're better now just 'cause you're squeezed into a gorgeous... what suit is this?" Lolo asked and stuck her hand into the back of Qhayiya's jacket collar.

"THULA SINDI! You're wearing THULA SINDI? Girl! How much are you getting paid?! Or is there a new man we should know about?" Lolo squealed excitedly.

"Q, you got a new man?" Nala echoed the question with a conspiratorial smile. "That would explain why you're looking slightly fuller than the last time I saw you. Someone's all loved up!"

"It's one of the bankers from your firm, isn't it?" Runako added as she pushed the trolley towards the elevator. "I knew you could do better than Junior!"

"Oh, my gosh! Can you all calm down? This is a gift from my mom. There's no way I can afford designer suits while I'm on the graduate programme. I mean, come on..." Qhayiya chuckled. "And please don't speak about my boyfriend like that. Not everyone measures their worth by their job title..."

"So you honestly see nothing wrong with Junior being fired from the embassy?" Lolo asked, turning to Runako and Nala with a raised eyebrow.

"Not at all!" Qhayiya responded defensively, shaking her head. "It's never been Junior's desire to get into politics and his father would have never let him resign. So, the easiest way to get out of it was to get himself fired."

"Face it, Junior's a bum, babe!" Runako opined primly as she pushed the elevator button. "Always has been, always will be..."

"Hey! You better watch your mouth, Runako!" Qhayiya barked, pointing her car key threateningly in Runako's face. "If you want to stay at my place this weekend, then I suggest you choose your words carefully."

There was an awkward silence on the 40-minute car ride from the airport to Qhayiya's one-bedroom apartment in Rosebank. Lolo and Runako had decided to squeeze together on the sleeper couch rather than spend the night with their mothers. Over the years, they'd learned that no matter how independent they may be, trying to leave the family home at night would ensue in a debate with the parents that was best avoided.

The cosmopolitan suburb of Rosebank was the hub of the most popular cocktail bars and nightclubs in Johannesburg's northern suburbs. After freshening up and letting their local friends know they were in town, the girls painted Joburg pink.

Qhayiya's apartment, Rosebank

8 am

"Ru… Ru….Runako!" Lolo croaked.

"Hmmm," Runako mumbled.

"That's your alarm."

"What?"

"Your alarm. Switch off your damn alarm," Lolo groaned.

10 am

"Hello…" Runako rasped into her mobile phone.

"Runako! Are you still sleeping?" demanded a voice both surprised and annoyed.

"Oh, hey, Mom!" Runako replied, clearing her throat and wincing at the pounding headache.

"We're already at Gert's. Where are you, girls?" Maita asked.

"Uhm… We're just getting in the car now," lied Runako, squinting at the bright sunlight outside the window. "But what do you mean, 'we'? Who's with you?"

"I'm with Ellen. Cora asked her sister to represent her today," replied Maita.

"Oh… my… gosh…"

Ellen Yaw-Boateng was Cora Mensah's younger sister and mother to Kuku and Fifi. Born and bred in Azalia, she attended the elite Azalia International Senior School for Girls, and completed her undergraduate studies at the University of Azalia, graduating with an honours degree in Sociology.

Her excellent marks secured her a scholarship with the British Council to read for an MSc in International Relations with the Royal School of Economics in London, which she attained with distinction. Ellen earned the title "Pow Yaw" while working as an intern at the Royal Department for International Development, and proved why as she rose through the ranks in her subsequent positions at the World Bank in New York City, the International Finance Corporation in Nairobi, before finally settling in Pretoria as the Regional Programme Manager for Azalian Women's Development Corporation.

A staunch Catholic since childhood, she very vocally disapproved of Kobe marrying a girl whose parents had allowed her to spend five nights at her boyfriend's family home in Kent.

Showing up at the dress fitting late, hungover and reeking of alcohol would further confirm Ellen's conviction that Runako was the modern-day reincarnation of Mary Magdalene.

"GUYS! Wake up! We're late! It's quarter-past-ten, and my mom's already at Gert's," Runako bellowed through the double-volume apartment.

"Leave me. I've changed my mind. Happy married life…" Lolo mumbled as she pulled the covers over her head.

"Q, WAKE UP!" Runako yelled, running up the stairs towards Qhayiya's bedroom. "Lolo! Nala! Everyone! UP!"

"Hey! Don't look my way," Nala said prissily as she walked into the living area from the balcony, holding a cappuccino in one hand and the latest Harper's Bazaar in the other. "I'm bathed, changed and was wondering when you lot would get up."

"How are you this person?" Runako wailed, and winced again as she made her way back down the stairs.

"I am this person because I didn't indulge in drinks that are on fire, that's how. You guys were drinking flaming what?"

"Lamborghinis," Runako mumbled.

"Fla-ming-Lam-bo-rghi-nis! And you thought you'd wake up feeling okay? Chancers." Nala chuckled and rolled her eyes.

"I'm gonna throw up…" Runako groaned, and ran to the bathroom with her hand over her mouth.

Linden, then Parkhurst

Qhayiya's Toyota Yaris zipped through Rosebank, then Greenside, and a short while later, arrived at Gert-Johan Coetzee Studios in the nick of time, thanks to Nala's surprisingly masterful driving skills.

The dresses were glorious. Gert and his team had painstakingly worked metres of lifeless champagne-coloured duchess satin into form-fitting, mermaid-tail gowns. The Belters transformed from coming-of-age to regal with one pull of the invisible zipper.

The day was going well until Ellen insisted on treating the party of six to lunch before parting ways.

Happily, she and Maita were oblivious that the choice of an Italian eatery over a health bar was a tactic for the girls to cure their excruciating hangovers. Pounding headaches, mixed with nausea, were also laced with the occasional tummy rumble. Only much later would the older women learn that the girls' oversized sunshades weren't part of some new Cape Town trend, but rather an attempt to hide the damage caused by Rosebank's Moloko Night Club in the wee hours of that morning.

Walking into La Cucina di Ciro at lunchtime on a Saturday, without a booking, was a gamble, but the waiter, hearing the desperation in his newest patrons' voices, managed to make up a table quickly on the porch. Before he had even fetched the menus, he was strong-armed into promptly serving four tomato juice cocktails 'with all the trimmings' and an extra shot – his patrons' sunshades and the wink from Lolo a dead giveaway of what the extra shot was of.

A few short moments later, Obedient lived up to his name and returned with four tomato juice cocktails, a kola tonic and diet lemonade, and a pot of Rooibos tea with honey and a side of fresh lemon slices.

"You girls are healthy, hey? All drinking tomato juice?" Ellen commented, unaware the order was in fact for four Bloody Marys.

"Hair of the dog, Aunty," Lolo mumbled under her breath.

"Lolo!" Qhayiya growled, clenching her teeth.

"What was that?" Ellen asked, having genuinely not heard what Lolo had said.

"She said 'hair of the dog', Aunty Ellen – we want our skin to shine like the hair of the dog for the wedding," Runako replied, intentionally misleading Kobe's aunt and ignoring her friends' awkward looks at the explanation that made zero sense.

"Speaking of the wedding, my sister and I have agreed that I should oversee the decor. It will save costs as I know how over-the-top Italian wedding planners can be," Ellen informed them.

Nala and Lolo spat out their drinks, Qhayiya choked on hers. Runako took an audible gulp at the thought that Ellen, who still had the famous porcelain trio of dogs from the 80s on display at her house, would be responsible for the decor at her wedding.

"Erm… decor? That's very kind, Aunty Ellen, but I think we're covered. I've already finalised it with Kobe," Runako replied.

"Oh! Is that so? I'm sure it's easy to go around finalising things when you are not paying for anything," the older woman retorted snidely.

"That's not true, Aunty Ellen," Runako hissed.

"Is it not? Are the groom's parents not the only ones that have paid for anything to do with the wedding so far? What are YOU paying for, my dear? Or has your family found itself a jackpot?" The awful woman sat up straighter, her expression smug.

"Excuse me, sister," Maita interjected mildly. "What nonsense! You know very well that Runako's father is facing some financial challenges at the moment. That's why we waived our requirement for dowry. We knew we're not currently in a position to offer the financial support we would have liked to."

"And may not be able to do so for a long time if your husband is found guilty of the fraud charges laid against him!" Ellen jeered.

"Enough!" said Maita coldly. "You're embarrassing Runako! And this is no place to be having this conversation."

Realising that she'd overstepped and that her nephew would be less than impressed at all the things she'd said to his fiancée, Ellen tried another tactic.

"I'm not fighting, my dear. I'm just trying to protect my nephew," she backed down. Or maybe not, because she turned to Runako and asked, "Runako, are you people signing an antenuptial contract?"

"Well…" Runako started, "we haven't decided that yet. But when we do, it will be something we agree on between the two of us, since it is about the two of us." She stared back at Ellen, pointedly.

"How can it be about the two of you when marriage is a union of families? In a few months, you will be a Mensah, a member of a very wealthy and powerful family, I might add." Ellen seemed to be waiting for an acknowledgement from Runako.

Runako nodded stoically.

"And when we welcome you into the family, you will have to behave in a way that benefits the whole family, and not just 'the two of you'," Ellen sermonised. "That's African culture, dear. What we all call *Ubuntu*[1]," she patronisingly wrapped up her lecture.

"What about my family? The Madzonges? They'll still be my family too," Runako said innocently, although her blood was boiling.

"Of course, dear, they will. And you will support them when they need help from the wealth that *you* build. Now, do you see why that antenuptial is so important? It protects the Mensahs AND the Madzonges," Ellen said, apparently well-pleased with herself.

"Yes, Ellen, but we'll be building TOGETHER, for us, not for our families. What happens if we get divorced or if Kobe dies –"

The young bride regretted her words as soon as they passed her lips, knowing she had played into Ellen's hands.

"DIES?" Ellen exclaimed. "You're planning on killing Kobe?"

"Ellen!" Maita interrupted. "We both know Runako has no intention of killing Kobe. She knows what chaos her grandfather's passing caused on our family's finances and she's just trying to plan ahead for hers."

"Plan ahead to kill my sister's son?"

Maita heaved a dramatic sigh of frustration. No one else dared to react, and the table fell silent.

Runako held back her tears, refusing to give Ellen the pleasure of seeing her cry.

Maita seemed to consider her next words carefully. Runako understood that Maita was trying to find a delicate balance. Ellen had to understand that Maita would not be messed with, but anything she said would be twisted to advance Ellen's agenda of painting the Madzonges as opportunistic gold-diggers.

"Ellen," Maita began, "I read a heart-breaking research paper recently, on the plight of Africa's widows and divorcees, and how they are disproportionally disadvantaged to married women.

"From Nigeria and Kenya to South Africa and even Azalia, the article shared similar cases of women that were forcibly removed from their homes, stripped of their possessions, and subjected to horrific rituals.

"The article called on women to rally together in changing the cultural norms that leave Africa's divorced and widowed women destitute.

The author concluded with a powerful quote by Eric Thomas: 'If there is no enemy within, the enemy outside can do no harm.'

"I wonder if Azalian Women's Development Corporation knows they have an enemy within their own structures... I wonder if these girls know the paper I'm talking about was written by you!"

Rome, Italy
July 2009

The pulsing thud of a modified sound system slowly faded into the distance as the pair of black Mercedes Vianos pulled out the St. Regis basement parking and headed for Janiculum Hill.

The Belters, together with Kuku and Fifi, had barely reached the first turn when Lolo pulled out six shot glasses and a bottle of Absolut Bling-Bling. Eying the bottle suspiciously, Qhayiya announced the no-phone policy for the night and collected everyone's devices for safekeeping.

Four shots each and twenty minutes later, the girls arrived at the entrance of The Sofonisba Towers and made their way to the top floor.

"Miss Runako Rose Madzonge," Lolo said in the voice of a game show host, "Welcome to paradise!"

The imposing penthouse doors opened, to reveal about thirty of Runako's friends and acquaintances from high school and university that had flown in for the wedding. The Roman sunset skyline created the perfect backdrop for the sea of Nefertitis and Nefertaris that were draped in swathes of white kalasiris-inspired dresses.

The quintessential gathering of Africa's social elite shimmied and swayed to the bass pulsating from the grand hallway, through the entertainment area, and out onto the wrap-around balcony.

"The Roc girls are in the building tonight!" Lolo sang along incorrectly to the Jay-Z classic, as she grabbed a glass of Santa Margherita prosecco from one of the waiters and made her way through the crowd. Runako was greeted with excited hugs and air kisses from friends and family that had flown in for the wedding.

"LOVING the waiters!" Qhayiya beamed, locking eyes with the gorgeous specimen approaching with a tray of prosecco.

"I'll say," Nala winked, as she grabbed a glass. She bit her bottom lip as she took a second look at the sculpted posterior walking away.

"Ladies, I have to admit, you've done a great job here," Fifi chipped in, both hands aloft in the OK sign.

"Are we allowed to touch them?" Kuku asked, making a grabbing motion with her hands at another sculpted waiter making his way past her.

What Kuku and many of the guests didn't know was that the waiters were, in fact, male adult dancers. In line with the Ancient Egyptian theme for the evening, they were all dressed in nothing but barely there white cotton shentis, golden usekhs that rested on their bare pecs, a pair of golden cuffs, and nemes headdresses.

There were a number of unfamiliar faces in the crowd, and Runako pulled Lolo to a private section of the balcony to ask who they were.

"Uhm, those are Alex's guests," Lolo explained sheepishly.

"And who on earth is Alex?" Runako growled.

"The owner of this place... Who also happens to be upstairs in the cigar lounge with his friends," Lolo grimaced, bracing herself for the potential explosion.

"You're JOKING!" Runako obliged, hissing through clenched teeth in an effort to keep her voice below a shout. "Lolo, you ALWAYS do this! You know Kobe will KILL me if he finds out we're being hosted by one of your sugar daddies! And what about João? Does your boyfriend know about this?"

"If you MUST know, João and I are on a break!" Lolo hissed back. "And even if we weren't, how on earth did you think we arranged all of this? The penthouse, cases of prosecco, decor, 'waiters'? Huh? I had to call in a favour – that's how! And how do you expect me to get Alex to throw you a party and then tell him he can't come?" Lolo demanded, throwing her hands in the air.

"I believe congratulations are in order," a deep, melodic baritone spoke from behind.

Runako was stunned into silence. The voice was familiar. The British-Nigerian accent distinct. Could it be? No,… it was impossible!

"Obi…" she whispered, turning around hesitantly, and finding her gaze irresistibly drawn to his eyes.

Lolo made a quick escape while Runako came to grips with being face-to-face with Obinna Okonkwo again. He was even more striking than the night she met him in London, standing head and shoulders above her. She compared him to her memories; his deep cocoa dark skin, full beard, and perfectly white teeth. And she never forgot his deep dimples when he smiled, as he was doing now.

"Aah, she still remembers my name," he chuckled in his mellow voice.

"Of course I do," Runako giggled uncomfortably, stepping back until she bumped against the balcony railing. "What are you doing here?"

"I'm in town for the summer with some of my friends. Uche's dad owns this place. You remember Uche, right? He was one of the guys partying with us at Two Degrees."

"Yes…," Runako coughed, realising Lolo was potentially having an affair with one of Obi's friend's dads.

"How have you been?" Obi said, taking a step towards Runako. He tilted his head to study her face. "It's good to see you."

"It's good to see you, too," Runako blushed, trying and failing to look away.

"Why did you run away from me?" Obinna asked, not once taking his eyes off hers as he took a long, slow, drag of his cigar and swirled his whisky with his other hand.

"Because… what happened was a mistake, Obi. It meant nothing," Runako stuttered under her breath, surreptitiously sliding along the railing to create some distance between her and the imposing figure standing over her.

"Are you sure?" Obinna asked, sending a shock down Runako's spine as his index finger rested lightly on her cheek. He slowly traced her jawline, stopping at her chin, where he gently tilted her face upwards towards his. Slowly, and without breaking his gaze, he continued until her lips were within a whisker of his. The sweet scent of whisky mixed with the smokiness of the cigar was on his breath, and Obinna's piercing stare reminded Runako why she had surrendered before.

Out the corner of her eye, Runako glimpsed someone peeking around the corner before disappearing again, bringing her to her senses. She quickly pulled away.

"Obi, I'm getting married this weekend, and I haven't spoken to you in nearly two years! Let's not pretend there's something here."

"Pretend?" Obinna laughed wryly and stepped closer. "So, you think everything that happened between us was pretence?"

Nothing about Obinna had been pretence.

The billionaire heir apparent who partied with international celebrities had shown her the best of London and given her a sexual experience like she'd never had before. He'd lived up to everything he promised over their three-day dalliance following their introduction at Two Degrees.

When she had casually gushed over a Christian Dior Saddle Bag in the Harrod's window, he arranged for it to be delivered to her the next morning. When she complained about dreading the long flight home on economy class, he upgraded her to the first class cabin.

Obinna had continued to phone and message her when she returned to Zimbabwe and South Africa. That is until the day she had to block him after Kobe caught her on the phone with him.

He was right, nothing about him had been pretence, and she believed his feelings for her had been genuine.

"Obi, I had a boyfriend, the same boyfriend I'm marrying. You and I were supposed to be just a holiday fling."

"And, is that all I was to you?" Obinna smiled cheekily.

Nala ran onto the balcony screaming, "Runako! What the hell are you doing!"

Fifi and Kuku ran up behind her, shaking their heads and silently mouthing, "Oh my God!"

Qhayiya soon followed, holding her hands over her mouth.

Runako pulled away from Obinna, puzzled by all the commotion. "What's going on?" she asked, perplexed.

"Come! Just come NOW!" Nala pleaded.

The girls ran into the expansive guest bathroom, and Nala locked the door while Qhayiya and Lolo just stood there. Both were shaking their heads. Fifi and Kuku had stayed behind on the balcony with Obinna, whom they hadn't seen in months.

"Why would you do this, Runako?" Nala asked as she rested her back against the wall and slid to the floor.

"Why, *chomi*[2]? Why?" Qhayiya exclaimed.

"After everything you guys have been through?" Lolo added emphatically.

"Guys, you're scaring me. What the HELL is going on?" Runako begged.

"It's Kobe. Look!" Qhayiya said, handing Runako her phone.

Ten missed calls from Kobe and a WhatsApp message: A blurry image of Runako's back with Obinna leaning in towards her. Beneath the image were the words:

The wedding's off

Runako tried ringing Kobe to explain, but numerous calls went unanswered. João, Blaise and Junior didn't answer their phones, either. Neither did her brothers Tawanda and Tongayi.

The next logical step was to try and speak to Kobe directly. Nala and Runako grabbed a cab to Il Palazzo Gentlemen's Club while the rest of the girls remained at the penthouse.

Thanks to their Egyptian costumes, a number of patrons mistook Nala and Runako as the next act on stage. Still, they were too flustered to be upset by the constant groping and wolf whistles they had to evade while searching for Kobe and his party.

Finally, one of the bouncers escorted them to a VIP booth where Kobe was being treated to a lap dance. Not having any desire to cause a scene in front of his friends and future brothers-in-law, Kobe quickly obliged Runako's request to speak to him outside.

"Baby, it's not what it looks like," Runako assured him, pleading with him to hear her out.

"Runako, listen to me and listen to me well," Kobe said brusquely. "I am giving you exactly three minutes and one chance, only one, to come clean about who, exactly, that is, and what you were doing with him."

Runako held her face in her hands as Kobe continued.

"And don't think I'm asking because I don't know who it is. I know very well! But I'm giving you a chance to prove whether I can trust you or not."

Runako looked over her fingertips when Kobe eventually stopped speaking. He was looking up at the night sky, his jaw muscles working, until he took a deep breath.

He scanned the parking lot unseeingly as he continued. "If there is even one piece of information that you hide from me or that is untrue, and I find out, you can consider your diary clear on Saturday."

Runako weighed up her options. She knew that coming clean would damage her relationship, but she didn't know how much Kobe already knew. She had no idea who had sent him that picture, to begin with.

"Baby, we were just talking –"

"WHO IS HE?!" Kobe bellowed.

"It's Obi," Runako said and burst into tears.

"Obi? London Obi?" Kobe asked, shaking his head.

Runako nodded, unable to speak through the crying.

"I thought you stopped talking to him."

"I did… I didn't know he'd be at the party. I didn't even know he'd be in Italy! I haven't spoken to him since you told me to block him…"

"When I caught you on the phone with him, you said he was just someone you met on a night out and that nothing had happened. It has since been brought to my attention that something did happen, in fact, many things," he spat. "This is your only chance to tell me everything, Runako, or I swear, by the time the sun rises, I will be out of your life forever."

Not knowing whether Kobe was bluffing or not, Runako caved and told him everything. From meeting Obi at Two Degrees, to giving him her number, to the dinners, the night at the club, the designer bag and finally – the sex. Kobe immediately stormed back into the club and told the bouncers not to let her in.

Nala, who had been secretly watching the exchange from out of sight, quickly grabbed her friend and told her it was best that they head home. She texted Lolo and Qhayiya to give them an update.

(01:20) Nala: It's bad. Taking her back to the hotel. Chat in the morning x

---

The St. Regis Hotel

It was 4 pm, and Kobe was still not answering Runako's calls or messages. She decided to take the girls' advice and give him space to cool off.

Maita and the rest of the family blamed a hangover for Runako's staying in bed all day, unaware that there was potentially no wedding on Saturday. Cora's phone call to Maita earlier that afternoon to finalise the list of hymns was Runako's only hope that the wedding was still going ahead.

She stole two of Maita's insomnia tablets and just as she was dozing off, received a text from Kobe.

(22:33) Baby Cakes: Meet me tomorrow, 06:30. St Peter's Square, Vatican City

---

By 06:15 am, Runako was already waiting at the entrance of St Peter's Basilica. The air was warm, and the sun already shining bright in the Roman summer sky. Runako was casual in a knee-length stone-coloured wrap dress, light cardigan and closed-toe espadrilles. Her oversized sunglasses hid her puffy eyes, a result of having cried through the night.

Kobe walked to the entrance at 06:45 am, and Runako knew better than to call him out about his tardiness. He was dishevelled, his hair was unkempt, and he was in a faded oversized tee shirt, grey chinos, and flip-flops. His eyes were bloodshot red. He had clearly been crying too. Or not sleeping. Or both.

"Hey, Baby Cakes," Runako whispered, stepping towards him to half-reach for a hug. Kobe ignored the gesture and walked past her. He turned right into one of the Doric colonnades and continued walking without checking if she was behind him. She wondered if he had purposely chosen the structure built to symbolise "the welcoming arms of the Church" as the location for her atonement.

"Look, I'm not going to waste your time," Kobe said coldly, still walking two steps ahead of Runako. "I'm open to the wedding going ahead, not because I still believe in this marriage, but because it would cause my parents huge embarrassment if I were to back out now."

"Thank you, baby!" Runako squealed, completely ignoring most of his words as she sighed with relief.

"Don't thank me yet," Kobe warned emotionlessly. "I said I'm open to it. On two conditions. One, Lolo cannot be your maid of honour, and two, Fifi and Kuku are banned from attending the wedding."

"What?" Runako exclaimed, horrified.

Kobe stopped and looked back at Runako. The morning sun streamed through the columns and illuminated Kobe's face. He was angelic as he uttered the words that contained pure evil. "Actually, Lolo cannot be part of the bridal retinue at all. She is welcome to attend as a guest, but I will not allow someone who disrespects my marriage to stand at the altar with me as I say my vows. The choice is yours."

"Kobe, no…" Runako pleaded.

"As I said, the choice is yours."

With that, the meeting was over, and Kobe walked back down the colonnade towards the exit.

Still dumbfounded by the quick turn of events, Runako stood in silence and wondered how she would tell her best friend that she was no longer allowed to escort her down the aisle. And how Fifi and Kuku, who had flown in from London specially to attend the wedding, would take the news that they had been uninvited.

Villa Reggio, Rome

The ethereal melody of Pachelbel's *Canon in D Major* filled the warm summer air as Runako took her first step down the aisle holding firmly onto her father's arm.

Each *sul ponticello*[3] and *sul tasto*[4] melted into the next under the skilful fingers of the Orchestra Sinfonica di Roma as she gracefully floated towards the altar. The diamante-encrusted straps of her Jimmy Choos dug cruelly into her toes as she slowly approached the man she so loved, but at this moment, so despised for separating her from her best friend on her wedding day.

There was no way Lolo would have accepted being demoted from maid of honour to ordinary guest at her friend's wedding. Her absence from the bridal retinue would have raised a slew of humiliating questions from friends and family, and Kobe knew this.

It was a case of damned if you do, and damned if you don't, and Lolo wasted no time informing Runako that she would subject herself to no such indignity.

The guests' faces were a blur as Runako fought back the tears, grateful for the Chantilly lace veil hiding her face from prying eyes.

Up ahead, Runako spotted a woman's face that caused a sudden rush of déjà vu. Runako's mind raced, trying to figure out who she was. Just then, the guest beside the mystery woman also turned around. It was CJ!

Despite Runako's best efforts to convince him otherwise, Kobe had been adamant that not only was CJ coming to the wedding, but she would also be bringing a guest! It suddenly made sense. The mystery guest, the girl giggling with CJ, was her younger sister, Amma.

OH MY GOD! At that moment, Runako knew exactly where she had seen her before. It was the face that had peered around the corner when she was on the balcony with Obinna. The bitch must have taken the photo of Runako and Obi!

Runako fumed at the realisation that the evil sisters were the reason her wedding was nearly called off, but she wouldn't give 'Anastasia and Drizella' the satisfaction of seeing her shaken up. Nor would she let them see any tension between her and Kobe. As she made her way past the two, Runako nodded to them gently while plotting revenge.

White rose petals floated back down to earth, to the sound of ululation, as the newlyweds made their way out of the chapel.

The Mensah and Madzonge families followed the photographer as guests swayed their hips, clicked their fingers and whistled along to Soweto String Quartet's *Millennia*.

On cue, a colony of stewards appeared, some carrying assorted canapés and others with trays of prosecco and Bellini's. On the starter menu were mini duck pancakes, salmon and caviar *blinis*[5], and *arancini di riso*[6].

On the other end of the wedding venue, young and old alike jostled for the perfect spot on the bridge. The photographer chuckled at the medley of accents that chorused, with everyone wanting to look their best for the first official family photograph.

"Blaise, scoot over," came an American accent from João.

"Oli, do I look alright?" Kate asked in her Fulham accent, adjusting her Philip Treacy fascinator in the reflection of her boyfriend's sunglasses.

"Lipstick *yangu* iri kupi?[7]" came the distinctly Zimbabwean accent from Maita.

"Qhayiya, *ngicela ubheke ukuthi is'peletu sisabambile*[8]," Nala whispered in her Zulu accent.

Yes, the excitement in the melodic voices from all over the world was almost infectious as the two families united. Despite the rocky start to the day, Runako took time out to appreciate this moment fully and what it meant to her.

"I wonder how much they paid for these flower balls," was Cora's backhanded compliment as she entered the reception venue.

"They're called pomanders, Mum, flower pomanders. Not flower BALLS," Kate automatically corrected.

"Whatever they're called, they look expensive," Cora sniffed.

"They must be," Ellen agreed, as she stopped at one of the tables to take a closer look. "There must be at least twenty red roses in each ball. Who decorates their whole reception with red roses?" she huffed.

"Exactly! It's clear the Madzonges wanted to show off to their friends using our family's money," Cora decided derisively.

"*Au sio?*[9] This is practically their wedding. They invited FIFTY-SIX people! We were told we can only bring forty-four. Imagine my embarrassment when I had to uninvite Ambassador Onyango and his wife! And they could still have come, now that Afia and Kuukuwa's seats are available," sighed Ellen. "Did anyone find out what they ate to get such bad food poisoning?"

"Ah! Can you not see? *Ni uchawi!*[10]" Cora declared. "Witchcraft!"

"What did your mom just say?" Oliver whispered to Kate.

"Doesn't matter. Let's go get a drink!" Kate replied, grabbing Oliver's hand to drag him after her.

The wedding planner and her decor team had done a fantastic job in transforming Villa Reggio into the Renaissance-inspired fairy tale Runako had asked for.

Life-size angel statues lined the walkway into the reception area, each holding a torch above its head. Inside, four French empire crystal chandeliers hung from the exposed wooden trusses creating a warm golden glow.

The ten round tables were draped in floor length ivory tablecloths with golden damask print. On each table, a large red rose pomander was elevated on a gilded candelabra, with red delphiniums cascading down like waterfalls.

To avoid the politics of which family members were allocated "Table 4" instead of "Table 3," the tables were named for some of Runako's favourite Renaissance-era artists instead.

The bride and groom's parents sat at table Anguissola. Siblings were at Teerlinc. Aunts and uncles were at Fontana and Sirani.

First cousins were seated at Gentileschi and Leyster, while friends sat at Peeters, Van Hemessen, Nelli and Galizia.

The DJ marked the end of the official programme by opening the dance floor with Oliver Mtukudzi's crowd-pleaser *Dzoka Uyamwe*. As the guests filled the dance floor and spilt over into the bar, Runako spotted Kate and Amma heading for the bathroom and decided it was the perfect opportunity to confront them about their attempt to sabotage her wedding day.

Runako quickly rounded up Nala and Qhayiya, and they followed her to the bathroom for the showdown. Qhayiya stood guard at the door as Runako walked slowly towards her newest arch-enemies.

"You have some nerve showing up here!" Runako said to Amma. "And you, Kate, you've had it in for me from day one. You need to get it through your head that I am Kobe's wife now. I don't care how badly you wanted him to marry your friend CJ. I am the number one woman in his life. ME! Runako!"

"Are you sure about that?" Kate taunted.

"What the hell is that supposed to mean?" Runako demanded.

"Just 'cause he married you doesn't mean you're number one in his life," Kate shrugged.

"Yes, I am! That's why he married ME, and not CJ!" Runako spat.

"Only because my sister has constantly refused to get back together with him," Amma laughed humourlessly, rolling her eyes.

"Amma, you had better watch your mouth before I ask security to escort you off the premises!" Runako bit back.

"Please do! You'd spare me from having to endure another second of your pretentious wedding…" Amma scoffed

"Almost as pretentious as Kobe's feelings for you," Kate winked as she walked towards the door. "Get the hell out of my way, you fat pig," she sniped at a speechless Qhayiya.

Runako sagged onto a toilet seat and started sobbing while her friends tried to comfort her. She had to wonder.

Was she really Kobe's second choice? Was he actually still in love with CJ?

Nala and Qhayiya returned to the dancefloor while Runako remained in the bathroom to touch up her makeup. Tailored suits and elaborate *dukus*[11] danced and swayed to the music, as the bride sat out of sight in anguish. Nala spotted Kobe at the bar with João. Junior had joined Qhayiya on the dancefloor, but Nala couldn't see Blaise anywhere. Blaise had left an hour before to fetch a change of clothing for Nala. She'd missed a step while taking photographs earlier, ripping the back of her dress in the process. Blaise's suit jacket was doing a good job as a cover up, but he had offered to make the trip back to the hotel as he also wanted to fetch the cigars he'd bought to celebrate Kobe's big day.

"Are Blaise and Olivier still not back?" Nala shouted to Kobe over the music.

"Haven't seen them. I thought they were with you," Kobe responded casually.

"I shouldn't have let Blaise drive in that condition!" Nala shouted back.

"Relax! He wasn't that drunk," Kobe replied, placing his arm over Nala's shoulder. "Besides, you know how easily distracted Blaise is when he's with his younger brother. I'm sure they're fine!"

The St. Regis Hotel

Nala opened her eyes and checked her phone. Blaise and Olivier had still not returned any of her numerous calls and messages. She had a sinking feeling in the pit of her stomach, but dismissed it as nothing more than her overprotectiveness getting the better of her.

She slipped quietly off the bed, careful not to wake Lolo, and tiptoed to her suitcase that was lying open. Nala changed into a pair of shorts and a tee shirt, grabbed the hotel slippers, and snuck out the door.

Silence. Nala had been banging on Blaise and Olivier's door for five minutes with no response. It was now 5 am, and Blaise had never stayed out this late before, even when he was with his younger brother who had a tendency to get carried away.

Tears started welling in Nala's eyes as she marched towards reception. Her mouth was suddenly dry, and there was a big lump in her throat. The elevator doors pinged open, and she ran towards the reception desk, fearing the worst.

"Excuse me, sir. I'm a guest, and I need you to call a guest in the Imperial Room, please," Nala huffed, holding back the tears.

"With pleasure, *Signorina*[12]," replied the gentleman whose name tag read Niccolo. "May I have a surname, please?" he smiled politely.

"Mine or the guest?" Nala huffed.

"The guest please, Signorina," Niccolo replied, holding the handset to his ear.

"Ilunga. Blaise Ilunga. He's also with the Mensah party." The world turned blurry as Nala watched Niccolo's hand slowly move away from his ear, and replace the handset on the receiver. Dread filled his face as he turned away from Nala, and his smile faded.

Something terrible had happened to Blaise and Nala broke down into tears before she even found out what.

"Phone my husband, Niccolo!" Nala shouted across the counter. "I said, phone my husband!"

"Signorina, please! Come with me." Niccolo escorted a now hysterical Nala towards one of the private check-in lounges. He explained that a call had come in about two hours before from St Gianna Ospedale, asking for the emergency contact details for two patients that had been brought in the previous night after suffering a car accident.

The room keys in their wallets pointed to which hotel they were staying at, and their drivers' licences served as identification. The hotel had given the hospital Brigitte Ilunga's details, details they had thanks to Blaise's obsession with providing emergency contact details whenever he checked into a hotel. Niccolo escorted a distraught Nala to the hotel shuttle, and after she gave him a list of people to call and update, she was soon on her way to the hospital.

Villa Reggio

A phone rang in the distance until Runako slowly opened her eyes and tried to figure out where she was. Kobe was snoring loudly beside her, still fully clothed in his wedding suit. The phone rang again.

She patted around the side table for her mobile phone and remembered she and Kobe had given both their phones to Qhayiya for safekeeping.

"Hello?" she groaned, into the landline.

"*Buongiorno, Signora*[13] Mensah. This is Giovanni from the front desk. I have a message for you, and I'm afraid it's not good news."

"What is it, Giovanni?" Runako asked, sitting up.

"There's been a car accident signora, and your friends Mr Blaise Ilunga and Mr Olivier Ilunga are at the St Gianna Ospedale."

"What!" Runako screeched, holding her hand to the forehead.

"May I call a shuttle to take you to the hospital and arrange for late checkout?"

"Yes. Please!"

"Oh, sorry, Signora Mensah, before you go, may we also please bring you the list of extra charges in the meantime for you to double-check as you will need to settle these on checkout?"

"Ok" whimpered Runako, trying to think what extra charges Giovanni was talking about.

"Kobe wake up! Blaise and Olivier were in an accident" Runako shouted, shoving Kobe awake.

"Where the fuck am I?" Kobe moaned, squinting as he looked around the room trying to make sense of his surroundings.

"Can you PLEASE focus?" Runako scolded, before relenting. "We're still at Villa Reggio. We booked a suite here. And now we have to rush to the hospital. Blaise and Olivier were in a car accident!" She burst into tears again.

"FUCK!" Kobe roared. He jumped out of bed, ignoring the pounding headache, and headed for the bathroom.

"How bad was the accident? Do you know?" he shouted over the sound of a flushing toilet.

"They didn't say. And I can't even call anyone cause Q still has our phones from last night," Runako shouted back.

"Then use the bloody hotel phone!" Kobe shouted with a mouth full of toothpaste.

"I don't know anyone's number off by heart!" Runako shouted back, frustrated.

Kobe walked out of the bathroom to find Runako already changed into a simple summer dress and tying the laces of her espadrilles. There was a knock on the door and a kind looking Giovanni delivered a thick envelope and offered to escort the couple to their shuttle.

The driver took off as Runako ripped open the envelope and scanned its contents.

"Five thousand Euros in extra charges? They're insane!" Runako shrieked.

"Let me see that," Kobe frowned, holding out his hand for Runako to pass him the invoice.

"These guys are taking chances!" Runako said as she leaned towards Kobe for a closer look at the bill. "Like this. Extended venue hire. Why are they charging three hours when we were only delayed by an hour?"

"I extended the reception hire and tab after you went to bed," Kobe explained.

"What? By TWO WHOLE HOURS?" Runako's FOMO exploded. "And what the HELL were you guys drinking for TWO THOUSAND EUROS?

"Hey, watch it!" warned Kobe. "My dad's covering that, so chill."

"Okay, then. But what about this suite charge? Our suite comes free with the package I chose so they can't charge us extra for that."

"Oh, that's for CJ and Amma."

"For WHO?" Runako seethed, having heard Kobe very well the first time.

"Don't make a big deal out of it. They were too drunk to take a cab home by themselves, so I offered to pay for a room for them," Kobe muttered defensively.

"Really, Kobe? REALLY? After everything those two have put us through?" Runako's voice rose as she spoke. "I KNOW Amma is the one that –"

"Don't even TRY to blame your inappropriate behaviour on Amma or CJ!" Kobe spat back. "YOU are the one that was sleeping with another man the very same week I introduced you to my fucking parents!"

The driver turned back to look at the commotion behind him, and Kobe lowered his voice in embarrassment.

"YOU are the one that met with him again in the week of our wedding!" Kobe hissed, "YOU are the one who kissed a man that nearly broke our relationship, and you will NOT fucking blame it on MY FRIENDS. DO YOU HEAR ME?"

"I did NOT KISS him!" Runako growled through clenched teeth.

"Only because Amma caught you! Lord knows if we would even be married now if she HADN'T found you when she did! And you had the nerve to DISRESPECT me a SECOND TIME in front of my COUSINS, after making a fool of me in London!"

Kobe was practically foaming at the mouth, and Runako knew better than to talk back at him when he was in this mood. She chose, instead, to reflect upon his words.

WOULD there have been a wedding had Amma not interrupted when she did? Although Runako had stopped speaking to Obi after she promised Kobe she'd block him, she thought about him long after that.

She had shared an unforgettable three days with him, and he had been nothing but kind, considerate and of course, extremely generous. She wondered if she had made the right decision in choosing her relationship with Kobe instead of exploring a new one with Obi.

Kobe was a much safer bet as Obi was definitely not the type of guy one settled down with.

How COULD he be? He partied with celebrities and had a string of girls from all over the world, chasing after him.

Why would he be serious about her, little old Runako who was born in the small village of Zvishavane? He probably couldn't even pronounce Zvishavane. But that was all speculation, and she had no proof that his feelings for her were not genuine.

It didn't matter now, though. She was married to Kobe and had no choice but to make it work.

St Gianna Ospedale

The smell of bleach and latex gloves was in the air as Nala paced up and down the emergency waiting room. Her heart stopped with each doctor that walked towards her, hoping it was news about Blaise and Olivier's progress. She spotted Qhayiya, Lolo, Junior and João down the passage, and ran out to meet them.

"Oh babe, I'm so sorry," Lolo sobbed, squeezing Nala tight.

"This is so terrible" Qhayiya added, wrapping her arms around both friends. They stood in place for a moment, sobbing silently, before peeling themselves off each other again. Junior stepped in for a quick but firm hug, and João placed his arm around Nala's shoulders as they made their way towards the waiting room again.

"Any news?" João asked. His eyes were puffy and red.

"Not yet," Nala choked. "They're both still in surgery. But I know they'll pull through. They just have to!"

"Of course they will, babe! There's just no other way!" Lolo reassured. Lolo tapped Nala on the shoulder before handing over her mobile phone. In the rush to get to the hospital, Nala had forgotten to return to her room to collect it.

She unlocked her screen and noted she had no new phone calls or messages. It was strange that Brigitte hadn't tried to reach her after being contacted by the hospital. Or perhaps she had been caught up in making emergency travel arrangements from Azalia. Knowing Brigitte and Jean-Pierre, they were already on a jet headed directly to Rome.

João was taking coffee orders when Kobe and Runako burst into the waiting room panting heavily. Runako immediately crouched at Nala's feet, and Kobe cried into João's shoulder.

"I'm so sorry, babe. I'm so, so sorry!" Runako whimpered. "He'll be fine, you'll see."

"Yeah. He can't leave Solal and me now. Our baby is not even a year old yet!" Nala said, bursting into tears again.

Time ticked by painfully slow as the friends waited for an update. Stretchers squeaked past and food trolleys clanked by. Machines beeped, and ventilators huffed to an invisible hospital metronome.

Nala opened her eyes to the silhouette of a tall, slender woman towering above her. Despite all the chaos, Brigitte arrived looking every bit her regal self.

She was striking in a floor length, batwing bubu dress. The cerulean chiffon popped against her ripe-plum-coloured skin. Crowning her already imposing 1,8m frame was an oversized, wax print head tie. Adorning her décolletage was a gold Adele Dejak statement choker.

Jean-Pierre was casual in navy pants, matching long-sleeved dashiki shirt, and brown leather Gucci Horsebit Loafers. He was already deep in conversation with the boys, who were standing in a corner, shaking their heads in silence.

"Nala," Brigitte nodded, looking down her aquiline nose at the young lady lying on the steel bench. Nala rose to her feet and gave her mother-in-law a hug.

"Hello, Ma," Nala rasped. Her voice was burnt from having cried all day. Brigitte took a seat, kindly offered by Qhayiya, and quizzed Nala on the events leading up to Blaise and Olivier leaving the wedding venue.

A middle-aged doctor with thick black hair and a peppered beard appeared and asked to speak to the Ilunga family in private.

Nala followed the Ilungas and a team of doctors and nurses into a private room. They were offered a glass of water as they took their seats. One of the nurses held a box of tissues behind her back, and Nala immediately knew it would not be good news.

The dark-haired doctor introduced himself as Doctor Rossi. He had led the team that performed surgery on the brothers when they arrived in the late hours of last night. After clearing his throat and paging through his clipboard again, Doctor Rossi began.

Olivier was conscious, but had suffered spinal damage that would leave him paralysed from the waist down. The seatbelt he was wearing had prevented him from being thrown out of the car when it rolled off the road.

Blaise hadn't been so lucky as he was not wearing his seat belt. Nala remembered how he'd always complained about the discomfort because of his height. As a result of not having worn his seatbelt, Blaise had been flung out the car during the accident and had suffered severe trauma to the head that fractured his skull.

A nurse offered Nala a tissue as she broke down into tears. Jean-Pierre and Brigitte held hands in silence as Doctor Rossi continued.

Doctor Rossi and his team had managed to stabilise Blaise. However, Blaise was still in a coma, and the fracture had caused him severe brain damage. If by some miracle, he did come out of the coma, he'd be in a vegetative state for the rest of his life.

It was up to the family to decide if they wanted to keep him on the ventilators for another 48 hours, to monitor his progress, or whether they wanted to take the decision to switch off the machines now. Dr Rossi offered to give the family some privacy to consider their decision.

"No! Switch them off," Brigitte said coldly, rising to her feet.

"No!" Nala screamed. "Don't switch the machines off. You need to do everything you can to keep him alive! He has a nine-month-old son that needs him! You keep him alive!"

Brigitte walked towards Nala and pointed her finger in her face.

"You witch!" Brigitte spat. "You killed him, and now you want to pretend you care about him?"

Nala looked on in horror as her mother-in-law rained insults on her. "You sent my sons onto the road, at night, after they had been drinking. What did you think would happen?" Brigitte turned to the stunned doctor, walked towards him and placed both hands on his shoulders, before repeating her instructions.

"Doctor," Brigitte began, her voice was deep and toneless. "I shall not repeat myself. As the mother of your patient, I am instructing you to switch off those machines. No son of mine will spend the rest of his life half dead!"

Nala jumped from her seat and wedged herself between Brigitte and Doctor Rossi.

"Doctor! I am the patient's wife!" Nala barked, "And I DEMAND that you keep those machines on for 48 hours. Please! Just 48 hours!"

"His wife, you say?" Brigitte said, folding her arms and smiling provokingly.

"Yes!" Nala coughed in between the crying, "I am his wife. Blaise and I are husband and wife according to South African customary law, and I have the right to decide what happens with my husband's life."

Nala pursed her lips, half impressed at her show of courage against her mother-in-law, and half fearful for the response she would receive. Brigitte took a step back and gave Nala an evil eye that bore into her soul.

The doctors and nurses shifted uncomfortably as the two women stared each other down. Brigitte paused for a moment before turning to the doctor.

"Doctor, let's listen to the wife. Keep the machines on for another 48 hours. But only on one condition."

Brigitte turned back to Nala. "Mrs Ilunga," she mocked, "if my son is not awake in the next 48 hours, we will switch the machines off." She paused to let the weight of her words sink in. "After we have switched the machines off, you, Mrs Ilunga, will come back to Azalia with us to mourn my son. And you shall follow ALL our mourning rituals. Since you have decided that you are his wife…"

5

RUNAKO ROSE

"Do not set sail on someone else's star"

— AFRICAN PROVERB

Kobe and Runako's Place, Cape Town
January 2010

*T*he first few months of marriage had been unkind to the Mensah bride. Kobe carried tremendous guilt that his best friend had lost his life on his wedding night. And, as much as Runako had tried to make up for the incident with Obi, her husband was far from over it.

He still looked at her as though he despised her, and in the six months they had been married, she could count on one hand the number of times they'd been intimate. It didn't help that they hadn't had any real time alone since the wedding.

Runako had spent many late nights and early mornings on campus to finish her master's research. Kobe had volunteered to take up a post on an oil rig in Mossel Bay, ONLY a five-hour drive from their home in Cape Town. From coming home every other weekend, Kobe started coming home once a month and sometimes only after six weeks.

Just when Runako thought they'd finally have solitude over the Christmas holidays, Kobe advised his parents would be visiting with them for three weeks as they wanted a "Cape Christmas."

Cora, who had been a nightmare to deal with in the buildup to the wedding, had been significantly more tolerable since the Azalian leg of the traditional wedding celebrations held the week after the celebration in Rome.

The Mensah half of the celebrations had been held at Kwame's village in Kikuyu State. As the first grandchild to get married, Kobe immediately attained celebrity-status with his *cûcû*[1]. The fact that his bride was from a foreign country, and the daughter of a senior politician, only served to cement this position.

Cûcû had looked approvingly at the slender, dark-skinned, Shona girl on her knees before her, as Runako presented a plate of *ugali*[2], *mukimo*[3], *sukuma*[4] and beef stew.

Ordinarily, Runako would be expected to wake up at dawn to prepare the meal herself on an open fire. But, having seen how doll-like her grandson's bride was, with her *Muzungu*[5] hair and artificial nails, Cûcû had decreed that Runako was not to be subjected to the archaic ritual again.

By the end of the third day at the Mensah homestead, Runako had gone from the bottom of the family pecking order right to the very top, thanks to the favour, which the family matriarch bestowed upon her. At Cûcû's side, all the drama, tension and insecurity of the previous months seemed to vanish.

Ellen's cruel words no longer held any power, CJ was a nameless entity, Kate was just another family member being sent about on this or that errand, and Kobe had even agreed that cutting Lolo out the bridal retinue had been a tad harsh.

But now, back in Cape Town, Cûcû was two thousand kilometres away, and Runako risked returning to her standing as the opportunistic girl with the questionable pedigree.

That evening, as Runako was clearing away the dinner plates, an email popped into her inbox with the subject line 'Offer of Employment'.

"*Pongezi*[6], bi harusi," Cora and Kwame said when Runako rushed in to share the good news.

"How much will these people be paying you?" Kobe asked, eagerly scrolling through the contract on Runako's laptop.

"There, under remuneration – R120 000 per annum. That's like R10k per month!" Runako squealed.

"Not so fast," Kobe cautioned. "That's the cost to company of your package. The cash portion will be much less. Did they attach a dummy payslip?" Kobe scrolled down to the end of the contract. "Aah! There it is!"

"SIX THOUSAND rand?!" Runako exclaimed. "I was promised a package of ten thousand rand per month during the interview!"

"I've heard this is what big companies do," Cora chimed in. "They attract candidates with big numbers, but when it comes to the offer, they give nothing close to what was discussed!"

Runako nodded enthusiastically in agreement with Cora, grateful for the ever-elusive buy-in from her mother-in-law.

"Well… were you promised R10k or did you assume R10k?" Kobe questioned. "Something I learned when I started working is never to budget using the CTC figure. It includes the company contributions paid on your behalf. Rather ask for the cash component, or better yet, the dummy payslip."

Runako sighed dramatically; disappointed that she would be receiving only two-thirds of the income she had bargained on. Kwame, whose eyes were fixed on Sky News, shook his head disapprovingly, his only contribution to the discussion.

"Well, at least you won't have to pay medical aid as you're already on mine!" Kobe said brightly, trying to cheer up his wife. "That's an extra R1 450 in your pocket every month."

"Really?" Runako sat upright, looking less dispirited. "Is there anything else I can get back? Like this 'Preservation Fund Contribution?'"

"I'm afraid not. That money goes towards your pension, life cover, disability, sometimes funeral cover as well," explained Kobe. "At induction, ask HR about your preservation fund benefits, and then maybe we can cancel any duplications when we next meet with our financial advisor."

Cora reached for the TV remote and lowered the volume. She turned to Runako and Kobe. "Do you two have a financial advisor? Did you hear that, Daddy?" Cora emphasised as she waved her hand to get her husband's attention.

"Just leave the children to discuss their household matters in private, Mommy," Kwame replied irritably. "And raise the volume, I'm trying to watch the news!"

Runako leaned closer to Kobe so she wouldn't have to shout over the broadcast. "I guess I can't do much about UIF and PAYE, right?" she whispered.

"Not at this stage. Your earnings are still pretty straightforward," Kobe confirmed. "Once they start getting complicated, you'll find there are ways to minimise your tax burden."

"Well, let me get on the phone with my parents to tell them their daughter has been accepted into legal articles. Thanks for helping with this, baby," Runako smiled, and gave Kobe a kiss on the cheek. She headed to the guest bedroom to phone her family to share the good news.

Clubhouse, Borrowdale Golf Estate
November 2010

Two crowned lapwings took flight as a golf ball came hurtling towards them. Another four-ball team was approaching the 18th hole, once again disturbing the birds that were trying to sunbathe on the putting green.

Runako watched fondly as the golfers went about their game, remembering the many mornings she spent watching her father indulge in his favourite pastime.

Being back on the Borrowdale Clubhouse balcony was bittersweet. It held fond memories from her childhood, but also reminded her of the many losses her family had suffered since her father was removed from office eighteen months before.

An elaborate scheme had been devised by one of his party rivals to kick him out of the Future Freedom Party ahead of the next general elections, as he was the party favourite to run as Presidential candidate.

George Madzonge had since tried and failed to secure alternative employment, as no one wanted to be seen lending their support to the enemy of the potential future president.

The political rivalry had also been used to frustrate Runako's brothers, who were managed out of their roles in public service.

A solution to the Madzonge family woes presented itself in the form of a senior posting for Kobe with the Mensah Renewable Energy Corporation (MREC) in Zimbabwe. After increasing disruptions to the solar farm development project, Kwame Mensah appointed his son to oversee operations as his "man-on-the-ground" and ensure its timeous completion.

Kobe wasted no time in overhauling the management team and appointing George, Tawanda and Tongayi in its place, simultaneously preventing his wife's family from falling into total financial ruin.

Runako hoped being around a group of familiar men would help Kobe with his depression, or whatever it was, he was suffering from since Blaise's passing more than a year before.

Blaise had been Kobe's closest remaining friend in Cape Town, and Kobe had become a recluse after his passing.

Runako was deep in thought when her cousin, Rory, walked onto the balcony. Mixed-race with hazel eyes, Aurora "Rory" Scott caused quite the stir whenever she entered a room.

Rory had the confidence of one that had never had their value questioned based on their skin colour. On the contrary, her years of growing up as an only child had given her an assuredness that was not easily shaken.

Her parents, Dawn and Nathaniel, had always given into their daughter's every whim, which could explain why, at the age of twenty-five, she had never left her parents' home. Nor held a job outside the family business. Nor maintained a romantic relationship for longer than six months.

"Hey, you!" Rory said. She gave Runako a peck on the cheek before taking a seat.

"Rory! How are you doing?" Runako replied, setting down her chai latte on the table.

"I'm good. Just happy to be out of the house! I swear Dawn and Nate are driving me up the wall!"

"Oh, really? Whatever is the matter now?" Runako chuckled. A waiter came by the table, and the cousins placed their brunch order.

"They're just always complaining about something or the other. 'Aurora, when will you settle down and get married? Aurora, maybe you should consider doing a Masters. Aurora, we've sheltered you too much, you need to get a proper job!'" Rory mimicked her parents, pulling a face.

"Oh hush, Rory! Leave my precious aunt and uncle alone," Runako chided, laughing at Rory's imitation. "They're clearly not as young as they used to be."

"Please! They've been annoying me my whole life. How are YOUR parents doing? Mom has been worried sick about her only brother's wellbeing."

"We're doing as well as can be. Kobe has hired Papa and my brothers to be his senior advisors on the solar farm his family business is building up here in Zim. Without my husband's intervention, our family would have been in serious trouble!" Runako said.

"That's amazing, cuz!" Rory exclaimed, patting Runako on the shoulder. "You really bagged a good one in Kobe. Hopefully, I'll be just as lucky when I get married. *If ever!*"

"I wouldn't be too quick to make that wish if I were you," Runako frowned. "Sadly, my relationship with my husband has been very different since I became a housewife. Well, since I haven't managed to secure a job here in Harare. Apparently, no legal firm wants to hire 'ousted Governor George Madzonge's daughter' as a candidate attorney. It's really putting a strain on my marriage, Rory."

"How so? It's not like you NEED to work. Kobe's from a rich family, no?" Rory enquired, cleaning the lenses of her gold reflector aviator sunglasses.

"True! But it's not so much about the money as it is about the quality of our relationship. I've never had aspirations of being a kept woman,

Rory. And going from the challenging life I had as a candidate attorney in Cape Town, to being a housewife that spends her days lunching and going to the spa, is really messing with my psyche. By the time Kobe gets home from work every day, I'm grumpy from doing NOTHING all day, he's grumpy from doing TOO MUCH all day. We're like two ships passing in the night!" Runako said, shaking her head.

"Have you tried spicing things up in the bedroom, maybe?" Rory winked. The waiter arrived and placed their drinks order on the table.

"I have. Numerous times! And as you can probably tell, that didn't go too well either. Can I tell you a secret?" Runako said. She leaned over her cousin's shoulder and cupped her hand over her mouth before whispering, "We haven't had sex in four months."

"What? I would die! I would LITERALLY fall over. And die!" Rory said with distaste, stirring her dragon fruit smoothie with her straw.

"I know..." Runako sighed heavily. "You are sitting in front of a woman that is slowly dying."

"How are you still sane?" Rory asked, shaking her head.

"Let's just say this girl's found some weird and wonderful contraptions to keep herself busy with," Runako said, smiling glumly.

"Oh..." Rory mouthed in surprise, taken aback by her conservative cousin's newfound hobby.

"Someone who's not having a problem in that department is Lolo. Speaking of, do you know she gave birth to twins last month?" Runako beamed.

"Really!" Rory exclaimed, her jaw dropping to the floor. "Is she still with her on-again-off-again boyfriend?"

"João? Yup," Runako nodded. "And apparently his family is SMITTEN with his boys. The Morreiras insisted the boys are born in the US, so Lolo has been living with the Morreiras for the past four months!"

"Hectic! And work?" Rory enquired. She cleared the table for the waiter to place their brunch order of avo on toast and a baby kale breakfast salad.

"She's taken six months maternity leave," Runako said, grinding black pepper over her avocado. "And apparently made it very clear that she's not giving up her career to move to Azalia or the US. It will be quite interesting to see how that plays out with the mighty Morreiras," Runako said, biting her bottom lip.

The cousins tucked into their meals and spent the next hour, catching up on the latest happenings in their lives.

Rory shared that her parents were considering adopting a baby, as they were afraid of being alone should their only child decide to up and leave them. It wasn't an absurd thought, since Rory was considering applying for a music scholarship to France.

Having spent her formative years in different countries around the world, Rory was starting to feel stifled by being in one country for so long.

Runako shared her concern over the increasing number of hours Kobe was spending at work. This wouldn't have been a problem if those hours were spent with his clients.

But more and more client meetings were turning into social meetings, to which Kobe would invite his female staff members, Danai, Tanaka, Chipedza, and Grace. Increasingly, Kobe's client meetings ended up being social meetings, with these four ladies in tow.

Runako was worried about the growing distance between her and her husband, but had convinced herself that she was letting her insecurities get the better of her. After getting a job, she would have something on which to focus her attention, and not let her imagination conjure up images of the worst.

The cousins were about to order last rounds when Rory spotted a familiar face taking a putt.

"Oh! There's Anesu. Remember him?" Rory said, pointing to a golfer on the putting green.

"Anesu…" Runako repeated slowly, trying, but failing, to place the name.

"Yeah! My friend from high school. I once brought him to your house for drinks when your parents were away," Rory elaborated and waited expectantly, eyebrows raised.

Runako still looked confused, so Rory tried again. "Anesu!" she insisted. "He stayed in Borrowdale Ridge. Friends with Blake? We once smoked weed with them at the tennis courts?"

"Oh! THAT guy. Is that him? He's looking way more handsome than I remember," Runako marvelled appreciatively.

"I know, right?" Rory giggled, looking over the balcony at the chiselled body down below. "And he is SO in the money! His dad bought into some IT company and made a killing. Dude got an apartment and a G-wagon for his 25th birthday! That's why he can afford to play golf on a random Wednesday morning."

"Get out!" Runako exclaimed, looking at Rory in disbelief.

"Let me get a waiter to tell him we're sitting up here," Rory replied.

The waiter was clearing the girls' plates when Anesu appeared on the balcony. Runako and Rory stared in awe as he walked towards their table.

He was a far cry from the scrawny high school boy Runako had imprinted in her memory. Instead, Anesu had transformed into a modern-day Riace warrior.

The base of his thighs popped into a 'V' under his white golf shorts with every step he took, while his chiselled torso made its presence visible with every swing of the arms. His shoulders filled the sleeves of his navy-blue golf shirt, whose collar sat neatly beneath his square jawline. His '70% cocoa' skin was soft leather in the sun. And his thick eyelashes fluttered beneath the peak of his white Titleist cap.

"If it isn't Miss Roar herself!" Anesu smiled. His voice was rich with a private school accent.

"Anesu!" Rory giggled, rising to her feet and accepting Anesu's invitation for a hug. Rory turned to Runako. "You remember my cousin, Ru?"

"Of course," Anesu said casually. "How can I forget my teenage crush?"

Runako smiled and rose to her feet to give Anesu a hug. A hug that lasted a second longer than it should have. Anesu had held on as Runako pulled away.

"Teenage crush?" Runako giggled as she sat down again.

"Yes. You didn't know?" Anesu said with a raised eyebrow. He pulled up a chair and joined the girls' table. "I thought I was being pretty obvious that night we came for drinks at your house?"

"Uhm… no," Runako smiled, containing herself from giggling again. "I don't remember you making a move."

"Well, there's no use in talking about it now, since, uh…" Anesu paused, cocking his head towards Runako's two-carat solitaire diamond ring.

"Yup. Too late now, I'm afraid!" Runako smiled, wiggling her fingers.

"Anyway," Rory interrupted. "We just wanted to say hi. I need to get going before my employers slash *parentals*[7] wonder where I've disappeared to. Ru, are you staying, or shall I call for the bill?"

"Go ahead and call for the bill please, darling! I need to head out too," Runako said, reaching for her bag.

"Leave the bill to me," Anesu said, rising to his feet and placing his hands in his shorts pockets. "I'll add it to my tab."

"Thanks, boo!" Rory said, giving Anesu a hug. "We should link up soon, yeah?"

"Yeah, that would be great!" he replied. He paused and looked at Runako. "You should come along too."

"Maybe. Maybe I will…" she smiled, before giving Anesu a hug goodbye. This time, it was Runako that held on a second longer than she should have.

House Boat, Lake Kariba
April 2011

The melancholy melody of Gabriel Fauré's *Pavane* floated through the Platinum Suite as the warm Zambezi sun streamed through the window. The pianist continued serenading the birthday girl as she slowly woke from her slumber.

Runako recognised the melody as the tune from one of her many childhood piano lessons. She smiled sleepily and wondered what else was in store as part of her much-anticipated birthday surprise.

She opened her eyes and standing at the foot of her bed was a boat steward with a pink peony in his hand. Runako slowly sat up and pulled the covers tightly around her chest.

The smiling steward walked around the bed, handed her the flower and walked back out to the living room. As he did, another steward entered the bedroom, also holding a peony in hand. The first steward returned, with a third peony in his hand.

This continued until Runako had 25 pink peonies in her hands, to match her new age.

These must have cost a fortune, she thought to herself. Peonies were seasonal flowers, available in Southern Africa only around October and November. *These must be imported.*

She laid her precious petals on her bedside table and felt the baby kick. Runako was only five months along, but her daughter had already taken to doing cartwheels in her belly! She gently brushed her tummy and then turned to her side.

"Thank you, my love," she said, and gave Anesu a soft kiss. She slid down the covers and nestled her head on his chest.

"Anything for my lady on her special day," he replied, planting another kiss on her forehead and wrapping his arms around her. "Did you like my special song request on the piano?"

"*The Pavane?*" she replied.

"Yeah. It reminds me of the night we came for drinks at your house. The first time I met you."

"Really? So, what's so special about that song?" Runako asked lightly, and turned onto her side to spoon back against his body. Anesu immediately turned too and wrapped his arm around her.

"Don't you remember my friend Blake had Amu's song *Attention* on repeat the whole night? That's the same melody," he replied huskily.

"Was it Blake's phone that had that song on repeat? I thought it was yours!" Runako remembered.

"Nope. It was Blake. It was so funny seeing a white guy so deep into hip hop," Anesu reminisced. "Blake loved that song so much, he went and bought all of Amu's albums!"

"Hilarious," Runako giggled.

"I take it you're spending the afternoon with your family, or do you have to make an appearance at the office?" Anesu asked, softly stroking Runako's arm.

"Nope, I'm only seeing them in the evening. As soon as we get back to Harare, I need to head straight to my gynae's appointment" Runako paused and sighed loudly. "It's so awkward having to see Kobe at EVERY single consultation!"

"Why is it awkward? Is he still asking that you two get back together?" Anesu asked casually, pulling away to lie on his back.

"Yeah. He is," Runako replied. Her voice was soft and sad. She turned around and lay her head on Anesu's chest again. "He makes me feel so guilty for not wanting to work things out with him. He keeps asking for another chance, saying he's a changed man. That he's ready to settle down and not mess around anymore."

"You mean not cheat anymore?" Anesu replied sarcastically.

"Technically he didn't cheat with Danai," Runako defended. "They were just friends and only started dating after I moved out."

"Runako!" Anesu said sternly. He rolled to face Runako and propped his head up with his arm. "You left your marriage BECAUSE of his relationship with Danai. Whether or not it was platonic at the time. And the very woman he told you not to worry about, is the one he hooked up with as soon as you moved out! I don't know how you define cheating, but it sounds to me that Kobe had a closer relationship with HER than he did with you! And that, to me, is cheating!" Anesu snapped.

"The same could be said about me and you, Anesu..." Runako replied defiantly, still lying on her side and using her arm as a cushion.

"I see..." Anesu replied. His voice fragile, like that of a defeated man.

He was silent for a long moment.

"So?" Anesu eventually posed the monosyllabic question in a cold but non-threatening way.

Runako waited for him to continue. He didn't.

"So, what?" she asked softly.

"So, are you considering getting back together with your husband, Runako?"

"Hey! Don't use that word!" Runako snapped. She sat up in the bed and fixed the cushions behind her back. "He's still my husband only because the court date hasn't been finalised yet. You make it sound like I'm having an affair with you when I'm actually trying to build something new with you!"

Anesu looked up at Runako, unmoved by her yelling and exaggerated gestures. He held her gaze until she looked away in discomfort. Then he continued, his voice cold and now threatening.

"Runako. Answer the question. Is there a chance that you will get back with Kobe?"

"I don't know, Anesu! I don't know!" Runako began to cry, an increasingly frequent occurrence since she fell pregnant. "I wasn't happy in my marriage, Anesu. I hadn't been happy for a long time. I can't honestly sit here and say Kobe and I would still be together had he not met her!"

Runako paused to grab a tissue from the side table. She wiped her nose and continued, "On the other hand, I owe it to my baby to at least try and give her a comfortable childhood. Look at my friends Lolo and João!

"They are THE most dysfunctional couple in history, but they got engaged and are trying to build a life together for their sons. Maybe God wanted me to stay with Kobe. What other reason could there be, for me finding out I'm pregnant in the very week I was planning on moving out?"

"Really! God created a whole new human life just to save your sham of a marriage? You seriously believe that?" Anesu demanded, before throwing back his head and laughing incredulously.

"I don't have time for this, Anesu," Runako evaded. "We need to get going otherwise I'll be late for my appointment." She climbed out of bed and walked into the bathroom. She was brushing her teeth when Anesu appeared at the door.

"Runako," he said calmly. "You need to choose. By 5 pm this afternoon, I want to know if you're building a life with me, or whether you're going to try and work things out with Kobe."

"Have a happy birthday," he said wearily, before turning around and walking away.

Great Zimbabwe Private Medical Centre, Harare
August 2011

The operating room was filled with chatter, beeping, and the sound of rolling wheels. Runako arched her back and held her head in her hands. The thought of an injection piercing her spine made her nervous.

Runako's obstetrician, Dr Dhliwayo, and her assisting doctor chatted animatedly in the background. Their light-hearted banter provided relative calm to Runako's shattered nerves.

The nurse dutifully applied a cold, numbing cream on Runako's back, and the anaesthetist walked around and pulled up a chair. A pair of blue surgical shoe covers appeared in Runako's field of vision as Dr Jones took his seat before her. He gently placed his hands on Runako's knees and explained the risks associated with an epidural.

Runako stopped listening when he spoke about the risk of spinal damage and potential disability. What was the point when she had little choice in the matter? Her daughter had to be born by Caesarean section, and that would not be possible without an anaesthetic.

Soon after, a stinging sensation shot through her body as the needle entered her spine. Runako willed herself not to move since that could cause spinal damage. A few minutes later, her body started going numb, and the nurse rushed to help Runako onto her back.

"Are Q and Junior still here?" Runako asked, adjusting herself into a more comfortable position.

"Yup! It's still so weird seeing them together as a couple," Kobe chuckled. "Q is all prim and proper, very first lady, you know? Michelle Obama!"

Runako nodded as she watched Kobe animatedly narrate their friends' appearances. He rose to his feet as he prepared to continue with the story.

"Now Junior, on the other hand, is walking around looking like Lenny Kravitz with his big dreadlocks and all those piercings and tattoos. He looks much happier since standing up to his father and following his passion for art. Such a pity it came at such a high price..." Kobe said, shaking his head.

"You mean his dad basically disowning him?" Runako opined.

"Yeah, and Junior having to start over. From scratch. With nothing!" Kobe sighed. "I can't imagine having to rely on your girlfriend for everything. Food. Shelter. Hell, even the bed you're sleeping on!"

"I think Q and Junior will be just fine. Q's always been an independent woman, and I don't think she sees anything wrong with being the breadwinner in the relationship. I mean, if Lolo and João can make a relationship work, ANYONE can!" Runako smirked, shaking her head.

"I was actually on the phone with them earlier! They send their regards. Look how big the twins are?" Kobe said, handing his phone over to Runako.

"They're too cute," she cooed. "I don't know how João survives the six-hour flight to Cape Town every three weeks though!"

"Not forgetting the layover in Johannesburg!" Kobe yawned, stretching himself before taking a seat at Runako's bedside again. "Seems my boy has manned up! I'm actually very proud of him. Of THEM. They did the right thing for the twins," Kobe smiled, taking

Runako's right hand into his own. "Just like we did the right thing for our little girl."

Runako shifted uncomfortably as her lower body started to go numb.

"How are you feeling?" Kobe smiled, rubbing Runako's hand.

"I don't know," Runako smiled crookedly, looking up lovingly at Kobe.

"You should be excited. This is what you've always wanted," he reminded her, gently.

"I know... It's just that..." Runako took a deep breath and absently catalogued the strange sensation caused by the anaesthetic and the doctors' preparations. "I'm a little scared."

Runako squeezed her eyes shut when the rough tugging and pulling at her stomach started. Kobe gently kissed the back of her hand and continued to stroke her arm.

"You've got nothing to worry about," he said softly. "You've got the best doctors around you."

Runako was not worried about only that, and she suspected Kobe knew this, too.

What was worrying her was whether this time would be any different. Whether Kobe was ready to settle down and let go of his philandering ways. Whether Kobe wanted to work things out because of who she was, or who she was carrying.

Kobe had been a saint since she moved back home three months ago. Whenever she called, he answered. Whenever she had a weird craving, he climbed in the car and went to buy it. When her back was sore, he rubbed it. When it was time for bed, he climbed in the sheets first to warm them up for her.

He didn't leave for work without asking if she needed anything. He didn't return from work without asking if she needed anything. By

6:30 pm, he was home, lying on the couch and watching soapies with her, just like they used to when they first moved in together.

So committed was Kobe to making his marriage work, that he'd even started staging scenarios for Runako to access his phone. He'd ask, "Please take a photo of your dad and me," or "I'm jumping in the shower. If my phone rings, please answer it." Runako's favourite was "What do you think this message means?" as he'd handed over his phone, already opened to his WhatsApp messaging.

There was no denying that Kobe was working hard to be the husband Runako wanted. He knew that Runako believed a child would rather be FROM a broken home that IN a broken home.

She had agreed to return on condition that they would build a loving home for their child, and should he break her trust again, she would have no qualms in ending the marriage. This time, for good.

But the truth was, she didn't want that, and she didn't want her marriage to end. She didn't want to lose the family she'd built.

Runako gently pulled Kobe's arm closer and kissed the palm of his hand. She vowed to put the past behind her, as Kobe had pleaded, and never raise it again.

A screech filled the room as baby Zina took her first breath. The doctor settled Zina on Runako's chest, and the new mom instantly fell in love. Zina was an unsightly little thing, with grey skin and a wrinkly face.

"Thank you for bringing us together, my girl," Runako whispered to her baby, before showering her with kisses, all over her tiny face.

She looked at her chubby cheeks and button nose and knew it had all been worth it. She said a silent prayer thanking God for the safe delivery of her daughter.

When the nurse came to fetch the baby to be cleaned, the new mom gave her little girl one last kiss and whispered a blessing:

"May your latter days be greater than your former my child."

Kobe spent the rest of the day at Runako's side and was back early the following morning. Runako waddled through the hospital passages towards the parking lot, per Kobe's request. She didn't understand why she had to walk all the way to the car to fetch the extra clothes Kobe had brought for her, instead of him just bringing them inside the hospital.

Her heart nearly stopped when she suddenly realised why Kobe had insisted that she meet him in the parking lot.

Parked in front of her was a brand new Porsche Cayenne SUV, with a giant red bow on it, and filled with red roses.

Kobe was on one knee in front of the car, holding up a box with the biggest solitaire diamond Runako had ever seen. Runako held her hand on her mouth at the sheer grandness of this gesture.

"Runako Rose Mensah," Kobe began, "will you 'marry' me? Again? Forever this time?" he smiled.

"Of course, Baby Cakes!" Runako squealed with glee, jumping into Kobe's arms, oblivious to the protest from her incision.

Savoy Inc., Harare
April 2012

The laptop screen lit up blue against Runako's face as she logged on and navigated to the Skype icon. It was nearly 7 pm and time for her weekly catch-up call with the girls.

Weekly Skype dates were the girls' attempt at offering each other ongoing support as their lives were becoming increasingly complicated.

Lolo and João were constantly fighting over where they would settle down. Lolo wanted João to move to Cape Town as he had a higher chance of getting a job there than she had of getting one in Azalia.

João wanted Lolo and the twins to move to Azalia. He was already earmarked to become a junior partner at his law firm. He was also spending more time serving on the board of his family business.

Qhayiya and Junior were adamant that marriage was not on the cards for them, but had decided on taking the next step in their relationship by buying a house together.

And Nala had missed the call AGAIN, which was such a frequent occurrence it was no longer surprising!

An hour had flown by, and it was time for goodbyes and for the friends to return to their lives. Runako ended the call and stared at her computer screen, scrolling aimlessly through news sites.

It was just after 8 pm, and she had long completed her work for the day. She raised her head and noticed the rest of the floor had gone home, except for two or three fellow candidate attorneys.

Nothing was keeping Runako at the office, but she just couldn't will herself to head home. She'd been staying later and later to avoid going home.

In just eight months, Kobe had reverted to his factory settings. Her marriage was back to what it was when they had decided to separate.

Every time Runako complained that Kobe had broken her conditions of returning to their marital home, he replied by saying she hadn't stuck to his conditions, either. Hers were simple:

1. **Monthly finance meeting:** Set short, medium and long-term financial goals for the household, and review household income and expenditure at the end of every month.
2. **Quarterly Assets and Liabilities review:** Every three months, they were to sit and go over their personal assets and liabilities. Runako had been scarred by the bank repossession of her family home shortly after her father was kicked out of office. He had maxed out the mortgage without her mom's knowledge to fund their extravagant lifestyle.
3. **Housewife Agreement:** If at any point Kobe wanted Runako to be a housewife, they were to sign a contract that he would transfer to her an agreed monthly amount into a bank account in her own name. This amount was to be accompanied by a payslip to ensure that she didn't lose her financial independence, especially if she ever wanted to apply for credit. Should he default on her payment for a maximum of three months, then she would be free to get back into formal employment again.
4. **Household Standards:** There were to be no double-standards. If Kobe wanted to go out with his friends three times a week, then Runako had the same right. If Kobe went on a boys' trip once a year, then Runako could take a girls' trip, too. The same rules were to apply to both husband and wife.
5. **Date Night:** They would have a romantic date night once a week, every week.

Kobe had drawn up his own list of conditions, which were more a set of expectations. These, he believed, would lead to a better marriage:

1. **Respect:** Although he agreed that he and Runako were equal partners, there could still be only one head of the household. He, therefore, had the final say.
2. **Family first:** Nothing should be placed above the responsibility to the marriage and the children.
3. **Marital roles:** The defined roles in a marriage were that the

husband is the provider, and the wife is the nurturer. Kobe's primary responsibility was to ensure that the family was financially taken care of, and Runako's primary responsibility was to take care of the day-to-day running of the household.

4. **Decorum:** Kobe expected Runako to dress as a wife should, avoiding clothing that was short or revealing. It also wasn't acceptable that she constantly partied with her single friends and cousins, except for special occasions.

They'd honoured each other's conditions for the first three months after Runako returned home but had started slipping after that. It became worse as the months went by.

When Runako asked for a sit-down to discuss household finances, he argued that he could not sit down with someone who didn't respect him. When Runako went out for a drink with her friends because Kobe was out having a drink with his friends, he complained that she didn't know the role of a wife.

It was a vicious cycle. The more they pushed to address their frustrations, the more frustrated they became. And so it continued, a pressure cooker of emotions.

Runako sometimes wondered if she'd made a mistake getting back together with Kobe, just as she often wondered if she'd made a mistake in choosing her relationship with Kobe over exploring a new one with Anesu.

She also wondered if there was any formula for a relationship, for choosing the right partner. Or, whether all relationships inevitably lost their magic.

During such introspection, Runako wished that she was still in touch with Anesu. Or even Obi. Someone to keep her company during the lonely times. But she also knew those conversations led down a slippery slope.

Runako was lost in thought when her phone rang. It was Kobe.

"Hey," she answered unenthusiastically, sagging back into her seat.

"Hey. How far are you?" Kobe replied, his tone no better than hers.

"I'll be another thirty minutes. I just have an urgent court application to finish up," Runako lied. She tapped on her keyboard to support her lie.

"Runako, I've spoken to you about staying at the office late," Kobe said irritably.

"Yes, but I have something to finish up, Kobe!" Runako insisted.

"When I started working, I was always done by five!" Kobe shouted. "If the work you're doing is so important they wouldn't have given it to a candidate attorney!"

"If you were done by five, then Lord knows what or who kept you until ten pm because that's when you'd come strolling into the house!" Runako replied bitterly. She stood up from her chair and walked into the kitchen area for some privacy.

"THIS is what I mean when I say you don't respect me!" Kobe shouted. "You don't know your place as a wife, and I'm tired of every conversation ending up in an argument, Runako!" Runako had to hold the phone away from her ear by the end of his statement.

"And you? Do you know how to be a husband, Kobe? An equal partner in the home instead of a gift-wielding dictator?" Runako retaliated snidely.

"Equal? You want us to be equal partners, Runako?" Kobe growled menacingly. "Let me tell you something. The day your salary is equal to mine is the day we can talk about being equal partners. Until then, I expect you to start behaving like a wife or to pack your bags and leave my house. For good!"

6

HAND TO MOUTH

"A man who uses force is afraid of reasoning"

— KENYAN PROVERB

Alpha Private Bank, Sandton
May 2012

*Q*hayiya paged casually through the day's business newspaper while Junior paced up and down the client waiting area. He feared his status as a foreign national, who was self-employed, would negatively impact on the home loan amount the bank would be comfortable granting them.

It had been more than a year since Junior moved in with his girlfriend. He'd hoped that his father would have accepted his decision to quit politics by now. Embrace his decision to nurture the talent he had displayed since childhood. But to Prime Minister Geoffrey Okello, art was nothing more than a hobby and he would have no son of his shame the family name by dedicating his life to "playing around with colours".

At 3 pm sharp, as scheduled, Olivia Harris appeared and invited the young couple into a private meeting room. Tall and slender, dressed in a grey knee-length pencil skirt, crisp white button-down shirt, and chestnut hair that fell on her shoulders, she was strikingly beautiful with dewy skin.

Qhayiya's private banker offered the couple some refreshments before taking her seat on the opposite end of the table. Qhayiya kicked off the meeting by introducing Junior and making small talk to soften up the woman that stood between them and their dream home in the trendy suburb of Hyde Park.

"Congratulations on your decision to buy a home," Olivia smiled. "I take it you brought along the documents I asked for?"

"Yes," Qhayiya said, pulling out two plastic folders, and handing them over to Olivia for her assessment of their application.

"Please let me know if anything is unclear," Qhayiya said nervously. She peered over the table to try to see what documents Olivia was frowning at. "We've put in an offer of R2 million on an apartment in Hyde Park, and we'd like to apply for 100% financing," Qhayiya volunteered.

"Got it!" Olivia said pointedly, paging through the folder containing their documents. "You're earning R700k per annum Miss Dana, and Mr Okello is on…"

"It depends…" Junior fired flatly. "I work as a freelancer, so my earnings aren't fixed."

"And you'd estimate your average earnings over the past two years to be around what?" Olivia pressed mildly, perhaps sensing Junior's reluctance.

"I would say around R1, 2million," Junior replied after some thought. "I was on R800k per annum when I left my last job. I've made about R400k since being on my own. So, I make an average of R600k per annum."

Olivia looked up quizzically, trying to follow the explanation. Junior explained that he invoices for his freelance work and art sales through a registered company that he's the sole shareholder and director of.

He also runs most of his expenses through the company bank account. He doesn't draw a monthly salary from the business as his income does not flow monthly. Instead, he draws a dividend as and when it makes sense.

Olivia investigated Junior's business bank statements for clarity and realised he had drawn only two dividends in the past twelve months, that he transferred to Qhayiya's account for their joint household expenses. The erratic nature of his earnings, coupled with the lack of at least two to three years' history of earnings, rendered Junior's income unreliable to advance credit against.

Olivia explained the couple had two choices. Either, they could proceed with the credit application relying solely on Qhayiya's earnings or, they could try again in the next twelve to eighteen months, provided Junior was generating a steady or significant income. In that time, Junior would also need to be drawing a consistent, monthly salary from his business, payable into his own personal bank account. In addition, Junior would need to create a clear distinction between those expenses that are business expenses, and those that are personal expenses. Only those expenses directly attributable to the running of the business would go through the business account, and those expenses of a personal nature would have to run through the personal account.

Junior and Qhayiya asked for some privacy to consult with each other. After a few minutes, they invited Olivia back into the meeting room to confirm their final decision.

"We'd like to see what we qualify for using only my earnings," Qhayiya said confidently.

"Certainly!" Olivia smiled, seemingly grateful that there was still a deal on the table. "So, using the three times' earnings rule for you Miss Dana," Olivia began, "we would theoretically be comfortable with a total combined debt level of around R2,1 million," Olivia said.

"That's great news! So R2 million will be easy, then!" Qhayiya squealed.

"Not necessarily. That's the TOTAL amount of debt we'd be comfortable you're liable for, given your salary, provided that you also have a good credit score. Do you have any car debt? That's what usually kills these deals."

"No. I mean, yes!" answered Qhayiya. "I have a small car that I owe nothing on, and Junior has a car that he owes R350k on. Well, I took out the financing in my name as the bank wouldn't approve a loan for Junior. But Junior transfers the money for both the instalments and the car insurance premium to me every month."

"I see…. Well, that immediately takes us down to R1.750 million we could theoretically lend to you." Olivia ran her finger down the pages as she flipped through Qhayiya's credit report. "Anything else? Any short-term debt?"

"I have about R30k in credit cards and store debt," Qhayiya confirmed. "And another R100,000 owing on a personal loan that I took out to help my mom relocate back to South Africa."

"Hmmm… That leaves us with only R1.620 million, provided we can prove affordability," Olivia thought aloud, tapping her pen on the table and pursing her lips. "Do you think you could negotiate the seller down?"

"I don't think so! R2 million is the offer we settled on after I negotiated them down from R2.2 million," Qhayiya replied in the negative. "I am however expecting a bonus of about R600k next month, so I can put down a deposit if needs be. I've also been earmarked for a promotion with a significant salary increase effective 1 September."

"Okay. So, assuming your bonus covers the shortfall we may still have a deal on the table. Let's see how much the repayment would be on a bond of R1 620 000." Olivia pulled out her diary and scribbled a note before punching numbers into her financial calculator.

"Okay. Your monthly repayment, at 10% per annum over twenty years, would be R15, 633.35," Olivia announced, turning the face of the calculator towards Qhayiya and Junior. "Do you have any questions, or can I calculate your monthly cost of ownership?"

"I hate this cost of ownership thing you guys do," Qhayiya frowned, slumping back in her chair.

"What's that?" Junior mouthed.

Qhayiya dismissed him by pointing to Olivia and mouthing back, "Listen."

"I know it's annoying, Miss Dana, but you know we do this because many clients land up in trouble after taking out a bond. They apply for the maximum instalment they can afford, only to be shocked by the additional cost of rates, taxes, levies, homeowner's insurance, and general upkeep," Olivia said, reasonably.

"I see," Qhayiya conceded.

For half a second, Qhayiya wore the fakest smile Junior had ever seen on her face. Then, tapping his feet under the table, he asked nervously, "And…do the numbers work?"

"I'll let you know in a minute. Just running some calculations," Olivia replied, not once looking up from her laptop screen.

"Okay! I have the numbers, let's see if you can afford repayments of between R17, 700 and R18 700 per month," Olivia said, and started going through the pile of papers to find the couple's income statement.

Olivia scrutinised the personal income statement alongside the bank statements. The way her face turned suggested she felt that the numbers presented in the Income Statement were not a fair reflection of her clients' spending habits. Qhayiya recognised the worried look on her banker's face and immediately moved to take control of the fast-declining situation.

"Olivia...Perhaps you can do the calculations and email us some options?" Qhayiya muttered nervously.

"Certainly! You'll hear from me by close of business," Olivia assured.

Qhayiya's apartment, Rosebank

Qhayiya arrived home from the office at 10 pm that evening. A late afternoon client lunch had turned to dinner and drinks with her colleagues, courtesy of their divisional head Stewart Delport.

Stewart was hilarious, and it was his charm more than his looks that made him attractive. He was agreeable with shaggy, chocolate-brown hair, tanned skin, and a crooked smile that gave away his naughty past.

Stewart managed his division with a rebellious streak, constantly pushing them to go harder and regularly dropping f-bombs much to EXCO's obvious horror! His charisma had all the girls on the floor swooning, while the guys wanted his approval. In short, every intern wanted to be selected to join Stewart's division.

The evening with her colleagues had been a welcome distraction from the disappointing feedback Qhayiya had received from her banker that afternoon.

She tiptoed up the stairs to her bedroom, hoping Junior was already asleep. Instead, she found him sitting in bed reading a crime novel.

"Where have you been?" he said calmly, barely raising his eyes from the book.

"I've been at a client lunch, like I said I would be," Qhayiya evaded, stumbling over the shoes she had just kicked off.

"A lunch that ends at 10 pm?" he continued sternly.

"As. I. Said." Qhayiya's voice dripped sarcasm. "I was at a work function. I was having fun and decided to stay longer. Am I not allowed to change my mind?" she murmured, rummaging through her cupboard for her winter satin pyjamas.

"I was worried 'cause your phone's been off since 6 pm."

"Battery died," Qhayiya informed him dismissively.

She hoped Junior would take the hint that she was in no mood to engage in one of his accusations. Lately, he had become increasingly suspicious of Qhayiya's movements.

He was constantly insinuating that her long hours at the office were due to something other than her increased workload. Their arguments were sometimes so heated that the complex security guards had knocked on their door with a noise complaint on more than one occasion.

"Did you hear back from that banker lady?" Junior put down the novel and shifted to sit on the edge of the bed with his feet on the ground.

"Don't wanna talk about it," Qhayiya deflected cheekily. She threw her work clothes into the laundry basket and walked into the bathroom. Junior followed her and stood and the door.

"Hey... Qhayiya, is everything okay?"

"No, Junior, everything is NOT okay!" Qhayiya fumed with her toothbrush in hand. "Because of YOU, I can't get the house I want!"

"What do you mean?" Junior asked. Qhayiya shot him a venomous look before storming past him. She grabbed her laptop bag off the floor and collapsed onto her bed. Loud sighs coupled with the occasional *nx!* could be heard as Qhayiya navigated to Olivia's email.

"There!" Qhayiya snarled. She turned the laptop screen towards the bathroom door where Junior had remained. Junior rolled his eyes and shook his head as he walked slowly back to bed. As he did, Qhayiya stood up and returned to the bathroom to resume her night-time routine.

From: **Olivia Harris** Olivia.Harris@alphapb.co.za
To: **Qhayiya Dana** QhayiyaDanaZA@fs.com
Date: **Wednesday, 09 May 2012, 17:34**
Subject: **Home Loan Options**

Dear Miss Dana,

It was a pleasure meeting with you and Mr Okello earlier.

Credit is very happy with your low level of personal debt and your high credit score. However, the monthly amount of R5,500 that you send to your mom limits your home loan affordability.

In addition, the car instalment and insurance premiums you pay on your partner's behalf, greatly hamper your ability to take out additional debt.

If you are willing to pause or lower the support you give your mother, and/or move Mr Okello's car finance and insurance into his own name, then I believe you can get your dream house.

Taking the above into consideration, please see below for the possible home loan facilities we can get approved for you based solely on your earnings:

OPTION 1: R360,000

Keeping everything as is, you qualify for a home loan of R360k.

OPTION 2: R1, 100, 000

If you pause the monthly contributions to your mom, you qualify for a home loan of R1,1m.

OPTION 3: R1,700, 000

If you move Mr Okello's car loan and premiums into his own name, you qualify for R1,7m.

Please let me know if you have any queries around this, otherwise, I look forward to hearing back from you once you're ready to proceed.

Regards,

Olivia Harris – Private Banker, Young Professionals

Qhayiya's ring finger lightly tapped La Mer serum onto her under eyes when Junior appeared at the door. She kept her eyes fixed on the mirror in front of her. He paused for a long moment, his head cocked to the side, and his arms folded in front of his chest.

"I'm sorry about the house," he said, eventually.

"Instead of being sorry, I'd rather you did something about it, Junior," Qhayiya growled through clenched teeth. Her voice was cold, and her eyes remained fixed on the mirror in front of her. Junior walked towards Qhayiya and stood behind her, looking into her reflection.

"What exactly are you saying?" he frowned.

"I'm saying it's time to get a job, Junior!" she snapped into the mirror. "I'm saying it's time to face reality and realise that I cannot carry on like this!"

"I never asked you to 'carry on like this', Q!" Junior grunted. "You're the one that practically begged me to move in with you after my father kicked me out and I told you I'm planning on moving to Berlin! Anyway, I don't want to fight. Let's chat about this when we're both in a better space to have a decent conversation." Junior walked out of the bathroom, and Qhayiya followed behind him.

"You want to live in Berlin HOW Junior? Huh?" she spat as she watched him grab a blanket out of the cupboard. "By teaching English? Writing a column? Being a waiter? Until when?"

"I'm not doing this with you, Q. I shared those things with you in confidence, not for you to one day use them against me," Junior replied wearily. He climbed down the stairs with the enthusiasm of a defeated man.

"I'll tell you until when," she pestered as she stomped down the stairs behind him. "You'll do that in Berlin, and New York, and every other city you've threatened to move to until the day you realise that the location is not the problem –"

"Watch it, Qhayiya!" Junior cautioned, propping up the cushions on the couch where he would be spending the night.

"No! I won't watch it!" Qhayiya barked, ignoring Junior's warning. "It's time you accepted that South Africa is not the reason your art is not selling. Your art is not selling because it's SHIT! There, I said it, you paint SHIT!"

Silence. Everything went silent. And black. What happened? Qhayiya slowly opened her eyes to a wall of white squares and black lines. Tiles. She was on the floor. She tried to lift her head, but it had turned into a ball of solid lead. She turned slowly and saw Junior standing over her with his hands on his head. The look on his face confirmed what had happened. Junior had hit her!

De Sousa Residence, Hartbeespoort Dam
August 2012

Of all the perks that came with being a wealth manager with one of the continent's most exclusive financial institutions, Qhayiya's favourite was the luxurious lifestyle.

How else could you wow Africa's 0.1% wealthiest individuals, if you weren't familiar with the next great painter to invest in, or the most exclusive addresses to call home? After all, they say you are only as important as the average of your six closest neighbours!

A home that was certainly at no risk of being in average company was the one sitting behind the palatial gates Qhayiya was pulling up to now – the new full-time residence of Mr Stanford De Sousa.

Johannesburg's newest billionaire resident had relocated to Africa just six months before, in an effort to be closer to his friends and family. Moving back to Azalia would have been too great a culture shock for the mining magnate who, for the past thirty years, had only known British and American infrastructure and efficiency. And although South Africa had its own frustrations, the ageing billionaire had managed to secure himself a lifestyle that placed him strictly in the first world pockets of this third world country.

There was certainly nothing third world about Stanford's ten-bedroom mansion situated on one of the country's most expensive equestrian estates. Set on what would undoubtedly soon be Africa's richest square mile, the manor house with a nine-figure price tag had all the usual trimmings one would expect from a four-storey trophy home; a sixteen-seater cinema, gym, a private night club that could comfortably host a party of fifty, a cigar lounge, elevator, and Qhayiya's favourite feature – a beauty spa complete with a hood dryer and manicure station.

It was Africa's answer to Carrie Bradshaw's famous walk-in closet from Mr Big. But, three months after Baba Big moved in, the spa remained untouched, despite Johannesburg's top models, businesswomen and female celebrities working tirelessly to secure their spot as the next "Mrs 4 Clydesdale Estate."

A gentle spring breeze caressed Qhayiya's face as she walked onto the runway terrace where her client was ensconced behind that morning's edition of The Business Times. Far from handsome but ever soigné, he was the picture of old money as he sat cross-legged in his khaki chino shorts, a crisp white collared shirt, and brown Tod's leather loafers. The sing-song of Cape Robin-Chats and the gentle trickling of water from the Apollo fountain created the perfect ambience for the picturesque afternoon.

Stanford was Qhayiya's wealthiest client by far, and certainly one of the top five wealthiest in the bank. However, playing banker to the 1% of the 0.1% meant jumping when summoned to a meeting at the client's residence with only an hour's notice, as was the case now.

"If it isn't the beautiful Miss Dana," Stanford greeted warmly, flashing a broad smile as he stood up and folded his newspaper.

"Mr De Sousa," Qhayiya smiled coyly, bracing herself for another session of inappropriate comment dodgeball.

"No need to be so formal..." Stanford chuckled, as he walked around to greet his banker with his signature Dutch kiss, before pulling out a chair for her to take a seat across from him, facing the pristinely manicured gardens. "May I offer you some tea?"

"Yes, please. Thank you," Qhayiya replied, feeling silly at the slight British twang her accent adopted whenever she was around her only British client.

Boisterous barking heralded the arrival of Lincoln and Kennedy, Stanford's King Charles Cavalier puppies. They charged through the door followed by another Charles. Stanford's son had been significantly rude to Qhayiya since his father appointed her to manage his global portfolio on João's recommendation. A role he had hoped to secure for himself.

Careful not to let the doting father catch her rolling her eyes at his less than agreeable offspring, Qhayiya quickly feigned a smile and stood up to greet the thirty-five-year-old FCA, CFA, MBA, who clearly thought that collecting three-letter acronyms behind his name would earn him his own identity, instead of being known solely as Stanford De Sousa's only son.

"I asked Charles to join us, I hope you don't mind," Stanford smiled, the expression on his face half apologetic and half 'You really don't have a choice in the matter.'

"Of course not! It's always a pleasure to see Charles!" Qhayiya replied unconvincingly, wondering if Charles ever got around to the assignment for which his investment banking employer had seconded him to Johannesburg.

"Baba, Miss Dana," Charles greeted, or rather nodded while taking his seat at the head of the table and propping up his iPad mini-tablet.

"I'll get straight to it," Charles began in a serious, toneless voice. "My father's landed himself in a rather precarious situation which we need your assistance in managing."

"Sure. What are we dealing with?" Qhayiya asked with her iPad unlocked and stylus in hand. She was ready for action.

"Maybe I should begin," Stanford said, clearing his throat. The usually cool gentleman leaned back in his chair and ran his hands through his salt and pepper beard as he looked out into the distance. The urgent meeting had come to an abrupt pause, and Qhayiya wondered how precarious the situation must be to warrant such concern from a man as powerful and influential as Stanford. A member of the De Sousa house staff appeared with the tea-time spread of crustless salmon and cream cheese sandwiches, spinach and artichoke quiche cups, and an assortment of lemon, passion fruit and pistachio macarons.

Stanford offered to pour his guest a cup of tea and proceeded to provide details of the situation that was troubling him.

"Let me recap, so I make sure I understand," Qhayiya began. "We have a thirty-three-year-old woman, who is three months pregnant with your son, and happens to be your new business partner Doc Kunene's daughter?"

"Yes," Stanford nodded.

"And although you've agreed to pay lobola for her in the next three weeks, you have no intention of actually marrying her?" Qhayiya continued.

"Correct! But her father must BELIEVE I intend to marry her otherwise this situation could get in the way of a very important business transaction that is currently on the table," Stanford added, pointing to Qhayiya with his index finger to emphasise his point.

"I see…" Qhayiya frowned, her face failing to hide her disbelief while she scribbled some notes on her iPad and took another sip of her tea. Charles folded his tablet away and placed his hands on the table.

"Our lawyers are concerned Frank will conduct the lobola negotiations in a way that renders my father traditionally married to his daughter." Charles paused and looked at Qhayiya, who nodded her understanding. "If that happens, she will apparently have access to half of my father's estate! Is this correct?"

"Yes. If the three conditions of a customary marriage are met, then in the eyes of the law, Stanford will be married in Community of Property."

"What three conditions are those?" Stanford asked, leaning in and listening intently.

"You must both be over the age of eighteen, you must both agree to be married to each other, and the negotiations must be finalised and/or the union celebrated according to custom."

"Would it still be a legally recognised marriage if the negotiations are conducted by someone that is not a marriage officer?" Stanford asked calmly.

"Yes," Qhayiya nodded.

"I read somewhere that the marriage would need to be registered at Home Affairs before a marriage certificate was issued though," Charles added.

"True, but even without a marriage certificate, the marriage would be legally recognised because not registering the customary marriage does not invalidate the marriage. Registration of the marriage is encouraged because it constitutes proof of existence of the customary marriage. As long as the three conditions I mentioned are fulfilled, you'll be legally married in Community of Property."

"Damn it!" Stanford growled, hitting the table with both fists. Qhayiya had never seen her client upset before, and this display of anger was unusual for the man that seemed to have his emotions always under control.

"Maybe we can register an antenuptial contract without her knowledge," Charles said condescendingly, his lips gently kissing the Hermes Cheval d'Orient teacup to take a long slow sip without breaking eye contact with his father. Qhayiya glared at Charles for a moment before remembering Stanford. She took a deep breath before giving her response.

"I wouldn't suggest you take that course of action as it would not only be illegal, but the contract would also be invalid," Qhayiya said, shaking her head at Charles' ludicrous suggestion.

"I've got it!" Stanford said, suddenly rising to his feet and placing both hands in his pockets. "Charles, get the lawyers to draft an 'ANC with Accrual' contract. Let's see how keen Frank will be to marry off his daughter when I open the discussions with a prenup in hand. Secondly, get them to move all my remaining assets into the trust. Also, speak to Fez about the most tax-efficient way to structure these donations." Stanford turned to Qhayiya before continuing, "Miss Dana, I'm disappointed you didn't point out that we need to think about the possible child maintenance claim as well. Frank's daughter has very expensive taste, and I don't want her thinking she will fund her lifestyle via my future son. So, I need you to make me look as poor as possible. Max out all my credit facilities and transfer the funds into the trust. Charles, tell my PA to set up an urgent board meeting for my salary to be cut in half with immediate effect. I'll run my lifestyle expenses through the company credit card. Is there anything else you can think of?" Stanford asked, standing with both palms of his hands on the table.

"Uhm… no, I don't think so," Qhayiya replied softly.

"Of course there is – the deal with Frank! How far are you with the loan application? We need to purchase that equipment quite quickly to secure the rock blasting contract."

"Yes, that. I was actually meant to present to Credit this afternoon, but I rushed here instead after you said you needed to see me urgently," Qhayiya chided gently.

"Silly girl! You should have told me you were busy with other, more important things," Stanford chuckled, knowing full well he wouldn't have accepted no for an answer. "Very well, then. I trust you will handle it tomorrow?"

"Yes, sir! Consider it handled!"

Qhayiya and Junior's place, Hyde Park

Qhayiya arrived home tired from her long day at work and noticed a number of envelopes had been slipped under her apartment door. She placed her bag on the marble kitchen counter and went through the mail. It was the usual; the electricity bill, some promotional material and a notice from the body corporate notifying residents of yet ANOTHER special levy.

Owning a home versus renting a home had proven to be far more costly than anticipated, and it didn't help that Junior was contributing less and less to their home. He was too proud to ask his family for money and too stubborn to realise his art was a non-paying hobby, and he needed to get a job!

Qhayiya put the kettle on and heard an email notification beep on her phone. It was the email she had been longing to see – CFA Institute. Inside were the results of her final board exams towards qualifying as a chartered financial analyst. A cold shiver went through her body as she clicked on the bolded email and scanned its contents for her results.

She sank down onto the cold tiles and looked at her transcript again. There had to be a mistake. But there it was. She'd failed to achieve the required marks to attain her Level III certification that year.

Tears trickled down her cheeks in steadily growing streams as she thought of the consequences.

The exam was only available again in December, meaning she was no longer eligible for the promotion she had been earmarked for.

What would her mom say? What would Chloe and the rest of her colleagues say?

What would Stewart say? He held her in such high regard and had groomed her for senior leadership over the past year. Now she'd have to face him as a failure. How would he ever respect her after these results?

And all of this, for what? A toxic relationship with a man that was increasingly jealous of her career success? Junior had been a nightmare to deal with since Qhayiya joined Stewart's division.

Over time, it had become clear just how intimidated Junior was by Qhayiya's meteoric rise at Franklin Securities, especially since his career was non-existent.

Stewart had taken Qhayiya under his wing, and in a few short months, she had begun working on top client accounts. Dinners with Africa's most powerful men and women were now the norm; travel to meetings by private jet was now a bi-monthly occurrence; and six-figure bonuses were now within reach for the woman that had previously feared she wasn't good enough for her group of friends.

But, as Qhayiya's confidence grew, Junior's waned, and in its place, hatred and aggression had found a home.

"Hey, MaMtolo. How was your day?" Junior asked, walking down the stairs in nothing but a towel around his waist.

"Don't touch me!" she barked. "Don't you fuckin' touch me!"

"And now?" Junior replied nonchalantly, striding over and dropping to his haunches to console Qhayiya, who was now hunched over and sobbing. He smelled like pine fresh shower gel, and his dreadlocks were still wet.

"You are the reason I failed my exam," Qhayiya wailed. "You and your stupid insecurity! Always making me feel bad when I have to stay at the office late. Always humiliating me when I'm with my study group."

"Not this shit again," Junior sighed. He rose to his feet and started walking away. Qhayiya followed him and continued raining anger on him.

"Don't walk away from me, Junior! I'm sick and tired of your bullshit! I'm tired of you accusing me of being in a relationship with every male colleague I introduce you to at my work functions. Tired of you dismissing my work achievements as unimportant. And you know what, Junior? I'm ESPECIALLY tired of being the only one that pays for anything around here. It's time you grew a pair and acted like a man instead of a little boy that wants to play around with paintbrushes all day and call himself an artist!"

"Careful, Qhayiya!" Junior warned, sliding open the door to their high-rise balcony and lighting up a cigarette to calm his nerves.

"Was it worth it, Junior? Huh?" Qhayiya spat. She shoved his shoulder angrily, and nearly slipped from the force of her action. "I thought our plan was to become a power couple. Be the best versions of ourselves without all the pressure of conforming to the standards set by society. Accept each other for who we are and not what people say we ought to be. But it seems the higher I climb, the harder you try and push me down. Are you happy now, Junior? Are you happy that I won't be better qualified than you? Become a bigger success than you as your father predicted? ANSWER ME, JUNIOR!"

Junior caught her wrist when she tried to shove him again. "I'm not going to warn you again," he sighed wearily, infuriating Qhayiya even more before he continued, "All I've ever asked, is that you show me a little respect."

"Respect? Respect! What the fuck do you mean by respect?" Qhayiya exploded, as she watched Junior throw his cigarette bud over the railing and walk back into the lounge.

"Respect, Q. You don't respect me as your man," Junior growled, pointing his finger threateningly in Qhayiya's face. "You're always working late and travelling with that Stewart character. You think because you're now a senior banker and make more money than me that you're senior in this house too. You need to learn to leave your fancy title at the door when you walk into my house!"

"Actually Junior, it's MY house," Qhayiya sneered, "It's MY name on the title deed, and it's MY salary that pays the bond. You can't even qualify for a bond, and you want to call yourself a man!"

The world went black as Qhayiya fell onto the floor. She slowly opened her eyes to a sight that had become all too familiar – a pool of warm blood on the porcelain tiles, and Junior towering above her. She placed her hand on her throbbing head and slowly sat up, balancing her back against the base of her couch. Junior knelt down beside her and held her face in his hands.

"Fuck! I'm sorry baby," Junior wept. "Why do you push and push and push me until I break and do this to you? To US? Huh?" Junior lay his head on Qhayiya's lap and pulled her arm over his bare chest.

"I love you, MaMtolo. I really do. But I can't stand the man you're turning me into," Junior sobbed. "Stop pushing me, baby. One day you'll push me too far…"

Junior held Qhayiya's arm to his chest with both hands, while she wondered when it would all end. The fighting, shouting, constant name-calling. And of course – the beatings.

It was something, always something. And she was tired. Her tumultuous relationship with her partner had all but destroyed her home life, and now it was destroying her career, too.

7

FLOWER POWER

"If the panther knew how much she is feared, she would do much more harm"

— CAMEROONIAN PROVERB

Franklin Securities, Sandton
August 2012

*M*ornings in the FS lobby were always a hive of activity. Bankers scurried about to grab a Flat White at the coffee bar, fetch their dry-cleaning from the in-house laundromat, put in a workout session in the in-house gym, or convince the Forex division that their client's transaction warranted settlement in T+1 instead of the standard T+3.

That morning, Qhayiya also raced through the turnstiles, determined to be first in line to present her most strategic deal of the year, that of Doc Kunene.

Dr Frank Vusumzi Kunene or 'Doc', as he insisted on being called, was a successful 60-year old businessman who'd made his money in the coal mining sector. Thanks to the Afro-Coal BEE deal that saw his consortium and three others acquire 26% of a company with a R100 billion market cap, he went from being a humble attorney to a multimillionaire overnight.

Doc was one of the early beneficiaries of BEE, the South African government's economic policy drawn up to redress the racial, economic exclusion policies of the pre-1994 apartheid regime. Doc was highly educated, having obtained his Bachelors, Masters and Doctorate of Laws degrees from the University of Azalia while in exile.

Highly connected in business and politics, Doc was well positioned to be invited to the consortium table when deals were being discussed. At their introductory meeting, Qhayiya had made the mistake of asking Doc how she, too, could be invited into a consortium, since her observations led her to believe that the wealthy black people in South Africa had made their money either from a BEE deal, or from subsequent business ventures they had funded through wealth generated from BEE deals.

"You see, baby girl," Doc had replied condescendingly, "This thing of BEE and consortiums and deals... is a very tricky one. You guys are lucky that you got a good education and the opportunity to join the workforce while you were still young. Look at you – a banker. And you're only... how old are you?"

"Twenty-six," Qhayiya had replied.

"TWENTY-SIX? I was still in exile at twenty-six, fighting for the freedom of this country, and for you – the Qhayiyas of the world..."

She nodded brightly and respectfully and pretended to be enthralled.

"… to be bankers with these top institutions, and make money as professionals serving our continent," Doc concluded his version of 'when I was your age'.

"Yes, Doc, but as young, black professionals, we still get shut out of the deals that make real money –" Qhayiya had tried to elaborate.

"No man, Qhayiya," he interrupted. "You're still young. And we need you in these structures. We need our youth to represent us in those credit rooms where the decisions are made." Doc had regarded her appraisingly before finally turning to the real purpose of the meeting.

"In fact," he confided, "there's a small project I want you to work on for me. Get this one right, and there'll be plenty more coming your way." Two weeks later, Qhayiya was about to present the most strategic deal of her career yet.

Checklist in hand, she went through the documents in the credit pack one more time as she waited nervously to be called into the presentation room:

- Client profile summary
- Client's Assets and Liabilities
- Client's ITC credit report
- 3 years' personal income tax returns
- Company 2 years' financial statements
- Client's investment portfolio valuation statement

A few minutes later, the phone rang, and Credit was ready to see her. Franklin Private Capital (FPC), the lending division of Franklin Securities, was located on the 10th floor of the FS building. The credit committee at FPC was made up of a number of credit officers, with different areas of expertise, who came together to assess the financial, legal and tax implications of a credit application.

That day's credit committee was meeting in boardroom 'Shilling', which had the same layout as all the other boardrooms on the floor.

As one entered, the room was dominated by a large oval glossy-oak boardroom table, and the credit committee sat facing the door with their backs turned to the glass wall overlooking the banking atrium.

To the right was a large monitor, for the committee members that would be dialling in from other provinces or regions. To the left was a large projector screen, where bankers could display any presentations or visuals in support of their application.

Opposite the committee, three multicoloured Nelson Makamo paintings adorned the pale grey wall, and below them stood an oak server with teas, coffee, water and biscuits.

The credit committee could spend anything from thirty minutes to six hours in session, and so refreshments, and sometimes lunch, were prepared for them. It was best to present your deal early before the fatigue and grumpiness set in. It was also advisable to open your presentation with an icebreaker, and Qhayiya had one prepared.

"Good morning, everyone! I'm hoping to make this quick and painless, since Moody's may give us a rough day tomorrow by downgrading us this evening!" she said with a smile, handing out the credit packs.

Lumka took a sip of his tea and answered, "Please do! The potential downgrade has us all in a tailspin." Lumka Sibanda was the Head of Credit, an accountant by trade, and the longest-serving credit officer at branch level.

"Thanks for finally showing up," Jonathan Smit added drily, paging through the credit pack. Highly analytical with a tax background, he was one of the fiercest credit officers in the room.

Priyanka, the committee's legal mind put her cup down and said, "I agree with Jonathan. You owe this committee at least an apology for adding your deal to the agenda yesterday, and then not bothering to pitch, even after we waited fifteen minutes for you."

"Apologies for that!" Qhayiya responded sincerely. "I was summoned into an emergency meeting with Mr Stanford De Sousa. He has a R100m portfolio with us, and I couldn't risk losing it."

"Don't blame the client," Priyanka snapped. "That's what your assistant bankers are for. You could have delegated the presentation to her!"

Qhayiya held her tongue as now was not the time to make enemies by giving a cheeky response.

"Right! Let's get to it, shall we?" said Leonard, a property valuation specialist with a cool and collected demeanour that was equally cold if a banker didn't have their story straight.

Without delay, Qhayiya presented the application. After giving the introductory information on Doctor Frank Vusimuzi Kunene, such as background and qualifications, Qhayiya advised that Doc needed to raise a small facility of R20 million to purchase a hydraulic rock blaster for his small-scale chrome mine.

The security he was putting down for the loan was a R60 million listed share portfolio.

A caveat was that the portfolio had very little diversification, with about 70% of his portfolio being made up of his Afro-Coal Ltd shares. The rest of the portfolio was made up of a variety of blue-chip, listed shares. To mitigate this risk, Qhayiya had proposed to the client that the deal would be structured with 3x cover, as opposed to the standard 2x to 2.5x the bank usually accepted.

"What's the total value of his properties, and are they bonded?" Leonard asked, inputting the erf descriptions into the Lightstone property valuation programme.

"He has four properties, total value at around R35 million. He has a R24 million primary residence in Bryanston, a R5 million investment property in Kyalami, and four tenanted flats in Greenstone that are valued at R1,5 million each. The Kyalami and Greenstone properties are still bonded, but that's only for the tax benefit.

"He has unit trusts with us worth R4 million and a cash balance of about R5 million in his money market account, but he doesn't want to touch that."

"And his tax returns – they're the latest?" Priyanka asked, putting on her glasses and paging through the pack, no doubt to find another silly question to ask.

"You don't get more recent than 2011 and 2012 when you are still in the 2012 calendar year," Qhayiya responded cheekily, referring to the South African tax year, which runs from March to February.

Qhayiya leaned back smugly, proud of the presentation that had garnered smiles from Lumka, Jonathan and Leonard.

"Ladies and gentlemen, what say ye?" Lumka asked. "All those in favour of approving the deal please raise your hands."

The hands went up all around the room. Lumka. Leonard. Jonathan. Priyanka. But not Daniel.

Daniel Anderson, the fifth committee member who had been busy with his tablet throughout the presentation, was a stockbroker by trade, and not one to throw curveballs during Credit. Qhayiya wondered what his objection could possibly be.

"Uhm, sorry, guys," Daniel apologised. "The markets are crazy at the moment, and I was just handling a crisis on the trading floor." He turned his tablet upside down on the table to avoid further distractions.

"Qhayiya, excellent presentation, I must say! I have just one request. May I see the latest portfolio valuation statement?" he asked.

Qhayiya tried hard not to roll her eyes at this unnecessary delay. "It's Annexure 4 in your pack, Daniel," she reminded him.

"But this is from two days ago. You didn't get a new valuation this morning?" Daniel insisted.

"No, because all our valuation statements are valid for 48 hours," Qhayiya said, puzzled.

"Yes, that's true Qhayiya, under normal circumstances. But the markets have been exceptionally volatile over the past 24 hours, and when the markets are volatile, we prefer the latest available statements."

The truth was Qhayiya had gone to bed early after taking strong painkillers for the pounding headache that came with Junior's blow. Instead of listening to the news on the ride into work, she'd listened to gospel music instead, gathering the strength she needed to get through the day without breaking down.

On the surface, she looked fine, and Junior had mastered the art of giving her blows without leaving a trace on her face. But inside, she was crushed, barely hanging on by a thread. Her plan was to get this approval and then take the rest of the day off. She said a silent prayer hoping the Afro-Coal shares had held their value, and her deal would go through.

"Don't look so panicked, Qhayiya. I'll quickly ask one of the stockbrokers to give me the latest valuation figure. Do you have the client's investment number?" he asked, dialling the trading floor on the Polycom SoundStation. Daniel put the phone on speaker for the rest of the room to hear.

"Yikes! This portfolio has taken a serious knock over the past 24 hours, hey?!" said the voice on the other end. "R40 million. That's the number. The total portfolio is valued at R40 million… Aah – it's the Afro-Coal Ltd shares. They crashed 40% this morning after news that their contract with SA Power hadn't been renewed. I'm surprised anyone is still holding on to these…" the voice continued. "Is there anything else I can help you with, sir?"

Daniel reached for the end call button and replied, "No, that will be all."

In just five short seconds, 'the voice' had left the whole room stunned. Lumka stupefied, had stood up from her chair and was pacing. Priyanka was slowly shaking her head.

Jonathan had pulled out his iPad and was typing something into the Bloomberg terminal, Leonard rested his elbow on the table and held his head in his right hand, and Daniel sat at the table with his arms folded, looking at Qhayiya with an expression of 'I told you so'.

"So," Lumka eventually resumed, breaking the silence that had followed the phone call. "Let me get this straight. You wanted THIS credit committee to approve a R20 million facility with only R40 million in security?"

Qhayiya held her head down in shame, her knees shaking uncontrollably under the boardroom table. She called upon every fibre of her being to help her fight against her overwhelming need to break down and cry.

"That's two times cover. Only TWO-FUCKING-TIMES-COVER!" Lumka spat. "On a portfolio with a significant concentration risk! Are you trying to get us all fired?"

Qhayiya looked up with tightly pursed lips. The credit committee did not take kindly to tears, and it took all her steel to hold them back.

Lumka fell into her chair, took off her glasses, and tilted her head back with her nose to the ceiling. She leaned forward and crossed her arms on the table. "Ms Dana, I don't know what is going on with you lately, but you had better fix it – and fix it fast – before presenting anything to this credit committee again." Her expression was glacial. "Now get the hell out of here!"

Qhayiya rushed to the bathrooms. After a good twenty-minute cry, she phoned Hayley, her assistant banker, to bring her handbag to the 10th floor bathrooms.

Qhayiya touched up the makeup that was now just a layer of black and brown mud, as Hayley looked on and asked what had happened in the credit room. After filling in Hayley and her cracked foundation, Qhayiya was ready to face the rest of the bank again.

"Oy, vey, Qhayiya! What will you do with Doc's deal now?" Hayley asked innocently as they walked back to their desks.

"I didn't become the top female banker in Gauteng by mistake, Hayley!" Qhayiya sniffled. "And I certainly didn't keep it that way through luck either. I will fix this. Today!"

Back to the drawing board, Qhayiya thought to herself. *It's just twenty million. Surely, I can raise twenty million from Doc's other assets.* She paged through Doc's assets and liabilities schedule.

She had to find a way to secure the funding Doc was applying for, or Stanford would be highly disappointed with her.

Afro-Coal Shares? Non-starter.

Other shares in the portfolio? Possibly. R18 million of Doc's other shares were blue-chip shares. Even with the current volatility in the markets, the fact that these shares had high trading volumes and were diversified across the telecoms, mining, digital and FMCG industries, meant that Credit should still be comfortable to lend against them at a 3x cover. But that would release only R6 million worth of funding. Qhayiya was still short R14 million.

Cars? Negative. The National Credit Act prohibited banks from issuing additional funds against cars. Qhayiya could do a vehicle finance takeover, but not release new cash.

Chrome mine shares? Impossible. The shares were privately held, and FPC lent out only against listed shares.

Think, Qhayiya, you've got to think. Take it back to basics. All you have to do is find safe/safe-ish assets the bank can take as security for the loan. It's not that deep, she told herself.

Property! Qhayiya could propose FPC takes out a bond over Doc's property. His primary residence wasn't mortgaged, and she could register a first covering mortgage bond over it. Given the risk associated with the deal and Doc's age, it was prudent to bond it at only 50% loan-to-value.

Qhayiya was getting close but was still short R2 million. Jewellery, art and furniture totalling R7.5 million meant absolutely nothing since she couldn't raise financing against them. *Unless he goes to a pawn shop? Fat chance!*

Two million rand. Where was she going to find two million rands?

Unit Trusts! Doc also had R4 million worth of unit trusts with Franklin's asset management division. Qhayiya knew Credit was comfortable at a more aggressive ratio of 2:1, meaning she could raise R2 million from doing a 2x cover deal on his unit trusts.

Okay! So, she had R12 million from the house, plus R6 million from his share portfolio, excluding the shares in Afro-Coal, plus R2 million from the unit trusts, equals R20 million. *Eureka!*

By that afternoon, Qhayiya had not only come up with an alternative deal structure for Doc Kunene but called in a favour with Credit so that she could present again at the end of the day. The deal was approved, re-instating her reputation as one of the top dealmakers in the bank.

It was exactly the kind of comeback she needed at the end of a long and gruelling week, and she couldn't wait to call Doc to give him the good news. Just as she was about to hit the dial button, her phone rang – it was the security from her apartment complex. She was in no mood to pick up, but it could be important.

"Hello! I can't chat right -" she answered coldly.

"Ma'am, there's an emergency at your apartment. You need to come home now!"

"What emergency?" Qhayiya panicked. "Is my partner-"

"NOW ma'am!" the voice urged, before hanging up the phone.

Qhayiya's hatchback raced down Rivonia Road as her mind worked through the possible reasons for the urgent summons. Junior wasn't picking up her calls, and she worried he had done something to hurt himself.

The gravity of the call suddenly became all too real as Qhayiya pulled into the underground parking and saw two men in official Azalian uniform stationed at the entrance, one with his hand on his hip and the other frantically waving Qhayiya towards a black sedan with tinted windows.

Qhayiya parked her car and ran towards the black BMW 7-series. She noted the Azalian coat of arms on the door. *Something must have happened to Junior,* she thought to herself, as she was ushered into the back seat.

The officials introduced themselves as members of the Prime Minister's office before reversing out the basement parking. No matter how hard Qhayiya pressed for an update on Junior, the officials remained vague, stating they'd been given strict instructions not to say anything until they reached their destination. The driver raced down the highway while the other official typed frantically into his phone.

The phone rang, and he answered with three words: "Start the hummingbird."

"I demand to know what's going on!" Qhayiya barked from the back seat.

"Ma'am, please just trust us," the official in the passenger seat replied sternly before he resumed typing into his phone.

Thirty minutes after they'd departed, the driver pulled into what looked like a large parking lot. Up ahead, a black helicopter was waiting with its blades turning. The driver jumped out of the car and held the door open for Qhayiya.

The other official escorted Qhayiya towards the helicopter. As she approached, she found Junior buckled into his seat, holding a bouquet of what looked like 100 red roses.

"What the fuck is going on, Junior?" Qhayiya barked from the door of the chopper. "I thought something had happened to you!" Her voice broke, and tears streamed down her face.

"I needed to say sorry!" Junior shouted over the sound of the turning blades. "This is the only way I could think of to get you to spend some alone time with me!"

Qhayiya shook her head as she climbed onto the aircraft. She was so angry at Junior for this stunt, SO ANGRY! But, he had clearly put great effort into orchestrating this gesture and for that he deserved some leeway. Qhayiya clicked her belt into the buckle as the helicopter rose into the air.

The BMW and the surrounding buildings slowly became tiny dots in the distance.

"I'm still mad at you, Junior!" Qhayiya shouted through the aviator headset, wiping the tears from her eyes.

"It won't happen again, MaMtolo. Promise..." Junior smiled.

When she switched on her phone on Monday morning, Qhayiya had a slew of text and voice messages from concerned friends, worried family members and irate clients – including Doc Kunene.

"Miss Dana! Where is my loan agreement? If you people don't want to loan me money, just say so instead of disappearing!" Doc blustered.

"Good morning, Doc! I'm so sorry I didn't get back to you on Friday. I had a minor car accident and lost my phone in the process," Qhayiya lied. "I managed to do a sim swap over the weekend but had to wait to get back to the office because I lost all my contacts."

"Oh, okay. I see. At least tell me you have good news for me? Then all will be forgiven," he relented.

"Yes, I do," Qhayiya confirmed cheerily. "I've thought up a better way to structure the deal, but I'll need to sit down and take you through it. I can get you a better interest rate and repayment term by looking at your other assets, instead of the share portfolio alone."

"BRILLIANT! That's very good news to me, Qhayiya. Listen, I'm having breakfast at Duke's with a friend, a gentleman who is far richer than me!" Doc chuckled. "Come join us and take me through this BETTER offer of yours, and if it's really good, you'll add another billionaire client to your book."

Duke's Restaurant, Melrose

Located in the affluent suburb of Melrose, Duke's Restaurant had cemented itself as one of Johannesburg's most popular upmarket eateries, the preferred dining spot for the city's elite. Its patrons ranged from politicians to international supermodels, from musicians to corporate executives, those with legacy wealth and those that were self-made.

At any time of the day, the restaurant's underground parking was worth more than most luxury car showrooms. Cayennes, Velars, Continentals and Phantoms all regularly made a temporary home there, as did Qhayiya's humble hatchback that day.

As she walked into the restaurant, she was offered a warm greeting and a table by one of the maître d's.

"Actually, I'm joining someone. Doctor Frank Kunene," Qhayiya said before she was interrupted by the sound of her name.

"Qhayiya!" came the familiar voice of the owner, Duke Maake.

"Papa Duke! How are you?" Qhayiya said, returning the famous hug with which he greeted all his patrons.

Papa Duke, as he was known to his regulars, was the owner of the Duke's Group of restaurants, with a presence in Sandton and Cape Town. In just two short years as a restaurateur, he had managed to disrupt the established and saturated premium dining industry with an offering that attracted diners from far and wide.

His approachable demeanour and constant fussing over his patrons could fool one into thinking his prices were friendly too – they were not. Duke's was known for a bar that served R100 shots of whisky when its competitors were charging half the price. Nevertheless, the premium was negligible for Joburg's elite, and Duke's restaurants only grew in popularity.

Papa Duke ushered Qhayiya to Doc's table in the cigar lounge of the restaurant, at a corner table with dark armchairs. The fragrance of cinnamon toast emanated from Cuban cigars.

"Qhayiya! My favourite banker!" Doc shouted with a cigar in one hand and a crystal whisky glass in the other. "*Hlala hlala hlala!*[1]"

"Thank you, Doc," Qhayiya smiled, setting down her bag at her side and placing her iPad on her lap as she took her seat.

"*Er… Gatsheni*[2], *uQhayiya Dana lo. uMaRhadebe.* A very special young lady," Doc introduced.

"*Awu*[3], MaRhadebe!" smiled Doc's guest, sparking an immediate rush of blood to her cheeks.

"Er… MaRhadebe, *lona ke uNdlovu*[4]," Doc continued. "Bernard Ndlovu. Chairman of –"

"Ndlovukazi Group Holdings?" Qhayiya interrupted, her mouth agape at realising with whom she was seated. Bernard needed no introduction. She knew of him but had never met him in the flesh. There were no internet images of him because he kept an almost obsessively low profile, a tactic Qhayiya was learning was the habit of the truly wealthy.

But those in the know, like Qhayiya, had learned to smell wealth. For instance, Bernard's Jaeger-LeCoultre AMVOX 2 DBS watch was the first giveaway. Another watch with a complex dial to the uninformed, but an indication that the Aston Martin DBS Qhayiya walked past in the parking lot was his, because the watch was, in fact, his car key.

His casual dress sense at one of Joburg's most fashionable eateries was another clue. Dressed in an unbranded white tee and navy cotton shorts, paired with navy sneakers, Bernard was much younger and more handsome than Qhayiya could have ever imagined.

She didn't know whether she was blushing from his dashing good looks, or whether it was the charm that came with being addressed by her totem. Doc snapped his fingers to get the waiter's attention and handed Qhayiya a menu.

She had no appetite but didn't want to offend her client. Qhayiya settled on ordering a Mimosa, and a half portion Egg White Florentine.

"Chief! You didn't tell me you were bringing me such a fine woman today," commented Bernard.

"No, Cadre... this is not the girl I was talking about. Miss Dana is a real professional woman. *Eintlik*[5], do you know whose banker this is?" Doc asked animatedly, pointing at Qhayiya with his thumb.

"*Ubani*[6]?" Bernard asked, shaking his head.

"Stanford. Stanford De Sousa. The guy we're doing the chrome mining deal with," Doc replied, elbowing Bernard with glee.

"Oh! The British-American!" Bernard exclaimed. "That man needs to stop stealing our women!"

"Excuse me?" Qhayiya asked, chuckling to hide her confusion at the statement.

"No, sweetheart, I'm just saying with the way you look, I wouldn't mind if you were also my banker," Bernard winked.

"The way I LOOK?" Qhayiya frowned.

"*Ag*[7], don't take it seriously, Qhayiya man!" Doc reassured her. "Gatsheni is just trying to pay you a compliment."

Qhayiya's frustration must have been evident because an uncomfortable silence suddenly fell over the table.

"Err… Chief! I need to make a call," Bernard said, and stood up to walk away.

"Look, Qhayiya, you're a very beautiful woman, and every man that comes around you can see that," Doc said as he conveniently rested his hand on Qhayiya's thigh. "And, I know that with a woman that's also as smart as you by my side, I could go very far."

"What do you mean by that, Doc?" Qhayiya said, shifting in her seat to dislodge his hand.

"I'll be honest with you," he said disingenuously. "I see a conflict of interest with you being my banker and also Stanford's banker."

"But Stanford was my client first, Doc!"

"You don't have to pretend with me!" Doc chuckled. "We both know that man is only after one thing. If you choose me as your client, I'll make sure to bring you the REALLY big deals. Maybe even get you invited into a consortium or two."

"EXCUSE me?" Qhayiya shrieked.

"Calm down, there's no need to raise your voice," Doc cautioned, looking around. "Look, we discuss these things as men, and I'm just saying Stanford will not be as lucrative a client as me once he gets what he wants."

"Excuse me, Doc," Qhayiya hissed. Flabbergasted, she pushed her plate away and proceeded to grab her bag. She stood up, adjusted her skirt and gave Doc a steely look. "Doctor Frank Kunene, I'd like to officially resign as your banker. Please expect a call from your new banker by COB today, who will take you through the merits of the deal that Franklin Securities has approved for you!"

Bella Restaurant, Chislehurston

Qhayiya was still fuming from the way Doc had treated her at their breakfast meeting earlier. In all her engagements with him, she had been professional and proven her smarts. Why then had he reduced her to nothing more than a pretty face and wide hips? To impress his friend Bernard?

Heads turned as Qhayiya pulled into the quaint parking courtyard, drawing attention from the patrons that were dining on the restaurant's peaceful terrace. It didn't help that the only available parking spot was right next to Lolo's loud and unmissable car.

The neon yellow Mercedes Benz G-wagon was a custom-ordered *Push Present*[8] from João. It was probably the only G-wagon in Johannesburg in that colour; certainly, the only one Qhayiya had seen, but to ensure that the public was never mistaken about the driver, it also had a personalised number plate: Lolo 7 – WP.

Qhayiya walked in to find Lolo diligently typing away on her Goldgenie MAC Book Air. Her 20-inch platinum blonde Peruvian lace wig and opaque Porsche Aviator shades were very "on brand" for the independent digital branding specialist.

Lolo hadn't held down a formal job since her departure as Head of Digital Content for a local magazine when she relocated to Johannesburg three months ago. Lolo and João had decided Joburg was the perfect compromise to their residence dilemma since Lolo was adamant she would not live in Azalia, and João had just made junior partner at his law firm.

This also gave him greater work flexibility and allowed him to spend three weeks working from the Joburg office, and three weeks working from the Azalian office.

Travelling between Azalia and Johannesburg was also significantly less stressful as the flight was direct, and shaved four hours off the total travel time.

Although she was still actively looking for a job, Lolo wasn't desperate for new employment. Her love of documenting her 'outfits of the day', international travels, and cute playdates with the boys on her Instagram account had positioned her as one of South Africa's leading fashion and lifestyle influencers.

As a result, she was toying with growing her role as an independent digital branding specialist from a hobby, into a full-time job.

"Miss Q is in the house!" Qhayiya blurted out and then giggled naughtily at her friend's startled reaction.

"Hey! I didn't see you come in. How are you doing?" Lolo chuckled, standing up to hug her friend. Lolo was chic in a black, white and gold Versace baroque shirtdress paired with black Valentino Rockstud heels.

"I'm good, and you, babe? How are the twins?" Qhayiya said, placing her shades on the table before perusing the menu.

"The twins are fine," Lolo smiled. "They're growing way too fast for my liking! Can you believe they're two in October? At this rate, they'll be groomsmen by the time João and I eventually settle on a wedding date!"

Qhayiya guffawed at her friend's statement, the first time she'd laughed in what felt like weeks.

"And? Are you guys any closer to finalising a date?" Qhayiya smiled.

"For the white wedding, no," Lolo said, taking off her shades. "But we've agreed on late November for the *Magadi*[9]. That's when Joao's uncles are available to come down for the lobola negotiations."

Lolo closed her laptop, and focused her full attention on her friend. "And you? What was up with you disappearing for the whole weekend? I was worried sick!"

Qhayiya sighed and suggested they place their orders so that they could talk without any disturbances. Lolo chose the roasted butternut and Danish feta salad, and Qhayiya, the halloumi-filled ravioli. The waiter departed, giving the duo the privacy they needed for the conversation that was about to take place.

"Junior took me on a surprise weekend away," Qhayiya began, her tone serious and voice shaky, "to say sorry…"

"For what?"

"For IT. One of his outbursts."

Qhayiya toyed with her napkin, weighing her words. "He hit me…"

"He did WHAT?" Lolo asked, eyes wide and mouth agape.

"Yes," Qhayiya whispered. "But we'd had a huge fight, and I said some –"

"Qhayiya don't you DARE excuse Junior's barbaric behaviour!" Lolo screeched before she calmed herself down after drawing eyes to her table.

"Qhayiya Dana, I swear, if you don't break up with Junior NOW, you'll land yourself in MAJOR trouble. Like, what the actual fuck?!" Lolo breathed incredulously.

"I know, babe! It's just… it's not as simple as you make it out to be," Qhayiya whispered

"Hold that thought!" Lolo said, and cleared the table for the waiter to set down their drinks order. "Continue."

"I was saying… it's not as simple as you make it out to be," Qhayiya insisted, taking a sip of her Aperol Spritz.

Lolo took a less-than-dainty sip of her Inverroche Amber with tonic and grapefruit before looking at Qhayiya piercingly.

"I'm listening," she said.

Qhayiya stared at a random patch of floor for a few seconds, before shaking her head and looking back at Lolo.

"Because I love him…"

"And?" Lolo persisted.

"And I can't remember my life without him. He's the only boyfriend I've ever had, Lolo, and he's the only one that was there for me when I first moved to Joburg."

"I don't know what to say, babe," Lolo said with concern, unable to hide her disquiet.

"Me neither, Lols," Qhayiya said, fighting tears. "I miss my man. My Junior, one of my best friends. Where is he, Lols? Where is my sweet, innocent Junior?"

The waiter arrived with their food, and the rearranging of the table afforded Qhayiya a moment to compose herself.

Lolo stared unseeingly at her plate before taking her friend's hands into her own. She contemplated their joined hands for another brief moment before looking up into her friend's eyes. "It's not my place to tell you how or how not to live your life," she told Qhayiya, quietly. "But I've heard…"

Lolo searched for words again, but apparently decided to speak bluntly. "João has told me about Junior's past. You're not the first woman Junior has physically assaulted. I've never mentioned it because I thought maybe he had changed and wasn't doing it to you."

"What do I do, Lols?" Qhayiya asked, chastised, feeling stupid and desperately helpless.

"Why don't the two of you go see a psychologist? Try therapy?" Lolo suggested after some thought. "But just know, if a man has it IN him to beat up a woman, he's almost always capable of doing much worse…"

The friends caught each other up on what was happening not only in their own lives, but with Runako and Nala as well. Lolo was worried that Nala had become increasingly reclusive since living in Azalia.

Qhayiya worried that things were only getting worse between Runako and Kobe. After another round of drinks, Lolo settled the bill, and the friends walked to the parking lot and promised to see each other more often, and not only when there was a crisis.

Qhayiya drove back to the office, feeling much better than she had on the way to lunch. Yes, from the outside looking in, Lolo's life was enviable: a doting fiancé, a set of adorable twin boys, frequent international first-class trips, a mansion in one of South Africa's most expensive suburbs, and no apparent problems or stresses.

But, living in Joburg as long as she had, and working with some of the continent's richest and most powerful individuals, Qhayiya knew not to covet her neighbours. No matter how perfect things looked from the outside, pain was no respecter of man, and was a constant companion on the journey called life.

8

SIXPENCE IN HER SHOE

"Starting a journey before others does not mean reaching before them"

— AFRICAN PROVERB

Lolo's Dad's House, Houghton Estate, Johannesburg
November 2012

*L*olo peered at her watch and figured she'd been resting for only a few hours, but she was too excited to go back to sleep. Her boys Kael and Noel were snoring gently beside her, their tiny button noses twitching every time they exhaled. Lolo slipped out of bed carefully, tiptoed into the en-suite bathroom to brush her teeth, and then quietly padded to the kitchen to fix herself a cup of tea.

The rest of the house was still sleeping, and, in the silence, the early morning sun streamed through the skylight in the double-volume entrance hall and put on a spectacular show. It *jetéd*[1] off the glazed porcelain tiles, *pirouetted* across the glass dining table, and performed hundreds off teeny-tiny *pliés* on the marble-top kitchen counter.

Growing up, Lolo and her sister would wake up early every Christmas morning to catch the dancing sun. It was a tradition instilled by her father, who told them the sun also celebrated that special day. Perhaps the Highveld sun knew that today was a special day too, the day the Motsepe and Morreira families would be united.

In the blink of an eye, the serene home turned into a bustling hive of activity. By 7 am the goat meat was cooking on the fire in the backyard, the bride was seated in the makeup chair, and the professional camera was clicking away.

Safely behind the guest bedroom door, Lolo could hear the familiar sounds of an authentic African celebration.

Cupboards were banging, shoes were shuffling, phones were ringing, babies were crying, and at regular intervals, Aunty Zodwa, Nandi's sister and self-appointed chief organiser would randomly shout *"Usugezile*[2]?", "Iphi i ayina*[3]?"* or the universal favourite, *"Ubani ophethe is'khiye sefridge*[4]?"*

The nostalgic sights, smells and sounds of a traditional African ceremony swept through the house and spilt out into the driveway, letting every passerby know that it was a day of celebration at the home of the Motsepes.

The Morreira delegation had been given strict instructions to arrive at 10 am for the conducting of the formal lobola negotiations and, according to custom, arrived promptly at 09:30 am.

They stood in the driveway singing Motsepe praises as they waited to be called into the house.

At ten o'clock sharp, Raul Morreira, accompanied by Stanford De Sousa and two of João's uncles from Isabel's side, were invited into the house.

They were warmly greeted by Malome Rodney, Harvey's younger brother, and ushered into the study, where Harvey and the rest of the Motsepe and Khoza uncles were waiting to receive them.

The elders resumed their discussion behind closed doors until around 11:30 am when João and Lolo were summoned.

When the word went around that the negotiations neared conclusion, the Khoza, Motsepe and Morreira family and friends started streaming into the snow peak marquee set up in the backyard, to await the commencement of *uMembeso*.

Although the gift exchange ceremony of uMembeso was practised in the Zulu and not Tswana culture, Harvey indulged his ex-wife's request to host the day's festivities in a way that honoured both sides of their daughter's heritage.

A Zulu traditional dance troupe provided entertainment as guests caught up with their old relatives and introduced themselves to the new ones.

The guests ululated and erupted into song as the Khoza, Motsepe and Morreira uncles approached, walking hand in hand with the newlyweds following closely behind them.

Speaking a Western language is taboo at customary ceremonies, but since the bride's family did not speak Portuguese or Swahili, and the Morreiras did not speak Setswana or isiZulu, Harvey had little choice but to make the expected announcements in English.

Hundreds of eyes sparkled with anticipation as the respected elder took to the stage. After clearing his throat, a polite way of asking the hopeful guests to quieten down and take their seats, Harvey began.

"*Mchana mwema*[5]," he greeted, to a loud cheer from the Swahili-speaking guests. "To the Morreiras, De Sousas and everyone else gathered here from near and far, I welcome you to the Motsepe home. You walked in as guests, but now, I am pleased to announce, you will leave as family!"

Clapping and ululations echoed through the marquee once again before calming down to pockets of whispers.

"Ordinarily, the conclusions of the lobola negotiations and the Zulu gift exchange ceremony of uMembeso aren't held on the same day. However, seeing that we have guests from Azalia, the US, and various parts of the country, we thought it best to combine the two."

"Did he just call us guests? So much for being family!" Isabel piped up.

"Oh, cut it out, Mom!" Eva shushed her mom.

"As you can see," Harvey continued, gesturing to Lolo, who stood next to him with her head appropriately bowed. "We have taken very good care of our daughter. From the homes she grew up in, the schools she went to, and of course, her plump figure."

The crowd broke into laughter, and Harvey squeezed her hand and whispered, "I said plump, not fat."

"We hope that, as you take her now as your bride, you will continue to look after her as well as we did. Thank you!" Harvey concluded.

"*Ntate*[6]," Uncle Stanford replied after receiving the microphone from Harvey, "may I humbly correct you? There is no bride being received by the Morreiras today, but rather a daughter. We will treat her like our own and assure you that she will remain plump. Just look at her mother-in-law!"

Isabel stood to her feet and twirled playfully before Stanford continued, "With your permission, Ntate," Stanford continued, "I would like to invite the Morreira women to collect our daughter, who is no longer a Motsepe, but now one of our own, and take her into the house to dress her according to our customs."

At a nod from Harvey, Stanford ushered Isabel's table towards the stage to commence with the age-old African tradition. "When Tshenolo emerges, she will be dressed as a Morreira," Stanford concluded poetically.

Nandi, holding Lolo's hand, escorted Isabel and her entourage out of the marquee and into the house. As they exited, the sound of the beating drum thundered through the crowd. The Zulu warriors soared through the air as they took to the stage.

"Matching? Wow! That's so sweet, Mom," Lolo exclaimed, keeping a contrived smile on her face by sheer force of will. Isabel was dressing Lolo in an outfit that matched her own, AND her sister Teresa's.

Eva and Sofia helped Lolo into the green and purple peacock-print mermaid-tale skirt, with matching long-sleeved peplum top and head wrap.

Runako and Qhayiya's laughter was masked by the crowd's ululations as the bride reappeared, flanked by Isabel and Teresa, with Nandi, Koketso, Eva and Sophia following close behind.

Once they had taken their seats, Stanford returned to the stage to continue with uMembeso by handing out the gifts, brought by the Morreiras for the Khoza and Motsepe families. The ceremony was intended to reinforce relations between the families and to thank the bride's family for granting their daughter's hand in marriage.

As was the custom, the bride's father was gifted with a coat, a hat, a blanket, an axe, and a bottle of whisky. In true Morreira style, only the most luxurious of these items were sourced. The coat was Belstaff. The hat, a Borsalino fedora. The blanket, an authentic Seanamarena. The axe, a handmade Karesuando Kniven, and the whisky, a rare bottle of Longmorn 1967. For the bride's mother, the Morreiras brought a Seanamarena blanket, a full set of AMC pots, a floral Marlow Home Co. apron, and two trolleys' worth of groceries. The bride's aunts received an apron and a blanket each, and Lolo's younger sister Koketso received a blanket and a designer outfit she had specified.

After the presentation of the gifts each, the guests enjoyed an elaborate spread of traditional Zulu and Setswana delicacies. There was *ting*[7], *idombolo*[8], *uphuthu*[9], and *bokgobe*[10]. The vegetable spread included *amadumbe*[11], *morogo*[12], sweet potato and pumpkin.

The slaughtered goat meat was served as a choice of *seswaa*[13] or curried, and *inhloko*[14] was set aside on *is'thebe*[15] for the uncles. For those that didn't eat goat, there was *umleqwa*[16], fried chicken drumsticks, and curried chicken feet.

To honour their new relations, Aunty Zodwa had also brewed *um'qombothi*[17] and ginger beer.

By the time the sun set, the DJ had the guests on their feet, ready to entertain them until the wee hours of the morning.

"Nala is starting to worry me, you guys!" Lolo frowned, playing with a patch of grass. She, Runako, and Qhayiya had decided to take a breather from the hurly-burly of the day by sitting in a darkened spot at the back of the house.

"Me too!" Runako sighed, taking another sip of the Savannah Dry cider she commandeered from Qhayiya.

"It's been over three years since Blaise passed," Qhayiya reasoned, "do you think she still blames herself for it?"

She leaned away from the wall to take a closer look at her friends for an answer.

"Maybe…" Lolo sympathised, "that would explain why she's literally dedicated her whole life to raising Solal in the Ilunga household."

"I… I just hope they're treating her well…" Runako stuttered, "she looked rather malnourished to me the last time I had a Skype call with her."

"Rather malnourished?" Lolo mocked, "Who speaks like that?"

Qhayiya cackled at Lolo's imitation of Runako's plummy accent, who simply scrunched her nose and rolled her eyes in response.

"I have an idea!" Lolo proffered proudly, lowering her chin and raising her eyebrows. "Since Nala's excuse for not seeing us is always a lack of money, and her discomfort at asking her in-laws for money, I will offer to cover the cost of her attending my bachelorette!"

"You will?" Qhayiya asked, with knitted brows.

"By me, I mean João. Duh!" Lolo furrowed.

"Got it!" Qhayiya winked mischievously.

"Lols, I, for one, think that's a FANTASTIC idea," Runako chimed in, "and I am fully behind it."

OR Tambo International Airport, Johannesburg
July 2013

The airport was its usual hive of activity as the Belters made their way through the international departures terminal. Their intentional uniform of black leggings, Converse sneakers, and slogan tees had them looking like a girl band going on tour.

The matching tees were Runako's idea of adding a special touch to Lolo's bachelorette celebration, much to the others' disapproval. However, they had finally relented, on one condition – they would each choose their own slogan.

As a result, the four friends were wearing their hearts on their tees. Runako's declared her irritation at the girls' initial reaction with a tee that read "THAT WASN'T VERY VERSACE OF YOU," Nala celebrated her natural beauty with the slogan "I WOKE UP LIKE THIS," Lolo's let onlookers know "YOU CAN'T SIT WITH US," and Qhayiya's tee rebelliously stated, "I DON'T WEAR SLOGAN TEES."

The sisterhood of the travelling tees caused quite a stir among the other patrons of the Shongololo Lounge before making their way to the boarding gates.

"Well done on securing the emergency row!" Nala said, smiling at Lolo. "The extra leg room is definitely appreciated."

"I insisted the travel agent give us the exit row since you guys are making me fly ECONOMY!" Lolo grumbled, struggling to fit her overnight bag in the overhead compartment of the full-to-capacity cabin.

"It was either fly business class or stay at one of Singapore's best hotels. I'm sorry, you were outvoted!" Runako rationalised as she buckled her seat belt.

"Actually, I would have preferred we do both. And WE COULD HAVE, had you all accepted João's offer to sponsor the trip!" Lolo argued, bragging brazenly. Runako gave her a firm kick on the shin for being insensitive to her friends' individual financial positions and turned to distract Nala, who luckily seemed not to have heard Lolo.

"Not a chance! We wanted to do this ourselves, and I'm glad we did," said Qhayiya, checking out the contents of the seat pocket.

Runako grinned, leaning forward to exchange her sneakers for the fresh aeroplane socks she'd found before adding, "Exactly! And what matters most is that we're all together celebrating your bachelorette."

Nala concurred, wiggling her toes. "And Lolo, we've had it with your 'I only fly Business…'"

"You mean FIRST…," Lolo interjected, unamused.

"Whatever," Runako said, touching her index finger to Lolo's lips to shut her up. "Although this trip is about YOU, it's actually for all of us to connect, let loose and have a good time. So I don't want to hear any more complaints from you over the next four days. Get it? Got it? Good!" Runako warned, giving Lolo a searing side-eye.

"I like the sound of that!" Nala giggled.

Pierre Balmain's Batik print Kebayas floated up and down the aisles as the Singapore Girls went about their business. The Belters marvelled at their iconic uniforms, porcelain skin, and impeccable grooming. They were ethereal. Their arms gently fluttered as they offered passengers a hot towel, and their faces glowed as they repeated, with patience and grace, the day's lunch option of Hainanese Chicken Rice or Fried Hokkien Mee.

Once all the trays had been cleared, the angelic figures dimmed the cabin lights and glided out of sight. The Belters settled in to watch a movie and Lolo realised her in-flight entertainment system was faulty. This gave her an idea.

International Arrivals Terminal, Changi Airport,
Singapore

Flight SQ 479 touched down at Changi Airport at exactly 06h10 local time, and three passengers started clapping. Not for the pilot, as is custom after a long or difficult flight, but for a fellow passenger. Tshenolo 'Lolo' Motsepe.

"I can't believe you pulled it off!" Nala giggled, folding her in-flight blanket.

"She's a legend. ABSOLUTE legend!" Qhayiya added.

"Shut up!" Lolo snapped, leaning over at Qhayiya seated across the aisle. "You're not supposed to speak English, remember!"

"Oh, yeah! Sorry!" Qhayiya whispered.

"And me? You said it's my first time flying, right? Remind me to look super-anxious when we disembark!" Runako snickered, throwing Lolo a thumbs up.

"And just because I've got natural hair you decided to make me the nervous fourth wife of Chief what's-his-name?" Nala asked, covering her mouth as she burst out laughing again.

"Ngonyama. Chief Ngonyama YeZulu of KwaZulu-Natal," Lolo said primly.

The cabin filled with raucous laughter as the friends recalled Lolo's antics in getting them upgraded to business class when only she had been eligible, thanks to her frequent flyer membership.

"You guys can laugh all you want, but you know my plan worked! I saved your asses eleven-and-a-half hours in economy class," Lolo smiled smugly, unbuckling her seatbelt.

Representatives from the Azalian High Commission were already waiting on the tarmac when the friends disembarked. The diplomatic welcome was a surprise arranged by Junior.

A pair of black Mercedes S-class sedans whisked them off the tarmac to the VIP customs clearing centre, and onwards to their hotel. A third vehicle, a Mercedes V-Class, followed with their luggage.

In the lobby of the Marina Bay Sands, residents had their phones out and were snapping away at the mystery guests that had arrived in a government convoy, convinced they were either royalty or celebrities.

After being escorted through a growing crowd of onlookers, Singapore's newest sensation arrived at their suite ready to tick off the first item on the day's agenda. Sleep.

Lantern Bar, Fullerton Hotel

The sky was a fire lily orange as the Belters strutted after the maître d' who was leading them to their table. The afternoon breeze added a windblown effect to their already VOGUE-esque entrance.

Located on the rooftop of the historic Fullerton Bay Hotel, the Lantern Bar was one of the Lion City's trendiest places to be. Widely regarded as the go-to spot for sundowners, it had panoramic views of the spectacular Marina Bay Waterfront. It also offered front row seats to the dazzling Spectra Water and Lights show held every night.

Dressed in their holiday look-book outfits of maxi dresses, high-heeled wedges and oversized hats, the Belters looked every bit the unrecognisable-but-definitely-famous girl group. By the time they'd taken their seats, many more locals had snuck in a picture of the foursome 'just in case'.

"Have these Chinese people never seen black people before?" Qhayiya asked irritably, frowning at a fellow patron who was pointing his phone at their table.

"Singaporean," Lolo corrected distractedly, paging through the menu.

"Well, I think it's nice to be getting a little attention for a change," Nala smiled sheepishly.

"Allow the locals to savour ALL of this melanin, *daaahling*," Runako said pompously, putting her nose in the air and fanning herself with the brim of her hat.

"Focus!" Lolo said, pointing to the menu.

"How hectic are these prices, though?" Nala blurted.

"Don't convert, babe. You'll give yourself a heart attack," Runako advised.

"And don't forget that you're in THE most expensive city in the world!" Qhayiya chimed in.

"Nala, I said the trip's on me, so don't worry about prices," Lolo said, waving to the waiter. "And girls, I'll get this bill, you've already sacrificed so much coming out here. It's the least I can do."

"Phew! That's a relief," Runako smiled gratefully.

"What do you mean a relief? Aren't you rolling on Kobe's black card?" Lolo teased.

"Nope. Afraid not. This girl is paying for herself!" Runako sighed, pointing her index finger at herself.

"Balling!" Qhayiya exclaimed.

"Try SAVINGS!" Runako replied huffily.

"Why's he making you pay for yourself?" Lolo demanded, grabbing the menu out of Runako's hands to get a better view of her face.

"Because! Kobe already pays for so much around the house. And the business is draining a lot of cash right now. We even had to change our marital regime just to make sure I'm protected."

"Make sure you're protected?" Qhayiya asked, eyebrows raised sceptically. Alarm bells immediately rang in her head when she thought back to her meeting with Stanford.

"Yeah," Runako nodded, frowning. "Why are you all looking at me like that?"

"Repeat that. You changed WHAT?" Lolo asked, turning her attention back to the conversation after placing an order of four Singapore Slings.

"Our marital regime. We changed from COP to ANC. WITH accrual, before you guys think he's trying to screw me over," Runako said defensively.

"That still doesn't guarantee you'll get what's rightfully due to you should you ever get divorced babe," Qhayiya mused. "I just hope he settled you your half share of the COP estate when you changed over. He *did* settle you, didn't he?"

"Ooh! The wings look good," Runako said, watching a platter being delivered to the next table.

"Ru, don't change the subject. Q's asking if he settled you," Lolo insisted.

"Settle what? We're married!" Runako snapped. "Why would he settle me from assets I'm still enjoying?"

"Because if he didn't, you have significantly weakened your financial position!" Qhayiya huffed. "Your behaviour is very confusing for someone that's supposed to be a lawyer, Ru."

"Did you at least consult with your lawyer before you signed? It's bad practice to rely on one's expertise when dealing with one's personal affairs," Lolo said gently.

"Oh, my God!" Runako snapped, holding her head in her hands. "Can you guys stop interrogating me? Please! You're ruining my trip!"

"Fine! I'll back off," Qhayiya said reluctantly, throwing her hands in the air. "But before I do, may I give you one piece of advice?"

Runako rolled her eyes and let out a loud sigh before nodding her head.

"Make sure you keep a close eye on your household finances. The best way to do that is to split the household bills not by nature, but by percentage. Don't fall into the trap of paying for utilities, groceries and other household consumables, while he pays for the big-ticket items like your home loan and vehicle finance.

Instead, pay a percentage of everything based on the ratio of your earnings. If Kobe is making four times what you do, then pay one-fifth of the bond, cars, insurance etc. That way, he'll be forced to hold those assets in your name too. And, you'll have access to those accounts. Promise me you'll do that and I won't raise the issue again!" Qhayiya concluded.

"I'll try…" Runako sighed.

"We're just trying to have your back, Ru. Some of us learned about these things the hard way…" Nala sighed, staring pensively over the marina.

"Sounds like there's something you'd like to tell us, Nala," Qhayiya said, clearing the table for the waiter to place their drinks.

"Not now…" Nala smiled awkwardly.

"I'd like to propose a toast!" Lolo said.

The tension was palpable as the girls raised their glasses. "To our children – well, future children for you, Q –"

"I'm not having any!" Qhayiya blurted.

"Whatever. Don't ruin the moment," Lolo winced. "Anyway, as I was saying, to our children. May their fathers always be rich, and their mothers always be beautiful. *L'Chaim*[18]!"

Marina Bay Sands

The suite was a mess.

Suitcases sat open with clothes spilling out. Wigs were hanging off chair ears. Stuffed Minions and lace bunny ears lay strewn on the floor. And although it was nearly 2 pm, the girls were still fast asleep.

Spending the day at Universal Studios, followed by an all-night party at Club Attica, had taken a toll on their bodies. They clearly no longer had the stamina of their university days.

Runako looked around the room in amazement. *Yup! This is what I call a girls' trip!* she thought to herself, as she tiptoed onto the balcony.

Their room had a direct view of the Gardens by the Bay, and Runako took a moment to marvel at the manmade Supertree Grove and Cloud Domes.

The gardens were magical, and reminded her of planet Pandora of *Avatar*, as if at any moment she would spot a Na'vi walking about.

But Runako was slowly learning that magic didn't really exist, and fairy tales held little truth. The real world was less colourful. And happily? Only in sprinkles throughout the ever after.

Runako pulled out her phone and dialled Kobe. She hadn't spoken to him or Zina since landing in Singapore on Friday morning. Not because she'd forgotten, or couldn't, but because she was enjoying her time away from them.

Time to be herself, and not someone's mom. Or wife. In the two years since Zina was born, it was the first time Runako had taken time for herself.

Kobe's phone rang with no answer, which wasn't unusual, considering it was only approaching 8 am back home. Runako had better luck with Mai Precious, the live-in nanny, who explained Kobe was still sleeping as he'd had visitors the night before. Kobe hadn't mentioned anything about hosting visitors, but Runako dismissed it as their texts had been brief anyway.

She spoke with Zina, who was not at all impressed that her mom had seen 'Shwek' without her. Runako promised to bring her along next time, and all was forgiven. *How quickly children forgive.*

The girls wrapped up 'breakfast' at Ku Dé Ta and walked across the Sky Deck to the famous Marina Bay Sands infinity pool. It was as marvellous as depicted in the pictures.

Perched 57 floors above the city, the world's longest elevated swimming pool offered guests the experience of swimming in the sky.

"Look at this view, you guys!" Runako squealed, as she walked across to the pool deck.

"How AMAZING…?!" Lolo agreed. "Our pictures will be INSANE!"

"I'm over Singapore and its prices, ya'll. Like, I'm DONE!" Qhayiya complained before spreading a towel over a poolside lounger.

"Okay, I will admit that those hand-reared, breastfed, cuddled-to-sleep Wagyu cows on the menu were a little pricey," Lolo chuckled, as she slipped off her sarong and slathered her body with sunscreen.

"Are you okay, Nala?" Runako asked. "You've been quiet all day. In fact, you've been unusually quiet all weekend!"

Nala sighed and lay back on the lounger, staring into the clouds.

"I don't want to go back to Azalia," she replied, and fiddled with the tassels on her poolside kaftan. "I've been thinking about it all weekend, and I've decided I'm not going back!"

"Why not? What about Solal?" Lolo exclaimed, taking a seat at Nala's feet.

"You guys have no clue what that family put me through," Nala said as her voice broke. "From the moment I arrived to mourn Blaise, they've treated me like a criminal. Brigitte still blames me for the accident and put me through the most horrible rituals to prove I did not have a hand in killing him." Nala hugged her knees and burst into tears as Lolo grabbed a towel and shielded her from prying eyes. "I can't even begin to tell you half the things she made me do!"

"What happened, babe? You can talk to us," Runako frowned, taking a seat next to Qhayiya on the lounger and placing her hand gently on Nala's knee.

"Yes, Nala," Qhayiya added softly. "We've been dying to find out if everything is okay with you, but you just seemed to push us away every time we reached out to you."

Nala rocked back and forth and took a moment to compose herself. She sat up, with the towel still over her head, and fiddled with her kaftan, wondering if she should come clean. She didn't want to ruin Lolo's trip, but she couldn't bear keeping the reality of her life in Azalia a secret any longer.

"Now I understand…" Nala croaked.

"Understand what, babe?" Lolo pressed gently, squeezing Nala's left hand with her right.

"Why Blaise kept saying his family is VERY traditional…"

"Okay…" Lolo nodded. The friends kept quiet and allowed Nala to take her time in opening up to them.

"I…I'm still not comfortable talking about what happened in the first year. But since then, I haven't been allowed to do anything but raise Solal. I still haven't finished my honours, and I'm not allowed to work. I can't date. I can't even leave Azalia for more than one week to see my family in KZN."

"Is that why you couldn't come to my traditional wedding?" Lolo asked sincerely, suddenly piecing the puzzle together.

"And why you couldn't make Zina's first birthday party?" Runako added, with equal revelation.

Nala nodded her head gently.

"But why?" Qhayiya asked sternly, still hunched over towards Nala. "Why are they treating you like a prisoner? Like they OWN you or something?"

Nala started rocking again. Her heavy breathing giving away that she'd started crying again.

"Because I refuse to do the stupid cleansing," she admitted, "and the Ilungas have threatened to keep Solal from me if I move back to South Africa without first being cleansed. I can't let them take my baby from me!" Nala was now sobbing again, and Lolo waved to Runako to pass her another towel so Nala could dry her tears.

"*Shhh…* Please don't cry babe," Lolo said gently, hugging Nala to her chest. "I know you have your religious beliefs, but maybe you should do the cleansing and get it over and done with!"

"Yeah!" Runako said, turning to Lolo and shaking her head in agreement. "Like, how bad can it be?"

"You guys don't get it!" Nala shrugged, pulling the towel away to reveal her bloodshot eyes. "The cleansing is me having sex with Blaise's uncle!"

The friends listened in horror as Nala explained the Ilungas practised the ritual of *kusasa fumbi*[19]. According to this practice, a widow is cleansed of the bad luck surrounding her husband's death by having unprotected sex with her brother-in-law, one of the late husband's relatives, a selected future husband, or a paid sex worker.

The ritual is believed to cleanse the widow of evil spirits that caused the death of her husband. Although outlawed in many parts of the continent, the ritual continues to be practised in countries such as Kenya, Zambia, Malawi, Uganda, Tanzania, Mozambique, Angola, Ivory Coast and the DRC.

The sun was beginning to set, and the friends looked out onto the Singapore skyline, dumbfounded by the revelation Nala had shared with them. The modern city buildings glittering in the Singaporean sunset stood in stark contrast to the archaic ritual holding their friend hostage in a foreign country.

The friends agreed to offer Nala the support she needed to leave Azalia and rebuild her life without the Ilungas. As the sun slowly set over the horizon, it was clear that although they lived on the same earth, the friends had clearly been living in very different worlds.

Kobe and Ru's place, Glen Hills Estate,
Harare

Runako pulled up to the boom gate, calling a greeting to the guard on duty as she placed her finger on the biometric scanner. Although she'd been in Singapore for only four days, her surroundings suddenly seemed unfamiliar to her.

From the outside looking in, she led a charmed life. She seemed carefree in her luxury SUV, wind blowing through her 18-inch

Peruvian hair, and face shielded from the harsh sun by her 'I got these at Selfridges' Chanel 5018 half-tint shades.

But, as Harare's high society knows, looks are often deceiving in this town. The poster girl for all things 'Happy Wife, Happy Life,' was, in fact, clutching onto a marriage that was now nothing more than PR. Runako was very well aware of this as she inched her way through the estate in her piece of Stuttgart.

She knew she would no longer be married to Kobe, had it not been for the promise of a changed man, her seven-figure Push Present, and two-carat Cheat Charm - a gift from a cheating spouse in exchange for a stay of execution and, hopefully, forgiveness.

The gesture was but a band-aid on a wound that had continued to fester and was now becoming toxic. Runako waved to the residents' cycling club gliding past before pulling into her driveway. She turned off the engine and sat in the car for a moment, willing herself to WANT her life as a mother and wife again.

Runako's home was located in the manicured Glen Hills Estate, where the skies seemed just a little bluer and the grass a little greener than in the rest of Harare. The front entrance had two imposing double-volume pillars. The double-volume design extended into the entrance hall and made the house seem much bigger than it really was.

The large, frosted window above the door let in a stream of light that bounced off the snowfall white porcelain tiles, creating a mystical glow and airiness. The kitchen was larger than those in similar homes and had the centre island all self-respecting homeowners now insisted upon.

Up the sweeping stairs were six bedrooms, all en-suite, with their own balconies that faced the calming water feature framing the pool.

The million-dollar mansion was evidence of Kobe's meteoric rise since moving to Harare. Along with the money and power, however, came girls that saw themselves as the next Mrs Kobe Mensah.

"Mama!" screamed Zina, as she came racing through the garage door.

"Hello, *mudiwa wangu*[20]! How are you, my baby?" Runako cooed, picking her up onto her lap and giving her a big squeeze.

They headed inside the house as Mai Precious appeared from the butler's pantry where she did her ironing.

"Hi, Mai Precious, how are you? Was everything fine while I was away?" Runako asked, opening the fridge to grab a bottle of chardonnay and already tasting the leathery liquid in her mouth.

"Yes, *Mai Zina*[21], everything was fine, thank you. How was your trip?"

"It was AMAZING Mai Precious. I didn't want to come back!" Runako chuckled.

"Miss Zina was such a good girl while you were gone. We played and watched Teletubbies. She even asked for a second bowl of *sadza ne gravy*[22] yesterday."

"Aww! She likes her sadza, just like her daddy!" Runako chuckled.

The fridge was looking unusually empty for a Tuesday, considering that Mai Precious and Baba Schumacher (the family driver) had done the weekly groceries just two days before. Runako reached for a wine glass and noticed that Mai Precious had made mince for dinner again, which Kobe despised.

"Mai Precious, why have you made mince again? Did you guys not buy other meat?"

"It's because the money *Baba Zina*[23] has been giving us for the past month is not enough to buy everything we need. So I just make a plan with the money we have."

"Why didn't you tell me this, Mai Precious?" Runako asked, somewhat exasperated. "I am the woman of this house. You can't just be having these conversations with Baba Zina without telling me!"

"Sorry Ma, I thought you both agreed to change the amount of money he gives us. He used to give us three hundred dollars for the week," Mai Precious explained. "Now, he says we must buy from the cheaper stores, but it's still expensive. Everything has gone up. *Zvodukya zvinodhura*[24]!" she exclaimed.

"It's okay, Mai Precious. I'll chat to my husband when he gets home tonight," Runako reassured her. "But please, next time, let me know."

7 pm.

8 pm.

9 pm, and Kobe was still not home. You'd think for someone whose wife had been away he'd be excited to get home early. The late-night meetings had become an almost daily occurrence. The fact that he answered his phone every time Runako called was the only ray of hope that her marriage was still intact. There was no evidence that he had moved on to someone else, but it was clear that he'd moved on from Runako.

It was nearly 10 pm when the garage door finally opened, and Kobe returned home for the first time that day. He walked through the door as he always did; carrying his newspaper, suit jacket and iPad mini. He placed them on the kitchen counter and made his way into the TV room to give Runako a kiss.

"Hey," he said matter-of-factly, giving Runako a peck on the lips. He smelled like red wine and garlic.

"Hey," Runako replied brightly, trying hard to contain her anger from the conversation she had with Mai Precious earlier. She decided to change her train of thought. "Guess what?"

"What?" Kobe replied, with his head in the fridge where he was digging for something to drink.

"Bumped into Chief Justice Moyo at the airport today."

"Oh... okay. And?"

"And he said he's heard what a good job I'm doing at Savoy Inc. and I should consider joining public office at some stage in my career," Runako said, walking into the kitchen.

"Oh. Nice," Kobe responded neutrally.

"Nice? Is that all you can say, Kobe?" Runako exploded. "I'm telling you one of the most senior legal heads in the country knows my name, and you're just going to dismiss me?"

"Runako don't do this!" he warned, loosening his tie. "I've had a very difficult day, and I don't want to be stressed by you as well." He poured himself a shot of 18-year-old Macallan from the crystal decanter they'd received as a wedding gift.

"STRESSED?" echoed Runako incredulously. "Do you have ANY idea how much stress I'm under, Kobe? Of course not! Because we hardly talk anymore." She deflated at hearing her own words. "You haven't even asked me how my trip was. You seem to have all the time in the world for everyone else but me, and it feels like nothing I say is important enough and nothing I do is good enough." Runako was quiet for a moment, pensive. "Is that why you keep all the girls around, cause I'm not good enough?" she asked softly, her voice trembling with tears.

Kobe sighed theatrically and collapsed onto the couch, turning on the TV and pointedly remaining silent. She grabbed the remote from him, turned off the TV, and threw the remote onto the floor.

"No, Kobe!" she shouted. "You will NOT ignore me. Not this time! I am talking to you, and I expect an answer. Will I EVER be good enough for you?!" she demanded, her voice rising to a screech, her eyes shiny with furious tears of betrayal.

"You'd better keep your voice down before you wake up Zina," Kobe growled. "I am sick and tired of your insecurities and your disrespect for me. What girls are you talking about? Huh? WHAT GIRLS?! I told you that I'm not cheating on you, but you keep going on about some girls!"

"Just because you haven't slept with them doesn't mean you're not cheating, Kobe," Runako said as the tears finally broke free. "You're cheating me out of my time with you because you're always giving it to someone else. You're cheating me of affection because you always have compliments for other women but none for me. You're cheating me of affirmation because you never congratulate me, but you're always commenting on other women's achievements on LinkedIn." Runako covered her eyes with her hands for a few heartbeats, before angrily wiping her eyelashes to continue.

"You're cheating me of intimacy because you haven't touched me in three months. THREE FUCKIN' MONTHS! How am I supposed to stay married to a man that doesn't sleep with me? I'm young and beautiful and desirable, Kobe! And you look at me like I DISGUST you!" Runako sobbed.

"Do you really expect me to discuss your little meeting when I've just lost a hundred-million-dollar deal? Huh?! Do you know how much stress I carry trying to keep this house afloat? To keep YOUR family employed?" Kobe countered bitterly.

"But you don't have to go through that stress alone, baby! I am here for you!" Runako reminded him, empathy and guilt softening her tone.

"You! You with a salary that only pays for Zina's nursery fees and our staff?" he snorted derisively. "Whose bank statement only knows Net-A-Porter and Craig's Studio? Because all you care about are designer clothes and expensive hair! You have no clue what things cost. Do you even know how much I spend just to keep you in this house?"

"But the mortgage is way less than what you make baby," Runako answered indignantly.

"Stop right there, before you embarrass yourself any further." Kobe leaned forward threateningly in his chair, his eyes filled with rage and practically foaming at the mouth.

"You think the only cost of owning a home is the mortgage? Ever heard of water, electricity, levies, rates, taxes, sewerage, household and homeowner's insurance? I guess not, because all you're ever worried about is your next nail and lash appointment and how you're going to 'show them on Instagram' with your fancy wigs and latest designer outfits!" Kobe accused, before storming off into the guest bedroom and slamming the door behind him.

Kobe's words, although harsh, were true. Runako couldn't help feeling disappointed in herself. She had been more concerned with her worldly appearance than the managing and sharing of the financial responsibilities of their household. Her husband had been silently suffering and she, his rock-star commercial law wife, had been too engrossed in emulating the imaginary life she saw on TV, where things 'magically took care of themselves', to notice. She felt physically ill.

She wondered how, being highly educated herself, she could have been so oblivious when it came to her finances. It was embarrassing to admit that she didn't have a handle on what life actually cost, and wouldn't know where to begin buying a car or shopping for insurance because although she knew the theory, she'd never actually gone through the process herself. Kobe had always taken care of such things.

She took a sip of the whisky Kobe had left behind, and decided to head to bed. She had to be at the office early the next morning and resolved to be a more involved partner going forward.

Kobe and Runako's place
October 2013

Kobe's car was parked in the driveway when Runako pulled up from another long day at the office. The sight that used to bring her so much joy was now a source of pain.

It felt as though every time Runako and Kobe were home together, they were fighting about some or other household issue, like the poor quality of Mai Precious's cooking or household items that ran out in the middle of the week and Runako had not replaced.

Holding her tongue that evening would be particularly difficult for Runako, but she didn't want to start a fight with Kobe on the night of Kate's birthday dinner. Kate and Oliver had taken a trip to Victoria Falls for her birthday and did a stopover in Harare before returning to London.

"Are you going to dinner dressed like that?" Runako croaked, her voice giving away her emotions and the statement coming out harsher than she had intended.

"I'm not going. I'm not feeling well," Kobe replied casually as he caught up on the day's news online. His laptop was perched on his chest as he lay in bed on his back.

"Not feeling well? Since when?" Runako said, irritably.

"I'm just highly-strung right now, and don't feel like being around people. Bad day at the office," Kobe explained without explaining.

Runako sighed loudly as she tried to contain her already highly charged emotions.

"But baby, you know that Kate has been planning this dinner for months! And my whole family is going to be there," Runako cajoled. "I just think it's so unfair that you've been skipping more and more family functions but are always available for a business THIS or a political THAT…"

"That's different. It's work," he replied curtly.

"And this? This is FAMILY! What happened to 'family first'? Hmm?" Runako taunted. "It would be nice if you actually LIVED your WhatsApp status, instead of just trying to sound deep…"

"Relax. It's not a big deal," Kobe retaliated. "I'll message Kate and tell her I'm not coming. She'll be fine – I'll send her some money so she can treat herself to something nice."

"Oh! Because that's how you fix everything nowadays, Kobe? By throwing money at the problem?"

"Oh, here we go again," Kobe sighed.

"It's the TRUTH, Kobe! Just throw money at the problem without EVER manning up to FIX IT!

"We have a big fight and instead of apologising you get your assistant to send me flowers. I complain that we're no longer having sex and it's 'Maybe we need to go on a holiday'. I ask that we spend time together and I get 'I have to work hard to give you this life.' Can't you see that's it's YOU that I want, Kobe? YOU!" Runako pleaded, impatiently wiping away brimming tears.

"Runako, don't you DARE be a hypocrite!" Kobe barked, getting out of bed and standing aggressively close to Runako. "Me? You say you want ME? I don't see you complaining when you flash your in-house gym or designer closet and first-class holidays on Instagram for your friends to see. I don't see you rushing to spend time with me when I AM at home. You're always on the phone with Rory or on WhatsApp with your girls or focused on Zina. When last did you phone ME to genuinely check up on how I am doing, and not to brag about your latest case or high-profile client?"

"But, Kobe –"

"SHUT UP and let me finish, woman!" Kobe roared. "I let you speak until you were done, and you will give me the same respect as your husband and as the man of this house! THAT'S your problem. You've forgotten how to be a wife! When last did you cook for me? Pack my clothes when I'm travelling? Sit with me while I watch football like you used to when we were still dating? Lie on my chest while I read the newspaper? Watch a new series with me? How many times have I BEGGED you to watch *Netflix* with me?" He shook his head without breaking eye contact, his face etched with pain. "Me? You don't want ME," he said dully. "You want the life I give you and your family so that you can be the envy of your family and friends. So don't come here acting all holier-than-thou and pretending that you are still in this marriage for anything other than the comforts it gives you."

Kobe trudged to the bathroom as Runako stood in shock, mouth agape and wondering how her husband could speak to her with such hatred in his voice and contempt in his eyes.

He was so angry! Why was he so angry? And what BS reasons he had given...! Cooking? Packing his clothes?! Why would that be so important to him now when it wasn't an issue before? Why would cuddling when he is watching TV be something he longed for when he used to treat me like an irritation when I did it? Was he gaslighting, or were these things he really wanted us to share? And what were the chances of us sharing such intimate moments when we could barely exchange more than four sentences between us before the conversation became an argument?

More and more conversations were ending this way. It seemed the more Runako tried to fix things, the worse she made them. It killed her to keep quiet, but it hurt more to speak.

Oh, God, please help me! I don't know what to do. I am watching my marriage crumble with each passing day...

"I'll see you at dinner," Kobe muttered, grabbing his keys and leaving the room, banging the door on his way out.

Runako stood frozen in place, in an awkward silence that was part anger, frustration, hurt, sulking, pride, disappointment, and mourning.

A while later, she snapped out of her trance and hurriedly threw on a pair of blue Hudson's distressed jeans, brown suede Sam Edelman booties, and a white Elie Tahari collared shirt, before rushing out of the bedroom to try to catch up with Kobe who had driven off ten minutes before her.

The Mensahs were already suspicious that things between them were less than rosy, and she didn't want her nosey sister-in-law in her business, pretending to be concerned but, in reality, looking for kinks in her gold-digging, Zimbabwean sister-in-law's marriage.

Fishmonger Restaurant

Kobe was already seated and having a drink when Runako arrived. Raised eyebrows and wry smiles around the table clearly indicated that the separate arrival had been noted and would be used as gossip fodder during Kate's next phone call to Cora. Runako paid her no mind and launched her own counter-attack to prove that she and her husband were rock solid.

"Kate! Happy birthday, sweetheart!" Runako cooed, leaning in for a hug and double air-kiss before handing the celebrant her gift of a duck egg stole.

"I hope you like it – it's 100% vicuña, softer than cashmere and rarer than Alpaca. I asked a friend to bring it for me on her last trip to London," Runako elaborated.

"Vicuña? Brilliant!" Kate chuckled disdainfully.

"Excuse me?" Runako hissed.

"Oh, nothing. I just find it fascinating that salespeople still manage to convince you Africans that expensive is better," Kate trilled, her arrogance almost comic.

"YOU Africans?" Runako verified, fortunately too startled to burst out laughing at the idiocy.

"Uh-huh! I mean, no Londoner would willingly pay, what… £2 500? … for a scarf, when a Marks & Spencer one would have done a perfectly good job, at a fraction of the price," Kate explained sanctimoniously.

"You're right, Kate! I don't know why I thought that, behind all that polyester, you'd have an appreciation for vicuña," Runako smiled angelically. "Next time I'm in London, I'll head straight to the Camden market for your birthday gift."

"Please, do! I have some exquisite vintage items from there. But then again, you may find shopping at a market tricky since it requires one to have an inherent sense of style…" Kate sneered, eyeing Runako up and down.

Runako sat down and gave Kobe a peck on the cheek, fascinated that two women could exchange lethal words and looks between them, while the men in the room remained completely oblivious of the altercation.

Knowing that her husband would never come to her defence, Runako had learned to return her sister-in-law's snide remarks as graciously and cunningly as they had been delivered.

Speeches, grilled bream, and bottles of Graham Beck Sauvignon Blanc later, the moment that would change Runako's world presented itself. Kobe checked his phone again, as he had done all night, sent a short text, and left it face-down at the table.

"Bathroom," he whispered, as he stood up and left the table.

"Sure, hun," Runako smiled back, uncomfortably. Something was very different with Kobe, and she knew his phone held the answer.

***

"Kobe's cheating on me with CJ, Mommy!" Runako sobbed into the phone, as she raced back home down Borrowdale Road.

"Watichi?"[25] Maita mumbled over the phone, obviously struggling to wake up.

"I said, Kobe is cheating on me with CJ!"

"How do you know, sweetheart?" Maita asked, still groggy.

"I saw a text from her come in while we were at dinner, and he'd been on his phone all night. And he's been having more and more work trips to London lately. And we're always fighting…"

"Calm down, Ruru. That is hardly confirmation that he's cheating on you…"

"He must be! Why else would he be chatting with CJ in secret? I didn't even know they still kept in touch," Runako mewled in despair.

"I hear you, darling," Maita comforted her. "Question is what are you going to do about it? I mean, if he really IS cheating, so what? All men cheat. You're the main house, the one wearing his ring, birthing his babies and carrying his surname. What's your problem?"

"Love, Mommy. What about love?" Runako sobbed.

"Who said he doesn't love you?" Maita asked pragmatically.

"If he loved me, he wouldn't cheat on me!" Runako insisted hysterically.

"Runako, be serious. Love and fidelity are two VERY different things. You have a beautiful family with a husband that treats you, your daughter and your family well. Your dad and two brothers are on his payroll for goodness' sake! He doesn't hit you, does he?"

"No…" Runako whispered

"He isn't an alcoholic, nor does he spend months on end away from his family. I'm struggling to see how you can say he doesn't love you." Maita sounded genuinely confused.

"That's not the kind of love I got married for, Mama," Runako explained again.

"What kind is that, Ruru?" Maita replied

"I don't know… the kind we had when we first met!"

"There's your problem. Every smart woman knows you don't build a marriage on that kind of love…"

"What kind of love do you build a marriage on then?"

"The kind of love you feel for a man when he's at his worst…" Maita paused to let her words sink in before continuing.

"Runako Rose Mensah, don't do anything drastic yet, because you have no proof that Kobe is cheating. Besides, Lolo's wedding is coming up in a few weeks, right? Why don't you use that time to bond with your husband? Reassure him that you're there for him and let him open up to you. If he does, you can have an open and honest conversation about what you are willing and not willing to accept, and take it from there."

9

THE MENSAHS' DILEMMA

"If a mad man takes your clothes, do not run after him naked"

— AFRICAN PROVERB

The Cape Grace Hotel, Waterfront, Cape Town
November 2013

*T*he piano played softly in the background as Runako made her way through the foyer of the Cape Grace Hotel. The Waterfront's grande dame was her home away from home whenever she, Kobe and little Zina were in town. Runako always felt pampered when staying at 'the Cape's Saving Grace' as she lovingly called it.

As she made her way under the three-tier candelabra chandelier, and past a pair of suited Chinese businessmen, she thought back to the many times she had sat at that table since first visiting the hotel back in 2012.

This was the first time that she wasn't with Kobe, who would only be flying in the following morning. On the day of his best friend's wedding. Although Nala and Qhayiya had done their best to keep her entertained the previous night, Cape Town just wasn't the same without Kobe.

Qhayiya had generously offered to sponsor Nala's travel and accommodation down from Shongweni where Nala was living with Granny Blossom. It had been four months since Nala had been back in the country and she was looking significantly healthier, happier and heavier than when Runako last saw her in Singapore.

The same couldn't be said for Runako though who felt she was watching her marriage crumble with each passing day.

The hotel felt empty without Kobe's running commentary about its history, or explanations of the different food items on the menu, or the hilarious recollections of his many university dating escapades that had gone wrong at the famous landmark.

Without Kobe by her side, the hotel didn't look and feel as luxurious as she remembered, even though it was just as spectacular as the last time she had stayed there. If not grander.

Runako felt glum at the thought that her best memories at the hotel may be behind her, and she feared the same could be true for her marriage.

Life had a funny sense of humour. Here she was, on her way to prepare for her friend's first step on the journey of marriage, while Runako wondered if she was on her last.

Runako carefully walked down the white marble stairs towards the entrance of the hotel. Nala and Qhayiya had arrived to pick her up for their grooming appointment, ahead of the biggest wedding the country had seen in years. Whatever the state of her own marriage,

Runako was in one of her favourite cities in the world, and she was adamant that she'd have a good time!

"Hey, guys!" Runako rasped in a burnt voice as she climbed into the back seat of Qhayiya's hired Mercedes Benz.

"Hehe, someone had a big night last night!" Nala tittered.

"Ah, man, it was crazy!" Runako agreed, before coughing.

"Shimmy's was LIT, hey? I haven't partied like that in years! And you better pray no one posts a picture of you twerking for Charles…" Nala teased.

"What? I was TWERKING? For Charles!" Runako squeaked in alarm, holding her hand against her pounding head.

"Yes, ma'am!" Qhayiya confirmed. "Ciara's *Body Party* came on and let's just say, there was definitely a party in Charles' pants once you were through with your little dance routine…"

Qhayiya and Nala giggled at the recollection of their friend's antics the night before.

"Oh, God, NO! My marriage SO does not need this," Runako begged frantically.

"Relax. We're just teasing," Qhayiya smiled. "Kidding about someone snapping a picture of you. NOT kidding about you shaking what Mama Maita gave you…"

"Not funny, Q! Oh, and can you not turn so much?" Runako winced.

"What do you mean 'not turn so much'?" Qhayiya replied indifferently, checking for cars before taking off again.

"All that turning! You're going to make me throw up!" Runako exclaimed, incredulous.

"There are traffic circles in the road, Runako. How else do you expect me to get around them?"

"You've been warned..." Runako acquiesced.

The V&A Waterfront shopping centre, located on the Atlantic shore, had cemented itself as Cape Town's premier shopping and dining destination. The complex housed a wide variety of salons, fashion boutiques and eateries, and provided the best in fashion, food and entertainment. The world's well-heeled regularly click-clacked along the centre's walkways to take advantage of the many attractions including a visit to the historic red and white Clock Tower, Two Oceans Aquarium, or simply taking in the variety of street and amphitheatre entertainment.

"Is everything with you and Kobe any better, Ru?" Nala probed, as they walked from the parking lot to the spa.

"I don't know, Nala. I saw a rather intimate text from CJ a few weeks back, and I think he's having an affair with her. In fact, I think he was with her last night, that's why he delayed his flight back from London," Runako replied sadly.

"Are you sure he's cheating, though, Runako? Maybe he really did have business to attend to like he told you," Nala suggested, pushing open the door into Life Day Spa.

"That's the thing," Runako replied, "I don't have any evidence. I have to go on his behaviour, and his behaviour screams that my husband checked out of this marriage a long time ago."

"Maybe you guys are just going through a bad patch. You survived your separation, I'm sure you can survive this too!" Nala reassured her.

"It feels different. In the build-up to the separation, we were still fighting. There was still attention. He was present. This time…. it's like I'm in this marriage alone, guys. I feel that I'm the only one standing on the dance floor of my marriage," Runako confided, holding back the tears she felt welling up.

"Well, maybe tomorrow he'll think back to your magical wedding day, and those memories will rekindle his love for you. Maybe tomorrow he'll walk back onto the dance floor with you," Nala smiled warmly as Qhayiya walked up to the welcome desk to announce their arrival.

The Conservatory, Franschhoek

Multi-award winning South African songstress Lira and her band took to the stage as the MC declared the dance floor open. The interlocking glass marquees hosting the six-hundred-odd guest list at The Conservatory immediately came alive as guests made their way onto the dance floor and the expansive, manicured gardens.

The bride was smashing in an ivory coloured Pronovias reception gown, her third dress for the day, as she danced and giggled with her father-in-law much to the crowd's delight. Few brides would be able to hide their excitement after their in-laws gifted them a five-bedroom house in the upmarket suburb of Sandhurst.

Runako couldn't help but feel a slight twinge of envy at the sight of her friend and her new husband. Perhaps she had married the wrong Muzungu, or perhaps, four years down the line, her friend would be sitting in the same position as Runako, looking longingly at another couple and wishing joy would once again smile upon her marriage.

"Dance with me," Runako asked Kobe, who had been sitting rather quietly throughout the day's proceedings.

"I'm tired," he replied neutrally.

"Please," Runako entreated. "We haven't danced in months. You've barely touched me in months. Why don't we forget about all of that for just one night, and be the Kobe and Ru we were at uni?"

"A lot has happened since we were in uni, Runako," Kobe pointed out impassively. "We will never be those people again."

"Fair enough," Runako allowed. "Maybe I should ask this, then – are you having an affair?"

"Excuse me?" Kobe replied, suddenly sitting up.

"You heard me. Our marriage is not perfect, and never has been," she admitted to herself as much as to him. "But something has fundamentally changed between us Kobe. So I'll ask you again, are you having an affair? With CJ?"

"Stop being ridiculous," he scoffed. "Are you making up all these accusations just because I said I wouldn't dance with you? I'm tired, that's all. I'm tired!" Kobe rose from his seat and walked away from the table.

"So am I, Kobe... So am I," Runako sighed, smiling dejectedly.

The Cape Grace Hotel

The sound of an alarm grew louder and louder as Runako slowly awoke and reached to silence her phone. The pain knocking on the side of her head was a reminder of just how much champagne she had consumed after she admitted defeat and resigned herself to the fact that Kobe was not joining her on the dance floor. Not last night, or ever. Runako had realised, watching her friends take their first dance, that she and Kobe had long ago taken their last.

She turned to her side and noticed her husband was not in bed. On his pillow was a short note: "Didn't want to wake you. See you at home. K."

Leaving without saying goodbye had become the norm, and Runako mocked herself for thinking that this trip would somehow magically mend her marriage. She'd hoped the time away from Harare would remind Kobe of everything they were before Harare. Before marriage.

Looking back, Runako realised that their problems started long before they moved to Zim. In fact, she felt her relationship had not been the same since Kobe found out about Obinna.

Was it all her fault? Had she cracked the foundation of a relationship that had otherwise seemed rock solid?

Did it even matter anymore?

She was too hungover to try and figure it out. Instead, she booked herself a massage and got ready to have breakfast and check out.

Kobe and Runako's house

Runako had been home for about three hours when Kobe eventually returned home from the 'business meeting' for which he had to leave Cape Town early. So important was this meeting that Baba Schumacher had fetched her from the airport, and not her own husband.

The five-hour journey back to Harare was significantly longer than the outbound leg, or perhaps it had just felt that way. Runako had spent the flight thinking of the best way to let Kobe know that she was leaving her marriage. For good this time.

"Hey!" Kobe said as he walked through the garage door and headed straight for the fridge.

"Hey," Runako replied softly.

"Sorry I couldn't fetch you from the airport. This deal I'm working on is really –"

"Kobe, you don't have to," Runako interrupted gently. "You don't have to explain anything to me. I think we both know that our marriage is over."

"What?" Kobe said, apparently genuinely surprised by his wife's statement.

"I can't do this anymore, Kobe. I'm done," Runako reiterated.

"You're DONE?" Kobe asked disbelievingly, walking towards Runako. "What EXACTLY do you mean by 'you're done'?"

"Done. With our marriage. I'm done fighting. Done pretending there's something here when there isn't. The love is gone, Kobe..."

"So you want a divorce." His voice was flat, toneless. A statement, not a question.

"I don't WANT a divorce, but I don't want to stay in a loveless marriage, either. I can honestly say I've tried everything I can but –"

"LET ME STOP YOU RIGHT THERE!" he thundered. "If there's anyone that hasn't tried in this marriage it's YOU! YOU haven't tried being a wife. That's the fundamental problem we have."

"I don't know how to be 'a wife', Kobe," Runako said, tearing up. "I just know how to be Runako! The same Runako you fell in love with in uni. The same Runako you shared your deepest fears and greatest joys with. The same Runako that dreamt of one day having children and also having a career. The same Runako that believes a successful marriage is a union of two people, that are allowed to grow into the best version of themselves. That's all I know how to be, Kobe." Runako stood in place, tears streaming down her face and arms hanging down her sides like those of a woman defeated.

"I will not allow you to shame my family!" Kobe said and walked towards the door into the garage.

Runako followed and halted in the doorway. "I'm serious, Kobe," she said softly.

The garage door hummed as it slowly rolled upwards, and Kobe opened the door to his car before turning around to face his wife.

"In case you forgot, we've just changed our matrimonial regime. If you leave now, you'll leave with nothing!" he spat.

Runako chewed her bottom lip as she considered her next words carefully. Then she sighed deeply before answering.

"You're wrong, Kobe, I'll walk away with the most valuable asset I have – my dignity."

Kobe slammed his car door shut and marched towards Runako, stopping only once he was right up in her face. He looked at her dead in the eye and tilted her face upwards by the chin.

"In that case, make sure to take your father and brothers along with you."

Ndoro & Associates, Harare
January 2014

The reception area of Ndoro & Associates felt very familiar. A centre island desk greeted Runako as she entered through the glass double doors. The firm's name appeared in bold grey letters on the wall behind it. To the right were floor-to-ceiling windows that looked out at the Harare skyline, and to the left was a suite of Dijon-yellow velvet chaises: a two-seater flanked by two single-seaters. Adorning the mist-grey walls was a pair of Mark Rothko-inspired paintings. Their sunset hues perfectly complemented the seating arrangement beneath them.

Elizabeth Ncube, in contrast, looked nothing like a cutthroat divorce lawyer when she walked into the reception area.

Runako had imagined that her divorce lawyer would resemble Jessica Pearson from *Suits* – tall and slender, dressed in a cream white suit and matching chiffon blouse.

Instead, Elizabeth was podgy, dressed in a sorghum-brown skirt suit and black block-heel Mary-Janes. She had big, round eyes that seemed to pierce through your soul.

Despite her underwhelming appearance, Elizabeth had an air that said she was ready for action! And this was exactly the kind of reassurance Runako needed after Kobe's threat.

Two young-looking ladies with pen and paper in hand walked in behind Elizabeth, and all four women made their way to the boardroom. As soon as the door shut, the no-nonsense lawyer got straight to business.

"So, what we have here are two professionals, married COP – which was later converted to ANC – that have one minor child, citing irreconcilable differences. Is this correct?" Elizabeth asked. She settled into her seat and paged through the document handed to her by one of the paralegals.

"Uhm… yes," Runako responded self-consciously.

"When did you change your marital regime from COP to ANC?" Elizabeth continued brusquely. She made eye contact only at the end of her statements to demand a brief answer with those piercing eyes.

"Uhm… Last year May," Runako replied, wondering if it was important. "Why?"

The woman's habit of looking up to glare at Runako only when waiting for an answer was disorienting. It felt as if the pile of documents in front of her was the person, and the flesh-and-blood Runako sitting across the table was an inconvenient accessory.

Runako thought carefully and weighed her words. "Well, my husband is self-employed, or rather employed by the family business, and was starting to sign as guarantor for huge amounts of debt to help fund the business," Runako explained. "He wanted to protect our family and me from that kind of exposure, so he suggested we change, and I agreed."

Elizabeth gave her two scribes a 'HOW STUPID CAN YOU BE!' look before continuing with her questions. "In your email to me, you wrote that you suspect his affair started when?" Elizabeth said sardonically, waiting for Runako to put two and two together.

"When he started travelling to London more frequently, which was mid last… OH, MY GOD!" Runako deflated and buried her face in her hands. She breathed heavily, her mind spinning, and felt tears welling up. She fought to control them, but they kept coming.

"Is he currently supporting you financially?" Elizabeth continued, indifferent to the implications of the bombshell she had just dropped on her newest client.

"Yes, he gives me seven hundred and fifty dollars per month towards my rent as he asked me to move out of our home," Runako hiccupped through the tears but managed to avoid sobbing.

"Does he provide any other financial support? For you or your daughter?"

Runako hurriedly wiped her eyes and nose and swallowed.

"Yes. He pays for my daughter's nursery fees and medical aid. He also buys her clothes and toys and whatever else she needs when she's at his house."

"And still gives you seven hundred and fifty dollars over and above that?"

"Yes," confirmed Runako.

"Sounds like a good deal to me," said Elizabeth and turned to a new page.

"No, it's not!" Runako objected. "He's not maintaining the lifestyle I'm used to!"

"Maintaining the lifestyle you're used to?" drawled Elizabeth. "I'm sorry, what area of law is that?"

"Isn't that what divorce law says?" Runako huffed. "That's certainly what I remember learning in law school!"

"Law school," Elizabeth nodded solemnly, pursing her lips. "This is not law school, Runako." Elizabeth pinned Runako with a deadpan expression.

"You're in Zimbabwe, in the real world, where the law is dynamic." Elizabeth condescendingly belaboured the point before returning her attention to the documents.

"Meaning?" Runako whispered.

"You have a full-time job, a law degree, and are earning two and a half thousand US dollars per month as an Associate at Savoy Inc. Correct?"

"Correct. What does that have to do with my case, if I may ask?" Runako asked timidly. Everything she thought she knew seemed to be wrong.

Elizabeth explained that courts have very wide discretion in terms of whether or not to grant a maintenance payment, how long the maintenance payment must endure, and the amount that will be payable. In making this determination, courts consider the following:

- The parties' existing and prospective means of generating an income;
- The parties' respective earning capacities, financial needs and financial obligations;
- The age of the Plaintiff (the person filing the matter);
- The duration of the marriage;
- The Defendant's conduct in so far as it caused the breakdown of the marital relationship;
- The parties' standard of living; and
- Any other factor that may have a bearing on the case;

Thereafter, the court will make a decision on whether or not to grant spousal maintenance and the amount. There is no automatic entitlement to spousal maintenance upon dissolution of marriage.

"Well," Elizabeth continued, "given my explanation, it will be very difficult to prove to a court of law that you need to be maintained beyond the amount Kobe's giving you."

"Are you saying I'll be punished for having gone to school and built a career for myself?" Runako asked plaintively.

"No. I am saying it will be difficult to prove that you cannot afford to provide for yourself."

"And what about the fact that he cheated, does that count for NOTHING?" Runako asked, turning to Elizabeth's scribes to look for allies.

Elizabeth looked up and sighed theatrically. "I'm afraid not," she answered bluntly.

"I see. I heard you're one of the best divorce lawyers in the country and I came here expecting a settlement that will make sure I'm okay," Runako said, suddenly looking and feeling very despondent. "So then, what AM I entitled to?"

"You'll be entitled to what your ANC stipulates: half the net value of the growth of the joint estate since May last year," Elizabeth said. She spoke slowly and patronisingly as if tired of repeating herself to a child. She shook her head before continuing. "The party with the higher net worth will pay out the other party so that each walks away with an equal share of the growth."

"I know EXACTLY how ANC with Accrual works, Elizabeth!" Runako pointed out cheekily. "What I mean is that with all his businesses, properties and cars, he's GOT to be wealthier than me, right?"

"That's not a given," Elizabeth said curtly. "You're entitled to a half share of the NET GROWTH in value of your estate from May last year, not the VALUE of the assets in your estate. Don't forget we need to take into account the debt in the estate as well."

"Is ANYTHING given, Elizabeth?" Runako hissed. "I'm feeling very nervous because you're not giving me any comfort that I will be sorted!"

"Hey!" Elizabeth snapped. "I'd appreciate it if you didn't take that tone with me. My job is not to COMFORT you. My job is to give you the FACTS. The facts regarding the law, and how we will APPLY it to get you the best possible settlement.

"But I've GIVEN you the facts and all you've done is just dismiss everything I say," Runako argued, feeling her eyes fill up with angry tears again. "Use the facts to get me a good settlement!"

Elizabeth and her team remained impassive. It was clearly not their first time at the rodeo, and they'd seen this scene play out before. The seasoned lawyer sat in silence for a few seconds after Runako had concluded her rant, letting her client register the awkwardness she had created.

"Runako," Elizabeth began, her tone calm, and her voice cold. "You engaged this firm to provide you with professional services. I expect you to conduct yourself with the same level of decorum.

"Now, I think we have covered enough ground for today, and I strongly suggest that you pull yourself together before our next consultation because I will not tolerate such behaviour in my offices again. Caroline will see you out when you're ready to leave. Have a good day."

Runako fell back in her chair as Elizabeth and her paralegals left the boardroom. She knew her lawyer was tough as nails. But Elizabeth was supposed to be tough on Kobe, not her!

The hour of interrogation had been gruelling, and she felt more anxious about the divorce process than before the consultation. Runako concluded that she had clearly been misinformed by all the assumptions she'd made about divorce law over the years.

Since a huge divorce settlement was no longer guaranteed, her future seemed increasingly precarious, ESPECIALLY since she was trying to get divorced from a man that seemed to be doing everything in his power to keep her married to him.

Runako didn't have the luxury of wallowing in self-pity, as she had to head back to work.

Savoy Inc., Harare

Runako sat at her desk, staring at the phone situated at her fingertips. The process was simple: lift the receiver, key in a number, and state her case. But stating her case to someone she hadn't spoken to in three months wouldn't be easy. Especially when said person was her sister-in-law, Kate. Kate was the only person Runako could think of, that could help her secure an interview with Cartwright Bank's Harare office. Kate was Chief Compliance Officer at the London headquarters, and Cartwright Harare was currently recruiting for a Risk Officer. The estimated 20% jump in her net earnings from Associate to Risk Officer would definitely help Runako with her living and legal expenses, especially since her family was offering no help or support in her quest to end her marriage to their darling *mukwasha*[1]. Swallowing her pride, Runako said a little prayer and dialled Kate's number.

To her surprise, Kate was extremely supportive of the move and confirmed she would be happy to assist.

Perhaps she'd misjudged her sister-in-law's character for all these years. Or, maybe, Kate was only too happy to help Runako rely less on her brother's precious money.

Sure enough, by close of business the following day, the HR department called confirming that Cartwright had received her CV and would like to invite her for the first round of interviews.

Runako was still recovering from her good fortune when another lucky break came in the form of Chipo Sibanda, Runako's deskmate, who offered to cover for Runako anytime she needed to step out of the office for interviews or appointments with her lawyer.

Grateful for her unexpected support, Runako concluded that all things considered, the week had worked out positively.

Savoy Inc., Harare
February 2014

Runako slipped into the weekly team meeting fifteen minutes late to find her teammates in loud applause. Wellington, one of the Senior Partners, was standing at the front of the room and Runako didn't understand why Chipo was standing next to him. Runako's puzzlement was interrupted by Chipo clearing her throat.

"Thanks so much, everyone, for your warm reception. I promise to do my best as your newest director."

CRAP! Runako thought, realising she was now reporting to Chipo, who knew Runako was currently interviewing with Cartwright Bank.

This was a DISASTER for another reason. April was bonus season, and Runako was relying on the windfall to fund the cost of her divorce. There was no way Savoy Inc. would give Runako a big bonus if she was a known flight risk, and she was barely getting by on her monthly salary.

When the meeting concluded, Runako made a beeline for the door, but Chipo caught her just in time. She asked her to stay behind for five minutes for a quick word with her.

Just my luck! she thought, resigning herself to an unpleasant outcome.

"Runako…" Chipo said, flashing a warm smile.

"Chipo…" Runako smiled back, no less worried.

"I think you know what this is about, right?" she continued, but unexpectedly, her voice was soothing and non-confrontational.

"Yes. I now report to you, which makes things awkward for me as you know I am currently interviewing with another organisation," Runako responded, falling into a seat.

"Well," she said, also taking a seat, "maybe not so awkward. You know we don't usually do this, but I've spent the last three months sitting next to you, and I know you're one of our team's best associates.

"I also know that Cartwright will make you an offer any day now. We will match whatever Cartwright is offering and promote you to Senior Associate. I'd like you to take over my old position,"

"Seriously?" Runako exclaimed, caught off-guard. She leaned over the table and tented her arms, hands supporting her chin.

"Yes!" Chipo affirmed, leaning forward and mirroring Runako's posture.

"And… you have authorisation to do this?"

"If, by authorisation, you mean do the rest of the partners know? The answer is yes, they do."

Runako fell back in her chair and clasped her hands behind her head. Chipo noticed Runako's distress at her betrayal and immediately explained her actions to put her at ease.

"Forgive me, but I had to mention it the minute my appointment was confirmed. I told them I'd take leadership of the team on the condition I wouldn't lose one of its star players."

Reassured by the apology and stunned by the compliment, Runako sat forward to lean on her forearms, at a loss for words. She absently tapped her fingers on the table.

"So, is that a yes?" Chipo said gently, reaching over the table to take Runako's hands into her own.

"Yes…" Runako said, but had to purse her lips to keep from crying. "Chipo, you don't know how much this means to me."

"Runako, it's not me who secured you the promotion. It's your history with the firm. It was a unanimous decision!" she confided, then grinned at her. "Your performance and dedication over the years haven't gone unnoticed. And we'll support you through this trying time in your life. You've earned it!"

Runako went back to her desk and immediately phoned Kate to advise that she was accepting a counteroffer from Savoy Inc. and would be notifying Cartwright Bank of same.

Runako's place, Borrowdale Brooke

After doing a transfer for her rent that evening, Runako settled down to draw up her new budget. Kobe was late with the interim maintenance, AGAIN, and receiving a Final Letter of Demand from her landlord was the wake-up call Runako needed to start taking her finances seriously.

She regretted having spent so much on furnishing her new place. She had also embarked on an emotional shopping spree to indulge Zina's every whim as her constant crying and screaming to go to Daddy's house was heart-breaking.

She wanted, as far as possible, to give her everything she had at her father's house, but he had an unfair advantage. A MUCH bigger paycheque.

Financially, Runako's spending was unwise but emotionally, she would do whatever it took to keep her baby happy and herself sane. Also, thanks to her new position, she'd be netting US$3,000 a month, US$500 more than she was netting before. She would now be able to live significantly more comfortably and afford her legal fees going forward.

Looking at the numbers, it was clear that the counteroffer had come just in time. She was grateful that her plan had worked out better than anticipated. God was still in control.

Saturday came and went, and as suspected, there was no deposit from Kobe. Sunday came and went and still nothing. The following morning, Runako decided to send Kobe another follow-up email, this time CC'ing her attorney.

*From: **Runako Mensah** Runako.Mensah@gmail.com*
*To: **Kobe Mensah** mensahk@gmail.com*
*CC: **Elizabeth Ncube** elizabeth.ncube@ndorolaw.co.zw*
Date: Monday, 03 March 2014, 13:44
*Subject: **Payment***

Dear Kobe,
Please advise the status of monthly interim maintenance.
Thanks,
Runako

*From: **Kobe Mensah** mensahk@gmail.com*
*To: **Runako Mensah** Runako.Mensah@gmail.com*
*CC: **Elizabeth Ncube** elizabeth.ncube@ndorolaw.co.zw*
*CC: **Elroy Kachingwe** ElroyKachingwe@kachingweinc.co.zw*
Date: Monday, 03 March 2014, 17:36

In a board meeting. Will revert tomorrow.
Sent from my iPhone

Runako had a knot in her stomach when she woke up on Tuesday morning. Something was off, and it had been a while since she'd felt this way.

She checked her phone to see if she'd received an email from Kobe, but still nothing. She checked her bank account, also nothing. She couldn't believe this had become her life!

She only had enough fuel to get to work and no way of getting home without a refill. Trying to borrow money from her friends would be met with judgement since they would ask how a hotshot lawyer could be too broke for fuel to get to and from work. Kobe had to deposit the money that day. He just HAD to!

Runako tapped her foot, the only sign of impatience as she quietly worked through her case file. It was already lunchtime and still no word from Kobe. She was anxious, and it showed.

A phone notification sounded. It was Kobe's long-overdue email response. She glanced and it and wondered why a simple response would be so long.

Well, this should be interesting, she thought to herself and clicked on the email to open it.

> *From: **Kobe Mensah** mensahk@gmail.com*
> *To: **Runako Mensah** Runako.Mensah@gmail.com*
> *CC: **Elizabeth Ncube** elizabeth.ncube@ndorolaw.co.zw*
> *CC: **Elroy Kachingwe** em@kachingweinc.co.zw*
> *Date: Tuesday, 04 March 2014, 13:23*
> *Dear Runako,*
>
> *Your email above refers. The interim maintenance amount of US$750 per month I was transferring to you was based on your earnings of US$2,500 per month. You have since secured a promotion where I believe you will be netting US$500 more per month. As such, I have adjusted the interim maintenance amount accordingly, and transferred US$250, the amount I will be sending you going forward. Effective immediately.*
>
> *Kindly note that Mensah Global is on a group-wide restructure and my earnings have been cut in half. I am happy to provide any supporting evidence you require.*
>
> *KM*

Runako went through the email again, slowly. Did Kobe really mean that instead of the US$750 she was expecting, he would deposit only US$250?

She quickly logged on to her banking app, and there it was, a deposit of US$250 with reference KOBE MENSAH.

Her chest went tight, her ears began to ring, and tears started welling up in her eyes. She grabbed her file and ran to the bathroom. She shut herself in the cubicle and tried to understand his calculations.

With one email, Kobe had taken her back to square one and eliminated the benefit of her two-month recruitment mission to improve her financial position.

She couldn't earn more from within Savoy Inc., since she had just received a promotion. She couldn't earn more from outside Savoy Inc. as she was on a market-related salary. She couldn't legally compel Kobe to contribute more because he was now on lower earnings and the divorce hadn't been finalised.

She was stuck, and she wondered if this was Kobe's intention. How did he find out about her new earnings? How would she finalise her divorce when she didn't have the money for legal fees?

Runako phoned her attorney to see if there was anything they could do. Elizabeth advised that, sadly, their case was weak as Kobe was now earning less, and Runako was earning more.

There was also no fundamental flaw in his calculations. In addition, the numerous shopping sprees on her bank statement and high-fashion pictures Runako was continuing to post on social media wouldn't be a good look for a woman claiming poverty in front of a judge.

On the contrary, Runako risked getting an order for even less than what Kobe was contributing, and the lawyer suggested Runako re-balance her finances and work with what she had.

Runako resigned herself to the downgrade her life would take post-divorce. It felt like Kobe was always one step ahead, like there was some 'Short Course in Divorcing Smart' he had taken.

It had been three emotionally and physically draining months, and she was now ready to put the divorce behind her and start rebuilding her life. Runako asked Elizabeth to draw up a settlement offer and close this chapter once and for all. She was ready to put it all behind her.

Savoy Inc., Harare
May 2014

A crowd susurrated in the distance as Runako lay in the dark, their voices growing louder and louder with every passing moment. Darkness morphed into a mishmash of colours as she opened her eyes and blurry faces coalesced as she slowly regained consciousness.

"Give her some air!" screamed a familiar stranger.

"Bring her some water," shouted another voice.

"Are you okay?" clamoured a third.

"What's happening?" Runako whispered to the familiar stranger, taken aback by all the distraught faces huddled above her.

"You fainted, dear," Chipo replied softly, gently helping Runako into a sitting position. "But don't worry, you're fine now, and the nurse is on her way."

"Fainted?" Runako asked puzzled, holding her head.

"Yes. You were on the phone and then…"

"Oh, my God!" Runako exclaimed, holding her hand over her mouth. Her chest went tight, she couldn't breathe. And she wanted to vomit. The memory of the phone call with Elizabeth had come flooding back, and the conversation was enough to make her sick.

"Okay, give her space, guys. And back to your desks please!" Wellington barked, waving the crowd of attorneys away. "Chipo, just walk her to the nurse. I don't want any more people seeing her like this."

Chipo escorted Runako to the staff wellness centre. The Savoy Inc. corridors were full of points and whispers as Chipo, and her dishevelled colleague went by.

When they arrived, the nurse apologised profusely for having been unable to leave her station. She had just finished up with another emergency case as Runako wasn't the first employee to suffer a breakdown in the office that day.

Chipo helped Runako onto the stretcher bed, and the nurse proceeded to take her vitals. Runako was dehydrated and slightly anaemic - indications that she hadn't been eating, and/or sleeping well. The nurse immediately put Runako on a saline drip and asked to be excused as she had another patient to attend to.

"Is everything okay, Ru?" Chipo asked with concern. She climbed onto the stretcher bed and sat next to Runako. Runako stared blankly ahead, and a lone tear slowly rolled down her cheek.

"He's coming for my baby..." Runako whispered, without shifting her gaze.

"What do you mean, coming for your baby? Aren't you already sharing custody?" Chipo asked, taking Runako's free hand into her own. Runako turned to Chipo and took a deep breath.

"He wants full custody." Runako started sobbing, and Chipo let her cry into her chest. She let Runako stay there until she had calmed down again.

"Don't worry, Ru," Chipo comforted. "He's just trying to scare you. No court will separate a mother from her child."

"Well, actually the courts can," Runako sniffled. She sat up before continuing. "I don't have an advantage over Kobe just because I'm Zina's mother," Runako blew her nose and took a deep breath. "Kobe has been phoning her on Mai Precious' phone when I'm at work late, and recording all the times Zina says she wants to come to him."

Runako paused again and took another deep breath. "Chipo, I need to work overtime, so I can bill more and provide for myself and my child. How will I do that when I can't focus at work because I'm always worried about LOSING MY BABY?"

"Oh, Ru..." Chipo commiserated, shaking her head.

"I can't compete with him, Chipo. I can't compete with Kobe."

"You're NOT competing with him, babe," Chipo tried to reassure her.

"Yes, I am. Yes, I am, Chipo!" Runako snapped. "It's me against his money. And his family. And his mansion. His fancy cars. Toys. Trips to Disneyland. Do you know he's taking Zina to Disneyland Paris this June, Chipo?" Runako cried. "I can't give Zina any of that! My own family won't even support me because they're too worried my father and brothers will lose their jobs. He's winning…"

"Runako… don't SAY that!" Chipo urged, hopping off the bed and turning to face Runako. "He's NOT WINNING, because it's not a competition. YOU are the mother of that child, you hear me? You!"

Chipo touched her index finger to Runako's chest as she made her points. "And because YOU'RE her mother, you will not go down without a fight!

"You will fight to protect her from a man who could be using this as a tactic to punish you for leaving him. You will fight to give her the best possible childhood, as you have been doing already! And you will fight because every child DESERVES to have their mother in their life!"

A faint smile appeared on Runako's face as she felt life returning to her body. Chipo was right. She would fight, with everything she had, to retain shared custody of her daughter.

"You're right, Chipo!" Runako nodded grimly. "I will fight."

"Good! VERY good!" Chipo smiled, squeezing Runako's hands. "I need to get back to my desk, and you need to take the rest of the day off. But before I go, I want to tell you something my *mbuya*[2] always told me when my brothers made me cry. She'd say 'Chipo when a coward sees a man he can beat, he becomes hungry for a fight!' Don't let Kobe bully you, Runako. Show him he picked the wrong fight!"

Runako's place, Borrowdale Brooke

It was well after 9 am when Runako opened her eyes the following morning. The best sleep she'd had in months – if not years! The sleeping tablets prescribed by the nurse had worked like a charm.

Chipo had graciously given her two duvet days, and Runako had every intention of spending this second one in bed.

Runako reached for her phone, and her mood soured almost instantly. Three missed calls from Elizabeth Ncube. She'd already ignored her lawyers' calls yesterday and knew she couldn't avoid the conversation any longer. But first, coffee.

"Ndoro and Associates, you're speaking to Caroline," said a lilting voice.

"Hello, Caroline, Elizabeth, please," Runako replied, dropping her dirty teaspoon into the sink.

"Certainly. May I ask who's calling?" Caroline responded cheerfully.

"Runako Mensah," Runako replied curtly, before taking a sip of her coffee.

"Runako! Oh! Hi! Elizabeth has been trying to reach you since yesterday. Are you okay?"

"Uhm… yes. Thanks for asking," Runako replied warily. "Is Elizabeth available now? I can chat now."

"I'm afraid she's in a consultation," Caroline said. "She did, however, leave a message asking that you set up an appointment to see her urgently, as this matter is time-sensitive."

"I see…" Runako sighed. She took another sip of her coffee. "I'll clear my schedule. Please put me down for the next available slot."

"Certainly! Let me pull up your file so I can confirm your details. One moment, please." Runako walked over to the couch and picked up the TV remote.

"Uh, oh!" Caroline exclaimed, still paradoxically cheery.

"What?" Runako asked automatically.

"Uhm… I'm afraid your account has been suspended because it is more than US$3 000 in arrears," Caroline replied delicately.

"I know that!" Runako spat. "But I can't settle my account if you guys don't get me divorced, can I?"

"I'm sorry, but you'll need to settle your arrears before I can schedule any appointments for you and Elizabeth," Caroline insisted firmly.

"Caroline, I'm in no position to settle anything because my husband pays me what he wants, when he wants! And the only way to compel him to give me my money on time is through a divorce order!" Runako's voice was rising. "But I can't get divorced without first going through this damn custody battle, and I won't get through this custody battle if you don't give me an appointment with Elizabeth!" Runako was now screaming into the phone and pacing up and down the living room.

"Runako, I understand your predicament –"

"No, you don't!" Runako barked. "He's taken EVERYTHING from me, and now you're letting him take my child too?"

"Runako –" Caroline tried unsuccessfully to interject.

"Caroline, you're going to stand by and let him take my baby? Is that what you're saying?" Runako hissed through tears. "Are you going to stand by and let him rip out my womb too?!" The phone fell silent, and Runako sagged to the floor.

"Ms Mensah," Caroline said calmly, "our hands are tied. Either you settle your arrears or find yourself another lawyer. Quickly!" she reiterated. "Alternatively, you can contact legal aid to see if there's a lawyer willing to handle your case pro bono. But I must point out that it's highly unlikely since you exceed the maximum monthly earnings for pro bono assistance."

Runako lay on her back, weighed down by Caroline's words. She stared blankly at the ceiling.

"I guess there's nothing further to discuss then, Caroline. He's done it – Kobe has won…"

10

CASAS IN THE SKY

"If you close your eyes to facts, you will learn through accidents"

— AFRICAN PROVERB

João and Lolo's holiday home, Bishopscourt, Cape Town
December 2014

*T*he Constantia Nek mountainside cast an imposing silhouette against the fiery Cape sunset. On its slopes, an Uber pulled up on one of South Africa's priciest roads and came to a stop in front of a modest-looking home. The Upper Sidmouth Avenue property had a deceiving street view, preferring instead to reserve its grandeur for its expansive backyard.

Lolo helped Kael and Noel out of the car as the Uber driver unloaded her luggage. It had been only twelve months since she and João got married, but she was already spending Christmas and New Year's Eve without him.

João and Lolo had planned to host friends and family for Christmas in their Johannesburg home and New Year's Eve at their Cape Town home when João's elderly grandfather suddenly fell ill. João rushed to Azalia while Lolo proceeded with their festive season plans, so as not to inconvenience their guests.

Nandi and Koketso would be arriving from Johannesburg the following day, giving Lolo a welcome window to be almost alone for the first time in a week.

Lolo placed the last of the bags in the twins' bedroom and took a moment to appreciate the splendour of her holiday home.

The modern manor home boasted six en suite bedrooms, three reception areas, a gymnasium, a sauna and a pool room. Best of all, it had a fully stocked wine cellar!

Alcohol, in all its forms, was taboo around her grandmother and drinking warm sauvignon blanc from a teacup, as Koko did, took away from the experience.

Although Lolo wouldn't be able to indulge that evening fully since she was alone with the kids, a glass or two wouldn't hurt. With one more after she'd put the kids to bed.

Kael and Noel were on the floor, happily rummaging through the giant bowl of cheese puffs Lolo had put out for them, while Lolo poured herself a glass of the 2008 Epicurean Bordeaux. The tranquillity brought on by the wine's silky notes was disturbed by a WhatsApp notification. It was a message from Neo, Uncle Roland's daughter. *That's strange,* Lolo thought to herself. Neo rarely messaged her. Perhaps she had changed her mind about spending New Year's Even in Cape Town and wanted to make arrangements for accommodation.

(17:21) Neo Cuz: Hey boo. How r u?

(17:23) Lolo: Hey hun! I'm good and you? Merry Christmas

(17:24) Neo Cuz: Lol! Ur only like 2 days late. Where are you?

(17:24) Lolo: I'm in Cape Town already. You?

(17:26) Neo Cuz: Oh ok! I just saw João & was wondering where u r

(17:26) Lolo: João? My João? Saw him where cause he's in Azalia?

(17:28) Neo Cuz: Nope. He's very much in Johannesburg. At my friend's braai in Bryanston to be exact.

(17:28) Lolo: Can't be! The kids Skype'd him this morning and he said he's in Azalia. Are you sure it wasn't someone else?

(17:29) Neo Cuz: It was João babe, he even greeted me!

(17:30) Lolo: IMPOSSIBLE! Who's he with?

(17:35) Neo Cuz: Uhm… he's with another woman.

(17:36) Lolo: Another woman? Probably one of our friends. What does she look like?

(17:36) Neo Cuz: Cuz… this is not just a friend. They're really cozy.

(17:37) Lolo: Send me a picture

(17:37) Neo Cuz: What?

(17:38) Lolo: Yes! Just send a picture. I'll know who he's with if you send me a picture.

(17:41) Neo Cuz: Ok hold on…

Lolo paced up and down the living room. Waiting for the picture. She took a sip of wine to calm her nerves. It had turned bitter.

Kael lay on the floor colouring in a picture, unaware of the storm threatening his future.

Lolo looked at her phone again – nothing.

Noel jumped off the couch, laughing. His favourite TV show had just come on – Paw Patrol!

Lolo looked at her phone again. What was taking so long? Her heart started beating so loudly in her chest that she was sure she could hear it. She could feel it. Painful. It was trying to burst out of her ribcage.

She looked at her phone again – still nothing. Only three minutes had passed since Neo agreed to take the picture. Why did it feel like hours?

Could it be? Was it possible? Could João really be in town with another woman? It was impossible, and now all she needed was for Neo to send the damn picture so she could figure out which of their friends João was at the braai with.

Lolo jumped when her phone went off again as a cold shiver shot from the base of Lolo's spine to the crown of her head. It was the message she'd been waiting for. Delivered in an envelope of relief and anxiety. She sat in place, paralysed by fear of what may be, and haunted by the hope of what may not. The latter grew stronger, and she turned the phone around. Ready to face the truth.

It was João alright, but Lolo couldn't make out the woman in the image. She was curvy with long, natural hair. Her features were indistinct, and any one of twenty mutual friends matched her profile.

Puzzled, Lolo decided she was being silly. João couldn't be having an affair only a year into their marriage.

(17:58) Lolo: Thanks babe. It's harmless. I know who that is. Have a good night! Mwah xx

(17:59) Neo Cuz: Ok cuz. Glad it's nothing. C ya soon xxx

The two cousins were lying to each other, and they both knew it. However, since they were both powerless at this point, it was better to find comfort in a lie than to face the discomfort of the truth. Lolo stared at the picture all night, wondering if it were possible. Was it possible?

Paranga Restaurant, Camps Bay

The sun was mockingly bright, and the sky a cruel, cloudless blue as Lolo carefully steered her Range Rover Autobiography down Kloof Nek Road. She wondered, with each turn, whether João was indeed having an affair.

Camps Bay had been their favourite hangout spot since university and was, therefore, THE worst possible place for Lolo to meet her mom and sister for lunch as it held many fond memories for her.

But meeting for a lazy lunch at Paranga was a longstanding December ritual, and it would be difficult to explain why Lolo was suffering a sudden change of heart. Especially since it was the only day her mom's long-lost friend, Aunty Nonceba could see them before she left for Mauritius. Aunty Nonceba had already graciously fetched Nandi and Koketso from the airport and brought them to lunch. Lolo couldn't possibly ditch them now.

"*Bathong*[1], guys! You're already on bottle number two, and it's not even one o'clock yet?" Lolo exclaimed. She leaned over to give her mom and Aunt Nonceba a hug while Koketso gushed over Kael and Noel.

263

"Hayi, man, Lolo, *keDezemba*[2]," Nandi rationalised. "And they're having a special on Veuve, so I thought, why not?"

"Just as long as you know I'm on a tight budget this December. My bank balance is more suited for *fampagne*[3] than the real thing," Lolo laughingly warned them before giving her sister a hug.

"That makes two of us, Lols!" Koketso chuckled.

"Don't worry. It's my treat," Aunt Nonceba smiled. "Anyway, how is *umkhwenyana*[4]?"

"He's okay, I think," Lolo sighed. Nandi and Koketso turned to each other with a puzzled look and Lolo debated whether or not she should share Neo's message. She didn't want to raise the alarm, but was also desperate for a third and fourth opinion on the matter. She decided to raise it casually and judge their reaction.

"You know, the funniest thing happened yesterday," Lolo said matter-of-factly, pouring herself a glass of champagne. "You remember Neo, right? Uncle Roland's daughter?"

"The one that used to dress funny?" Nandi asked.

"She still does," Koketso added cheekily.

"Yeah! Her!" Lolo confirmed. "Anyway, she sent me a message last night saying she saw João. Last night. In Joburg."

"In Joburg? How when he's in Azalia?" Koketso exclaimed.

"Yeah… And he was at a braai. With another woman," Lolo admitted fatalistically. She helped Noel with his strawberry milkshake, a distraction to keep from making eye contact with her mom and sister.

The table fell silent and sensing the tension, Aunt Nonceba excused herself to make a phone call. Lolo lifted her eyes just in time to catch her mom and sister exchanging concerned looks. The same cold shiver from the day before ran up and down her spine. This was not the reaction she was hoping for.

"Guys," Lolo chuckled uncomfortably, "what's going on?"

"He's now coming to South Africa with her?" Nandi asked. She was looking down at her hands, meticulously folding her napkin as an excuse for not making eye contact.

"Coming to South Africa with WHO?" Lolo asked breathlessly. A lump had suddenly grown in her throat.

"HER! His girlfriend, obviously. Isn't that who you're talking about?" Koketso replied.

The chitter-chatter of the restaurant turned into a faint buzz and then disappeared altogether as Lolo's world fell silent. Everything went into slow motion, and she willed herself to face her mother. Nandi's face was blank. With great effort, she turned her now heavy head towards her sister. Koketso looked back at her without blinking. She seemed surprised by Lolo's reaction.

Kael slowly stirred his vanilla milkshake with a straw. Noel fought with a piece of salmon sashimi that kept falling off the nigiri rice. The cars on the promenade inched past. People in twos and threes slowly made their way past each other in opposite directions. *His girlfriend…* The words jolted Lolo back to reality, and a fistful of air punched her in the lungs. She started shaking uncontrollably.

"His WHAT?" Lolo shouted. Tears ran down her face. "You said his what?"

"Koketso, quick, take your sister to the bathroom," Nandi ordered. Koketso escorted a now wailing Lolo to the bathrooms while Nandi waived down Nonceba and asked her to look after the boys. She then followed hurriedly after her daughters.

"Tshenolo, my baby, we thought you knew. Everybody knew," Nandi said soothingly. She rubbed Lolo's back to console her. Koketso rolled more toilet paper off the holder and kept it in her hands.

"EVERYBODY knew what?" Lolo sniffled. "What are you guys talking about?"

"Oh, crap…" Koketso winced.

"So… You didn't know that João has been seeing another woman in Azalia? We thought that's why you're spending December apart," Nandi said gently.

"No…" Lolo moaned. She threw her head into her hands and cried great, wracking sobs. Her throat ached, and her chest heaved so that she gasped for painful breaths between broken whimpers.

"Oh, my baby! I'm so sorry…" Nandi enveloped Lolo in an embrace. Koketso rubbed Lolo's back, and handed her more toilet paper to wipe her tears.

"Me too, Lols," Koketso said, almost in tears herself. "I honestly thought you knew! Otherwise, I would have NEVER just blurted it out like that!"

Lolo composed herself. Her breathing steadied enough for her to construct a sentence.

"How long have you guys known?" she whispered.

"It's been a few months now," Nandi said regretfully.

"That long?' Lolo asked, as if repeated confirmations would make it hurt any less.

"Pretty much. My friend Irene who's based in Azalia kept seeing him with the same woman," Nandi confessed. "She told me about it, but knowing your history with João, I decided to stay out of it."

"The same person?" Lolo breathed, starting to gasp again.

"Yes. Always the same person. Curvy. Fair-skinned with long natural hair," Nandi replied.

"Wait… I have a picture." Lolo paused and gathered some strength. "Koko, get my phone from the table. I have a picture. I want to know if it's the girl in the picture."

Koketso returned a few moments later. Lolo unlocked her phone and pulled up the picture. She turned the phone over to Nandi and Koketso.

The way they looked at each other was all the confirmation Lolo needed.

João and Lolo's holiday home, Bishopscourt

The kids were finally asleep. Nandi and Koketso had retired for the night, and Lolo was finally alone.

She had waited all day to be alone. There was nowhere to hide. She had to face the truth.

Everyone knew... EVERYONE. KNEW. Everyone but me....

How could João humiliate me like this? After everything, we have been through?

While I was busy playing 'Happy Family' for Facebook and Instagram, they were laughing at me. Is that why he never liked or commented on my posts? Why he never posted ME, only sports and the kids?

Did he already know? Was his heart already somewhere else? While I was fighting to build our marriage, had he already checked out? While I was buying lingerie and trying to spice up our sex life, did he decline my advances because he had already checked out? While I was trying new recipes to make his favourite traditional meals, were none of them good enough for him because he had already checked out? While I was buying new outfits and trying new hairstyles, is the reason I was never beautiful enough for him because he had already checked out?

Did I nearly drive myself insane trying to keep a man that had already checked out...

It all suddenly made sense. The signs had all been there. Coming home late from meetings in the three weeks he was in Joburg.

Corporate events that were suddenly 'No partners allowed.' A phone that was constantly off from a flat battery, when he had a car charger.

The growing number of hours spent downstairs by himself. Reading. Or watching sports. Or catching up on work. Or just not yet ready to go to bed.

More and more work meetings on Saturdays. Even Sundays. More and more missed flights that extended his stay in Azalia by a day here or a night there.

The signs had all been there. They'd whispered. Then nudged. Then screamed. Then shouted. She hadn't heard them. Or maybe she'd chosen not to listen.

Now her world had been pulled out from beneath her feet, her whole life seemingly a lie. Her whole universe nothing but make-believe.

She lay in bed, staring at the ceiling.

Kael and Noel snored away, unaware that their world was changing as they slept. She'd done the same in her tumultuous relationship and marriage with João.

Today she woke up. And found that the world she built was all in her head.

It was 11 pm, and she had been crying for two solid hours, with no sign of slowing down. She had so many questions for João. So much that she wanted to ask him. But she figured it was too late.

What explanation could he give that would make sense? All he deserved was a text letting him know she knew about the affair.

A curt text. Cold. Free of emotion. She was shattered, but she would deny him the pleasure of seeing that. Ever!

> Lolo: I know about your girlfriend. I think we can both agree
> getting married was a mistake.

João read the message and responded almost immediately.

My love: Ok.

Ok? Ok? Two kids and a marriage with someone and it all ends with an 'Ok'? All of a sudden, the tears gushed out uncontrollably. Her body started shaking painfully. A cloud of confusion came over her as if she had been thrust deep into the ocean. Her whole body felt like jelly, and her legs collapsed under her as she tried to climb out of bed and head to the kitchen.

She couldn't stand, but she had to get away from the children. She started crawling on the floor. Crawling aimlessly. She was trying to get away. From what exactly, she didn't know. She felt like a madwoman and was glad no one else was around to witness her in this state.

She was trying to get away from herself.

She crawled to the kitchen and pulled herself up onto a bar stool, and rested her head on the kitchen counter, cradled on her folded arms.

Her head was spinning. She didn't know whether she was hungry or whether she was full. She didn't know whether she was nauseous or just tipsy. She was trying to scream, but no sound was coming out. She wanted to sprint a marathon, but her legs had turned to lead. She was gasping for air but couldn't breathe. She felt her head was going to explode. She wanted to make it stop.

Please, someone, make it stop.

But it didn't stop. She cried. She paced. She sat down. Stood up. The clock struck midnight. She sobbed.

1 am. She was now just panting.

2 am. She sat rocking silently on the couch. Tears still flowing.

3 am. Her body was no longer her own. She was a spectator to this mass of flesh still crying on the floor.

4 am. The skin under her nose and around her eyes had started peeling from the constant wiping.

5 am. The lounge glowed a warm orange, and she heard the birds chirping. She slowly lowered her head to look down at her chest and saw a growing dark patch. The tears were still flowing. By themselves.

6 am. Nandi's alarm went off in the distance. Lolo quickly snuck into her bedroom, she didn't want her mother seeing her in this state. She didn't want anyone's pity, she just wanted a chance to come to terms with the truth.

The next two days were a blur. The rest of her family and friends had arrived, and Nandi volunteered to look after all the kids under eighteen, while the rest of the family crew went on their annual pilgrimage to one of the biggest events on Cape Town's social calendar for summer – the party at Asoka Bar and Lounge on the last Tuesday of the year.

It was the first time since finding out about João's affair that Lolo mustered the willpower to dress up and don some makeup. She was sure she had shed more tears in the last three days than her whole life combined. She decided that tonight she would let loose and have fun.

She took her time in front of the mirror, determined to use the outing as an opportunity to remind herself, and the world, just who she was!

She laid out her tools. Bobbi Brown face base. NARS liquid foundation in Macao. MAC Studio Fix contour palette in medium. MAC blush in Raizin. Anastasia Beverly Hills Glow Kit. MAC eye pencil in Engraved. Eylure Lashes No 143. Two pairs, for good measure. MAC lip pencil in Cork. MAC lipstick in Velvet Teddy. And to round it all off, a generous spritz of her signature fragrance, French perfumer Mathilde Laurent's creation – Cartier Baiser Volé.

Who the hell does João think he is, anyway? Just because I loved him like he was the only man in my life doesn't mean he was the only man that wanted me. Many men would kill to wife me. There are plenty of men that said so over the years. Some still say so, even now!

Since I'm single again for the first time in five years, I'm going to go out and have fun. For the first time in a long time, I can accept drinks from anyone. I can dance with anyone. I can kiss anyone. I can fuck anyone.

Lolo, you're back! Let's go show the world how badly João messed up by losing you.

And for what? A chick that disrespects herself enough to be a mistress?

What a joke!

Asoka Restaurant, Bar & Lounge, Kloof Street

Heads turned as Lolo worked her way through the crowd in a mini bodycon dress. The posse of ten siblings and cousins slipped into the private room where four bottles of Grey Goose Vodka and four jugs of cranberry juice were already waiting for them.

Lolo decided to scout the crowd by making a pretend trip to the bathroom before settling in. Nick Holder's *Summer Daze* had the crowd on their feet. Dancing and singing along to the house classic, she squeezed her way through the packed dance floor and past the olive tree in the centre courtyard.

She was about to turn into the ladies' bathrooms when she felt a tap on her shoulder.

"Lolo!" a voice said. It was unmistakable. Even before turning around, she already knew whose face she would see.

"Mamba!" Lolo exclaimed. She gave him what she thought would be an innocent hug. He returned it by pulling her close to him by cupping her bottom.

"Uhm... what was that for?" she asked with a flirtatious smile.

"Well… word on the street is that you're single now, so I wanted to be first in line," Mamba said with a half-smile.

Lolo had known Lumumba 'Mamba' Zulu since her early teens. She'd first met him at one of the many pool parties he hosted at his home in Northcliff. But by the time her braces were off, her pimples cleared up, and her breasts fully developed, he'd left to finish school in the US.

It didn't help that he was friends with Junior. Lolo had often bumped into Mamba whenever Junior and Qhayiya hosted a gathering at their place.

She'd always found him incredibly hot, and tonight was no different. He stood at 1.9 metres tall, his physique broad and muscular thanks to his college rugby days. His head was kept clean-shaven, and he sported a thick, lush beard.

And when he smiled, he smiled with his eyes that closed up into a squint and cheeks that reached for his temples. When he laughed, it sounded like a congress of dondo drummers in the depths of his belly. Mamba's words replayed in Lolo's mind and jolted her back to reality.

"What did you just say?" Lolo grimaced, suddenly pulling away from his embrace.

"Yeah… A friend of mine bumped into your ex and his new woman at a party in Bryanston last night. He told us you guys are divorced. Big up to the two of you for handling it so well," Mamba said, leaning in even closer. Lolo pushed him away angrily.

"That's because we're NOT divorced. I haven't even moved out of our home, for goodness' sake!" she snarled.

"Oh, wow! I didn't realise. I'm sorry to hear that. Are you okay though?" he asked, putting his arm around her shoulder. It felt sincere.

"Not really…" she admitted, and realised with horror that she was starting to cry again. She dropped her forehead to his shoulder and started sobbing.

"Hey. Don't cry," he said gently. "Come. Let's get some fresh air."

Mamba took Lolo by the arm and led her to a quiet section on the patio. When they were seated, he called a waiter and ordered her a double Glenfiddich on the rocks. One of her cousins came out to the patio for a smoke, and Lolo told him she'd re-join the crew later. An hour went by, and Mamba sat at her side, listening intently to every gory detail of her failed marriage.

"You guys always looked so happy, though," Mamba remarked, bemused. "I mean, everyone knew you guys were on-and-off for a while, but you seemed to get each other. Like you would eventually settle down with each other." Mamba moved to the edge of his seat and played with his whisky glass.

"I thought so too, Mamba," Lolo concurred. "João is the only man I've ever seen myself spending the rest of my life with. And I'll admit, we put each other through a lot of shit before we got married, but I thought things would be different once we settled down. I really love him, Mamba!"

"Come here." Mamba wrapped his arms around Lolo and held her tight. They stayed like that for a little while. Lolo lifted her head and looked straight into his eyes. She hoped he would see her soul screaming, 'Save me!'

Mamba lowered his lips onto hers and gave her a long, deep, passionate kiss. She let out a low moan and threw her head back. The pulsating in her core intensified as he kissed her neck. She certainly hadn't been kissed like this in what felt like decades.

Mamba placed his hand behind her neck and pulled her in, kissing her even deeper. Intensely. Passionately. His lips tasted sweet. It was the cognac. The taste pulling her in deeper. He groaned and took another deep breath before gently biting on her ear. Then running this tongue down the side of her neck. Across her clavicle. And back to her lips.

"Make love to me, Mamba," she moaned. Her thoughts escaped without due regard to the consequences they would bring.

Mamba smiled. "Not yet… You're not ready."

"I am," Lolo begged. "Make love to me, like REALLY make love to me. Now. And tomorrow. And the day after. And forever!"

"Woah, Lolo!" Mamba said sternly. He peeled her arms off his neck and sat back in his seat. "Uhm… I think you're a little drunk and I need to take you back to your cousins. Where are they sitting?"

"Fuck you, Mamba! I'm not drunk!" Lolo spat. She stormed off and ran for the bathrooms. She was embarrassed. No, offended! She felt rejected by her husband, and now by Mamba, too.

The queue of women standing in line gave way to the obviously distressed woman who barged in, sobbing. Lolo closed the cubicle door behind her and broke down. She looked at herself in the mirror and cried.

Mamba was wrong. She wasn't drunk. What she was, was hurt. And desperate. Desperate for something, anything that would numb the pain coursing through her body.

Even with all the makeup and sculpted dress that turned heads, she felt ugly. She felt unwanted. She felt rejected.

Every man at Asoka that night could have made a move on her, and she would still have felt ugly because the one man whose approval she yearned for had given it to someone else.

The one man she wanted to want her, wanted someone else.

The one man that could heal her from this pain was the same man who had caused it.

The pain she was feeling at that moment was the same pain she felt when her father chose another woman over her, her mom and her sister.

First, her father. Then João. And now, Mamba.

She looked at herself in the mirror and wondered if Mamba was right. Maybe she wasn't ready to make love to someone else. What she was sure of, though, was that she wanted to be wanted. NEEDED to be wanted.

Is that so bad…?

Cavendish Square, Claremont

The Woolworths cashier hurriedly rang up Lolo's sheer black stockings and black viscose shawl. It was already after closing time, and she needed to cash up for the day.

Lolo handed over her credit card without saying a word. She had said very little in the past few days.

Her phone went off, a WhatsApp notification. It was a message from Runako asking if she was free to chat.

Lolo hoped Runako hadn't found out about the affair as she was also in Johannesburg for New Year's Eve. She had intentionally kept the affair from the Belters, having no desire to go through the intense scrutiny that would follow the announcement.

The girls would want to know who and how, when and where. All details that would pick at the festering wound. Lolo herself had barely come to terms with this new revelation and was not ready to discuss it with her friends. It felt as though announcing it to them would make it official, and right now, it still felt surreal.

Lolo had actually never SEEN João with another woman since they started their long-term tumultuous relationship. As a result, her mind was unable to comprehend his BEING with another woman.

In fact, she was still silently hoping it was all a big misunderstanding. Hoping that João would call her asking to work things out, and to explain that the mystery woman was nothing more than one of their university mates. The hope was dwindling, but it was still there. She messaged Runako back, and her phone rang almost immediately.

"Hey, hun! What's going on? Is everything okay?" Lolo greeted.

"Babe, I should be asking YOU that," Runako replied severely.

"Excuse me?" Lolo said, caught off-guard.

"Why are you going around throwing yourself at men in the club?" Runako asked derisively.

"You've GOT to be fuckin' kidding me," Lolo chuckled, relieved, as she grabbed her shopping and made her way to the parking lot.

"Well, I'm glad ONE of us finds this funny. Why would you tear down your marriage like that?"

"ME? Tear down my marriage? How, exactly, would I do THAT, Ru?" Lolo challenged, getting irritated.

"Kobe told me that you were throwing yourself at Mamba last night at some club. Asking him to take you home and make love to you," Runako prissily repeated the gossip. "All the Muzungus are talking about it, including João. Why would you DO that?"

"Hmmm. Interesting!" Lolo replied sarcastically. "Tell me, Ru. Are all the guys also talking about how João's been cheating on me for the past six months? HUH? Are they talking about how he's parading his mistress all around Joburg?" Lolo's voice was steadily rising as she got angrier and angrier. "Are they? Are all the guys talking about how João is prancing around town telling everyone we're divorced when I haven't moved out my house yet? I bet they're not talking about THAT, are they!" Lolo was now screaming into the phone.

"Lolo, STOP! Just stop it. Please!" Runako shouted back. "What are you saying? What do you mean João has a girlfriend?"

"Yes, Ru! JOÃO has a GIRLFRIEND!" Lolo shouted. A few passers-by turned to see what the commotion was about. Lolo lowered her voice to avoid drawing more attention to herself. "I guess he conveniently forgot to tell you THAT part!" she seethed.

"Oh, my God, you guys. I can't take this," Runako said fervently.

"What's happening with you two? I thought everything had settled down since you got engaged and now you're telling me he's got a girlfriend, and you're busy hooking up with someone else!"

"Ru! Be serious. João having a relationship is hardly the same thing as me kissing someone last night!" Lolo snarled. "And by the way, MAMBA made the move ON ME because João is busy telling everyone we're divorced! Don't even TRY to make it the same thing," Lolo warned.

"I'm not making it the same thing," Runako evaded. "I'm not making it anything. I'm just trying to understand why two of my closest friends would hurt each other this bad!"

"Hurt each other? Is João HURT? By WHAT?" Lolo demanded in disbelief.

"By you kissing Mamba! He's SHATTERED," Ru replied perplexingly. "And don't think he didn't have his suspicions about you being attracted to Mamba. Or to Charles. Babe, the guys are talking about your history."

"Slut-shaming? How original," Lolo fake-yawned.

"I'm serious, Lolo. This is really not a good look for you!"

Lolo slumped back to lean against her car, too dumbfounded to move.

"Runako," she said in a low, icy voice. "Did I hear you correctly? Did you just say, 'not a good look'?" Lolo bit her tongue, but Runako was mute. Lolo exploded.

"NOT A FUCKIN' GOOD LOOK?! Runako, I've just told you that my husband and father of my kids has been cheating on me for half our marriage, and you reprimand me for kissing a guy, just yesterday, who João told we're DIVORCED, because it's NOT A GOOD LOOK? So we'll just ignore João's part in all of this then, HUH?" Lolo's mind reeled with the temerity of it all.

"Lolo, you're a woman," Runako said reprovingly, "with a rather colourful history. You can't be seen to be throwing yourself at other men, especially not at a time like this." Lolo clenched her jaw, her chest heaving with fury, and managed to stay silent while Runako obliviously exacerbated the double standard.

"Men cheat all the time," Runako continued, matter-of-factly, "but as the wife, you need to keep a low profile, otherwise people are going to think that YOU'RE the reason your marriage didn't work out."

"Runako Rose Madzonge Mensah," Lolo hissed, steel bands of self-control barely containing her rage, "if you would like us to still be friends at the end of this conversation, I suggest you pick your words extremely carefully. Because right now, the shit that's coming out of your mouth is making me question how I am friends with a woman with such archaic beliefs."

"You can end our friendship if you'd like, Lolo. But you and I both know that's how society works." Runako said solemnly.

Lolo sank into the driver's seat of her car, threw her arms over the steering wheel to cradle her face, and started sobbing.

How conveniently Mamba had gone around twisting what she'd said to him.

But more than disappointed, Lolo felt betrayed. Betrayed first by her husband, and then by a man, she'd known for half her life and considered a friend. What she had wanted from him was to be comforted, not humiliated. Again.

Lolo started the car, and as she put it into reverse gear, her phone rang again. She shifted back to neutral and pulled up the handbrake.

It was João. He hadn't called her directly since she texted him about knowing about his affair. She suspected his call had something to do with Mamba.

She dreaded answering the call but ignoring it would only make matters worse. She willed herself to stop crying and answered, bracing herself for the worst.

"Hello," Lolo croaked.

"Hey! Do you think you can be out of the house by Monday afternoon?" João asked casually.

"Out of the house? What house?"

"The Joburg house," João replied matter-of-factly.

Lolo could not have predicted that it would be this bad.

"Dude, how the hell am I supposed to move out on Monday when I land on Sunday night?" she retreated into practicality. "And what movers are open now? It's a Saturday evening, and they don't open on Sundays."

"I don't know man. I'm just saying that by Monday sunset, you, and all of your stuff, must be out my house!"

Beluga Restaurant, De Waterkant

Lolo stared into the distance as the party of twelve sang 'Happy Birthday' to her mom.

She didn't remember driving back home from Cavendish. She didn't remember getting dressed in all black, in line with the theme. She didn't remember doing her makeup. She didn't remember the ride to Beluga where the birthday dinner was being held. She didn't remember taking her seat or ordering the half-eaten Lobster Bisque that was in front of her.

It was as if she'd suddenly teleported to her seat from another time and place. It was happening more and more often, bouts of blacking out during the day only to 'come to' later on. She was functioning, but she wasn't present.

Maybe the mind, just like the body, goes numb when it feels intense pain. Maybe her mind was shutting down as a way of coping.

Whatever the reason, she wished it would shut down for longer spells. Right now, maybe even for good.

João and Lolo's house, Sandhurst
January 2015

It was 11 pm by the time João pulled up to the driveway from fetching Lolo and the kids from the airport. Kael and Noel were snoring in their car seats in the back, and Lolo and João had exchanged nothing more than "Hey" when he picked them up.

He stayed behind to unload their luggage while she carried Noel into the house and tucked him into bed. On her way back to fetch Kael, she noticed something strange about the picture frames hanging on the wall.

Many of them were empty. Pictures of João were in the frames. Pictures of Kael and Noel were in the frames. None of her. João had removed all pictures with Lolo in them from their frames and left the empty frames hanging on the wall.

She was a ghost in her home. She was no longer welcome in her home.

As she walked past the TV room and into the garage, she noted her absence from the pictures sitting on the plasma unit too. João was there. The kids were there. All the pictures of her, or with her in them, had been turned face-down.

Why was he treating her like a criminal when they had both agreed that the marriage wasn't working? Why was SHE being erased when HE was the one that had started another relationship during their marriage? Why was SHE the one who had to leave their home and not him?

She felt herself going numb. Her mind was shutting down again, and she went onto autopilot. She would process the emotions later. For now, she had to get her sons tucked into bed and get herself ready to start packing her belongings in the morning.

She changed into her pyjamas, and just as she was about to climb into bed, João walked into the room and stood at the door.

"Uhm…" he started, and cleared his throat. "Can you sleep in the guest room?"

"Oh… okay," she mumbled. She had no fight left in her.

She was tired, having barely slept in a week. She was tired from travelling with the kids. She was tired from the emotional rollercoaster of dealing with João and her family and Mamba and Runako. She was just tired.

She felt like a leaf blowing in the wind. Anything he could have asked of her at that moment, he would have received. If he wanted her to sleep in the bathroom, she would have. If he had asked her to sleep in the maid's quarters, she would have. If he'd asked her to sleep in the car in the garage, she would have. Right now, she was operating on battery saver mode.

She had no will to fight. No will to live. She had checked out and was now a spectator to her own life. She would check back in again when she could make better sense of what was going on, and how to survive it.

Off to the guest bedroom she went, where she cleared away laundry and lingerie that wasn't hers and slept beneath a wall covered with more empty picture frames.

———

The alarm went off in the distance, and Lolo opened her eyes and tried to figure out where she was.

Oh, yes, the guest bedroom, she hadn't imagined coming to sleep here last night.

Or imagined kissing Mamba. Or imagined finding out João had been having an affair. Or imagined deciding to leave her marriage.

It was all real, and she was waking up to the same never-ending nightmare.

As she made her way upstairs to shower and change, she saw her house in a different light. All of a sudden, she saw it in stark detail.

Everything stood out, perhaps because it was the last time she would be looking at it. She walked past the bar stools and noticed they were a little worn. The entrance hall could really use a new Persian rug. The large-frame mirror was streaky, whoever had polished it last was clearly an amateur.

The grout between the tiles on the stairs needed refilling. A pity she never got around to frosting the large window looking into the staircase with the Morreira crest. The runner rugs in the passage needed a deep clean.

She stood at her bedroom door, not sure whether to knock or whether she was free to walk in. She stood at the entrance. Paralysed. She was about to walk into her bedroom for the very last time. She had no idea what lay waiting for her when she walked out.

11

CHRISTMAS IN JULY

"The roaring lion kills no prey"

— NIGERIAN PROVERB

Aunty Nandi's Place, Lonehill
January 2015

*I*s this really my life?" Lolo croaked, pulling up the covers and looking at the walls of her teenage bedroom. "What happened to my man? The naughty but loving Azalian boy I married?"

She paused, desperately searching her friends' faces for an answer, any answer, to help her make sense of the mess in which she found herself.

"Who is this cold, arrogant monster that has replaced my husband? I feel like I've been brought face-to-face with Satan…" she lamented self-pityingly.

"Oh, babe, if my clients' divorces are anything to go by, you've only just pulled up to the gates of hell," Qhayiya replied with blunt commiseration. Her words stood in stark contrast to the gentleness with which she rubbed her friend's back.

"That's a bit harsh, Q" Runako admonished, straightening up from the dressing table she'd been leaning on. "Not all divorces are ugly, Lolo, and I guess you and João just need to try and sort this out amicably."

"Amicably?" sputtered Qhayiya. "With the same guy that gave his wife 48 hours to move out of her home?"

"He *did*?" Runako asked in disbelief.

"Yeah," Lolo replied tonelessly.

"And notice anything missing from her ring finger?" Qhayiya continued sarcastically, pointing to Lolo's left hand. "He stripped her of her wedding ring, saying something about it being a family heirloom even though he'd bought it for her and not inherited it…"

"You're joking!" Runako choked. "Please say you're joking!"

Lolo's face crumpled into anguished and extremely messy tears.

"Let's be real, babe. It's not going to be amicable," Qhayiya opined dispassionately. "João's gloves are off, and Lolo, if you're not ready to put up a fight, you will lose more than you already have." Qhayiya lifted the covers and climbed out of bed to pour herself another glass of wine, and continued, "Taking back your car was bad enough. I know how much you loved your 'Lolo 7'. But kicking you out the house and stripping you of your wedding ring was below the belt. You know people will ask why you're now using your mom's run-around, right?"

"I don't care what people think right now, Qhayiya!" Lolo blubbered. "They can talk all they want, I don't care. I just want all of this to be over. I want to be divorced, get what's due to me so I can start over and focus on my kids and my career. Stuff what people have to say!"

"Are the boys still with him?" Runako asked softly.

"Uh-huh…" Lolo sniffled. "Three weeks with him, three weeks with me. João's decided to stick to his routine of spending every three weeks in Joburg."

"What an ass!" Qhayiya grimaced. "So the same guy that used to complain about spending three weeks in Joburg is now all too happy to do it? Let's see how long he'll survive having a pair of four-year-olds on his hands."

"Agreed!" Runako concurred, nodding her head emphatically. "João clearly wasn't ready for marriage. Well done for deciding to face the truth and leave him, friend."

"I didn't DECIDE to leave Runako," Lolo cried, "João made it impossible to stay!"

"And why did SHE have to move out? The man must move out, especially when he's been cheating," Qhayiya maintained.

"Says who?" Runako sighed, shaking her head. "You pretend to be all independent, but you're really backwards when it comes to money issues, Q. Did you REALLY think the cutthroat Morreiras were gifting Lolo a house with an 8-figure price tag? OF COURSE NOT! It was a marital benefit – hers to enjoy as long as she was married to João. She should have known that when she left João, she was going to leave all the benefits that came with being his wife." Runako placed her glass on the dresser before turning towards Lolo and looked her straight in the eye. "Lolo, when you left your last job, did you take your desk, chair and company car with you? No – you didn't. Guess what? The Morreiras operate on the same principle. I learned that the hard way when I tried to leave Kobe…"

"Doesn't the law favour the innocent party if your marriage ends because of cheating?" Qhayiya sneered, climbing back into bed next to Lolo.

"You watch too many movies, Qhayiya," Runako replied in exasperation.

Runako explained that South Africa operates on the 'no-fault' system of divorce. This means that a divorce will be granted if one of the parties believes that there has been an 'irretrievable breakdown of the marriage relationship', with no reasonable prospects of restoring it.

Although each case is assessed on its own merits, the law does not 'favour' the innocent party. It is the marital regime of the parties that determines how the assets owned by the spouses, will be divided upon dissolution of the marriage.

Qhayiya fixed Runako with a glacial stare, before deciding to let up. "Babe, you'll be fine," she comforted Lolo, instead. "João may have taken these things from you now, but all you need to do is get yourself a good lawyer, and take it from there."

"I will, thank you," Lolo sniffled. "I'm really exhausted now so if you don't mind, I'd really like to get some rest."

"Sure," Runako agreed. "But before we go, can I ask you for one favour, hun?" She looked at Lolo earnestly and tenderly. "Please keep a journal. A journal to help you work through your thoughts and emotions because we won't always be here."

Runako rose to her feet and took a seat at the foot of Lolo's bed. "I'm heading back to Zim in a couple of days, and will only be back in three months for my bulk grocery shopping again. Qhayiya has a hectic work schedule. And Nala, well, she's working through her own problems trying to rebuild her life. We may not always be available when you need us to be, and journaling will be a great source of comfort for you."

"I hear you…" Lolo said softly.

"On the real, though," Runako pressed, "promise me you'll journal. Even if it's just taking down your thoughts on your Notes app. It's helped me a lot through my drama with Kobe, and I promise it will help you work your way through this awful time."

"Okay. I'll try," Lolo acquiesced.

"That's a great idea," Qhayiya added. "I'll actually start journaling as well."

"Trust me," Runako smiled, "it's one of the most precious gifts a woman can give herself these days."

Monday 05 January 2015, 22h17

Take your time…

Tuesday 06 January 2015, 19h50

Hmm… not sure what to write.

Thursday 08 January 2015, 23h34

I miss my babies 😢

Friday 09 January 2015, 18h21

It feels like I'm walking around holding my beating heart in my hand, I feel all the elements – hot, cold, windy, all on and in my heart…

Monday 12 January 2015, 18h55

No mother should ever be separated from her children, ever…

Tuesday 13 January 2015, 23h48

Doesn't the body run out of tears? Tired of crying…

Thursday 15 January 2015, 23h36

Formally appointed a divorce lawyer today, but her first available appointment is only mid-Feb! Turns out January is the busiest period for divorce lawyers as that's when most applications for dissolution of marriage happen. Guess João, and I aren't that special after all. We're just another statistic…

Friday 16 January 2015, 22h18

I have my babies back; all is right with the world 🙂

Saturday 17 January 2015, 12h22

Hurts to hear the twins ask if I know Aunt Oyana. Kids aren't stupid hey. But I don't know her and frankly don't give a damn about her. She owes me nothing. João, on the other hand, made a vow to me that he broke. So be it, he will face the music later in life, I won't be waiting for that day though, I have a life to lead. In leading that life, I am reading newspapers that have Mamba's father on the cover. Seriously? Can I go a week without thinking or reading about Mamba, or having my sister send pics of him tagged by groupies? Urgh!!! I really wish I'd never bumped into him at Asoka, never had him hold and kiss me the way he did. No one man should have all that power… Maybe I should accept his invite for us to meet and clear the air…

Sunday 18 January 2015, 21h56

Think I'll sleep without crying tonight…

Wednesday 21 January 2015, 10h28

So proud of myself. Handled the school drop-off like a boss today. Walked the boys into class dressed to the nines and with my head held high. Reminded those gossipmongers who I am. #inothernews. Viewed some houses online today and went back into my box very fast. This whole living alone exercise will be rather expensive, and I am out here trying to get my teeth whitened and my vjayjay waxed, I better chill - and HARD.

Thursday 22 January 2015, 20h43

It gets easier and easier every day 😊

Friday 23 January 2015, 18h45

When you're already hurt, disappointments are even more pronounced, and one feels them in HD. When you know that, it makes it easier to cope. I'm so disappointed that Mamba moved our drinks date to Sunday night. He has a life before me, and I must remember that. I must also be careful not to make him my life as well. I must come back to the middle, so I don't obsess over anything as a coping mechanism - not even work or the kids. The brain tries to find something to obsess over so it can escape the present. I must live in the present, it's my new reality and my new future. I must deal with my shit, clean it up, not hide away from it. The time has come to clean up all my shit, it's time for growth.

Saturday 24 January 2015, 13h42

Raw Again. I'm so lonely. This is the part I must push through. Freedom can be lonely 😢

Sunday 25 January 2015, 17h18

Mamba just sent a message cancelling our drinks date. He didn't give any explanation. I'm crying and trying to figure out why cause it's not like I am in love with the guy. I guess I was using him as a distraction, pain killer. Painkillers - although they provide the same feeling as healing - are not healing. I mustn't focus my energy on painkillers, but rather focus my energy on healing.

Monday 26 January 2015, 03h39

"I'm not your enemy…" – Moneoa, Yekelela

Wednesday 28 January 2015, 21h31

I cry every day. Every. Blessed. Day.

Friday 30 January 2015, 17h32

Lord, when will I catch a break? When will the tears stop flowing? When will the pain end?

I feel I'm also on the cross taking lashes for a crime I did not commit. Just saw a picture of João, Oyana and the kids at the twins' school. So Oyana is good enough to be on his WhatsApp profile picture and not me? Wow! If he didn't want me anymore, why didn't he just leave me instead of constantly cheating on me and subjecting me to years of misery and loneliness in our relationship? This man had actually wanted to be in a steady relationship, just not with ME. He's now going around making a public declaration of his new family. This is the family he wanted, the one without me in it. You give someone the best years of your life and they can just throw you to the dogs! The faster and further I run from João, the better....

Saturday 31 January 2015, 00h17

Everything is as it should be…

Sunday 01 February 2015, 00h17

I officially and solemnly declare that last night was the second-worst cry I would have had, the first being 28 December in Cape Town. I will not cry like that again - I refuse.

I vow I'm not coming back here again; I vow!

Monday 02 February 2015, 12h34

They say you can't fall from the ground;

I want to reach the ground now...

Tuesday 03 February 2015, 18h35

Decided to see my mom's shrink today and one of the things she asked me is if I'm okay with the fact that I'll be single. Like alone. Alone in the shops, at the movies, at the kids' school meetings. I will not stay in a bad marriage because I'm afraid of being alone, not a chance. I'm not okay with being alone, but I do not fear it.

Friday 06 February 2015, 16h00

Survived another week. Well done baby girl, I'm proud of you. xoxo, Lols

Saturday 07 February 2015, 01h15

I'm on the up and up. Today was a good day. Think I'll sleep without crying tonight 😊

Sunday 08 February 2015, 13h05

The answer is always "He is just trying to hurt you."

Monday 09 February 2015, 15h45

Phoned a recruitment agency today. Meeting with them next week. Feels so weird 😊

Foresight Talent Offices, Woodmead - February 2015

By 10:15 am, Lolo was parked at the Foresight Talent offices, even though her appointment was only for 11 am. The last time she'd gone for a job interview was when she was applying for her internship at the end of 2008! Lolo marvelled at how different she was to the person she was then. Back then, she was fearless, confident, clear on where she wanted to be "in the next five years!".

Now, she had no idea who or where she wanted to be in the next five years. She was unsure of herself, unsure of her abilities, and unsure she could measure up to the very many graduates that had since joined the talent pool.

Lolo knew her limited work experience meant she would need to apply for a junior position. The people applying for the same position would be much younger than her, likely to have much higher grades than hers, and wouldn't be weighed down with family commitments. She was an old, single mother of two looking to fill a position that a young, unencumbered professional could too. What sane hiring manager would prefer her over that?

These thoughts weren't helpful, and Lolo knew she had to distract herself from letting her thoughts cause any more damage than they already had. Instead of fretting, Lolo used the time to make sure that not a single hair was out of place. She pulled down the car mirror and did a meticulous assessment of her appearance.

Her usually dramatic makeup was today subtle, in natural tones. Her cornrows were tied up and away from her face in a side bun. Her David Tlale collared shirt was a crisp white, and no shadows of her undergarments were visible. She looked down at her freshly pressed pencil skirt and noted it was "black black." She smiled, knowing how her mother loathed faded blacks.

The matching jacket hung safely off the coat hook in the back seat of her mom's fifteen-year-old Opel Astra. Her Ferragamo round-nose court shoes were comfortable and free from any scuff marks. And she had rounded off her neat, professional look with a single spritz of Kilian's *Love Don't Be Shy*.

Qhayiya had advised Lolo not to wear her usual overpowering floral fragrance. Apparently, even something as personal as a fragrance could make or break an interview these days!

Lolo looked at the time again. It was only 10:30 am. Still too early to make her way to reception.

She decided this would be the perfect opportunity to go through Qhayiya's interview coaching tips again. She pulled out her phone and navigated to her WhatsApp messages.

1. Avoid the use of filler words like "uhm." Speak with confidence and clarity.
2. Don't rush into an answer. Rather say "I'd like to take a moment to think about this."
3. Know your flaws, and how you will manage them, so they don't affect your productivity within the organisation and the team.
4. Don't badmouth your last organisation when explaining why you left.
5. Ask at least two questions when asked if you have any questions for us.

Lolo had gone through three rounds of mock interviews with her mom and felt confident she would nail this one. At 10:45 am, she made her way to reception, ready to make an impression and start a series of interviews that would hopefully result in her securing a job.

Lolo's heel tapped on the marble flooring as she waited in the lobby. At long last, the receptionist let her know that Mapule, the senior recruitment specialist, was ready to see her. Mapule smiled as Lolo approached, a genuine smile meant to put Lolo at ease. It didn't work as Lolo was suddenly even more unsure of herself.

Mapule had the same effortless style all corporate women seemed to possess. She was chic in high waist wide-leg navy pants, paired with a white collared shirt. The sleeves were rolled up and the collar open, reminiscent of Carolina Herrera. Her face was dewy, without a smidgeon of makeup. And her natural hair brushed into a side part, fell to her shoulders.

"You look lovely," Mapule said cheerfully, holding open the door to the glass-walled boardroom.

"Thank you. So do you," Lolo replied nervously, immediately feeling awkward at her response, although she meant it.

"May I offer you some tea or coffee?"

"Coffee, please. Actually! Water. Just water. Still."

Lolo remembered reading somewhere that still water was the safest drink option when in an interview. Coffee could leave a stain, and a bottle of sparkling water could bubble over when opened. There were so many rules to follow. So many things to remember. She didn't remember it being this difficult before.

Mapule turned to the receptionist and placed an order for one still water and a double espresso. She invited Lolo to take a seat and closed the door behind her before commencing with the meeting. As if she wasn't beautiful enough, Mapule smelled like fresh laundry, too. *Why is this woman so damn perfect!*

"I'm curious as to why you've been unemployed for so long," Mapule asked, once she, too, had sat down.

Lolo's stomach turned into a knot. *Did she have to go for the jugular and start with one of the most difficult interview questions?*

Lolo considered her options: be honest and say it was because she couldn't land a job after moving to Johannesburg, or provide a PR-friendly answer and say she decided to focus on raising her children?

"Uhm…" Lolo began, immediately breaking one of Qhayiya's interview rules and willing herself to sound more confident. "I wanted a better work-life balance as I'm a mom to twin boys. So, I decided to put my family first and left my full-time job. I have been blogging and working as a digital content creator since. You may know me as *@LolosLuxeLife*?" Lolo smiled expectantly. A woman as stylish as Mapule would surely have heard of her.

"No, I'm afraid not," Mapule replied casually. The little shred of confidence Lolo had mustered flew out the window. "And you won't be putting your family first with the role we find you?" Mapule continued without batting an eyelid. Lolo choked. The bitch was ruthless.

"Uhm… Well…" Lolo mumbled. The door opened, saving Lolo from her ramblings, and the receptionist placed a tray with their drinks on the table. Mapule thanked her and turned to Lolo, handing her a bottle of water and an empty glass. She reached for the bottle and fixed her eyes on the cap as she struggled to twist it open.

"I'm actually going through a divorce right now, so I don't really have a choice but to start earning a stable income."

"I see. I'm sorry to hear that," Mapule said sincerely, pausing for a moment before continuing. "I see you're interested in pursuing a career in digital media. Any particular reason why?"

"Well, digital media is a platform, I mean an area that I'm familiar with…" Lolo began, frantically digging into the skin on the side of her thumbnail. She took another sip of water, and yet her mouth remained dry, and her tongue still felt too big for her mouth.

She took a deep breath and continued. "I feel I understand digital media as my blog has been very successful, and my thesis, I mean dissertation, during my honours year, was… I'm sorry, Mapule," Lolo said, placing both hands over her mouth and willing herself not to cry. "I'll be honest with you, I'm very nervous. I haven't done this in years, and I'm desperate to get a job and start making some money to look after myself and my kids."

"I can tell," Mapule smiled, folding her iPad away. "And there's nothing wrong with being nervous because I care less about interview technique, and more about the actual answer you are giving me."

"What do you mean?" Lolo asked, relieved that she hadn't completely blown the interview.

Mapule swung her chair to the side and crossed her right leg over her left. "You see, many candidates focus on preparing for the interview itself. Stressing about details such as 'Don't use too many uhms' or

'Only drink still water because tea or coffee may stain'," Mapule winked. She'd noted Lolo's earlier change of heart, and knew the reason behind it. "But at Foresight Talent, our philosophy is that candidates must prepare for the ROLE."

"Well thank goodness for that!" Lolo sighed with relief. She placed her hands on the table to stop the room from spinning. "I thought I'd completely blown this interview!"

"Not at all!" Mapule replied, folding her iPad away. "Look, you've clearly put a lot of effort into today's meeting. The way you're dressed. Perfectly groomed. Arriving on time."

Lolo couldn't help but smile at Mapule's kind words of affirmation.

"But that's all packaging. It means very little if the contents don't match up. And this is where many candidates fall short," Mapule paused to take a sip of her double espresso.

"That makes so much sense," Lolo said softly. She suddenly regretted not having ordered an espresso for herself. "And how does one achieve this, preparing for the role and not the interview?" Lolo thought aloud, nibbling on the skin around her thumb.

"It's simple. Yet also kind of complex," Mapule said, shaking her head from side to side. "I say it's simple because all you need to prove is that you have the skills and competence for the role being advertised. On the other hand, one could say it's complex because you'd need to have insight into the role being advertised before actually being in it."

Lolo nodded her head in agreement, and Mapule took another sip of coffee before continuing. "You'd also need to show that you'll thrive in the culture of the organisation, as the culture not only impacts your work-life, but your home life as well."

"Is that why you started by asking about my family and priorities?" Lolo asked, half talking to herself. She looked away for a moment as she connected the dots.

"Exactly!" Mapule nodded. "It wasn't me just trying to be a bitch and give you a hard time."

"Do you like, read minds or something?" Lolo exclaimed, sitting back in her chair.

"No. But I do read body language, and your body language snitched on you earlier," Mapule replied firmly. "That's another critical yet often forgotten method of communication."

"For the record, I think you're a very lovely person, even though you don't recognise me from Instagram!" Lolo teased.

"She has a sense of humour too!" Mapule winked. "Look, I like you. I think you're smart, but more importantly, I think you're teachable, and hungry to make a success of yourself. THAT for me is a non-negotiable when it comes to candidates."

Lolo breathed a sigh of relief.

"So," Mapule continued, "I'll work with you. Instead of trying to find you a role, we'll pitch you to various organisations where your skills and expertise will be of value. In the meantime, I need you to start putting together a list of all the successful digital campaigns you've run, together with their performance metrics."

"The surest way we'll land you a position is to show potential employers that you're already good at what you're applying for. Stick with me, and within the next few weeks, you could be walking into your new job!"

Lolo skipped back to the car, filled with excitement at the prospect of starting a new job by the time April was through. She jumped in the driver's seat and immediately reached for her phone to let her mom know how well the meeting had gone.

Lolo was dialling her mom when a WhatsApp message from an unknown number came through. "Greetings," the message read. *Maybe it's a wrong number.* She clicked on the profile picture to see if she could figure out who the message was from. And there he was. Stanford De Sousa.

De Sousa Residence, Hartbeespoort Dam

The De Sousa mansion was more marvellous every time Lolo paid a visit. From the wooden doors imported from an ancient castle in Peru, right down to the Ercuis silverware used as everyday cutlery. No expense had been spared in the luxury home.

Lolo walked up to the front door, and as she was about to knock, a uniformed young lady appeared and invited Lolo to follow her. The crystal basket chandelier twinkled as they walked by. Lolo couldn't help but brush her hand against the smooth curves of the grand piano as she tried to keep up with her escort.

They walked onto the patio where the table had been set up with candles and a fresh bouquet of white Single Early tulips. The kind young lady excused herself, leaving Lolo by herself.

The soothing sounds of Miles Davis' *Blue in Green* played gently in the background. Lolo closed her eyes, imagining the rustling sound from the Apollo fountain was applause. She was lost in the enchantment of her imaginary concert when Uncle Stanford's booming voice called out to her.

"Mrs Morreira, how are you doing?" he enquired politely, as he walked towards her with his arms outstretched for a hug.

"It's MS Morreira now," Lolo corrected, annoyed. She gave Uncle Stanford an air-kiss and quickly pulled away from his embrace.

"Oh, yes. Pardon me," he chuckled. "I heard about you and João, and seriously, I am truly sorry." He looked anything but.

Uncle Stanford walked towards the table and pulled out a chair. "Please, take a seat," he gestured. "It's rude to keep a woman of your stature standing."

"Thanks, Uncle Stanford," Lolo replied curtly. She sat down and placed her handbag on a footstool next to her.

"Would you like to start with a glass of champagne now, or will you wait for dinner?"

"Dinner?" Lolo echoed dubiously.

"Yes, dinner between old friends. Is that a crime?" Uncle Stanford taunted.

"I guess not… But what's the occasion?"

"Must there be an occasion for me to see an old friend?" Uncle Stanford replied, melodramatically clasping his hand to his heart and rolling his eyes in fake surprise.

"Oh, come on, Uncle Stanford! You've never invited me to your house by myself before," Lolo challenged.

"Well, in all these years you've always come as a 2-for-1 package," Uncle Stanford teased. "Now that you're single, I'm able to invite the person I truly want to see, without all the superfluous parties."

"I see," Lolo smirked.

"Look," Uncle Stanford said, now serious as he adjusted himself in his seat. "I heard what happened and I'm sorry. The reason I called you here is that I'd like to offer my support."

"That's kind, thanks."

"No, I don't think you understand." Before he could elaborate, another uniformed young lady appeared with a bottle of champagne. Uncle Stanford waited for her to pour the champagne and then walk out of sight before he continued.

"As I was saying, Lolo, I would like to offer you my support. Financial support, that is."

Lolo had never been offered any gifts by Stanford before. And as much as he could afford to offer his support without it shifting a comma in his bank balance, Lolo had been around long enough to know that everything came at a price. No matter how benevolent the donor.

"Again, that's very kind, Uncle Stanford, thank you. But I can't accept it."

Uncle Stanford must have picked up on the anxiety in Lolo's voice, and hastened to reassure her.

"Please, don't think I'm expecting anything in return," he said, placing his hand gently on Lolo's arm. "It's just that I know how expensive divorces can be, and I would like to help you get through this."

"Uhm...I just don't feel comfortable doing it."

"Look," Uncle Stanford sighed. His face turned serious. "I understand you're uncomfortable, but I believe that your situation is grossly unfair."

"Uncle Stanford, I can't..."

"Lolo! Now is not the time for appearances!" Uncle Stanford barked. "Stop being stubborn and let me help you. Divorce can be a very messy exercise, and nowadays one of the more commonly used strategies is to drag out the proceedings so as to bankrupt the financially vulnerable party. By the time an offer is made, the weaker party is so broke that any offer seems attractive!"

Uncle Stanford waited for his words to sink in, before continuing in more measured tones. "You're on your own now. You need to wake up!"

Lolo stared into the distance as she considered the offer. She wondered if her husband was really capable of being that cruel to her.

She knew João was a cutthroat lawyer, but could he be as cold when it came to HER? The mother of his sons? His university sweetheart?

But what if João and her in-laws found out about this arrangement since they had introduced her to Uncle Stanford?

On the contrary, Lolo argued with herself. *Uncle Stanford is the one who should feel uncomfortable.* He was the one trying to thwart what could be his godson's strategy. If he didn't feel bad about it, why should she?

"Alright," Lolo murmured huskily, before clearing her throat. "Alright, Uncle Stanford. I'll accept your help."

"Good. I'm glad. The journey you're on is not an easy one, and you'll need to navigate it carefully because it affects the rest of your life. Now tell me, how much do you need a month?"

"Uhm…" Lolo mulled it over for a few moments. "I don't know. I haven't really thought about it."

Uncle Stanford sighed and gave Lolo a disapproving look. "Okay. Let me ask this. How much does your life cost you every month?"

"Well, I'm still staying at my mom's place right now. So it does not cost me very much," Lolo replied.

"Is it big enough for you and the kids?" Stanford asked sincerely.

"No. It's a three-bedroom townhouse. The boys are sharing a bed with me."

"That's not good!" Stanford said, rising to his feet. He walked to the edge of the patio and looked out onto the dam. The moon shone brightly in the cloudless sky, glistening off the black pool of water beneath it. Lolo wondered what Stanford was thinking, as he stood with one hand in his pocket and the other holding up his champagne glass. With a gentle nod, he motioned Lolo to join him. With each step towards the towering gentleman, she wondered what direction the conversation would take.

"Tshenolo," Stanford began, still staring out onto the water, "you need to get your own place. A secure place where the children will be comfortable and well taken care of."

"I'd love to, but I can't afford my own place right now, not until I get a job or interim maintenance," Lolo reasoned, praying Stanford would make eye contact so she could read his mind. Stanford maintained his position and continued solemnly.

"Those boys are Morreiras, and knowing João and Raul as well as I think I do, I wouldn't put it past them to want full custody of their heirs."

"João wouldn't. He'd never take my babies from me," Lolo squeaked. Her voice broke, and tears welled up in her eyes.

"How much do you need to get a comfortable place for you and the children?" Stanford asked gently. Finally, he had made eye contact, and Lolo saw pity in his eyes.

"Rent, electricity, food, the nanny…" Lolo counted out loud, she tilted her head back, using the stars as the beads of her mental abacus. "Thirty. I would need R30,000 per month," Lolo replied.

"Well, then, that settles it. Thirty thousand it is! I'll give you thirty thousand for three months. That should give you enough time to get a job or finalise your interim maintenance application. After that, you're on your own."

Uncle Stanford called for one of his staff members to bring him six 'bands' from the safe, as he and Lolo walked back to the table to take their seats. Shortly after that, yet another uniformed young lady appeared carrying a brown envelope, which Uncle Stanford motioned she should hand to Lolo.

"There should be R60,000 in there," he said. "You'll need money for a deposit on your new place, and all the extra costs that come with a move."

Lolo peeked inside the envelope. It contained six stacks of R100 notes, each secured by a rubber band.

"Thank you, Uncle Stanford. Really, thank you," Lolo said softly, stuffing the envelope in her bag.

"Make sure to text me your banking details before you leave. I'll have my assistant transfer the money to you on the first of every month."

Lolo smiled slightly and nodded. Stanford raised his glass to offer a toast. "To new beginnings, my dear."

"To new beginnings," Lolo beamed. She clinked her glass to his and took a generous sip of her bubbly.

Walking back into her mother's townhouse that night, Lolo was overcome with a sense of freedom. The money she had in her possession gave her the freedom to treat Kael and Noel to a new PlayStation so they wouldn't throw tantrums claiming 'But there's a PlayStation at Daddy's house!'. Freedom to hop on a plane to Harare and spend the weekend with Runako whenever she was tired of hiding from the world. Freedom to take a trip to Cape Town with the kids whenever the pressure of being in Joburg became unbearable.

Best of all, it gave Lolo the freedom to finally start rebuilding her life by moving into a place of her own. Being back under her mother's roof after living on her own for nearly a decade had been extremely difficult.

And though her mother was sure to protest her moving out before being financially stable, it was a risk Lolo was prepared to face.

What had originally seemed a huge sum of money suddenly evaporated when she drew up a list of her current obligations. All in all, she was sitting with a total of R110 000 in debt. This made her extremely nervous, but she thought it best to keep as much cash as possible for the move to her new place, as she did not know where her next paycheque was coming from, or how long her divorce would drag out for.

Saturday 14 February 2015, 10h32

Father Christmas! That is all…

Monday 16 February 2015, 16h45

Saw my lawyer today. Looks like I'll walk away with nothing since João drew up a watertight prenup. Focus now is to get myself back on my feet. Wish this whole recruitment process would be faster!

Wednesday 18 February 2015, 22h40

I wanna love and be loved so bad…

Tuesday 24 February 2015, 12h34

Just got feedback from my first job interview, and it went well. Cross fingers xxx

Sunday 01 March 2015, 22h40

Just finished moving into my new place. Feels so weird being alone again…

Monday 02 March 2015, 21h18

There's a quiet strength in knowing that I'm okay alone. I don't fear it, I draw strength from it. Life goes on, quietly…

Thursday 05 June 2015, 21h18

Got a paying social media campaign today. At least I'll have some money for next month. God is still in control.

Sunday 08 March 2015, 20h38

So yesterday morning Q gave me a call and asked what I'm up to. I told her I have no plans, and she asked me to meet her at Hyde

Park. I thought she's taking me for breakfast, but when I arrived, she was waiting at Woolworths with an empty trolley and told me to buy everything I need. That's the sweetest thing anyone has done for me. I've been so scared to ask my friends to help me with more money, especially since I already owe them. We then came back to my place, and she spent the night.

How sweet

Wednesday 11 March 2015, 19h25

Just come back from Spur with Aus' Moipone and the kids. I couldn't even honour their wish of taking them for supper as I don't have the money for all of us to have had supper there. Instead, we had supper at home and went out for dessert. If you had told me a year ago that I'd only be able to take my kids out for ice cream and not burgers, I would have laughed in your face. But look at me now.

How the mighty have fallen!

Thursday 12 March 2015, 22h49

Tomorrow I'll be alone again as the kids are going back to João and Aus' Moipone is going home as I can afford to keep her for only the three weeks that they're with me. This is now my new life, being alone for three weeks at a time. It's sinking in. It's painful. It hurts. I don't know whether I'm coming or going. I'm always anxious, my heart beats hard in my chest, it's painful. I'm always quarter to tears. I'm an optimistic person, but this is depressing. I can't focus, can't work, can't still my mind long enough to be productive at anything. I'm always running...

Wednesday 18 March 2015, 02h15

I get anxious when I'm going to be around my kids 'cause I have the situation rubbed in my face...

Thursday 19 March 2015, 22h40

Went for my final interview today. Please, God, let me get this job. IJN I pray

Saturday 21 March 2015, 12h34

Just saw a picture of J&O having dinner with João's parents. In our home in Sandhurst. At the table we used to sit at. I was foolish to think João's parents will stand on the side of fairness instead of their son. Maybe Charles was right. There was nothing special about being introduced to João's parents. I was and always will be just another girl. Who would have thought that out of all those people in the room the day I met the Morreiras, only Stanford would stand at my side...

Tuesday 24 March 2015, 23h35

Guess who's moving to Joburg next week??????
NALAAAAAAAAA! Will be so good to be in the same town as my bestie again. She got a job at a call centre (poor thing), but at least it's a start. So glad to see her rebuilding her life. Nala had gone so dim, a shadow of her former self. I hope this divorce doesn't do to me what Azalia did to Nala 😔. One day she'll be brave enough to return to that God-forsaken place to face the Ilungas and fetch her son. Hopefully...

Friday 27 March 2015, 15h55

I GOT THE JOB! YAAAAAY! Start work on 15 April 😊 And it's my birthday next month. I think this calls for a celebration 😊 😊 😊

Mousiki Night Club, Rosebank
April 2015

Method Man and Redman's *Y.O.U.* blasted through the posh establishment which had been transformed into a New York City hip hop club, in keeping with Lolo's 90s theme.

Scores of waiters scurried about to make sure 'Carlton Banks' didn't wait too long for his vodka cranberry, 'The Spice Girls' had their champagne topped up, and the detectives from *New York Undercover* were given Tabasco sauce to go with their chicken wings.

Lolo took another sip of her complimentary champagne and sat back on the black lounger in the dancer's change room, where she was waiting to make her grand entrance.

There is a lot to be thankful for, she thought to herself. In the last three months, she'd moved into her own place, secured herself a job, and had one of her childhood best friends move to Joburg.

Besides, her financial arrangement with Stanford was working like a charm, and, true to his word, he had given her three 'bands' at the beginning of every month without asking for anything in return.

It was also thanks to Stanford that she could afford to throw herself a lavish 30th birthday party for eighty of her closest friends, family, and colleagues. Even Runako had made the trip down from Harare to celebrate with her.

It was a pity Kobe had a prior engagement that kept him from being in attendance. It would have been nice for Junior to have his friend around.

Lolo's excitement grew as the minutes went by. It was the first time she would be making a social appearance since January, and she planned to put on a spectacular show.

The severe stress of the past five months had an unexpected benefit, and much to her delight, she was fifteen kilos lighter than in

December. Her birthday party presented the perfect opportunity to showcase her 'revenge body', and mark her entrance into the Dirty Thirties as a single girl.

Lolo waited in the change room with Star and Destiny, the two professional vogue dancers, who had choreographed her entrance routine and would be performing it with her. In the middle of sharing a joke, there was a knock at the door.

"Who is it?" Lolo called.

"Stelios!" replied a voice behind the door.

Lolo unlocked the door and gestured for Stelios to enter, but he stayed where he was.

"We need to talk," Stelios said curtly and ran his tongue along the top of the Rizla before deftly rolling it around the tobacco.

He stepped inside and glanced at Star and Destiny, acknowledging their presence with half a nod. The look on his face said the two weren't welcome, and Lolo asked them to give her some privacy. They obliged without comment.

"You look nice," Stelios said, pulling up a chair and flicking open his Zippo to light his cigarette.

"I know!" Lolo smiled.

So do you, she thought to herself, taking a good look at the man she'd only ever seen in dim lighting. She'd met with Stelios a few times during the planning of her birthday party. He was always dressed in the same ill-fitting blue jeans, classic New Balance sneakers, and a black Mousiki branded t-shirt.

Tonight, he'd made a simple but striking effort in a black turtleneck, matching skinny jeans; and Mexico 66 sneakers. The white ones with the blue and red lines. His greying mane, usually hidden under a cap, was gelled back and for the first time, she saw his blue-grey eyes.

Under normal circumstances, Lolo would be uncomfortable, alone in a room with a man like him, especially in her revealing outfit of black hot pants, matching lace bodysuit and crystal lace-up heels.

But Stelios had never been inappropriate, in all the times she'd met with him, and she didn't think it likely he would start now.

"Your friends are enjoying the party?" he asked, taking a drag of his cigarette.

"Yup! Been chatting to them on WhatsApp and they're very impressed!" Lolo winked.

"Good. I'm glad," he said, his Greek accent still heavy after twenty years in South Africa. "So, the 30k budget was right?"

"Yeah. Spot on! Especially since the WHOLE guest list decided to show up!" Lolo giggled, trying to ease the awkwardness in the room.

"You brought my 50% balance then?" he continued coldly.

"Yes! But it's in the car. I didn't want to be carrying all that cash around, you know? We can go fetch it now if you'd like?" Lolo explained nervously.

"No, there's no rush. I don't want Mr Party to get upset seeing me walk out with his girl," Stelios teased. He sat back in his chair and used his arm to cushion his head.

"There's no Mr Party, Stelios," Lolo informed him archly.

"You're paying for yourself?" he asked.

"Duh!" Lolo replied, chin up and daring him to doubt her.

"Why didn't you tell me?" Stelios sat forward to rest his elbows on his knees, still holding his cigarette.

"What difference would it have made?" Lolo shrugged.

"Two minutes," Stelios said. He jumped up and walked out the door without waiting for a response. Lolo shifted uncomfortably in her chair, wondering what was going on.

A few minutes later, Stelios returned with a slip in his hand and his cigarette hanging out the side of his mouth.

"There," he said. He handed Lolo the small piece of paper.

"Paid in full?" Lolo asked, looking up at him with confusion.

"Yup. You don't owe me anything. I'll ring up the bottles at cost and cover the difference myself. It's my birthday gift to you," Stelios smiled.

"Wow… I don't know what to say!" Lolo giggled and blushed. Then, in a softer, more pensive voice, "Thank you, Stelios."

"You're welcome. You look like an honest, hardworking girl. Don't change…"

Stelios sat down again and pulled out his tobacco to roll another cigarette. He lit up and took a long drag of his modified oxygen. His eyes met Lolo's, and as he slowly exhaled up towards the ceiling, he smiled, with his eyes crinkling, not once breaking eye contact.

Lolo was still seated upright on the lounger. His gaze was piercing, so piercing that she giggled and looked away in discomfort.

Immediately, she felt silly for giggling and allowing the man to stare her down. She turned back to him and indulged in his power play, matching his stare, determined not to back down again.

And so they sat, staring at each other in silence. The Greek bad boy, and the disillusioned Motswana princess.

The crowd cheered, jeered and gasped as Lolo, Star and Destiny performed their dance sequence, choreographed to Beyoncé's *Grown Woman*. Lolo had chosen to declare her entrance into the Dirty Thirties with a stage performance that symbolised her once again taking ownership of her body, her decisions, her sexuality, and her future.

As she dipped, gyrated and ran her hands suggestively down her toned thighs, Lolo caught sight of Stelios staring at her from across the room. He was leaning against the wall with his shoulder, arms folded across his chest.

She held his gaze and exaggerated every suggestive dance move even more, determined to make him look away first this time.

He didn't. He fixed his eyes on her until the end of her dance routine. She imagined herself as Rachel Marron, and he, her loyal bodyguard.

Tuesday 05 May 2015, 21h37

So today I had the weirdest day ever at work.

I went to the office wearing mismatched shoes. Who even freakin' does that! Anyway, my team leader called me aside to ask what's going on as my shoes don't match, and she's also noticed I've been "off."

Long story short, I came clean about moving out and the whole divorce thing, and I was very surprised at how supportive she was. She said if I needed any extra leave days, she would sign them off, and that she would sign off extra sessions with the company psychologist and legal counsellor as well (didn't even know we had one). I'm very glad she could be honest with me and put my needs first instead of just giving me the typical manager PR story about how the company cares about me without actually putting their money where their mouth is. Looks like God is on my side! 😊 xoxo

Thursday 07 May 2015, 18h17

Really universe? Just like that - hey neighbour, my name's Dennis! 😊 😊 😊 Oh my gosh, he feels just like sunshine... That's it! He's my Vitamin D!

Monday 11 May 2015, 19h36

I need to slow down. Vitamin D's got me going all giddy, and I don't even know him - haven't even seen him since Friday. Can't be distracted from my healing process. I need to keep on track ito fitness, education, spiritual wellbeing. I need to establish a routine and stick to it- I'm very topsy turvy and fragile right now. It's been four months since I moved out, which is nothing really, but enough time to have let things go to shit. I need to finalise the way forward. I need self-discipline otherwise I won't achieve everything I want to...

Saturday 16 May 2015, 18h45

I need to go on a boy fast. Aaaah I've been using crutches, I don't know if I know how to be 100% single. Eeish!!! I need to process that... Not that "Look at me I'm single" single, but that "I'm not even thinking about the fact that I'm single" single... Eeeeish... Faaaaaark I think the shrink may need to be called upon. Oh my gosh! Oh my gosh! Oh my gosh! BREAKTHROUGH Acceptance 😀 😀 😀 😀 😀 😀 Stages of grieving, I'm making progress AAAAITCH 🕴 🕴 🕴 🕴 🕴 🕴 🕴 🕴 🕴 I'm single, I'm single, shout it from the rooftops I'm single. I accept it, I embrace it, I live in the moment, I'm single!!! 😵

Now what?

Tuesday 19 May 2015, 16h45

Introducing a new character: Stelios! Been seeing him when I go clubbing at Mousiki with Nala and Q, and been ignoring his requests for dinner. Like. Me? Dinner with Stelios? In what world? Anyway, I was bored and finally agreed, and he took me to dinner Tuesday night at La Campagnola. He fetched me from my house, we had a 3-course meal, good wine, chilled by the fire and this one lady said we look so comfy with each other, how long have we been together 😄 😄 😄 😾 . First time I went on a date with a white man and as Nala said: He's just a human being, don't worry about what people will think! Eek!

Thursday 21 May 2015, 13h56

Submitted settlement offer today. I'm so tired of fighting. I just want out. It is well.

Monday 25 May 2015, 11h34

Had another meeting with my lawyer today. João declined my settlement offer saying I earn way more than I've stated. He's asked we both submit our bank statements. What the hell!

Thursday 28 May 2015, 10h22

Got an email from my lawyer. Apparently, the money from Stanford and my salary and the campaign make me look way richer than I actually am. João is offering ZERO, nothing, per month in alimony. How is this even fair!

Friday 29 May 2015 17h21

I've been knocked down so hard I can't even pray…

Wednesday 03 June 2015, 09h20

He's coming for my kids! Uncle Stanford and Runako warned me, but I didn't listen. He's used the same damn predictable strategy Runako warned me about in his custody application:

Slut-shaming: He's claiming I was also having an affair during our marriage and that I decided to leave the marriage because I have some rich boyfriend. WHERE? He even referenced the situation with Mamba to support his claim. Seriously…

Alcoholism: He's used our pictures from the past and pictures from my party to claim I'm an alcoholic and therefore, incompetent mother. He's even requested I submit a toxicology report from the hospital to prove I'm not an alcoholic.

Financial Frustration: I suspected João would stop my monthly allowance once I left him, but I didn't think he would kick me out of the house and take my car too. The cost of having my own place is killing me, and without Uncle Stanford's money, I won't be able to continue with the legal battle to retain shared custody of my boys.

I should have listened to Runako and prepared for this… I should have kept my money from Uncle Stanford instead of wasting it on a stupid party. Now I don't know how I'll pay for everything and still afford my legal fees. Maybe I should ask Uncle Stanford to help me out until this custody situation is over. Just for the next three months. It's not like he can't afford it.

De Sousa Residence, Hartbeespoort Dam
June 2015

Lolo hadn't been back to Uncle Stanford's house since the meeting where he first offered his help. The next two payments had been made via bank transfer.

As she walked up to the door, Uncle Stanford himself welcomed her and ushered her into the living room where he invited her to take a seat on the couch. Lolo noticed another striking difference in the reception she received with this visit. No staff members were scurrying about, and there was no elaborately laid table.

At the initial meeting, Uncle Stanford had been dressed formally, in a tailored navy-blue suit, a lilac shirt, and lilac and navy floral tie. Today he was casual, in a baby blue collared shirt, khaki chinos and classic brown Hermes loafers.

"May I offer you something to drink?" Uncle Stanford said. He stood with his hand over his heart and resembled an English butler.

"No, thank you, I'm fine," Lolo replied curtly. She was hoping to get this meeting over and done with as quickly as possible. She wanted to avoid being held hostage by an unfinished bottle of champagne.

"I hope you won't mind if I pour myself a glass of wine," Uncle Stanford assented.

"Of course not. Please, go ahead," Lolo replied.

Uncle Stanford whistled away in the kitchen as he fixed himself a drink and returned a few moments later with a glass of red wine and a coaster. On the few occasions she had been in his presence, she noted that he was very clean and neat. Obsessive, even.

"What's that João up to now?" Uncle Stanford began, lowering the volume on CNN.

"You were right, Uncle Stanford!" Lolo began, "not only is João dragging the divorce out, but he's now also coming for full custody of the twins. And on top of that, he stopped sending me money after he found out that I'd started working, Uncle Stanford," Lolo said petulantly. For a moment, she felt like a little girl ratting out her siblings to Daddy. "I had actually reworked my budget just two days ago and was breaking even with his contribution. Anything less and I'm screwed."

"Oh! That's TERRIBLE!" Uncle Stanford commiserated, shaking his head. "How are you going to cope?"

Lolo was taken aback. It was not the response she was hoping for, but she decided to play along. He had helped her before – perhaps he needed her permission to help her again.

"Uhm… I know we'd agreed that you'd help me for only three months. But I was wondering if you could help me for another three months? Just until I figure out my next move. I'm in arrears with the legal fees, and now I need to pay extra for us to go through the custody battle," Lolo said ruefully.

"I see…" Uncle Stanford nodded. With leisurely, measured movements, he took a sip of wine and carefully placed the glass back on its coaster. Lolo stewed in her discomfort, feeling smaller and smaller by the second.

Excruciatingly slowly, Uncle Stanford stroked his beard with thumb and forefinger. At long last, he cleared his throat.

"I'm willing to help you," he said ponderously.

"Thank you," Lolo exhaled with relief. She hadn't realised that she was holding her breath. "I really appreciate it…"

"But this time I want something in return." Uncle Stanford's voice was toneless, his expression calculating. The power that had been Lolo's refuge now made her feel caged and threatened.

"Sure. Yes. Certainly!" she answered. "I'm willing to work for it. Maybe help out at your office? Or offer some of my marketing expertise? Just name it. I know nothing comes for free. What can I offer in return?"

Uncle Stanford responded immediately and without batting an eyelid, "You."

Tuesday 09 June 2015, 19h45

Eli Eli lama sabachthani[1] 🌑

Wednesday 10 June 2015, 16h35

One day at a time…

Thursday 18 June 2015, 18h56

Just came back from a Parent-Teacher meeting and João and Oyana were there. He was so normal like he's not trying to take my kids from me. How can one human being be so cruel? How can she just stand by? Black woman, you're on your own…

Friday 19 June 2015, 18h10

Was feeling down and so sorry for myself and just got a text from Stelios inviting me to Mousiki for a drink and dinner before the club opens. Cute 😊

Wednesday 24 June 2015, 04h10

Is this even my life? 😖

Monday 29 June 2015, 20h20

Who am I? Where am I? Where am I going?

Thursday 02 July 2015, 21h34

Just came back from dinner with Mr "I'm not the romantic type and shit." But who's the one fetching me from my doorstep and holding open doors for me? LOL! Funny how Stelios knows how to shield me from life's loneliest moments. I like that he's not trying to save me, but rather that he keeps me company as I learn how to save myself. *Efharisto*[2] my love, efharisto…

Sunday 05 July 2016, 21h40

John 15:13

Lolo's Place, Canary Estate, Hurlingham

It was 3 am, and Lolo couldn't get back to sleep. Lolo watched Kael and Noel gently snoring on either side of her. So cute. The usually independent Kael had decided to join his brother in sleeping in his mom's bed every night, and the scramble had settled on having Mom sleep in the middle so that they could both cuddle with her.

Kael still snored when sleeping, as he had done since he was a baby. Noel still clutched onto Lolo like a baby monkey. He was her little monkey. They were her everything.

Lolo couldn't let them go. She WOULDN'T let them go. She would rather die than let them go.

Lolo peeled Noel's arm off her chest, careful not to wake him up, and gently slipped out of bed. Quietly, she tiptoed down the stairs in the dark, using only her phone's torch for light. Turning on the lights would wake Aus' Moipone, who would insist that Lolo get back to bed and get some rest, and Lolo was in no mood for that conversation.

Once downstairs, Lolo lowered herself quietly onto the couch and wrapped the throw around her feet.

There has to be another way, Lolo thought to herself and went through her options again.

Her credit lines were maxed, and her last two requests for an increase in her overdraft had been declined by her bank. She had long exhausted all savings arranging first the move to her mother's place, then another one to her own.

Her father was having his own financial troubles with a business deal that hadn't turned out as anticipated. Her mother would ask the same question as Qhayiya – why was Lolo still staying in such an expensive place when she could simply move back home?

Nala was a non-starter, and Runako had reacted strangely when Lolo had asked her for a mere R5,000 during the move, citing Zimbabwean foreign currency restrictions or something of the sort.

She had one option left.

With hands shaking, she opened WhatsApp and drafted a deceivingly simple four-word message to the contact named Father Christmas.

Lolo: I'm ready to talk

CRIMSON BRIDES

"Do not look where you fell, but where you slipped"

— AFRICAN PROVERB

Lolo's Place, Canary Estate, Hurlingham
July 2015

Kael and Noel were happily devouring their Saturday dinner treat of Domino's pizza, while Lolo stood in the shower feeling like a lamb getting ready for the slaughter.

No matter how hard she scrubbed, she felt dirty. Dirty at the thought of what was to occur. Something that went against everything she had worked so hard to become. Everything she wanted people to believe she was.

She reluctantly got out of the shower and dried herself, looking at the stranger staring back at her from the bathroom mirror. Was it really a stranger? Or just a side of herself she had kept buried all these years?

She pulled out a black lace thong and its matching bra.

The irony. It was the La Perla set João had bought her for Valentine's Day, two years before. Now she was wearing it for his godfather's enjoyment. The same João, who used to protect her, was the one from whom she now needed protection.

Tears streamed down Lolo's cheeks as she sped down William Nicol drive. She was late, and Uncle Stanford didn't take well to tardiness.

The gate automatically opened as she pulled up, like in those horror movies when the main character enters a haunted house.

Maybe she WAS entering a haunted house. Maybe Uncle Stanford was an evil spirit, and she, his victim for the night. Or maybe she, too, was evil, and this was a coven of sorts.

Lolo pulled up behind Uncle Stanford's car and noted that the front door was ajar. She turned off her engine and took a moment to reconsider her decision one last time.

At that moment, she wanted nothing more than to ask God to *let this cup pass me by*. But prayer, at this time, was useless. She'd left God on her front doorstep twenty-two minutes ago.

Besides, she didn't feel like a conversation with God right now, because He would tell her to read Proverbs 3:5. And that even if João was successful in taking her children, Apostle Paul's words in Romans 8:28 would still hold true.

Since the verses were no comfort, she decided to handle matters her way. There was only one prayer fit for such an occasion, and she hoped it reached God, wherever He was.

Forgive me, Father, for I'm about to sin.

Katz & Katz Attorneys, Sandton

There was something significantly different about the Lolo Morreira that walked into the offices of Katz & Katz that Tuesday morning.

On all the other occasions that Khanyisa, the receptionist, had welcomed her, Lolo had been timid, vulnerable, withdrawn and unsure of herself. This time, she walked tall, with her chin up and her shoulders back. She was chic in black pants and a matching slit-sleeve cape, a white cotton shirt and oversized black sunshades. Liz's youngest client, who was usually soft-spoken and preferred to sit quietly and wait to be called into a meeting room, was now walking threateningly towards Khanyisa's station.

"Khanyisa, morning," Lolo said crisply. She took off her shades and hooked them over her lapel. "Look, I'm sorry for my outburst at your offices last week. I panicked at the thought of losing my children. It's no excuse, but I hope you understand and accept my apology."

"Morning, Lolo. You're forgiven," Khanyisa smiled sincerely. "I take it you're here for your 10 o'clock with Liz?"

"Yes. Yes, I am. And as promised, I have the money to settle my arrears and take my account into credit by R10 000. You take cash?" Lolo replied, placing a thick brown envelope on the reception counter.

Liz kicked off the consultation by clarifying that the depiction of custody in (mostly American) movies, was not an accurate reflection of how the law works in South Africa. Instead, the concept of parental responsibilities and rights, as contained in the South African Children's Act of 2005, applied. The Act divided parental responsibilities and rights into four broad categories: care, guardianship, contact, and maintenance.

Liz explained that the principle of care referred to a parent's decision-making powers over a child's day-to-day life, including the food they eat, schools they attend, and the religion they practise.

The principle of guardianship alluded to the legal powers that a parent exercises on behalf of their minor child, without the consent of the other parent.

The principle of contact, which João was contesting, entailed the parent's right of company and communication with their child or children, and specifically the right to their residence.

Lastly, the principle of maintenance encompassed the financial responsibility of each parent towards the maintenance of the child or children.

Liz explained that João was applying for the right to provide primary care for the children, meaning that they would live with him full-time.

Lolo would have visitation rights, as deemed appropriate by the courts. This would, however, not strip her of guardianship rights – João would still need her consent for certain things. He could not apply for their passports or take them out of the country without Lolo's permission, for example.

Furthermore, it would not absolve her of her responsibility to contribute financially towards the maintenance of the children.

"So, you're telling me he can strip me of my children AND make me pay maintenance for them?" Lolo queried with raised eyebrows, leaning forward in her chair and resting her elbows on the boardroom table.

"Yes," Liz said, bluntly.

"How do we stop him?"

"By showing the court that your current shared residence arrangement is in the best interests of both children. He has made a formal application via the office of the Family Advocate, and it is in your best interest to press through all the resultant processes meticulously and TIMEOUSLY." Liz looked pointedly at Lolo, obviously alluding to Lolo's delay in returning her calls and scheduling the consultation.

"I'll jump through every hoop you tell me to," Lolo assured Liz. "Where to from here?"

"The legal obligation is to perform an investigation into the current care, contact, and guardianship arrangement. "First, we'll send a reply agreeing to the assessment, on condition that we nominate the investigator. Secondly, we'll state that the investigator's fees, and the fees of any other experts that may need to be called upon, will be for João's account, as he is the one that is insisting on an investigation."

"And he won't be opposed to us appointing our own person?" Lolo enquired, nibbling on the side of her thumb.

"It won't be 'our own' person," Liz corrected. "It will be an independent person that we just happen to appoint. Investigators are usually forensic psychologists. They are duty-bound to be impartial and unbiased and are highly unlikely to put their professional career on the line for the appointing party to win their case. In fact, there are many cases where the investigator has submitted findings that recommend primary care be taken away from the party who appointed and/or paid them."

"Really?" Lolo said, her face showing a glimmer of hope.

"Yes. Besides, João's attorney must confirm she's happy with the person we've nominated before we proceed. And, if any party is not happy with the investigator's conduct or outcomes at the end of the case, they can submit a complaint to the relevant regulatory body, such as the Health Professions Council of South Africa." Liz said, running her hands through her fiery red hair.

"How long will this whole thing take?" Lolo asked, feeling much more confident.

"Plus-minus three months. It depends on everyone's availability."

"Everyone?" Lolo asked.

"Yes. Yourself, João, the children, Oyana –"

"OYANA?" Lolo sputtered indignantly.

"Yes, Oyana," Liz confirmed drily, as if she had answered this question a thousand times. "She's a primary caregiver to the children and will also be interviewed."

"Wow…. So you're saying my ex-husband's SIDE-CHICK will play a role in determining whether I keep my children or not?" Lolo screeched, shocked.

"I'd drop the drama, if I were you!" Liz snapped back. "It won't serve you well in your interactions with the investigator. You need to use your HEAD, and not your heart, now." Liz's voice grew less sharp as her words had the desired effect.

"Be calm and factual in all your communication. Act normal, and never, ever, try and discuss anything with the investigator 'off the record'. He or she is NOT your friend. EVERYTHING you discuss will be on the record and can be used against you in a court of law.

"Also, you cannot be seen to delay, frustrate or influence this process. Move whatever you must in your calendar.

"Finally, relax. If you are anything like the type of mother I have come to know in the short time I've spent with you, you have nothing to worry about. Let the process run its course, and you'll come out just fine."

Lolo leaned back and stared at the ceiling, willing herself not to cry in her lawyer's presence again.

It seemed never-ending. The pain, the humiliation, and now the reality that João's mistress could have a hand in stripping Lolo of her children, too.

She had played strong, walking into Katz & Katz offices that morning. Played strong in bed with Uncle Stanford over the weekend. But she didn't have the strength to pretend she could live without her babies.

Coetzee Residence, Randburg
August 2015

Estelle Coetzee was nothing like Lolo expected. Instead of the podgy retired-cop image she had in her head, Estelle was elegant, with a petite physique and shoulder-length silver-grey hair. She was more Helen Mirren than Sherlock Holmes. More tea and crumpets than doughnuts and coffee. More Pringle twinset than Belstaff trench.

Estelle invited Lolo to take a seat on the patio and asked if Lolo was okay with her beagle, Charlie, being around. Lolo couldn't help but wonder if the investigation had already begun, and whether this question was set up to test her character in some way or another.

Would hesitance to be around dogs mean she was unaccommodating of others and put her own needs first? Or that she would deny the kids pets because she didn't like animals?

Lolo replied that she had no problem with Charlie sticking around during the interview and added that she had dogs growing up, two Maltese poodles names Snoopy and Fluffy.

Estelle didn't take Lolo's bait to establish rapport. She simply replied, "Thank you," and flashed a genuine but fleeting smile.

After introducing herself and explaining the purpose of the investigation, Estelle went on to describe the procedure.

"How the process works is that I will put together a report from information gathered through interviews. These will take the form of play therapy with the kids; psychometric tests, collateral information like school, medical and psychologists' reports; and finally, a home visit. Is there anything you would like to ask me before we proceed?"

"Yes, please. I believe you will be interviewing myself, João, and his fiancé, Oyana. I would like to request that you include the children's nanny, Aus' Moipone, since she is also a primary caregiver, and has known me and my household since before the break-up," Lolo said, lightly patting Charlie, who had decided to settle at her feet.

"Oh, yes, of course! She is on the list of people to be interviewed. We also need to interview your close family members. João has put forward his mother, Isabel, and best friend, Junior. Are there any family members you would like to nominate?" Estelle asked.

Bastard! He's chosen my two arch-enemies. People he knows will have nothing good to say about me. Who will I choose…?

Bingo!

"Yes, I'd like to nominate my mom, Nandi, and my best friend, Qhayiya. She's not blood family, but we've been best friends since we were teenagers, and she's a big part of the children's lives."

"Noted. Please make sure to give me their contact details before you leave," Estelle requested.

"I will," Lolo promised, wondering if she was supposed to do so right away. "I have another question, please. When you say 'psychometric tests', what do you mean?"

"Personality tests. They are multiple-choice questions that you will need to complete during one of our sessions. You can't prepare for them so please don't try. All I would advise is that you get a good night's rest, arrive on time, so you're not flustered, take your time and answer as honestly as you can. They are designed to pick up manufactured or manipulated responses."

"I see. Oh! One more, if I may. You mentioned a home visit. Could you please clarify?"

"Sure. I will set up a time to come to your home and observe the children and their interaction with you in their home environment."

"So, you're coming to watch us?" Lolo asked uncomfortably.

"To observe you. I'll have some activities for you and the children and record my findings of their interaction with you."

"Uhm… okay."

"Again, Lolo, just be yourself," Estelle reiterated reassuringly, while still maintaining her professional decorum. "Pretend I'm a family friend coming to visit and go about your business as you normally would. Please don't prepare anything or try to put on a show, because I will see through it, and it may jeopardise your case."

"Okay. I think I get it," Lolo replied deferentially, nodding.

Estelle proceeded with the day's interview and asked Lolo to detail her background and family history.

She interrogated everything; where and when Lolo was born, her parents' relationship status at the time, who raised her, the schools she went to, and the nature and quality of her relationships with her parents and immediate family.

It was harrowing. Lolo wondered if the fact that her parents were divorced would count against her. Also, Lolo and her mother had both left their marriages. Could that be interpreted to mean that Lolo was a bad example to her kids? That they'd have a better outcome if raised by João, who came from a still intact nuclear family?

Lolo mused over all these things again as she drove home from the interview. She replayed everything in her head and evaluated what she could have done better.

It was torture. She felt like a criminal without a charge. A convict without a crime. Guilty, of being an unfit mother, until proven innocent.

The next few weeks were a blur as Lolo tried to play model mom to the children. She put her social events on hold for fear that João would use these to portray her as an absent mother. Runako had also advised her to stop posting her alcoholic beverage partnership on social media, as alcoholism was an increasingly popular method used by fathers against mothers when claiming for custody during a divorce battle.

Lolo had spent six weeks co-operating with all requests from her lawyer, the investigator, and family and friend. Now, she had one final hurdle to cross – surviving the home visit.

Lolo's Place, Hurlingham
September 2015

The Highveld's autumn sun rose as it did every day. The hadedas sounded their call as they did every morning. The low-pitched hum of the washing machine sounded the same as it did every Saturday. But for Lolo, this morning was different. Critical.

This was the day on which the everyday goings-on would be observed by a stranger, to determine whether Lolo was a good enough mother.

By the time the estate security called at 11 am sharp, Lolo was showered, changed and already on her third deal with God. She'd figured a prayer was too routine for a situation as delicate as this and had thus decided to make deals with God instead.

First, if God brought her through this situation, she would dedicate her career to helping other women be better prepared for divorce. Second, she would be a better mother to her children and take them to church every Sunday. Third, and perhaps most tempting to God, she would never sleep with another married man again, no matter how desperate her circumstances. She'd made as compelling an offer to God as she could think up, and now it was up to Him to ensure the investigation found her to be a fit mother to retain shared care of her children.

Everyone had taken their positions when Lolo let Estelle in. Aus' Moipone was busy in the kitchen washing the breakfast dishes, and Kael and Noel were in the living room playing on their iPads. Lolo offered Estelle a cup of tea, and, after accepting, Estelle sat down and took Lolo through the morning's agenda.

"What we're going do to today, is observe the children's living conditions and their interactions with you. I will need you to take me on a tour around the premises, and when we return, we will play some games with the children."

"Sure, no problem," Lolo replied, hoping that she sounded suitably earnest and co-operative.

The cup of tea sat, neglected, on the coffee table while Lolo took Estelle on a tour around the house, starting in the kitchen.

Estelle looked through the fridge, the freezer, and the cupboards, and studied the children's artwork, framed and displayed all around the kitchen. Lolo silently thanked herself that she'd insisted on taking half of the children's art from her marital home.

Next, they proceeded upstairs, to the bedrooms. The twins' room was first, and Estelle looked around at the lime green linen and plush toys, picked through the papers and colouring books strewn on the desk, and finally checked the cupboards – rummaging through the clothes, and pulling out the bed linen and curtains stored in the top shelf.

The petite investigator asked for the desk chair and climbed on top of it to get a clearer view of what else may be hiding out of sight.

Estelle moved to Aus' Moipone's room, where the same meticulous procedure was followed. She looked through Aus' Moipone's bedside table and opened the cosmetics containers, taking a sniff to determine if the contents matched the packaging. She looked through the cupboards and again asked for a chair so she could check for everything stored at the top of the cupboard.

In the children's bathroom, Estelle looked through the medicine cupboard, paying attention to the contents and reading the product labels of the various products stored there.

Finally, Estelle entered Lolo's room. She noted the books on the bedside table, scanned the pictures in the frames, went through the books on the desk and, finally, went through the cupboards.

This time, she started with the top of the cupboard and again asked for a chair. She went through Lolo's clothes, and Lolo's shoes, opening the shoeboxes to check what was inside. A momentary fear ripped through Lolo's core.

She kept cash from Uncle Stanford in a shoebox. Luckily, she had paid it all to her lawyer. How would she have explained thirty grand, in cash, sitting in a shoebox?

They went back downstairs, and Estelle asked Lolo to give her a tour of the yard. She noted the pool didn't have a pool net, to which Lolo quickly replied she was happy to ask the landlord to supply one. She walked around the garden and noted it was well-maintained, asking how often the garden was serviced, who serviced it, and how Lolo had appointed her garden service. Was Estelle worried that the gardener would pose a risk to her children? Was she testing Lolo's interpersonal skills?

Lolo's mind was playing games with her. Every word she uttered, every gesture she made, might determine whether or not she would raise her kids, going forward.

Estelle and Lolo returned from their tour and Estelle apologised to Aus' Moipone for having let her tea go cold. Aus' Moipone was only too happy to offer another cup since Lolo had briefed her about their mystery guest on Saturday morning, and the power she wielded.

As Aus' Moipone was brewing a fresh pot of tea, Estelle asked Kael and Noel if they could show her a game they played with their mom. It could be any game – a card game, board game, hide and seek, whatever. As long as it was something they regularly did with their mom.

Luckily for Lolo, her meagre finances and resultant downgrading of her cable TV package meant she'd resorted to playing card games with the kids.

'Porridge' and 'Snap' were their favourites since they were high-intensity but still simple enough for the kids to understand. The trio decided to play 'Snap' as 'Porridge' would take too long to build up.

Kael and Noel giggled with glee as their mom intentionally lost the game and gasped at how well they were doing, oblivious to the observant onlooker, sipping her tea and taking notes.

Apparently, Estelle had seen enough, and she asked for one final activity before she concluded her investigation for the day.

"Kael, I'd like you to please rub this lotion on your mommy's hand, and when Kael's done, Noel, I'd like you to please rub this lotion on your mommy's other hand. Do you think you can do that for me?" Estelle asked in warm tones.

"I'll go first," Noel squealed.

"No, Noel! The lady said I must," Kael asserted.

"Noel, let Kael go first, please," Lolo mediated in the calmest, 'fit mother' tone she could muster. "When he's done, then it will be your turn. Okay, my boy?"

"Okay, Mommy," Noel yielded, with a brilliant show off smile at Lolo.

Kael proceeded slowly and gently to rub lotion on his mother's left hand, all the while giving her a warm smile and looking lovingly into her eyes. Noel, having seen his brother and never one to be outdone, proceeded to do the same, with an even more exaggerated smile and intensified affection.

Estelle put down her teacup and announced that she had all the information she needed to conclude her report. She thanked Lolo for her hospitality and departed.

After she'd shut the door, Lolo broke down into tears and gave her confused children a long and lingering hug. *It's true, you don't know what you have until it's gone,* Lolo thought. She had never loved and appreciated her children more than she did at that moment.

Yes, they were a lot of work, and yes, they were annoying at times, but oh, my God, she would never, ever willingly give up the privilege of raising them and watching them grow.

A sense of calm and relief overcame her as she collapsed onto the couch, as the hours of tossing and turning the previous night suddenly caught up with her.

Estelle had been warm but not familiar. Firm, but not cold. She was there to get the job done, and her disposition had remained the same throughout the interview and the investigation process.

"I think we did well, Aus' Moipone," Lolo mumbled with a yawn, "I think we did well."

Nala's apartment, North Riding
May 2016

"Shall I call the Uber, ladies?" Nala asked as she scrolled through her Instagram feed.

"Why so early? You know I hate waiting around at these concerts, babes," Qhayiya said casually.

"No, it's a good idea to get it now. It took me an hour just to get from Beyers Naudè to here. Traffic is a nightmare!" Lolo countered.

"Okay. I've requested it," Nala said. "It says it's twenty minutes away."

"Who needs a top up?" Runako asked, as she walked back into the living room with a freshly opened bottle of champagne in her hands.

"Me!" Lolo exclaimed, shooting her hand in the air even though her glass was still half full.

"You may as well top all of us up. We've got at least another hour before Mariah gets on stage," Qhayiya added.

"Fair enough," Runako replied

"Well, in that case, ladies, I propose a toast," Nala said, raising her glass. "To a friendship that's stood the test of time. Seen us through the best and the worst that life has to offer. From fabulous weddings in Rome to horrendous rituals in the bushes of Azalia…"

Qhayiya shook her head as she held her glass to her chest. "Nope! I'm not toasting to that unless you're willing to finally reveal what happened to you in that year of mourning."

"Are you sure you want us to go that deep? Cause I don't think ya'll can handle *me* going deep!" Lolo said, shaking her head.

"You're right," Nala smiled softly, "It hasn't been all bad. Just look at Runako. She's managed to survive two separations and prove you can still have a happily ever after…"

"I wouldn't be too quick to use Kobe and me as the barometer for good marriages, darling!" Runako said.

"But that's exactly my point," Nala argued, taking a seat next to Runako on the emerald velvet chaise. "Good marriages are not *perfect* marriages. They are a union of two forgivers that love each other through all of life's messy parts."

"Guys, can I tell you a secret?" Runako said in a low voice before democratically interrupting herself. "Actually, I'll share my secret only if you promise to share yours, too. I know I'm not the only one with skeletons in her closet…"

"Okay… this should be interesting," Nala drawled. "I'm in."

"Don't look at me!" Lolo resisted, kicking off her ankle boots and pulling her feet under her thighs. "I've never been one to hide my dirty laundry."

"Oh, there MUST be something we don't know, Lolo," Nala fished.

"Ok. There may be one or two things… But I'll only share them if your secrets aren't pap," Lolo teased.

"I'm in," Qhayiya said excitedly, leaning forward on the couch she was sitting on next to Lolo. "Spill!"

"Pinkie-swear?" Runako insisted anxiously. She was rewarded with a solemn, silent hook-up of four hands, a shared gesture that had become familiar over the years.

"So..." Runako began, sighing while she evaluated her words. "The only reason I'm still with Kobe, well other than the fact that he threatened to fire my father and brothers from his company if I went through with the divorce, is that I'm in a relationship with someone else."

"WHAT!" Nala exclaimed.

"With who?" Qhayiya added, her jaw dropping to the floor.

Runako was silent for a moment and then smiled awkwardly. "Anesu."

"Good for you!" Lolo cheered as she raised her glass in the air.

"Why cheat instead of just leaving if you're not happy?" Nala asked innocently.

"Because... I've already tried that TWICE!" Runako said ruefully, shaking her head. "I tried. You guys know how hard I tried to leave Kobe. But by then, it was too late. I'd given him too much power. He had power over my family and our finances. Power over my father and brothers' livelihood. Power over my ability to provide my baby Zina with the comforts she had grown accustomed to. Power even over my very ability to leave him, as I could not afford my life without his financial support." Runako paused, stunned by the power of her own words. She placed her champagne glass on the coffee table in front of her and stared at the floor. She continued, speaking more to herself, than to her friends. "I gave Kobe too much power. And by the time I wanted to take it back, it was too late."

"Aren't you scared of what will happen if he finds out?" Nala asked, gently brushing her friend's back.

"Frankly I couldn't be bothered," Runako said matter-of-factly, sitting back up and leaning against her seat.

"Say what?" Lolo exclaimed, choking on her drink.

"What's he going to tell me when he's happily having an affair with CJ?" Runako asked breezily.

"Who's also married! I give up!" Qhayiya sighed, holding her hands on her head.

"Don't be judgemental, Q. If it works for them then we have no right to say anything on the matter...." Nala reprimanded

"And while you have the mic, why don't you tell us what your big secret is, Little Miss Perfect Nala?" Qhayiya turned the tables.

Nala bit on a hangnail as she debated whether or not to share her secret with her friends.

"Okay," Nala said and cleared her throat uncomfortably. "I see things."

"As do we..." Lolo said sarcastically, looking around the room.

"No, Lols! I mean SEE things. Spiritual things. Like visions and stuff."

"Hayi! Hayi! Hayi! Nala! *O tlo re loya yanong*[1]!" Lolo screamed as she jumped up and ran towards the door.

"Oh my God..." Runako yelped, dashing after Lolo. "Please don't read my mind!" she begged, holding her head in her hands and squeezing her eyes shut.

"You're a *sangoma*[2], friend?" Qhayiya asked with eyes wide open.

"No, well I don't think so..." breathed Nala. "I don't know what I am. I have visions. And premonitions. And can see the future, if that makes sense."

"Then you should be able to tell us exactly where the Uber is!" Lolo teased, eyeing her friend suspiciously and still clutching onto the door handle.

"Stop being silly!" Nala chuckled. "It's a little uncomfortable to be honest, knowing things people would prefer you didn't. Like the vision I keep having of you, sitting on the shoulders of a giant man, as he carries you into a deep lake…"

"THAT is just freaky. Guess it's my turn, then!" Lolo exclaimed, walking back into the living area and standing in the centre of the room. Runako followed and took a seat, still mouthing "Don't read my mind" to Nala.

"My big secret, ladies, is that I slept with Father Christmas," Lolo confessed, chin in the air and lips pursed.

"Cancel the Uber! It's going to be a long night!" Runako exclaimed.

"No!" Nala shrieked.

"What?!" Qhayiya screamed.

"Don't make me feel bad. I had to," Lolo said plaintively. "Sometimes, I still have flashbacks of his beard scratching the back of my neck, and I can smell his fragrance coming from over my shoulder. It's the most disgusting feeling ever. The absolute worst feeling."

"What do you mean, you HAD to?" Runako asked sceptically.

"I needed to settle my legal bill that was already twenty thousand in arrears before Liz would attend to my custody matter. And Stanford wouldn't give me more money unless… you know, I slept with him."

"And why didn't you ask US for help?" Runako exclaimed.

"Yeah!" Nala concurred.

"Exactly!" Qhayiya added, shaking her head. "You had plenty of options, Lolo!"

"Because YOU Qhayiya, would have reminded me that I'm living beyond my means!" Lolo said, cocking her head to the side and scanning her face. "And you Nala, would have helped me with money from where?"

"I guess you're right..." Nala sighed sheepishly.

"And let's come to you, Runako. How I have longed for this day," Lolo said. She placed her glass on the table before straightening up and folding her arms in front of her chest. "Please explain to me how you, would honestly expect me to reach out to you for any kind of support when you have been openly fraternising with João's fiancé?"

"What do you mean?" Runako replied awkwardly, straining her neck to look up at Lolo.

"You heard me. I've seen your Instagram pics. Hosting her at your house for dinner. Laughing with them at the Polo in January. I'm listening." Lolo was now standing over Runako and bowing threateningly over her face.

"I wasn't hosting HER," Runako replied defensively. "I was hosting my husband's best friend, who just happened to be engaged to the woman that broke your marriage."

"So, knowing full well what João and that woman have put me through, you still have no problem smiling for the cameras with them!" Lolo spat. Tears were now rolling down her face. "Knowing full well, they took my kids from me, Runako! Knowing full well they put me through the very thing that's keeping you chained to your sham of a marriage? That's the REAL reason you're still married to Kobe, isn't it? Because you're afraid, he's going to take Zina from you!"

"Stop it, Lolo!" Runako screamed, rising to her feet. "What choice did I have? Huh? João is one of Kobe's best friends. I would have risked troubling my marriage if I refused to hang out with him and his fiancé. I had to put my marriage and my family first."

"No, Runako. You could have chosen to put YOUR best friend first, just like Kobe put HIS best friend first!" Lolo spat, shoving her friend in the chest. Runako fell back in her chair, tears rolling down her face. Qhayiya and Nala looked at each other in horror, paralysed by the showdown unfolding in front of them.

"I'm sorry Lolo, but we're not in uni anymore. We don't make decisions on what's best for the squad. We have to make decisions based on what's best for-"

"Ourselves. Clearly!" Lolo interrupted

"Our children," Runako said quietly. "I was going to say we have to do what's best for our children."

Lolo sank to the floor and hugged her knees to her chest. There was an awkward silence as Lolo gently rocked herself back and forth.

"I wish my dad had put his children first," she said pensively, looking up to the ceiling as she did. "I wouldn't be in this position if he'd been there for Koko and I... just to give us guidance, not even money, you know?"

"Yeah..." Runako said softly. She crouched beside her friend and held her to her chest.

"At least you still have your dad..." Qhayiya whimpered, her voice breaking through the tears. "I've spent the last few years in a shitty relationship trying to fill the void my father left when he and my mom broke up!"

"What do you mean, babe?" Runako asked gently.

"I mean Junior..." Qhayiya sniffled. "He's the first man I fell in love with, the first man to make me feel wanted, the only person I could lean on when I first moved to Joburg. And I've stayed with him even though things are bad. Like REALLY bad."

"Is it nothing you can fix?" Nala coaxed gently.

"Yeah, how bad can it be?" Runako prodded. Lolo and Qhayiya exchanged awkward looks before Qhayiya shared her secret.

"Phew! Okay," Qhayiya faced up with a deep breath. "Where do I start?" she vacillated, scrunching her face, and pursing her lips.

The room fell silent as the friends waited to hear what secret Qhayiya had been keeping.

"Junior hits me…" Qhayiya sobbed.

"No, Q! No!" Nala cried. She pulled her friend into her embrace and held her tight. "What the hell is wrong with that guy?"

Runako joined in and wrapped her arms around both Qhayiya and Nala. "Why didn't you say anything?" she begged.

"I don't know…" Qhayiya quavered, and blew her nose inelegantly. "I just kept thinking it will stop. Once his art was selling faster. Or he'd made up with his dad. Or decided to get back into corporate. I don't know…"

The girls sat on the floor with their backs against the chaises.

"Well, you shouldn't place yourself in danger while he figures himself out!" Lolo screamed. "Leave, Q! Break up with Junior and carry on with your life!"

"Exactly! And you should report him to the police too!" Runako added, emphatically.

"I can't…" Qhayiya frowned. "I just can't bring myself to do it."

"Why on earth not?" Lolo spat. "Put this guy behind bars for what he's done to you!" She turned to look at Nala and Runako for support.

"Guys, these things are often complicated," Nala pointed out. "Let's give Q a chance to respond. If she wants to. At the end of the day, she doesn't owe any of us an explanation."

"Because…because I love him –"

"Spare me!" Lolo sighed.

"And I have no witnesses," Qhayiya shrugged. "It was only ever just the two of us when it happened, and it's near impossible to prove a case of assault when there are no witnesses."

The friends shook their heads in disbelief at what they were hearing.

"The best I can do now is get as far away from Junior as I can, and try to make sure that what happened to me, doesn't happen to someone else."

INNER ENIOLA

"Do not stand in a place of danger trusting in miracles"

— AFRICAN PROVERB

Franklin Securities, Sandton
July 2016

*T*he Franklin Securities auditorium had many stories to tell. Over the years, it had hosted several results presentations, graduate inductions, long-service awards, and client product launches.

While the auditorium held stories, the adjoining bathrooms held secrets. When there was no event being held in the auditorium, its bathrooms were an oasis of absolute privacy – far from the prying eyes and swivelling ears of fellow Franklin Securities bankers.

It was in one of these bathroom cubicles that Qhayiya sat with hands shaking, hunched over the single sheet of paper that held the power to change her destiny forever.

It was this power that had her second-guessing a decision she had taken over three months ago. She shifted uncomfortably on the cold toilet seat beneath her thighs and went through the letter. Again.

Unit 6A The Towers
Park Lane
Hyde Park
2196

54 Gwen Lane
Sandown
Sandton
2031

Wednesday, 15 July 2016

LETTER OF RESIGNATION

Dear Mr Stewart Delport,

Please accept this letter as notice of my resignation from the position of Wealth Manager at Franklin Securities effective Wednesday, 15 July 2016, 30 calendar days from the date of this letter.

I would like to thank you for the opportunities and support afforded me during my tenure at Franklin Securities. I would like to offer whatever additional assistance may be required from me during this transitional period.

This includes helping to recruit, train and hand over to the person
that will be taking over from me in my role.

I trust you will find this in order.

Sincerely,
Qhayiya Dana (Miss)

"I'm scared, Hayley!" Qhayiya trembled. She looked up at Hayley, who was standing at the cubicle door. "I… I want to leave. I know I have to leave, but I'm still scared."

"Of course you're scared," Hayley responded. "This is scary. Change is scary. But you've prepared for it. That's the difference." Hayley smiled encouragingly if a little sadly.

"You're right," Qhayiya said less glumly, sitting up straight. "I HAVE prepared. I have way more than six months' salary equivalent sitting in my investments…"

"Exactly!" Hayley nodded. "And you have a strong personal brand in the finance community…"

"Yeah. Kinda…" Qhayiya said, waving her hand in a see-saw motion.

Hayley paused for a moment, thinking of another consideration she could use to motivate her colleague who was looking up at her expectantly.

"You had a solid performance last year, so you're not leaving on bad terms! That's always a good thing," Hayley smiled inquiringly.

"True! Very true!" Qhayiya nodded excitedly.

"You've finally let go of that loser boyfriend, so nothing is stopping your climb to the top!"

"I would be so far in life if I'd just let him move to Berlin when he first suggested it!" Qhayiya chuckled, shaking her head.

"And Q, I believe this is your *ikigai*[1]!" Hayley added.

"My WHAT guy?" Qhayiya squinted at Hayley, puzzled.

"Ikigai. Your purpose. The Japanese believe your purpose lies at the meeting of what the world needs, what you love doing, what you're good at, and what you'll get paid for," Hayley said, counting the four points out on her fingers.

"FANCY, Hayls!" Qhayiya teased, walking out of the cubicle and leaning against the marble bathroom counter. "Where did you learn about ikigais?"

"Online! One minute I'm searching for a Hamantaschen recipe and next thing I'm reading about the ikigai," Hayley chuckled.

"Right... maybe you should stick to having your Shabbos meals delivered, Hayls," Qhayiya suggested cheekily.

"You'll be fine, Qhayiya," Hayley repeated, resting her hands on Qhayiya's shoulders. "And many women will benefit from you starting your own women's financial wellness consultancy. I'm going to leave you alone now. You're going to count to ten, and then you're going to walk straight to Stewart's desk and hand him that letter. Deal?"

Qhayiya walked out of the bathrooms, taking the long route back to her floor. Her heart was racing, her body was trembling, her palms felt sticky, and the voices in her head were on overdrive.

Your life has changed so much in the past year. Why the hell are you leaving your job? Franklin Securities is the only stability you have!

But do I really want to sacrifice growth for stability?

It's not like I can't have both. I can simply change positions within Franklin Securities or get another job at another bank. In fact, I can work ANYWHERE!

And I want to throw all of that away, to start a new career as what? Someone that teaches women about the importance of being financially independent? Is there even a title for that?

Who cares what I call myself? It's what I'll be known FOR that's more important.

Some people rely on a title for power, some people breathe power into a title.

"I can't say I'm surprised, Q," Stewart said, holding the letter he had just finished reading. "But this is still quite a shock. Not to mention disappointment."

"I can understand you're disappointed, Stewart," Qhayiya replied, taking a seat at her superior's desk. "Especially since you guys groomed me throughout my whole career. I'm hoping you can understand why this venture I'm embarking on is so important to me, especially given my history with my ex. I believe it's my life's calling to start a consultancy that not only helps women gain and maintain financial independence but also assists in providing the necessary legal and psychological support for the challenges that come with being a financially independent woman."

She flashed him a warm smile before continuing. "With that being said, I still love banking very much and trust you me, if my little project doesn't work out, I hope I can still knock on your door and have my old job back."

Stewart chuckled. Qhayiya's plan had worked.

"Of course!" Stewart said, standing up and adjusting his pants. "You're one of our star performers, and we would be foolish not to take you back."

"Thank you!" Qhayiya blushed.

"I guess your mind is made up then?" he asked seriously.

"Yes. Yes, it is, Stewart," Qhayiya replied softly. "I'd hate myself if I didn't at least TRY and see where this takes me."

"Fair enough. I'll submit your resignation to HR and arrange for your exit interview. I'll miss you. Am I allowed a hug?" Stewart asked, with an exaggerated pout and outstretched arms.

"Of course you are!" Qhayiya laughed.

———————

Qhayiya didn't know what to expect as she walked into meeting room 'Dinar' that morning. The last time she'd been to the HR division was when she joined Franklin Securities seven years back. Now that she had resigned, she was contacted by HR to discuss the transfer of her benefits.

Norman Samuels, the employee benefits consultant, was already waiting when Qhayiya walked in. A friendly man with a small frame, his pale blue shirt and dark grey suit pants was a welcome departure from the attire Qhayiya had become accustomed to. Franklin Securities' unofficial dress code for male bankers was a dark suit, crisp cuff linked white shirt, and dark tie. And all the males on Qhayiya's floor strictly adhered to it.

Norman's eyes darted about behind his ill-fitting glasses as Qhayiya gave him a handshake. She helped herself to coffee and biscuits as he pulled up her benefits statement on his laptop. After inviting her to take a seat next to him, Norman meticulously worked his way through the document. He explained with great care each element of Qhayiya's benefits, and what she was walking away from as a result of her resignation.

"Why does my statement say 'Provident Fund' when you're talking about my pension fund?" Qhayiya asked curiously, pointing to the top of Norman's screen.

"Well, I actually haven't spoken about a pension fund, only your pension monies, which are sitting in a provident fund," Norman explained, pushing his glasses up the bridge of his nose.

"I'm confused," Qhayiya frowned.

"Let me explain. Pension monies are monies that will be paid out at retirement age. Depending on the organisation's retirement policies and procedures, the company will transfer them to either a pension fund or provident fund," Norman said confidently.

"What's the difference?" Qhayiya asked, taking a sip of her lukewarm coffee.

"With a pension fund, you can withdraw only a third of your investment at retirement. The balance is paid out as a monthly income that is meant to last you for the rest of your life," Norman spelt out, absently tugging at his collar.

"And the other one?"

"With a provident fund, you can withdraw the full investment at retirement. But you must bear in mind that you will be taxed on the lump sum pay out, which will probably put you in a higher tax bracket, as opposed to a lower monthly amount," Norman concluded as if that explained everything.

"This is all so confusing," Qhayiya lamented. "Anyway, what's going to happen to my pension now that I'm leaving Franklin Securities?"

"Well, you'll need to decide if you're transferring the full amount over to your new employer, or whether you would like to access some or all of your monies now," Norman answered intelligibly, for a change. "Either way, the funds will be disinvested from the group provident fund as you'll no longer be an employee of Franklin Securities."

"Uhm... I'll be working for myself," Qhayiya said nervously. "What happens then?"

"You'll need to speak to a financial advisor to transfer the monies to a retirement annuity or preservation fund for you if you're self-employed," Norman replied.

"I see..." Qhayiya nodded. "Can you explain these other death and disability benefits as well? Do I need to transfer those too?"

Norman explained that Qhayiya would be forfeiting the company benefits because they were not transferable.

Franklin Securities' Provident Fund came with a Death Benefit that entitled Qhayiya's beneficiaries to five times her annual Pensionable Salary, plus the total value of her Fund Credit, plus tax replacement cover. Doing a quick calculation, Norman showed this equalled roughly R4,5 million before tax.

The disability benefit would pay out if illness or accident rendered Qhayiya unable to perform her current job, or a similar one, subject to a three-month waiting period. If she were temporarily or permanently disabled, she would be entitled to a monthly disability benefit until the earlier of recovery, death or Normal Retirement Age. Franklin Securities' benefit, additionally, would have continued to make monthly provident fund contributions during the period of her disability.

Finally, had Qhayiya passed on while an employee of Franklin Securities, the provident fund would have also paid out towards the cost of her funeral.

"How didn't I know about any of these benefits?" Qhayiya asked, embarrassed that as a banker, and financial literacy advocate, she had such a skewed understanding of her own financials.

"Because you guys don't do an annual check of your benefits, Qhayiya. And worse, when you become self-employed, you forget to replace these benefits," Norman said piously.

"Well, I wish I HAD checked, or even asked for an explanation because you've broken it down so nicely, it's not as complicated as I thought," Qhayiya said, brightening up and smiling at Norman.

"That's kind," Norman blushed. "But at least you're here now, and I hope you won't make the same mistakes now that you'll be self-employed."

"What do you mean, Norman?"

"I mean, I hope you won't forget to make sure you have this cover in place. ESPECIALLY since you'll be self-employed!" Norman exclaimed, the passionate response a surprise from the usually shy consultant.

"Norman, I've changed my mind about you being a nice guy," Qhayiya sighed as she fell back in her chair. It had just become clear she had grossly miscalculated the amount of money she would need to match her cost to company at Franklin Securities.

Nelson Mandela Square, Sandton
July 2017

It had been a year since Qhayiya embarked on her entrepreneurial journey. Self-employment had turned out to be significantly different from life in corporate. Clients that had previously answered her phone calls on the first ring were now impossible to get a hold of.

Days that were filled by a never-ending to-do list were now a blank canvas that stared back at her in anticipation. Qualifications and experience played second fiddle to who you know and more importantly - who knows YOU!

The biggest surprise of all on the road of self-employment, was the loneliness. Not only had Qhayiya left the comfort of 44 floors' worth of colleagues, but she'd also left a relationship with the only guy she'd ever seriously dated. Over the past twelve months, she'd spent most of her days alone. She was lonely. And it hurt.

Friendship didn't offer much comfort, either. There was only so much complaining her friends could take as they were busy with their own lives too. Lolo seemed to be thriving in her role as a full-time social media influencer.

Losing custody of the boys had hit her hard, and her performance at work had started slipping. Badly. She ended up being managed out.

Nala, on the other hand, had used the solitude to her advantage. Solal, being based in Azalia with the Ilungas, allowed Nala to work her way quickly up the call centre ladder. In the last three months, she'd landed herself a promotion to HR manager. According to her calculations, she was now just one inflationary increase away from affording a lawyer to help her bring Solal back to South Africa.

Runako and Kobe's "arrangement" seemed to be working well. So well in fact that Runako was now pregnant with her second child. She'd resigned herself to spending the rest of her life with Kobe. Whether or not they were in love was far down her priority list.

Qhayiya was a mix of emotions as her Manolo Blahnik Misto pumps click-clacked across the scalloped marble floors of the Flamingo Room. She took a sip of her welcome glass of bubbly as the waitress mumbled something about the day's *amuse bouche*[2].

Nala walked in to Qhayiya making doodles with the leftover balsamic reduction from the complimentary goat cheese and roasted beet appetiser. She teased her friend for looking like a woman who'd been stood up. It was only after Qhayiya explained she'd lost the pitch to provide financial wellness services to a large corporate, that Nala understood the reason behind her friend's mood.

"Actually... maybe you should pitch your service offering to Franklin Securities," Nala suggested.

Qhayiya tapped a waitress walking past and mouthed 'Two Turkish Delights, please' before turning back to Nala, intrigued. "Continue..." she requested.

"I'm thinking you could turn your old employer into a client," Nala said, leaning forward on the table. "You have an advantage because you have an intimate understanding of the organisation and its operations. Pitch your service offering as a solution to specific pain points, and you'll convert them into a client."

"That is flippen' BRILLIANT, Nala Pauline Kalenga!" Qhayiya shouted, beaming. "Your new role as an HR manager is already starting to bear fruit for me."

"Hey! Don't you EVER use that name in public again," Nala chuckled.

"Ladies!" Lolo trilled, appearing out of nowhere. She blew Qhayiya and Nala kisses before taking a seat.

"Is that a new bag I see?" Qhayiya asked accusingly. She peered under the table for a closer look at the item Lolo had tried to sneak in discreetly.

"Maybe," Lolo replied unhelpfully.

"Maybe? I've seen that bag," Qhayiya exclaimed. "It costs like R30k a pop!"

"Qhayiya," Lolo reprimanded cheerily, "we're in a public establishment. And you're shouting. Not a good look!"

"Tshenolo..." Qhayiya said sternly. She closed her eyes and shook her head slowly, something she did when extremely frustrated. "Explain to me, please, how you have a new bag worth R30k when you still owe me five grand from nearly a year ago?" she enquired archly, opening her eyes to pin Lolo with a hawk's stare.

"And just last week you were complaining about needing money to get your new e-commerce website up and running," Nala added, with the tone of a tell-tale sibling.

"Can everybody relax!" Lolo defended, pointing to her friends with both index fingers. "Q, I'm pleased to announce that I have your money. Right here. In full!" Lolo smiled smugly. She lifted the hood of her new bag to reveal wads of R200 notes.

"I don't even want to know..." Qhayiya sighed, shaking her head.

"I do!" Nala interjected. "There's way more than R5 000 in there, Lols. Is there a new man?"

"Yes. AND no," Lolo began. "This took smarts. So I met this guy in the club last Wednesday – "

"Oh, boy..." Qhayiya groaned, dropping her head into her hands.

"He caught my eye with his traditional clothing, fancy watch and Nigerian accent. You know when I spot that combination, I immediately smell ka-ching!" Lolo smiled, rapidly brushing her thumbs against her fingers to signal money. "Next morning, we're shopping in Sandton – "

"How are we at the next morning?!" Qhayiya challenged, clapping her hands onto her head.

"Do you want the story or not?" Lolo asked glibly, pushing back her chair as if to leave the table.

"Of course! Please continue," Nala backed down with a long-suffering smile, gripping Lolo's chair.

"Good. As I was saying, we're in Sandton, shopping for his wife and kids and I help choose the most gorgeous items for them. Designer only. Cause I'm not stingy, you know," Lolo explained.

"Uh-huh," Nala murmured encouragingly, her hand over her mouth to hide the occasional snigger at Lolo's story.

"We get back to the hotel, and I say I'm so sad we didn't get time to buy something for me because I really liked the bag we both gawked at. He feels bad, especially after I've been so nice in picking out clothes and gifts for his family, and bingo, I'm sitting with R30k in my hands. Cash!" Lolo smiled smugly at her friends who were dumbfounded by her escapade.

"Okay…" Qhayiya said and cleared her throat. "So, if you bought the bag, how do you still have so much cash?"

Lolo threw back her head and laughed uproariously before taking another sip of her bubbly, still snickering.

"You amateur!" Lolo began, touching Nala's forearm condescendingly. "Everyone knows you don't buy the real thing when you've been given cash!"

"It's fake!" Qhayiya cottoned on, her mouth wide open.

"Yip! Bought it from one of my dealers for three grand. Sent a photo to 'Uncle Abuja' as evidence. Pocketed the difference which I'll use to repay you and set up my new e-commerce website!" Lolo beamed, raising her glass high in the air to toast herself.

"Why weren't you just honest with 'Uncle Abuja' from the start? Surely he'd have more respect for you, knowing you would spend that amount of money on a business and not a bag?" Nala asked innocently.

"Oh, Nala… Sweet, SWEET Nala," Lolo replied mirthlessly. "Do you not know that most men would rather give you money for a handbag than a business plan? For an iPhone than Apple shares? He will NEVER respect me as a businesswoman."

"That's not true. Did you even give him a chance to get to know that side of you?" Qhayiya argued too, shaking her head.

"Babes! Let's just say that in my thirty-two years on earth, I've yet to meet a guy that will take me from the bedroom to the boardroom," Lolo replied firmly. "I've learned that once a man has decided that he wants to bed you, trust me, there's a very slim chance that he's going to see you for your brains…"

"Damn," Nala reluctantly sighed.

"I guess I was lucky to find a man that sees me for my brains!" Qhayiya nodded.

"You mean Stewart?" Nala asked, looking up from the menu.

"Nope! Peter. My mentor. He's invited me to accompany him to Nairobi next month, so he can help me expand my business into the rest of Africa," Qhayiya said proudly.

"You know how I feel about your so-called mentor," Lolo said, signalling the waiter and changing the subject to a lighter topic with her usual frivolous insouciance. "Can the waiter hurry up? I've been dreaming of the salmon fishcakes all day!"

KFM, Nairobi City Centre, Kenya October
September 2017

The Nairobi sky was sunny and cloudless as Qhayiya's flight made its approach towards Jomo Kenyatta International Airport. A chance meeting when Qhayiya was pitching her business offering at Treynor Wealth Partners had resulted in Mr Peter Manyika, CE Rest of Africa and Middle East, offering to assist the young entrepreneur with her start-up, and help her expand her operations into the rest of Africa. The ever-enterprising Qhayiya used the all-expenses trip to Nairobi to schedule a radio interview before the lunchtime meeting that day, and host a women's event that evening. Qhayiya tuned her watch to 8:05 am local time and realised she had less than sixty minutes before going on air on KFM.

It would take a miracle for her to make it on time, as she still needed to clear customs, order an Uber, and navigate the notorious morning traffic along the A104 – one of Nairobi's major highways. Seeing the panicked look on her face as they waited for their luggage, the kind gentleman Qhayiya had chatted to at the airport lounge offered her a lift to her destination.

The air-conditioned interior of the black Lexus SUV Qhayiya was travelling in stood in stark contrast to the heat outside. Scores of sweaty passengers rode by in elaborately decorated *matatus*[3], overloaded *bajajs*[4] and barely roadworthy *tuk tuks*[5]. The morning traffic along the A104 did not disappoint, and Qhayiya reached her destination embarrassingly late.

With just thirty minutes of the show remaining, she raced into Lonrho House. The modern ocean-blue mirrored building that stood out in Nairobi's ageing skyline was the home of KFM, where Qhayiya would be interviewed.

On arrival, she was hurriedly escorted past the friendly security officers at reception, straight to the 19th-floor studios. A pair of headphones was immediately placed around her neck in preparation for the live broadcast.

A Coca-Cola advert blasted through the studio as Qhayiya exchanged pleasantries with Renee and her co-host Obama. The studio was a small room with dark grey, wall-to-wall carpeting, a cluster desk with four microphones, and a large west-facing window that looked over the city. True for every self-respecting breakfast radio show, copies of Kenya's top newspapers – the Daily Nation, The Standard, and The Star – lay strewn across the presenters' desks, and Qhayiya browsed through them as she waited to go on air.

"You're still on KFM breakfast with myself Renee and of course my co-host Obama, and as promised, our guest is in studio, all the way from Johannesburg, South Africa, to share with us a very inspirational and necessary story."

"That's right!" Obama smoothly continued. "Renee has been RAVING about this young lady since returning from the Graça Machel Trust conference in Tanzania a few weeks ago, and as a man, I'm excited to hear what women discuss at these closed-door events. Qhayiya – a pleasure to welcome you to KFM."

"*Asante*[6], Obama and Renee, thanks for having me. *Jambo*[7] to your listeners and I must say, I am very excited to be in Nairobi! It's my first time," Qhayiya said, managing to control her voice so that it didn't squeak with excitement.

"You are very welcome, Qhayiya!" Renee said, "and it's such a pleasure to see you again. We have exactly twenty-four minutes left on the show, and I would like to get straight into your story of overcoming a physically abusive relationship and what it has taken to rebuild your life since then."

Qhayiya's head bopped involuntarily to Octopizzo's hit track *TBT* as the Uber made its way from the centre of town to the affluent suburb of Westlands. The hotel security guard walking around the car with an under-vehicle inspection mirror served as a reminder of the ever-present threat of terrorist attacks on Kenya's capital. Having survived a crippling attack on the Westlands shopping mall a few years before, the city was still on high alert.

The receptionist typed in Qhayiya's details into the hotel computer as Qhayiya immediately logged on to the Wi-Fi to check in with Peter, with whom she hadn't spoken since leaving Joburg. A slew of emails, SMS and WhatsApp messages came flooding in, and, of course, one from the sender she was anticipating most.

"I thought you'd changed your mind about me," Peter joked as he answered Qhayiya's WhatsApp call.

"No, I hadn't changed my mind about COMING TO NAIROBI," Qhayiya emphasised. "My roaming didn't activate, and I'm only getting to the hotel now. That's why I hadn't contacted you before."

"Why only now? I thought your flight was delayed by only an hour," Peter said, genuine concern in his voice.

"It was! I had a radio interview this morning, remember?" Qhayiya replied.

"Oh, yes! Sorry, I have a lot on my mind," Peter acknowledged. "How was your flight? Did you enjoy business class?"

"It was alright, I guess."

"Hmmm… Some girls are hard to please!"

"Peter, I've told you many times that you don't need to do anything to please me except mentor me in running a successful start-up," Qhayiya replied firmly.

"Learn to take a joke, Qhayiya," Peter chuckled drily. "Anyway, I'm still out at meetings and will be back at around… 4 pm. You can go to the spa in the meantime. It's one of the best I've been to in the world."

"Spa?" Qhayiya asked, confused. "What happened to me attending meetings with you today?"

"About that," Peter began uncomfortably, "I thought about it, and it won't be a good look. Kenya is a very conservative country, and no matter how we explain it, my colleagues would have their suspicions."

"Oh… I see," Qhayiya said without masking the disappointment in her voice.

"Look, how's about we have a strategy session after your event tonight? I'll fill you in on my meetings, and we'll talk through some of the opportunities that may be available for you in Kenya. Deal?"

"Okay, that sounds fine. As long as it's business mentorship and nothing else, Peter. I'm SERIOUS!"

"Relax! What kind of a man do you take me for?" Peter chuckled again. "I'll see you later, baby. I've got to go. Bye!"

Peter always straddled the line between appropriate and inappropriate, which wasn't unusual for men of his stature. Qhayiya had experienced it countless times during her days in banking and had figured how to manage it, while still getting down to business.

With Peter, however, it seemed that flirting was where their engagements ended. He always had the upper hand. A rush of fear shot through her at the realisation that she was in a foreign country, with a man she barely knew, and one that had always managed to have things go his way.

Sure, she had friends in Nairobi, but she'd met them only a few weeks earlier. And they certainly didn't know she was in town with a married man. How would they react if they knew that their new acquaintance, who often preached about the devastating financial consequences of divorce on a woman's livelihood, was making international trips with a married man? Yes, she hadn't slept with Peter. And had no plans to do so. But perhaps Peter was right – the two of them being seen together wasn't a good look.

A scrawny-looking porter struggled under the weight of the bell cart as he escorted Qhayiya to her suite. The suite was the size of her first apartment back in Johannesburg and was tastefully fitted with dark-wood furniture, crisp white linen, and calming green accents in the couches, cushions and curtains.

After a quick room tour, Qhayiya showered, changed, and headed down to the terrace to sample some of the local cuisines. The waiter looked puzzled when the corporate-looking guest with her braids in a side bun, oversized Marc Jacobs sunshades, and a charcoal skirt suit ordered a bottle of Tusker Lager to accompany her meal of ugali, *kachumbari*[8], and *nyama choma*[9].

"Jambo, *rafiki yangu*[10]!" Qhayiya shouted over WhatsApp video calling.

"Hey, boo! How goes it in the wild, wild east?" Lolo responded, shifting her position and revealing a bare chest under her white duvet cover.

"Would you mind covering up!" Qhayiya gasped, turning her head away from her screen.

"Whatever, man. Nothing you haven't seen before!" Lolo teased, cupping her breast to provoke Qhayiya even more. "Anyway, how did your meetings go? You're looking very convincing in that shirt and jacket."

"I haven't been to any meetings, babe," Qhayiya said sulkily. "Peter decided against it because Kenya is apparently very conservative, and it would be a bad look for us to be seen together when I'm not one of his staff members."

"Wasn't the whole point of the trip that you'd accompany him to his meetings?" Lolo asked, looking puzzled.

"I know…" Qhayiya said.

"Hmmm…. I'm beginning to seriously dislike this Peter character. He's trying to get the best of both worlds," Lolo said pensively.

"What do you mean?" Qhayiya asked, taking a sip of her beer.

"Well, if you were a straight *Runs Girl*[11], right, he'd need to remunerate you for your time and of course the sex. A woman like you who's well educated could easily take him for R100k a month. But now, he's getting out of doing that by pretending to be a business contact. But I don't see any business happening. So basically, this guy is getting a premium travel buddy, without forking out a cent. Gotta hand it to him, he's good!"

"But I'm not sleeping with him, Lolo," Qhayiya responded.

"I bet Peter will try and shag you tonight," Lolo predicted fatalistically.

"What? Don't be silly! We flirt, yes, but I've made it VERY clear that this is strictly business," Qhayiya said, pulling her face to let Lolo know how offended she was.

"Okay. I won't argue," Lolo relented. "But I hope you packed condoms, 'cause the over-fifty crowd likes to hit it raw."

"I forget how disgusting you can be sometimes," Qhayiya said, shaking her head in annoyance. "Bye, Lolo!"

"Good luck for tonight, babe. Your event, I mean. Love you!"

By 6 pm, the who's who of Kenya's female business and social elite was already streaming into the hotel lounge for registration. The terrace was set up to welcome guests for Qhayiya's *Women and Wealth* fireside chat.

What was meant to be a ninety-minute informal discussion turned into a three-hour session of sharing the horrible truths that hid in some of the mansions of Muthaiga suburb.

At the end of the evening, newspaper journalists and magazine editors gathered around Qhayiya for one-on-one interviews. Photographers snapped away at the women trying to hold back their tears while swarming around Qhayiya for a hug and their two minutes with Nairobi's newest star.

In just one day in the country, she'd managed to do a radio interview, sneak in a spa treatment and host an event. She was back in her room, scrolling through the profiles of the women that had subscribed to her blog when she heard a knock on the door.

"I come bearing gifts," Peter announced jovially when she opened the door. He was carrying a bottle of red wine and two goblets.

"Peter! What are you DOING here?" Qhayiya replied, shocked. It was nearly midnight, and she'd forgotten all about her planned catch-up with Peter.

"You look surprised to see me. I thought we agreed to meet after your function?" Peter said, as he walked past Qhayiya and invited himself into her room.

"We did. But not in my room!"

"You'd rather come to MY room?" Peter teased, raising his eyebrows, and giving her a naughty smile.

"You know what I mean," Qhayiya said disapprovingly.

"Oh, don't be a party-pooper! I'm just an innocent guy trying to celebrate all your hard work. Why are you always so hard on me?"

"Fine, we can celebrate," Qhayiya relented, closing the door and leaning against it for a moment, willing herself not to feel uneasy.

Qhayiya turned back to find Peter standing practically on top of her. His sternum was inches from her nose, and without her shoes on, she realised that he was much taller than she.

Qhayiya raised her head to look up at him, and before she could ask what was going on, he grabbed her by the back of her neck and thrust his tongue into her mouth. His other hand cupped her buttocks as he pressed his fully erect manhood against her stomach.

"Peter, NO!" Qhayiya shouted, trying to pull away from him.

"I know you want this," he breathed, thrusting his tongue into her mouth again and pulling her even closer.

"NO! I DON'T! PLEASE STOP!" she insisted. His arms were wrapped tightly around her, and she was struggling to breathe.

"You wouldn't have come here if you didn't want it," he huffed. He smelled like garlic, wine, and stale musk.

"Let me go!" she screamed. She slipped under his arm and ran to the couches, the furthest point in the room.

"I like a woman that plays hard to get," he growled, his voice distinctly different to any tone she'd heard him speak in. "I'm going to enjoy fucking you."

Peter walked threateningly towards Qhayiya and pinned her onto the couch. He pulled her skirt down as she fought to keep it up. He used the full weight of his body against her, and she struggled to get free.

He held both her wrists above her head with one hand and pulled down her skirt with the other. His knee pressed down on her thighs and prevented her from kicking him.

"You're hurting me!" she cried.

"I would never hurt you, baby," he growled. "Stop fighting and give Daddy what he wants."

Qhayiya's skirt was now sitting at her ankles. With one quick move, Peter spread her legs and pinned her right thigh onto the back of the couch with his right knee. His eyes were drunk with lust as he stared directly at her mound, shielded now only by her black lace thong. He shoved his index and middle fingers into Qhayiya's canal and growled.

"If you don't want me, then why are you wet?"

"Please don't do this..." Qhayiya whimpered. Her wriggling was useless underneath the wiry man pinning her down. He fingers thrust harder and faster.

"I said, if you don't want me, then why are you wet?" he rasped. He was smiling pleased with himself for getting Qhayiya's body to surrender to him even though her mind insisted on fighting.

Peter's left hand pressed Qhayiya's wrists above her head, and with his other, he unzipped his pants, his knees still pinning her thighs apart. He was looking straight into her eyes, unmoved by the tears streaming down her face.

Peter had decided he was going to have sex with her, with or without her consent. Qhayiya considered her choices. If she screamed and caught the hotel staff's attention, she risked having her Kenyan community realise she had travelled to Nairobi with a married man. She stood to lose her newfound friends and kill her fledgeling brand.

If she remained quiet, it wouldn't be long until Peter was inside her. No matter what she decided, a part of her was going to die that night - her career, or her core. The choice she faced was no longer between life and death, as death was certain. The only choice left, was whether she was going to be killed publicly by scandal or killed privately by rape. Picking up the pieces of her shattered self would be a less public exercise, and so Qhayiya made up her mind – Peter would be the executioner.

Qhayiya had been standing under the shower for thirty minutes, frozen by what had transpired over the past five hours. Peter had not come to take one round of sex, he came for many.

The weapon that Qhayiya had selected for her death hadn't killed her in one fell swoop. It had bludgeoned her to death. Repeatedly. Relentlessly. Ruthlessly. And all the while she just lay there, motionless, silent, holding on to the only power she felt she had while pinned down on her back – she denied him the satisfaction of hearing her moan.

As she dried herself, she noticed his scent was everywhere. She could smell Peter on her skin. On the towel. On her hair. He seemed to be seeping out her very pores.

She walked to the closet and absently noticed that the room was still pristine, with no tell-tale signs of the crime that had been committed there throughout the night. Apart from the cushions on the floor, everything was still in its place, even the bottle of wine that Peter had brought with him supposedly to celebrate. It was still standing, sealed, in the very spot he had placed it when he walked in.

The hotel Mercedes cruised down the A104 as Qhayiya reflected on a question Junior had asked her when she had revealed the extent of the pain and torture João was putting Lolo through during their divorce and custody battle.

It was a simple question: "Where are the men in her life?" That's it.

The men that were supposed to rally around her and protect her from João. From life. Where WERE they?

Junior was aware that Lolo had a less than healthy relationship with her father, and that both her grandfathers were late. But what about her uncles, her cousins, friends? They had remained in the shadows as she navigated her divorce from João. Remained in the shadows as she fought to rebuild her life on her own.

And those that did come out of the shadows, like the Stanfords of the world, they came to take. Even when Lolo had nothing left, they had still taken. Just as Junior had taken from Qhayiya. And as Peter had taken last night. Qhayiya concluded that there were only two types of men in life – those that stayed in the shadows, and those that stepped out to TAKE.

The driver pulled up to the TV studio entrance, and Qhayiya looked over at him. Her heart was filled with rage and hatred as she wondered which type of man he was, to the women in his life. Did he stand by and say nothing in the face of injustice? Or was he the perpetrator of injustice? Bystander or perpetrator?

Qhayiya walked into the television studio and began filling out her details in the security register. She paused to look up at the uniformed male security guard manning the desk. His face filled her with the same rage and disgust. Bystander or perpetrator?

Qhayiya had a steely look on her face as she sat silently in the makeup chair. The unassuming artist meticulously transforming the tired face for TV. She had no idea of the battle taking place beneath the canvas she was working on.

Nairobi. What was supposed to mark a turning point in Qhayiya's entrepreneurial journey, a milestone as her first international speaking engagement, was now a dark memory she would rather forget.

Had she known the actual price for the trip she was about to embark on two nights ago, she wouldn't have boarded that plane because it was not worth the price she had to pay.

She could think of nothing that was worth the price she had paid. And would continue to pay every time she viewed her blog. Every time she scrolled through her messages from Peter. Every time she heard his interviews on the business news channels. Every time she saw his face in business publications. Every time the events from the early hours of that morning replayed in her mind.

Her so-called mentor, the man she looked up to in business, the man that had the power to open doors for her and help set her up, had RAPED her.

She had the brains, the qualifications, the experience and the track record to be a successful understudy. But he didn't see any of that when he looked at her. Instead, he saw one thing – his next climax.

A part of Qhayiya had died in the wee hours of that morning, and in its place, a new part had been born – one that hated all men and resolved to make them pay. Qhayiya pulled out her phone, and sent a text to the one person she knew would help her on her quest. Lolo.

Lagos, Nigeria
November 2017

Nigeria. A spectacular crashing of worlds where traditional values live alongside hedonistic excess, the world's poorest buys *agbado ati agbon*[12] alongside the wealthiest, and radical evangelists' practices are eerily similar to those of the sorcerers they so condemn.

Rich in history, art, music and fashion, Nigeria proves that anything the world can do, it can do *badder*. Despite the federal headquarters being moved to the purpose-built city of Abuja at the end of 1991, "Lasgidi" was still very much the capital city of Nigeria.

Its dilapidated infrastructure notwithstanding, the heartbeat of Africa's most populous city was truly the city that never sleeps – perhaps even more deserving of the title 'the New York of Africa' than the city of Johannesburg upon which it is bestowed.

From the bustling nightlife to the high fashion, Lagos had an answer for everything quintessentially Big Apple. Nike Art Centre's five

SAMKE S. MHLONGO

storeys with a collection of eight thousand artworks rivalled the Museum of Modern Art.

Bergdorf Goodman's loyalists from the upper crust of Manhattan Island would probably be just as impressed with The Polo Avenue in Victoria Island. Local fashion authorities Lisa Folawiyo and Lanre Da Silva Ajayi's creations were just as comfortable in the pages of VOGUE as those of Diane von Furstenberg and Vera Wang.

There was no shortage of money in Lagos. Neither was there a shortage of men who were willing to spend it. The arrival of the two South African ladies in town for only five days, increased the options available to such men. From the diplomatic protocol welcome at the airport to the six-car motorcade speeding towards their hotel, Lagos had already turned out to be better than the very many international trips Qhayiya had taken in her lifetime.

As Lolo and Qhayiya sped down the Third Mainland Bridge to the hotel they'd be staying at for the week, and knowing how unsophisticated her friend could be when it came to this sort of thing, Lolo gave her best friend a single piece of advice: DON'T. FALL. IN. LOVE.

Lagos, Nigeria
November 2018

Qhayiya lay on her back and stared up at the ceiling, reflecting on the past year. Not only had Qhayiya heeded her friend's advice, but she'd also made it her founding principle for the past year. It was the year the two friends had decided to seek revenge for the pain inflicted on them by the men in their lives. By Peter. And João. And Junior. And Mamba. And Uncle Harvey. And Qhayiya's estranged father. And all the other men that had hurt and disappointed them throughout their lives. Including the one snoring away next to her.

Their plan had worked. Between them, they'd travelled to many destinations with many different men, returning home each time with a bigger bank balance and their hearts still firmly encased in ice.

Dubai. Marrakesh. Mykonos. Abuja. Monaco. The Maldives. Accra. London. Nairobi. New York City. Harare. Los Angeles. Zanzibar. Their escapades from that year alone would fill a sensational book!

And here she was, back in Lagos, on the anniversary of the trip that first gave her a taste of how good life can be when you shut your heart and focus on using men just as they use women.

The city was still as fast-paced as she remembered, the parties and *owambes*[13] as extravagant as before.

Qhayiya's local *toasters*[14] had waited at her beck and call, ready to send a driver with instructions to collect her and attend to any and every need, before dropping her off at the *'guesthouse*[15]'.

She'd always return to the hotel the following morning, feeling empty. Dead. *Deader* than the night before, if that was at all possible. But this morning was different, thanks to a chance encounter last night when she met up with her local girlfriends for drinks at the Federal Palace Hotel. Qhayiya had walked in, dressed casually in a black, bubu gown and matching turban. As she made her way to her seat at the Explorers Bar, three waitresses commented on how regal she looked and agreed on giving her the name *Eniola*, translated as 'person of wealth' in the Nigerian language of Yoruba. Despite her protestations, Bukola, Fatima and Blessing insisted on referring to her all night by that name.

The meaning couldn't be further from Qhayiya's true circumstances. In the eighteen months she'd been an entrepreneur, she still hadn't managed to secure a single corporate client to take up her financial wellness offering. Her savings had all but disappeared from funding her monthly living expenses, servicing debt, and supporting her mom and her increasing medical costs.

Her spirit was still reeling from having been crushed by Peter the year before, and none of the men that had entered her life since then seemed to see anything of value, except the one thing all women possessed anyway.

Qhayiya didn't feel wealthy. Not in monetary terms. Not in self-confidence. Not even in hope.

"I don't have wealth," Qhayiya had argued, when the three women agreed that 'Eniola' was the perfect name for her.

"We are not saying you HAVE wealth, Madame," Bukola had replied. "You ARE wealth."

Lying in bed that morning, with a foreign being at her left side, and a brand new designer bag worth a small apartment on her right, the women's words rang in Qhayiya's head again.

This time, she understood them. Even with all the air miles and gifts she had collected throughout the year, she still didn't feel wealthy. To her, wealth was no longer something you attained. It was something you WERE. At that moment, Qhayiya decided to stop chasing wealth and finally accept that she WAS wealth, she was valuable, and she had much more to offer than the warmth at the meeting of her thighs.

Peter had killed off a part of her in Nairobi, but she had continued offering other men the same opportunity throughout 2018.

Yes, Peter had cast her into a dark hole, but Qhayiya had kept digging. She had been dealt a heavy blow but had come back for more.

She was trying to punish others but ended up hurting herself. She'd had enough. She wasn't going to do it anymore.

Starting that morning, she would no longer resent men for not having come to save her. Instead, she was going to save herself.

International Departures Lounge, OR Tambo International Airport
November 2019

Qhayiya paged through the SAWUBONA magazine as she sat in the SLOW Lounge, waiting for her boarding time. As she licked a finger to turn the next page, her eye caught sight of a pair of familiar faces sitting across from her.

She scrunched her face as she wracked her brain, trying to remember who they were.

"Pamela?" she said, thinking out loud, the moment it hit her.

"Qhayiya! How are you?" Pamela replied with a warm smile on her face. She rose to her feet with arms outstretched.

"Oh, hi, Qhayiya! We haven't seen you since our internship," Funeka added, also rising to her feet with a surprised expression.

Qhayiya wrapped her arms around Pamela, feeling absolutely mortified about how she had treated the two women when they were young interns on the Banker Development Programme. After giving Funeka a hug, too, Qhayiya took a step back to admire the two women that looked nothing like the young girls they were when she first met them a decade ago.

Pamela was Hamptons-casual in fitted khaki chinos, a white collared shirt and a baby pink woollen jersey draped over her shoulders. Her long natural hair was tied into a high bun, and her skin was glowing and makeup-free.

Funeka was Parisian-chic in black wide-leg pants, white open-collared blouse and three strings of pearls around her neck. Her bob-cut wig peeked out from underneath her black beret, and she topped off the look with black square-frame reading glasses.

"You guys look amazing!" Qhayiya exclaimed, feeling exceptionally underdressed in a black cotton jumpsuit and matching leather moccasins.

"So do you," Pamela replied politely.

"You always looked good though," Funeka added offhandedly, taking her seat.

"So, where are you guys off to?" Qhayiya asked. She shifted to the front of her seat to get closer to her ex-colleagues.

"We're headed to Boston," Pamela replied. "The annual CFA Institute conference is being held there this year."

"You guys are CFAs now?" Qhayiya exclaimed, her jaw dropping to the floor.

"Yup!" Funeka confirmed.

"And still both at FS in Cape Town?" Qhayiya pressed, pouring more Tanqueray into her suddenly not-strong-enough G&T.

"Yes, we are," Pamela smiled. "I now head up the Africa M&A team, and Funeka heads up the Fixed Income desk."

Qhayiya pursed her lips to hide the envy that would show on her face. The two women, who she had dismissed as feeling sorry for themselves, had not only qualified as Chartered Financial Analysts but had gone on to attain leadership positions at their firm. Their grace in engaging her now made her feel even worse because she deserved nothing but contempt for the way she had treated them.

"Uhm... I don't know what to say," Qhayiya nodded pensively. "Congratulations. I'm so proud of you. Really."

"Thank you," Pamela winked. "It wasn't easy, but we decided the best way to open up the industry was to climb to the top and grab the key."

"Exactly," Funeka concurred, passion and commitment evident in her voice as she elaborated. "We've implemented measures to ensure Franklin's environment is accommodating to people from all walks of life. We've even increased our black CFA throughput by 30% over the past five years. So, if ever you change your mind about qualifying as a

CFA, come back to FS, and we'll make sure you do!" The group chuckled at Funeka's light-hearted teasing.

The women spent the next thirty minutes catching up on what was happening in their lives, and in those of their ex-colleagues.

Chloe decided, despite qualifying as a CFA, to follow her true calling and changed careers from balancing portfolios to balancing chakras, as a yoga instructor. Caitlyn was thriving as a Senior Associate at Franklin's New York office. And Brooke's CFA certification was on the wall of her Palo Alto mansion after marrying a tech start-up investor she met while jogging along the Sea Point promenade one December.

Qhayiya looked admiringly at Pamela and Funeka as they spoke. The two young women from the township had placed themselves squarely in the driving seat of the agenda they'd set out to achieve, and Qhayiya couldn't deny being proud of them. Perhaps even slightly envious.

Pamela and Funeka had direction, resolve, purpose. Each had grown up knowing she had to fend for herself because no one else would. Not for long, anyway. Each was the master of her own fate, much like Qhayiya had been before that fateful night with Peter. Much like Qhayiya had resolved to be once again.

Lagos, Nigeria

The smell of diesel when you enter an Uber. The sound of non-stop car hooters on Ozumba Mbadiwe Avenue. The home of wax print fabrics accessorised with authentic Chanel.

And best of all, a cuisine so distinctive that it can not be described by taste alone... 'pepper snails that dance in the mouth as one newly in love'; '*egusi*[16] with the aroma of a happy childhood'; and 'jollof that satisfies like a mother's embrace'.

Lagos. Qhayiya was back in her favourite city in the world. She looked out of the window of the speeding Toyota Corolla and realised that much had changed in the twelve months since she'd last visited. Not much had changed with the city, but the woman she was had been transubstantiated.

The last time she had visited Lagos, Qhayiya had come to take.

No.

She had come to plunder.

To leave with as many designer brands, bands, and broken hearts as she could fit in her 2 x 32 kg baggage allowance.

She'd plundered – followed the definition of the word to a tee, and 'taken the goods of another by force as in war.' The goods had come in designer paper bags. Taken from all the men that fell victim to the South African temptress. The force had been the lure of her seduction. And the war, well, that had been within herself.

Qhayiya had since come to a truce with herself. No longer was she at war with the parts of her life that she did not like. Her fears had learned to live alongside her courage. Her hopes lived up the road from her disappointments. Her success was polished and on display alongside her failures. Her seesawing soul was finally at rest.

Lady Lagos had been kind to this foreign child. Kind, even when her own children were ill-treated in the foreign child's home. Qhayiya had not forgotten Lady Lagos's hospitality. And this time, she'd come to give.

The Toyota Corolla pulled up to the entrance of the Federal Palace Hotel, the treasure of Victoria Island.

There was something charming about staying in a 'palace', especially when, deep down, you still considered yourself a princess.

Qhayiya walked up the marble stairs to the entrance as a porter pushed her luggage up the ramp on the far side of the stairs. The doorman beamed as Qhayiya walked by, to enter the familiar expansive hallway.

Imposing marble columns, and a grand staircase, were the unmistakable features of the establishment built to be the country's premium international hotel during British colonial rule. The warm lighting created a golden hue throughout the expansive hotel lobby, emanating a royal charm of old.

Qhayiya checked in and proceeded to her room. She immediately headed to the window to take in the view of the ships lighting up the Atlantic Coast. She had learned very quickly to specify 'Sea View' when making her booking. Nothing compared to watching a spectacular Lagos sunset over the sea.

Qhayiya logged on to the hotel Wi-Fi and navigated to her banking app. She checked the balance, and it was still R64.32. She had over R250 000 from three different sources in delayed payments. The money was supposed to have cleared two days ago.

She decided to get some rest and follow up in the morning.

Qhayiya woke up hungry and craving the scrumptious breakfast buffet. It was the first time she'd been in Lagos this long without indulging in *dodo*[17], for breakfast, or a piña colada at the Explorers Bar.

She checked her balance again, and it hadn't changed. One client said there had been a problem with the server, but the money had been paid and would clear the following day. Another client said the woman in charge of processing the payments had fallen ill and left early for the day. The last client was out of the office.

The proceeds from the shares Qhayiya had asked her wealth manager to trade would only be clearing the following day. Qhayiya had grown enough, and was now attuned enough, to know when the universe was sending a signal. She'd also learned exactly who to reach out to when those signals weren't making sense – her good friend Nala.

"Nala, something is going on," Qhayiya said into the phone hurriedly, pacing up and down the hotel room.

"Why? What's up?" Nala responded calmly. Lately, she was always calm.

"I'm sitting in a foreign country with sixty-four rand in my account is what's up. I'm not used to my account not having a six-figure balance, and now I'm too embarrassed even to go down for breakfast because I could only afford to settle accommodation and not put a credit in my account for incidentals," Qhayiya explained, panicked.

"Okay, then. So fast…"

"EXCUSE me?" Qhayiya said shrilly.

"Excuse what?" Nala asked drily.

"Excuse that! You normalising hunger, and the fact that God is depriving me of my daily bread when I'm out here doing the Lord's work!" Qhayiya shouted.

"Okay," Nala chuckled.

"It's not funny, Nala," Qhayiya deflated, falling onto her bed.

"It's not, but you are," Nala chuckled. "You've learned to see using your spiritual eyes, but you insist on using only the physical ones."

"I'm not following," Qhayiya said cantankerously.

"What are you in Lagos to do?"

"I'm here to moderate a panel at WIMBIZ," Qhayiya replied in a sing-song voice. Why was Nala being obtuse?

"Why?"

"Because they INVITED me." Qhayiya rolled her eyes and crossed her arms in annoyance since apparently, Nala was intent on playing the WHY? game like a five-year-old.

"Why?"

Bingo.

"Because they've seen the female empowerment workshops I've been hosting all year and wanted me to speak about the importance of African women developing a wealth mindset," Qhayiya replied with clenched teeth.

"Why?"

"Because without it, they face many types of abuses. Physical. Emotional. Sexual. Psychological." Qhayiya's annoyance turned to anger, and its target was not Nala.

"Why?"

"Because powerlessness attracts abuse. Power corrupts. And absolute power corrupts – absolutely."

"So, I ask you again, what are you in Lagos to do?"

Qhayiya paused for a moment as the gravity of her trip crystallised in her mind.

"I'm here to shift power…"

The phone fell silent as Qhayiya's words echoed in her conscience. Nala gave her friend a moment to take in the magnitude of the task that lay ahead.

Satisfied that Qhayiya understood the significance of her words the following day, Nala continued the conversation.

"Qhayiya… if you had that money in your account today, or even the money you have on a normal day, tell me. What would you have spent the day doing?"

Qhayiya chuckled out of embarrassment.

"I hate it when you do this…" Qhayiya drawled, grudgingly smiling. "The plan was to get my outfit for when I go on stage tomorrow."

"Elaborate, Qhayiya"

Qhayiya rolled her eyes.

"Okay! I was meant to go to Nakenohs Boulevard and buy a dress from Ilàré. Then treat myself to a new lacewig from Kuku's Hair. Pick up a pair of Valentino slingbacks I'd set aside at The Polo Avenue. And then meet Vimbai for sundowners at Shiro because she's leaving for Calabar in the morning."

"I see... So, you prepare to shift power by getting a new outfit and meeting a friend for cocktails?"

"I guess not..."

"Or would you, perhaps, prepare by taking the day to clear your mind, body and soul of all distractions? Fill them with the weapons you need to fight the injustice before you? A broad base of information. Calmness of spirit. Clarity of thought. Attitude of servitude."

"I guess you're right."

"Don't be a slow learner, Qhayiya. God is a very patient teacher."

Eko Convention Centre
Present Day

Qhayiya sat nervously in the front row, her face fixed firmly on the stage for fear of seeing the over 2500 women behind her.

Considered Africa's largest conference of women in business and leadership, WIMBIZ had always drawn large crowds at its annual conference. Qhayiya doubted it would be different this time.

She could feel her heart pounding at the thought of getting on stage in the next fifteen minutes. Especially since she was probably the only South African in the room; not because South African women did not attend the conference, but because tensions between the two countries were high. There had recently been outbursts of violence in South Africa, between locals and Nigerian nationals living there.

She shifted in her seat to pull down her dress discreetly. She'd gained some weight since the last time she'd worn the dress. It no longer sat below her knees – making it an inappropriate choice for a raised platform in a conservative country, as a visitor from the country currently at war with their own.

Adrenalin coursed through Qhayiya's body. She'd even forgotten that she hadn't eaten in nearly two days. Food was the least of her concerns at the moment. Not offending 2 500 of some of the continent's most powerful women with her speech, was.

The crowd clapped politely as she made her way onto the stage. She took her seat at the far end of the panel. She sat at an angle with the side of her body to the audience, to avoid presenting a direct view up her skirt. It was the first victory of the day.

One by one, the rest of the panellists made their way on to the stage. A few minutes later, the Programme Director said the words Qhayiya dreaded, "I now hand you over to our Panel Moderator."

Qhayiya's tummy rumbled as she walked across the stage to the podium. The crowd murmured in confusion. *What was she doing?* Moderators spoke from their seats and not the podium. THAT was reserved for the Programme Director and keynote speakers.

Qhayiya put one foot in front of the other, praying to God that she would not trip and fall. She hated the shoes she was wearing and had packed them 'just in case'. Over time, the suede had softened, and the back of her heels kept popping out as she walked.

This is why I needed the Valentinos, God, Qhayiya prayed silently, still bitter about how harshly her Father in Heaven had grounded her the day before.

The glass podium was now in front of her, the conference spotlight firmly fixed on her.

Qhayiya had traversed over 42 563 nautical miles, made 726 diary entries and cried 147 tissue boxes worth of tears to stand at this podium.

Crystal clear on the culture she had to shift on her friend Nala's behalf. Crystal clear on the laws that denied her friend Lolo justice. Crystal clear on the stigma that was holding her friend Runako hostage in a lifelong sentence. And Qhayiya was crystal clear on the debt she had to settle on this podium, once and for all.

She no longer worried about the reaction of the audience. She was here to speak her truth. She was here to speak her friends' truth. She was here to speak women's unspoken truth.

"In my culture, it is rude to address your elders while seated," Qhayiya began. "Programme Director, I pray you'll thus forgive me for taking to the podium without your permission."

A few polite chuckles came from the floor. Qhayiya took a deep breath and opened her notebook to her speech.

"Conference Chairperson. Honourable dignitaries. WIMBIZ Chair. Board of Trustees. WIMBIZ Executive Council. Ladies and the few very brave gentlemen in the room. All protocol observed. Good morning."

The hall was silent. Qhayiya took another, even deeper breath, and plunged into her speech.

"It would be remiss of me to stand here and address you today, without first apologising for the way some of my countrymen have treated your brothers and sisters that call South Africa home.

"I stand here, not to debate whether the violence was xenophobic, or targeted at curbing the illicit drug trade run, unfortunately, by a few Nigerian nationals.

"I stand here instead, to apologise for the historical lack of hospitality my country has shown your people, when I have experienced nothing but the greatest welcome every time I have landed on your shores, the first of which was back in November 2017.

"At that time, I was a thirty-one-year-old woman, who'd recently left a physically abusive relationship. A relationship that had soured with my growing career success. The more money I made, specifically the more money *than my partner* I made, the worse the beatings.

"My partner accused me of not respecting him as the man of the house, of forgetting my place as a woman, now that I controlled our household's purse strings. I've often wondered if my relationship would have turned out better had I not been as financially independent and astute. The evidence around me points to the contrary.

"I look at my best friend Lolo, who lost custody of her children during her divorce, as she did not have the financial muscle to take on her hotshot lawyer husband. I consider the case of my friend Runako who's stuck in an unhappy marriage, held hostage not only by the stigma associated with divorce, but also by the financial dependence she, her father, and her brothers have on her husband and his company.

"The situations I've described are not unique to my friends. Studies show that over half of all women worldwide defer long-term financial decisions to their spouses, putting their own financial security at risk. Less than a quarter take the lead and even less share long-term financial decisions equally. Research indicates that the majority of married women prefer to stay out of long-term financial decision-making, as they believe their husbands know more about financial matters.

"You may be thinking that surely, as female education and income levels rise, this trend will be reversed. You would be wrong. Because millennial women are faring worse than the generations before them.

"These statistics wouldn't be so scary if the incidence of divorce wasn't at historical highs. In South Africa, four out of every ten marriages end in divorce before their 10th anniversary. And in the US, 40-50% of all marriages end up in divorce.

"In Nigeria, the actual divorce statistics remain unknown, given the high number of traditional marriages that are not governed by law; the requirement for two years' separation before a couple can apply to be legally divorced; and the high value that Nigerian society places on the institution of marriage – and fights to protect – even under circumstances that other societies consider the justification for giving up.

"Ladies and gentlemen, I'm not here to be alarmist. Nor to be the prophet of doom, as very many marriages will have their 'happily ever after'. But while divorce is a possibility, death is a certainty. Meaning, while many married women in this room may not end up being divorcees, they may very well end up being widows.

"According to a *World Bank report*[18], by age 65, there are as many widows on the continent of Africa as there are married women. By age 80, 80% of Africa's women live in widowhood.

"It is unfortunate that many women's attitudes towards long-term financial decision-making changes only after one of these two catastrophic events. The majority of widows and divorcees surveyed REGRET not having been involved in their financial planning while married, saying they would encourage married women not to make the mistake they had made.

"I don't need to remind you of the plight faced by Africa's divorcees and widows. From being stripped of their property and belongings in South Africa and Zimbabwe, to the forced sexual cleansing ritual of *kusasa fumbi* practised in some parts of Kenya, Zambia, Malawi, Uganda, Tanzania, Mozambique, Angola, Ivory Coast, the DRC and Azalia. It is this very practice that has kept my best friend Nala from seeing her son in over seven years! She has been denied access to her son, as she refuses to be RAPED, by her late husband's uncle. The rituals don't end there, because even as we sit here today, a woman may be forced to drink the water her husband's corpse was bathed in – to prove she is innocent of killing him.

"'Are you planning to kill him?' This question remains one of the most effective ways to discourage a woman from making financial decisions about her life, and planning for a future without a man by her side.

"Ladies and gentlemen, I was invited here today to moderate this panel that will discuss how we redefine the wealth mindset of African women. I trust my opening has highlighted the importance of our discussion today - we are here to shift power back to Africa's disenfranchised women."

Explorers Restaurant, Federal Palace Hotel

Qhayiya rushed into the Explorers Restaurant of the Federal Palace Hotel. She had only ten minutes before the buffet was cleared. The restaurant had already emptied out, except for a gentleman dining alone.

She was about to sit down when she heard a loud voice shout. "Madame Eniola! When did you arrive, Madame?" Bukola said, squeezing Qhayiya so hard she could hardly breathe.

"Wednesday night, Buki," Qhayiya wheezed, her lungs crushed under the embrace of the ample-bodied, chocolate-skinned woman.

"We missed you, Madame. We haven't seen you in so long," Buki said. She released her grip and took a step back to get a better look at her favourite South African patron.

"I know, Buki, me too. Things were a little bit tough, and I had to focus on work. But I'm doing much better now," Qhayiya smiled.

"Yes, oo[19], see Madame's nyash[20]. It's grown so big," Buki teased.

"Yours too, Buki!" Qhayiya returned the compliment, chuckling.

"I'll phone Halima and Blessing to tell them Madame Eniola is here. They must make sure to book a good, good table for you at dinner," Buki smiled.

"That's kind, Buki. Thank you."

Qhayiya was filled with mixed emotions as she tried to stomach her well-deserved lunch of pounded yam and *banga*[21] soup.

Her conference address and panel had been a resounding success, yet she still felt uneasy. Scores of women had come up to her after the conference, confirming that they carried the scars of being an African divorcee or widow.

One woman, in particular, was gnawing on Qhayiya's conscience – an elderly woman in a washed-out two-piece suit and torn shoes. You could tell she was dressed in her Sunday best for the occasion. She'd walked up to Qhayiya, squeezed her hand, and said, "Thank you."

Her sunken eyes and weary face had told the rest of her story on her behalf. Her rough hands painted a picture of the horrors she had endured. Her frail body and sagging shoulders whispered of the burden she still carried. And her image had continued to haunt Qhayiya as she smiled for pictures and basked in the glory of her victory.

I've done what I came here to do! Qhayiya said to herself. Or, perhaps, to God. She wrestled with her conscience that didn't seem to be at all satisfied.

She'd met her end of the bargain with God on numerous occasions, and on numerous platforms, around the world. She was ready to put her relationship with Junior behind her for good and focus solely on the next chapter of her life.

She was rolling another ball of pounded yam when the gentleman dining alone stood up and walked towards her.

"Hi," he smiled. "I'm Kamanu."

EPILOGUE

DECEMBER 2019

Sushi Restaurant, New York City, USA

*W*hat's this outstanding debt you keep talking about?" Qhayiya frowned. "My car is paid off. My rent and credit cards are up to date. I've repaid everyone that's helped me out when my business was having cash flow problems, so I don't understand. There is no one on earth that I have an outstanding debt with!"

The psychic returned Qhayiya's irritation with a blank stare. She had come to Qhayiya's table and insisted on giving her a reading. Dismissing it as a gimmick, Qhayiya and Kamanu had agreed.

"Your debt is not ON earth. It is not a monetary debt," she replied calmly.

"Huh?" Qhayiya winced, more baffled than before.

"You cannot start the next chapter..." she paused, looked at Kamanu and turned back to Qhayiya before continuing, "without closing the old one first."

Qhayiya shook her head in confusion.

"888. That's the number I keep seeing on the cards. What does 888 mean to you?"

"Nothing! I'm not Chinese. I've only ever seen that number on Chinese people's car registration plates," Qhayiya said dismissively, getting more annoyed by the moment.

"It's significant for you. Where were you on 8 August 2008?"

"The actual day? How am I supposed to remember?" Qhayiya frowned. "I had recently moved to Johannesburg and was in the first year of my internship. WHY?"

"And 8 August 2018?"

"Uhm… Let me check my diary entries" Qhayiya sighed, and did so. She scrolled through the Notes app on her phone until she reached the entry corresponding to that date. "Oh, I had been speaking at a Women's Month event and noted that my friend, who is a medium, said the very same thing you're saying. That I have an outstanding debt from this day."

"So it must be from before. What other year has the number eight in it? 1998? No…, you were too young to make a binding covenant at that age. Eight…. 2015! Yes! Two plus zero plus one plus five equals eight! Where were you on 8 August 2015?"

"Seriously!" Qhayiya huffed, scrolling through the Notes app despite her irritation. "I had come back from class and was energised and journaled about my class photo and that I have renewed hope I'll be successful and that I feel in five years' time women will be reading… oh, my God…"

Author's actual journal entry:

Saturday 08 August 2015, 22h50

*Well CHAAAAYLD! Got our class photos last night and
    when I saw "the prize" I was re-energised. It is amazing
    how powerful seeing 'the prize' is. It's such a powerful tool
    that I need to engage more often. Thank you, universe, for
    the lesson. I am going to trust my journey. But I swear I
    feel I am being prepared for something massive, massive,
    massive, massive! I feel like everything I am writing here,
    and journaling will be published in a book that will be
    distributed worldwide. I feel like I will be on talk shows
    and the voice for women. I feel like you are reading this,
    and I am thinking, yes, I know you will be reading this.
    You, tired woman, fighter of a woman, warrior of a
    woman, who can't seem to catch a break. And I am saying
    to you I feel 100% silly typing this, and would be
    embarrassed if someone read it now, but I feel in the next 5
    years, you will be reading this and making sense of it all.
    And I will be looking back and saying I knew; I knew the
    journey was preparing me for something great. And how
    do I know? Because all good stories start off with trying
    times. Because I can't be going through all this hell for
    nothing, because the extreme growth curve I am on now
    cannot be for nothing, because the universe wouldn't have
    shaken up a whole household for nothing - it doesn't work
    that way. Because that hope is the only thing that keeps me
    alive. And if I am wrong- well, at least I would have used
    my dream to get me through these trying times. Either
    way, I win...*

ACKNOWLEDGMENTS

Non mihi, sed tibi, gloria

Thank you: To God almighty for your divine providence always. To Thato Kgatlhanye for heeding the call to sit me down and give me stern instruction to write this book. To Sarah Mosidi for running my household and being mother to my children when I was studying, and working, and writing. To my children, Ntemi Nyasha and Simanga Thandolwakhe, for your patience and unconditional love. To my editor and publisher Bridget Lötz, for your wholehearted dedication to this project. I pray it continues paying you dividends long after this version has collected dust and been relegated to the back of the bookshelves. To my legal team at Fluxmans, Ntate Jack Phalane, Jerome Levitz and Fikile Sithole, for enduring the rollercoaster of emotions I put you through with this project. To my professional contributors Nondumiso Phambuka and Musi Skosana (Financial), Nyasha Matewe and Advocate Gift Mncube (Legal), Dr Zsofia Borsanyi (Psychological), Dr Shavina Frank (Medical), Cebile Xulu and Ayanda Seboni (Employee Benefits), Mapule Malau (Recruitment), I am forever indebted to you for your time and expertise. To my book reviewers Valentine Njoroge (Kenya), Ruvheneko Parirenyatwa (Zimbabwe), Zama Luthuli, Zolani Mtshali,

Visoni Luneta and Daniellia Schaller (South Africa), for schooling this maverick on the cultural nuances and sensitivities of the regions contained in the book. To my personal "Belters", my childhood, high school, university and life friends with whom I've shared the most memorable experiences, thank you for making my life colourful. I hope to see you guys in every lifetime. To my TNC Wealth team, you are very brave souls to put up with me year after year. I wouldn't change you for the world. To my family for your unwavering support. To my social media community, this book is testament to my love and respect for you. You expect nothing but excellence from me. I hope I have delivered. Finally, to the woman I was back in March 2015, thank you for holding on when the pain seemed unbearable, and hope faintly whispered, "What you seek is seeking you". Thank you for overcoming your fears and stepping into your purpose. For facing your faults and having the bravery to live your truth. For that is the only true victory, the victory over self. And it is only against self that you can ever truly say, I win!

ABOUT THE AUTHOR

Samke Mhlongo is founder of TNC Wealth Partners, a consultancy specialising in employee financial wellness. She is the voice behind the weekly Financial Wellness Feature on Talk Radio 702 and has been featured on international media outlets including CNBC Africa, Channels TV (Nigeria), and K24 TV (Kenya). Samke has over ten years' experience in the personal finance industry, with seven years spent as a private banker at Investec Specialist Bank and Asset Manager. She holds an Honours in Financial Planning, and an MBA completed with a dissertation titled *Factors contributing to over-indebtedness of black South African females*. Her business accolades include being named United Nations MIPAD Top 100 Most Influential Persons of African Descent, Entrepreneur Magazine Top 50 Black African Women Entrepreneurs to Watch 2018, and Brand SA "Play Your Part" Ambassador.

Samke is a divorced mother of two and lives in Johannesburg.

Ringfence is her debut novel.

NOTES

1. ONCE UPON A TIME

1. Rents: an abbreviation of parents.
2. South African exclamation of surprise.
3. South African slang for "Isn't that so?".
4. 'Phuza' is the Zulu word for "drink". Phuza Thursday is a slang phrase to describe Thursday nights, which have become the most popular party night amongst South Africa's youth.
5. French title or form of address used of or to a French-speaking man, corresponding to *Mr* or *sir*.
6. French title or form of address used of or to an unmarried French-speaking woman, corresponding to Miss.
7. Slang: A casual sexual relationship that is not a defined, romantic relationship.

2. ROW E, CLOUD 9

1. Bride (Swahili).
2. Xhosa expression that can be loosely translated to mean "Isn't it?".
3. Cooked white maize meal.
4. Mopane worms (Ndebele). A delicacy in many Southern African countries.
5. Broken maize kernels boiled until soft.
6. Kenyan fried flour balls (African doughnuts).
7. Rice cooked with onion, garlic, tomatoes, and stock (West African).
8. Carnival dancer (Portuguese).
9. Brazilian cheese bread (Portuguese).
10. Daddy (Portuguese)
11. Mommy (Portuguese)
12. Slang for extramarital affair
13. "Hey, you!" In Xhosa and Zulu.
14. Sister (Zulu), used casually as a way to address any woman.
15. "Let's go" (Zulu).
16. Gatsby: A popular Cape Town, foot long, submarine sandwich
17. A term used to address a female from the Mtolo clan.

3. THE MOTHER WOUND

1. Zulu term of endearment meaning little one.
2. May I please talk to you (Zulu)?
3. In the kitchen (Zulu).
4. Hey, not at all! (Zulu).
5. How? (Zulu).
6. Me, I (Zulu).
7. In my account (Zulu).
8. Yesterday (Zulu).
9. What's the matter? (Zulu).
10. An exclamation of surprise (Zulu).
11. So, what do you say we should do? (Zulu).
12. Watch how you speak to me! (Zulu).
13. Your ceremony (Zulu).
14. Sssh, my love (Zulu).
15. Traditional African celebration (Zulu).
16. The mouth opener (Zulu). A series of games, including a gift or money, to entice the bride's family to start talking.
17. The groom's negotiators (Zulu).
18. A square piece of cloth folded and worn as a headscarf.
19. Do you know these people? (Zulu).
20. Yes, Uncle (Zulu).
21. That's fine (Zulu).
22. You may go now (Zulu).
23. We will call you if we need you (Zulu).
24. No (Zulu).

4. AZALIAN HOSPITALITY

1. The quality of humanity and compassion (Zulu and Xhosa).
2. Slang for Friend (South African)
3. A musical direction for stringed instruments to produce a nasal tone.
4. A musical direction for stringed instruments to produce a soft tone.
5. Small pancake (Russian).
6. Deep-fried rice balls (Italian).
7. Where's my lipstick (Shona).
8. Please check the safety pin is still in place (Zulu).
9. "Is it not so?" (Swahili).
10. "It's clearly witchcraft!" (Swahili).
11. African headwrap
12. Italian title or form of address used of or to an Italian-speaking woman, corresponding to *Miss*.
13. Good morning, Mrs (Italian).

5. RUNAKO ROSE

1. Grandmother (Swahili and Kikuyu, pronounced "show-show").
2. Cooked maize meal (Swahili).
3. Mukimo is a popular food in Kenya made with potatoes, peas, corn and onions.
4. Braised collard greens.
5. Caucasian, European (Swahili).
6. Congratulations (Swahili).
7. Slang for parents.

7. FLOWER POWER

1. Sit, sit, sit (Zulu)
2. Gatsheni (Ndlovu totem), this is Miss Dana (Zulu)
3. Oh in Zulu
4. this one is Ndlovu (Zulu).
5. actually (Afrikaans)
6. Who? (Zulu)
7. oh (Afrikaans).
8. A gift given to a woman by her spouse or family, to mark the occasion of her becoming a mother.
9. Dowry negotiations (Tswana).

8. SIXPENCE IN HER SHOE

1. A dancing jump in ballet (French).
2. Have you bathed yet? (Zulu).
3. Where's the iron? (Zulu).
4. Who has the key to the (mobile) fridge? (Zulu).
5. Good afternoon (Swahili).
6. Father (Tswana).
7. Fermented porridge (Tswana).
8. Dumpling. A traditional Zulu bread made with flour and cooked using the steam on the top of a stew.
9. Crumbly maize porridge, made from mielie-meal, and cooked until dry and crumbly with the consistency of dry polenta.
10. Samp and beans cooked in melon.
11. A high-protein root vegetable which is cooked much like potatoes.
12. Spinach (Tswana).
13. Pulled meat (Tswana).
14. Cooked head of an animal.
15. A wooden board used to serve meat and dumplings to male elders.
16. A traditionally hand-reared chicken of which the meat is firm in texture and distinctive in taste.
17. Fermented sorghum beer (Zulu).

18. Here's to life (Hebrew)
19. Sexual cleansing (**kusasa fumbi**) is an African tradition in which a girl or woman is expected to have sex as a cleansing ritual after her first menstruation, after becoming widowed, or after having an abortion.
20. My love (Shona).
21. Mother of Zina (Shona)
22. Cooked white maize meal with gravy (Shona).
23. Father of Zina (Shona).
24. Food is expensive! (Shona).
25. Shona for "What did you say?"

9. THE MENSAHS' DILEMMA

1. Son-in-law (Shona).
2. Grandmother (Shona).

10. CASAS IN THE SKY

1. Exclamation used to express surprise, disbelief or dissatisfaction. (Tswana)
2. South African slang: It's December!
3. Fake champagne. Slang for Méthode Cap Classique.
4. Son-in-Law (Zulu)

11. CHRISTMAS IN JULY

1. "My God, my God, why hast Thou forsaken me?". One of the sayings of Jesus on the Cross.
2. Thank you (Greek)

12. CRIMSON BRIDES

1. You're going to bewitch us! (Tswana).
2. Traditional healer (Zulu).

13. INNER ENIOLA

1. Reason for being (Japanese)
2. A complimentary bite-sized portion of a dish of the chef's choice (French).
3. Minibus taxis (Kenyan slang).
4. A brand of two- and three-wheel vehicles used as taxis in Kenya.
5. A motorised rickshaw used as a taxi in Kenya.
6. Thank you (Swahili).

7. Hello (Swahili).
8. fresh tomato and onion salsa (Swahili)
9. Coal-grilled meat (Swahili)
10. Hello, my friend (Swahili)
11. A **Nigerian** Slang use to refer to a girl who likes to **hangout**, party and most times have sex with different men for money and other **benefits**. They don't hang out with broke men.
12. Nigerian street snack: Corn and coconut
13. Owambe: a lavish traditional Nigerian party
14. Nigerian slang for a sugar daddy
15. Nigerian slang for a secret property kept by a married man for extramarital affairs
16. Dried ground melon seeds (Nigerian)
17. Fried plantain (Nigerian)
18. 2015 World Bank Africa Poverty Report
19. A Nigerian colloquialism that can be loosely translated as "My friend".
20. Buttocks (Nigerian slang)
21. Soup made with palm nut extract (Nigerian)

Made in United States
Orlando, FL
18 May 2022

17996119R00243